D1733383

My Garment of Praise
for Your Spirit of Heaviness

Traci Wooden-Carlisle

MY GARMENT OF PRAISE
FOR YOUR SPIRIT OF HEAVINESS
(Promises to Zion Series) ⁃
KDP ISBN: 9781717803658
Copyright © 2018 by Traci Wooden-Carlisle

Editor: Paula – paulaproofreader.wixsite.com

This is a work of fiction. Names characters, places, and incidents are either the product of the author's imagination or are used fictitiously, and any resemblance to actual persons, living or dead, business establishments, events or locales is entirely coincidental.

When the perishable has been clothed with the imperishable, and the mortal with immortality, then the saying that is written will come true: "Death has been swallowed up in victory."
"Where, O death, is your victory? Where, O death, is your sting?"

1 Corinthians 15:54-55

DEDICATION

I dedicate this book to my Father in heaven
and my daddy on earth.
To the women of Zion who have touched soul, sowed into my
life and inspired me to share my testimony.

CHAPTER 1

Paige leaned against the window frame staring out at the waves breaking against the shore. She felt hypnotized by the receding water and imagined she could feel the drag of the waves pulling her in. She closed her eyes to escape the sensation and hugged her robe closer to her chest as the morning sun became shielded by some fast-moving clouds. It had the potential for such a lovely day, but even as it beckoned to her she felt detached, withdrawn and very much alone. Something was missing. A piece of her was misplaced. No, that spoke of the possibility of her finding it. This piece was absent, gone from her, dead.

She placed her fingertips against the window and resisted the urge to pull back when she encountered its iciness. Her heart sank like lead in her chest, and she couldn't help but wish she could find some way to lighten it. She sketched the outline of a heart with her left forefinger and colored it in with the fog from her breath. The diamond on her ring finger glinted and reflected off of the pane, catching her attention, but before she could study it, her other senses came alive. A warm shiver walked along her spine then webbed out along her nerve endings.

Her mind grew sluggish even as the hairs on her arms began to stand on end. She felt movement behind her, and as the person drew nearer she could feel their heat reach out to her. It engulfed her right before their arms did, and she leaned back into the embrace wondering why her skin began to light up like fireworks.

This wasn't what Brandon felt like, she thought to herself. His kisses warmed her from the inside out and cocooned her in his passion. This feeling... She grasped the description. This feeling was like sparks of electricity running across her skin. It was the same feeling as the moment she met...

"Are you going to watch whatever is outside that window, or are you going to come back to bed and let me light you up again?" said the sleep-heavy voice as it whispered against her neck while the arms around her waist squeezed gently. A sense of unease rolled over her even as her body sprang to life. She turned in the arms of her supposed husband and looked straight into a pair of familiar hazel eyes.

Paige woke with a start. Her heart was hammering in her chest, and she opened her eyes to an unfamiliar room. Fright skittered across her nerves right before memories from the day before came in like a flood, and she forced herself to take deep cleansing breaths. She took an assessment of her body and surroundings noticing a weight across her middle and warmth at her back. She forced her body to relax and felt the arm flex just before the body behind her snuggled closer. She released one final, deep breath and let her body melt into the heat surrounding her.

"Good morning, Mrs. Tatum," murmured a deep and drowsy voice from behind her ear. The weight at her waist moved languidly between her hip and ribs. She tried to shake off the dream and enjoy this first early morning with her new husband, but remnants of the unease she felt clung to the edges of her consciousness.

"Good morning, Mr. Tatum," she replied, snuggling deeper into his embrace.

He moved away allowing her to roll onto her back so he could look at her, then his lips returned to her ear. "That's Brandon, or husband, to you," he whispered before planting kisses on the underside and nipping the lobe before tracing a path toward her collarbone. She arched her neck giving him better access to a spot he'd found the night before that wiped all cognizant thoughts from her mind. Hopefully, it would do the same this morning, and she could forget the fact that she had been dreaming of another man on her honeymoon.

She felt him pull back, and she opened her eyes to watch him gazing at her in mild concern. "Are you alright?" How did he know? She opened her mouth to voice the question, but felt even that would be an admission of thoughts she desperately wanted to forget. "Yes, why?"

He continued to hover over her, scanning her face. She could tell he was searching for something, and she blinked a few times as she sent the thoughts to the recesses of her mind and turned the key. This was Brandon, the man she loved and vowed her life to just yesterday, and she meant it: every word, every promise, every kiss.

She shifted her leg, rubbing it against his as she skimmed his side with her fingertips. He made an odd noise and shifted as he took her hand away from his skin and kissed it. "I don't know. It felt like you were a million miles away for a moment there."

He was so observant and intuitive. It was one of the things she adored about him, but not this morning. She shrugged and pulled her hand free wanting nothing more than to change the subject. She brought her fingers back to his ribs to test out an observation of her own. She strummed his ribs lightly and felt the shudder move across him before he gave into the chuckle she watched him try to suppress.

"You are ticklish," she announced. He took her hand again even as she lifted her other to rub against his flat stomach. They began to wrestle playfully. She used her speed and small frame to wriggle her hands and arms out of his hold and find new spots to tickle until he trapped her wrists in one of his hands and used his body to hold her down on the mattress. She laughed as she flexed her fingers toward his chin and neck in a futile attempt to elicit more chuckles from him. She freed one leg and wrapped it around his calf bringing her heal to the back of his knee, and he almost bucked off of her. She laughed louder, spurred on by her small victory, but missed the gleam in his eyes right before he raised her captured hands above her head, resting them on the pillow. She squirmed against him, too wrapped up in creating enough space between them to rub any part of her body against him to make him laugh.

Too late she realized the precarious position she'd put herself in when his free hand slowly rubbed along the underside of her arm. Her eyes widened when she recognized his intent. She was breathing heavily from her exertion one second and not at all the next. *He wouldn't dare,* she thought to herself as his fingers continued to inch toward the sensitive skin just beneath her armpit. She voiced her thoughts hoping to dissuade him, but he just shook his head. "My turn." His fingers crawled closer, and the tension in her body ratcheted up.

"Please," she entreated softly. He shook his head.

She tried again. "I'm sorry. I won't tickle you anymore. Please." He seemed to give it some thought.

"What would you give me if I stopped?"

"Why should I have to give you anything? Why can't you just, out of the kindness of your heart, stop."

"Why didn't you?"

Mmmm, because it was too much fun finding out that little tidbit about this strong and beautiful man. That confession wasn't going to get her what she wanted though. She shrugged instead.

His fingers met her armpit and skipped across her skin with cruel intent. She tried to hold her body still and lips tight under the onslaught of the painful pleasure. All too quickly it was too much and she found herself laughing and begging for him to stop, and he did.

"I love the way your eyes light up when you laugh," he said almost reverently, shifting the mood from playful to intense. She

4

sobered and took a much needed breath as his hand slid down to rest at her lowest rib, skimming across at least one erogenous zone on its way. She tugged slightly on her hands, but instead of letting them go he leaned in and kissed her deeply. She wanted to wrap her arms around him and drink all of him in, but he refused to release her, so she pressed herself closer to him, and after a couple of swipes of his tongue across her lips she decided to follow his lead to see where this went.

*   *   *

Brandon pressed a lingering kiss to her temple as he finished pushing her seat closer to the breakfast table. Could it really be called breakfast at eleven thirty a.m.? She didn't care. She watched as he sat across from her, and she was hit by another wave of warmth and love. She was happy, and dreams or not, she wasn't giving this up without a fight.

A thoughtful expression crossed Brandon's features as he placed his napkin across his lap. She'd only caught it because she'd watched him over her heaping plate of eggs, sausage, country potatoes, grits, and fruit, waiting for him to situate himself and offer grace. All of the delicious smells had her stomach growling even as they walked through the buffet line. She continued to stare at him curiously as he settled himself and caught her gaze. He smiled apologetically, and she barely contained her laugh. She knew he was raised with good manners, but she'd never met a man with such staunch dining etiquette. She wondered why she hadn't noticed this when they'd gone out to eat before. She bowed her head when he did and joined him in saying grace over their food.

She was halfway through her meal before her hunger let up enough to allow her to slow down. She couldn't remember the last time she was so hungry. It was probably the boat... well, and last night. She couldn't stop the smile that formed.

"Those potatoes must be really good," Brandon said. She could tell he was working to contain his smile, but it didn't matter, she still blushed to the tips of her ears. He had mercy on her and changed the subject.

"So, I was wondering how Victoria found out about my latest test results," Brandon said right before taking a bite of his muffin. Paige studied his face to see if he was upset, but only saw confusion.

"I'm not sure, but she does have a lot of connections. It doesn't make it right because she shouldn't have been able to gain access to your records but thank goodness she didn't say anything to the family before we talked to them.

"I'm not too comfortable with you spending time with her." He lifted up his hands when she opened her mouth to reply. "Hear me out. I'm not saying I will keep you from seeing her. I wouldn't consider telling you that you couldn't go somewhere. I am only stating my discomfort with you interacting with her. I don't trust her."

Paige understood exactly how he felt. If the tables were turned she would be just as concerned. Victoria was complicated, at best, and Paige wasn't naïve enough to think that now that she'd given her life to Christ she would relinquish all of her manipulating ways. Sure, with the filling of the Holy Spirit she would be convicted and give more thought to her actions, hopefully before she did anything, but Paige knew the change wouldn't happen overnight. It was a process and there were plenty of chances where Paige could get caught in the crossfire before Victoria allowed God to fully take over the reins in her life.

Paige nodded her head. "I know how you feel, and to be honest, I'm feeling a little hesitant myself after what she said to me before our ceremony." She moved the remaining food around on her plate, while she thought of her next sentence.

"But she just gave her life to Christ, and though I know Richard will be there to answer any questions she has, sometimes women want a woman's perspective on things, and I don't think it would be right to turn my back on her now."

She looked up to see Brandon watching her with a gentle expression on his face. He shrugged and to her surprise went back to eating. She sat there confused for a moment. "That's all, just a shrug?"

"What do you want?" Brandon asked between bites.

She wanted him to stop eating and give her his undivided attention on this matter, so she could tell if he was being sincere.

"I want to know what you really think about what I just said," Paige replied as evenly as she could.

Brandon looked into her eyes for a moment before setting his fork down and wiping his mouth with his napkin. "Paige, I told you my concern with Victoria. We both know things come very easy for her, and it may be too much of a temptation to do things on her own instead of waiting for direction from God. I think at this stage in her relationship with God, there is a greater chance of you getting hurt by her. Whether it is directly or indirectly doesn't matter to me. I just want to keep you safe." He reached forward and took her hand, his brown eyes warming as they skimmed her face.

"You, Paige, are my treasure. You hold my heart in your beautiful little hands." He leaned forward slightly so he could touch his lips to her knuckles. "I love that you are generous and fearsome when it comes to those you care about, but I want to give you a word of caution." His eyes shone with something she'd seen only one other time.

"If anyone tries to hurt you, and I don't care who— anyone in your family or my family included—I will do whatever I can to stop them."

Paige was surprised at this admission, though she shouldn't have been. Brandon, for all his gentleness and kindness had a stubborn streak that carried with it a conviction so strong she loathed to come up against it ever again. She knew her threat did little to dissuade him from breaking up with her earlier in the year. It was nothing short of a healthy dose of tough love from Pastor Lawrence and a miracle from God that caused him to change his mind.

His slight tug brought her attention back to him. "Paige, I'd rather not use my energy chasing after or inflicting revenge upon someone because you put yourself in a precarious situation."

Paige shivered at the intensity in his eyes. She tried to lighten the mood a little. "You wouldn't do that. God said vengeance was His, and you pride yourself in doing His will."

Brandon's gaze didn't waver. "I love God, Paige, and no, I don't wish to grieve Him, but like I said, you hold my heart in your hands, and I am fiercely possessive of both." He turned her hand over and kissed her palm. "I take my role as your husband and protector very seriously, Paige. I will always fight for you if I think you're in danger. There will always be situations that will arise that we have no control over and those I am more than happy to place in God's hands." He began massaging her palm with his thumbs, and she watched as his face lost all expression.

The coolness in his eyes sent a shiver down her spine. "But be warned, Paige, if you follow your heart into a precarious situation, I will do all I can to make sure you get free from said situation."

Paige stilled, unable to fully comprehend what he meant. Before she was able to put a voice to her thoughts, Brandon blinked slowly, kissed her palm again and when he looked up at her the warmth had returned to them. If she hadn't just witnessed it for herself, she would have thought she imagined the last few minutes.

She watched as Brandon released her hand and looked at his watch. He glanced at their plates. "Are you still eating?"

She looked down at her now unappetizing plate and shook her head to the negative. "Are you sure? You still have quite a bit left." Brandon said after taking a healthy swallow of his apple juice.

"I'm sure," Paige said, surprised it came out sounding steady. Her appetite was sure and truly gone now.

Brandon pushed back from his chair and came over to help her out of hers. "Alright," he said, showing no signs of there ever being an intense conversation between them. "Come with me." He took her hand and gently pulled her to his side, so he could wrap his arm around her shoulders as he led her out of the dining room.

"I have a surprise for you," he said whispering in her ear.

In a slight daze, she let him guide her, thinking to herself that little could top the surprise he'd just given her.

CHAPTER 2

"So you want me to believe that you've never met that woman, in your life?" Victoria said none too quiet, as she closed the door to the suite and followed him into the bedroom.

Richard didn't even look at her as he sat on the side of the bed and began to untie his black suede shoes. "For the third and, hopefully, final time, yes I do because I *have never met her*," Richard said, placing an emphasis the last four words, "and I'm getting tired of your accusations."

"Richard." She came around to stand in front of him. "She addressed you as if she knew you. How would she know those things if you'd never met? Why would she approach us like she did?"

Richard looked up at her, and she saw the exasperation mixed with concern that took her anxiety to a whole new level. He placed his hands on either side of her waist and flexed his fingers. This was something he did early on in their marriage when she would worry about Rachel, the farm, or anything else that wasn't going as smoothly as she liked. Immediately, she took a deep breath, falling back into their old ways. "Another," he said while he flexed again. She obeyed and slowly let it out. He then pushed her away slightly, so he could stand close to her.

"I know Grace just about as much as you do, and if she could find out enough to try and blackmail you into giving her money when Vivian was young, then she can sure find out enough about me to know that I had her investigated."

Victoria went still. She knew her face drained of all color, but was helpless to stop it. Richard knew about the blackmail attempt?

How? Her thoughts must have shown on her face because Richard shook her slightly before he said, "Paige told me. Well, I guess I should say she confirmed it. I knew something happened when you started looking into Vivian's medical history because you stopped so abruptly. It wasn't, and isn't like you to let things go, but what I couldn't figure out was what Grace had against you to blackmail you with. Paige didn't seem to know either.

Victoria tried to move out of Richard's hold, but his hands tightened. She placed her hands on his shoulders for leverage in case she needed to push, but he pulled her closer. "Victoria, don't you think we should be honest with each other, now more than ever? We are still sorting through the devastation in our marriage, but despite that we just renewed our vows and are starting fresh with no lies, no secrets, and no deception. You even accepted Jesus Christ into your heart. That alone should be a catalyst.

"What Grace tried to blackmail me with wouldn't stand up in a court of law. Therefore, she didn't have anything on me," Victoria hedged, trying to buy some time.

Richard's body tensed and she looked up to read his face. His jaw was tight, and she could see impatience threaded throughout his features. He moved to set her away from him, but she knew she was teetering on a line, and she couldn't afford to lose his alliance, especially with Grace making herself known. Now that she had stepped into the foreground, so to speak, there was no telling what she would do.

Victoria wrapped her hands around Richard's neck to stop him from distancing himself. "Okay, okay," she capitulated, taking a deep breath, her gaze flickering back and forth between Richard's eyes and shoulders. Richard didn't continue to try to separate them, but he didn't soften toward her either. She encouraged herself with that small victory.

"Rachael wanted a baby." She shrugged her shoulder, feigning nonchalance. "I wanted to make sure she got what she wanted." She hesitated for a moment, but when Richard shifted his weight, she continued.

"I just used my connections to push them up on the adoption list. It was for the best; the other families didn't wait too much longer than they were already going to. I asked." She went quiet, but was unable to look up at him.

"If they wouldn't have waited too much longer, as you say, why did you really push them closer to the top, Victoria?"

She knew she had a perfectly good reason for what she did thirteen years ago, but at this moment it didn't shine her in the most perfect light. What could she do now, though? If she continued to hesitate, Richard would think there was more to it once she did share her reasoning. *Just get it over with.*

She looked up into his face, still not quite meeting his eyes. "I saw Vivian's mother's bio a couple of weeks before Vivian was born." She took a deep breath. "Or what I thought was to be her bio." She finally chanced a look at Richard. His expression was impassive.

"I thought the child would be perfect for Rachael."

"Why?" Richard asked with a note of apprehension. He shook her slightly when she paused too long for his liking.

Her heart was beating widely in her chest. Why, after all this time was she so concerned about what Richard would think of her in regards to her decisions in this matter? She knew her hesitation wasn't helping, but she loathed to see that look of disappointment on his face.

She shifted her eyes to look over his shoulder before she began. "The bio I read stated the birth mother was of mixed heritage; African-American and Italian, and the biological father was of Spanish descent."

She felt more than saw Richard's shoulders tense. "And?" His voice was quiet.

"I thought a mixed-race child would be a beautiful match for Rachael, with her fair features and Mason with his looks. It seemed right at the time."

"Was that the only reason you picked a child with those nationalities?" The question startled her so much she looked back into his eyes.

"Yes. Why?" She watched as he searched her eyes. What was he looking for?

After a few seconds the tension seemed to leave his body, but now she was curious. She watched him try to school his features and was afraid he would avoid the question. She ran her fingertips along the nape of his neck before applying pressure to keep his attention.

"Why, Richard?" She continued to search his face for what he was trying to hide.

He blew out a deep breath, obviously regretting opening whatever door he'd just unlocked. He reached back and disengaged her hand from his neck, holding it tightly in his grasp. "I thought you might have picked the child due to her mother's African-American and Italian heritage because of Brian and his father."

Victoria sucked in a deep breath, almost choking on the air. "What?" What was he saying? Did he really think she would manipulate the adoption process to bring that bloodline mix back into their family?" She worked to free her hand from his gasp, but he clasped both hands and pulled her closer.

"Listen to me, Victoria. Please, I want you to see it from my side. You used your 'connections.'" He paused for emphasis, and she knew if his hands were free he would have given the word air quotes. "To place this child with these particular traits into your daughter's life and our family. You yourself never let go of the child you were forced to give up. Every piece of information you could buy or steal is in a file in your office. It wouldn't be too far-fetched to think you might want to keep any part of that past."

Victoria stopped fidgeting as something in his voice registered within her. The anger that was rising as a result of the offense she was feeling at his words began to dissipate. "Even thirteen years ago it was too long to hold on to in such a way that I would deliberately try to keep a piece of either one of them, be it ever so small, in my life. Do you think I was trying to keep something of Brian in my life or his father?" She continued before he could answer. "Did you not believe me all of those years ago when I told you I held no torch for him? Did you not believe me when I told you that his betrayal and lies killed any love I had for him?" She moved into him, allowing her closeness to emphasize her words. "No, I wasn't thinking of Brian nor his father when I chose the child for Rachael."

She waited for his nod while she rethreaded her hands in his then brought them up to her cheek. "I simply wanted to help them avoid more questions. You know how people look at what they assume are interracial couples. It is magnified when they adopt a child representing only one or the other race. I wanted to spare them that."

"You interfered with something that could have had irrevocable repercussions, and you opened the door for a threat against our family. It didn't matter that it was unfounded. It was there nevertheless"

The wind was knocked from Victoria's sails. She took in the words and found there was no room for breath. "Are you blaming me for Grace being in our lives?" She warred with herself, not knowing if she wanted to know the answer, but unable to breathe until she received it.

"No one is to blame for this Grace person acting as she does, but now that she is in our lives we need to stand firm with each other and consider all sides." He slipped one hand away from her body and turned to lead her out of the bedroom.

"Let's go out into the living room so that we don't allow this subject to permeate our resting space." He squeezed her and wiggled his eyebrows. She gave him a brief smile, knowing he was trying to lighten the mood a little. She allowed herself to be led to the couch and didn't object when he allowed as little space as possible between them.

"Now, what we do know is Grace is Paige's grandmother which makes her Vivian's great-grandmother. Although she has no legal right to interfere with Vivian's life, she doesn't seem like the type to allow things like the law to get in her way when she wants something." He gave her a wry smile before continuing.

"We also know that she has her own connections if she knew I was investigating her."

Victoria thought of something she knew would cause him pain, but she needed to voice it. "Do you think you might have a mole?"

He seemed to consider this before speaking. "I sincerely doubt it. No one in my group has anything to gain by betraying me, and we've worked with each other for many years. Unbeknownst to them, I have background checks done on them bi-annually just in case someone runs into hard times. That way I don't have to question their fidelity. I already know."

Victoria looked at her husband with new eyes. She knew he had a savvy business mind, but this no tolerance work ethic was intriguing. It made her wonder just how much he knew about her investigative ventures. Maybe she would put Mike on it. He seemed to be the most competent of her investigators so far. She figured it was time she did a little background checking of her own.

She caught Richard watching her and sought to waylay any suspicions he had about the turn her thoughts had taken. "I was wondering if you or your people have come up with anything else about Brian." She leaned into him, laying her head against his shoulder for comfort and to hide from his gaze at the same time.

She felt the tension flow back into his body, but refused to look up. "Not yet." She felt the rumble of his words as they vibrated through his body. Should she let it go or lead the conversation to get the answers she wanted? She considered the fact that she second-guessed her motive a testament to her new faith and renewed relationship with her husband. Normally she would have twisted the conversation to meet her needs without a moment's hesitation. She knew the ultimate challenge would be whether or not she continued. She weighed that against the strength of her desire to see if Richard was hiding anything from her and compromised. She fell quiet.

Two minutes later she felt a small jostling as Richard shook his shoulder to get her attention. "Are you still awake?"

"Yes, just thinking," she replied, without giving any hint as to what she was thinking about.

"Would you like to share?" Richard asked as he leaned back and raised his arm and placed it around her shoulders.

She raised to an upright sitting position on the couch and looked him square in the eye. "You would tell me if you found something out about Brian or Grace, wouldn't you?"

A look of surprise then wariness crossed his features. She could tell he was considering schooling his expression, but must have thought better of it. He stared back her with sincerity. "Yes, I would.

Satisfied, Victoria leaned in to kiss him, but he pulled back and placed a staying hand lightly on her shoulder, his thumb sweeping back and forth along her collar bone. "Since we are asking questions, I have one for you."

Victoria tried to hide her apprehension but was sure she failed. "Sure, honey."

"Have you ended all plans to take Vivian from Mason?"

Victoria worked to keep her breathing steady. She was happy her face was still averted from his otherwise he would have known right away she hadn't.

"I am not pursuing court action against Mason." She purposefully left out "at this time." She knew his new lease on life and latest endeavor to remain sober wouldn't last, and she would be waiting for him to stumble.

16

She received a small shake from Richard and knew he'd read her correctly.

"Victoria, Vivian and Mason belong together. "Richard looked at her intently. He held her by her upper arms." He's been working hard to overcome some of his vices so he can be a better father to her. He is all she has known as a father and immediate family. She's lost her mother. It wouldn't be fair…"

"Fair?" Victoria interrupted. "Fair is Vivian growing up to know both her parents. Fair is Vivian not having to take medication for the rest of her life to make sure that she doesn't reject her kidney."

Richard let her go to raise his hands in surrender. "Okay, maybe 'fair' wasn't the right word, but you know what I mean. Vivian and Mason belong together. Remember, Vivian didn't just lose a mother. Mason lost a wife," he finished with resolve.

Some of the strength went out of Victoria's voice as she spoke. "Mason should remember that."

"Victoria." Richard's voice was beseeching.

She didn't want to waste this time thinking about Mason when she and Richard had much more important things, and people, to deal with.

"Yes, yes." She turned away and headed toward the sliding glass door leading to the balcony. "I will suspend all legal proceedings." She paused as she grasped the handle then turned to look at him over her shoulder. "Unless he shows himself unfit to care for her. I will not allow my granddaughter to be raised in a neglectful environment." She turned back and continued outside.

Richard worked his shoulders back and forth. His wife may have accepted Christ as her Lord and Savior, but he could tell the process would be slow going unless she began to release the unforgiveness still occupying her heart. He sat back down on the couch as he sent up a prayer for God's help.

CHAPTER 3

Mason walked through the hall to the elevators. He pressed the button to call the car heading down. He was in deep thought and had been fighting to stay focused for the past week and a half. His conversation with Brandon had rocked him to his core and had been replaying itself over and over again in his mind. How could a man who claimed to love someone so vehemently seek out the competition? Brandon was either the most selfless man he'd met, or Mason truly had no understanding of the Lord , Brandon said he served. Either one would make Mason, in his present state, inadequate for Paige. It was all too much. He wished Brandon had never placed the responsibility of Paige's well-being on his shoulders in the event of Brandon's passing. More than that. He wished he hadn't accepted.

He glanced at his watch as the elevator took him to the first floor. He had a date with Tabitha this evening, but first he had a lengthy "to-do" list for Vivian's surprise pre-birthday slumber party before she came home from vacation Bible school. He'd made a deal with one of his neighbors that he'd supply all of the food if she held the party for Vivian and her friends at her place. If he'd been in a better frame of mind he could have handled 8 precocious, giggling, thirteen-year-olds for one night and morning, but he wasn't, and Vivian had been hounding him about having a sleep over with her best 8 friends.

He knew he'd been preoccupied and wanted to surprise Vivian with this party to begin to make up for the lack of attention he'd given her since Paige's wedding. In fact it was the least he could do with her leaving at the end of the following week to share her birthday with her twin sister and mother in Los Angeles. When Vivian first approached him with her desire to spend her birthday with Paige and Gladys, Mason had his reservations. Not only was she going to be away from him on her birthday, she and her sister would be spending a week with Paige during the first month of Paige and Brandon's marriage. With Vivian's constant pressing he'd had a brief conversation with Paige and was reassured that it was her idea. After some pleading from Vivian and Gladys he relented and made plans of his own to help Vivian celebrate her entrance into the world of teenagers.

He bought a few orders of Vivian's favorite kung pao chicken, fried rice, and lemon pepper chicken wings to go with the pizza he'd scheduled to be delivered later that evening. The cake was ready for him when he arrived at the bakery, and all that was left was to drag her presents from under his bed.

"What time do you pick the girls up from the church?" Samantha asked as she placed the party favors of colorful toiletry pouches on a table in the living room. She told him they each were filled with a travel-sized toothbrush, toothpaste, shampoo, conditioner, scented bodywash, lotion, body cream, comb, brush, and hair decorations featuring the same animal on the pouch.

Mason glanced at his watch. "The bus should be pulling into the parking lot in half an hour. I'll bring Mirabelle and four of the girls here after I drop Vivian off at Polly's house. She still thinks they will be spending the night together after going with her parents to drop off packages to some of the sick people from their church. Imagine her surprise when they arrive here."

Mason continued to take in the decorations Samantha was putting up. It was beginning to look like a mythical wonderland with hanging butterflies, unicorn wall stickers, and twinkling lights bordering the huge bay window with the rainbow decal.

"Boy, Samantha you outdid yourself. Are you sure you don't want me to do something else?"

"Naw, I love doing this and it keeps my mind busy." She glanced up briefly while organizing the utensils. Mason saw a light sheen in her eyes. "Greg's deployment was extended, and I'm doing anything to make the time go faster." Mason's gut twisted. He liked Greg and Samantha and as much in love as they were it was hard to think of them spending so much time apart. "How much longer will he be gone?" he asked.

"Five more months," Samantha answered with a sigh. "I was hoping he would be back for Mirabelle's first day of school. They have a kind of ritual." She sniffed. "Hopefully, he will be available for a Skype session."

Samantha moved on to the refrigerator and began to pull out stalks of celery and carrots.

Mason moved the stack of forks a little to the right. "I'm sorry Samantha. If you or Mirabelle need anything all you have to do is ask."

She peered around the door. "Isn't it time for you to go pick up the girls? You don't want to be late."

Mason took a deep breath knowing he'd been dismissed. "Okay, I'll see you soon," he said as he headed to the door.

His hand was on the doorknob when Samantha spoke again, "Mason?"

He looked her way.

"Thank you for caring. It helps more than you know." He returned her small smile with one of his own and walked out the door.

*   *   *

"Surprise!" The screams reverberated around the room as Vivian continued to make her way into Samantha's townhouse. Mouth agape and eyes wide, her head swiveled right and left until they landed on Mason. He wondered briefly if she had just hit the age when hugging her father in the presence of her friends was no longer done. His concern vanished as she made her way to him, hugging him fiercely.

"Thank you, Daddy." She squeezed him a little tighter before letting go.

"You're welcome, hon," he whispered before releasing her.

He watched as she went around hugging all of her friends, as well as Samantha, exchanging a few words with each before going to the next. He saw so much of Rachael in her. She always made sure everyone felt welcome. She looked around the room, going from one decoration to the next exclaiming that everything was "perfectly beautiful," her new go-to words for anything sublime.

He sat in the kitchen with Samantha until the pizza was delivered. He'd shared with Samantha he had a date, but would be available by phone. She shooed him out the door, wishing him luck and trying to assuage any concern he had about the girl's night.

He walked back to his townhouse slowly replaying the look in his daughter's eyes when she spied the birthday cake and food. He'd done well and his baby was happy. He still wasn't too happy about her leaving him after the next week, but he needed to show he could give a little.

He decided he had enough time to run under the shower and go by the flower shop before meeting Tabitha at the restaurant. He wasn't thrilled about not being given permission to pick her up at her home, but he would take what he could get.

He thought about that as he put on a fresh shirt. What was it about Tabitha that made him want to jump through her hoops? Was she another elusive chance at a meaningful relationship? And if she wasn't, what would happen when... if...he needed to fulfill his promise to Brandon? He closed his eyes tightly trying to shut out the thought. This was supposed to be a night of new possibilities. He deserved at least one night to see what a living dream felt like.

*   *   *

Mason sat in the waiting area of the restaurant. He glanced at his watch for what seemed like the 10th time in the last two minutes. She had six minutes before he could officially call her late. Boy, he hated being early, especially when he was the first one there. This was nerve racking. He noticed his knee was bouncing and stopped it with the palm of his hand. He took a deep breath and was preparing to release it when he glanced at the door and caught sight of her. The breath forgotten, he stood up and took a step toward her. His hand felt different so he turned to see what had changed. That's when he realized he'd forgotten her flowers. He picked them up and continued his approach.

"Hi," he said on the long-kept exhale.

"Hi," Tabitha responded with a smile and slightly exasperated sigh while she tried to right displaced locks of hair.

"Are you alright?" Mason asked, taking in the wisp of curls at her temples that had escaped her bun and her deep green eyes made darker by smoky eye shadow.

She sighed and waved her hand side to side. "It's nothing that a good dinner and conversation won't fix."

He considered whether or not to push it briefly but decided to let it go for the moment.

"Well, I believe I can guarantee the first and hope I can supply the second." He offered the crook of his elbow she took it.

"How long have you worked at MarsdenTech?" Tabitha asked right before placing a small bite of chicken marsala in her mouth.

Mason thought about it for a moment and was surprised to realize it would be 10 years in two weeks. He shared this with Tabitha.

"Wow, congratulations. Are you going to do something special?"

He gave it brief consideration. "I guess it depends on whom I have to celebrate with."

She looked confused. "What about your daughter?"

"She'll be spending the week in Los Angeles with her biological sister and mother." He sipped his water, hoping it came out with the nonchalance he wished he'd felt.

"Are you and Vivian's mother close?"

He was a little surprised by the question, but Tabitha seemed to be a woman who spoke her mind. He knew he would be able to hide very little from her.

"We have a daughter together and that calls for a certain amount of interaction. In that regard, we are pretty close."

Tabitha eyed him warily, and he knew she found his answer lacking. He eyed his half-eaten steak and hoped the conversation would veer in a direction that wouldn't take away his appetite because it tasted amazing. He tried again. "I'm new to the dating scene, and I don't know what is considered appropriate to share at what point. I'm really enjoying myself, and I want us to get to know each other. It's just that I'm still getting used to having Paige, that's Vivian's mother, in our lives as well." He ended with a lame shrug, hoping Tabitha would let it go.

Tabitha watched him for a moment then smiled and went back to eating. He took this as the end of the discussion and went back to his steak.

"You know," she began slowly. "I totally understand your hesitation. These days you don't know what to expect when you're first getting to know someone." She smiled hesitantly. "That's why I think I'm so straightforward." She took another bite of her meal and chewed it slowly before continuing.

He understood where she was coming from, but there was no way he would tell her about his feelings for Paige. He didn't think he had the skills to make her understand that though the only reason he was single right now was due to the fact that Paige had chosen Brandon over him. Tabitha had caused him to take another look and then another chance. At this point he didn't know if it would last, but he was looking forward to her company, her wit, and her honesty.

The conversation picked up again between dinner and dessert. She'd talked about her sibling and he told her he'd been an only child. There was no need to open that can of worms. This time he asked the questions. "Are you close with your sister?"

A little of the light dimmed in her eyes. "We are kind of close. I wish we were closer, but the competitive streak she had as a child tends to rear its ugly head in our adulthood."

"How so?"

"Shannon and I favor one another. We have the same dark, curly hair and pea-green eyes except she has this air of confidence that men find very attractive. She also has three inches on me." She began stirring her coffee. "My last boyfriend found her a little too appealing for my taste."

Mason's water glass froze halfway to his mouth. He placed it back down on the table and waited for her to look up. When she did he could see a bit of sadness.

"What happened?" he asked.

She shrugged and looked away as she took a sip of her coffee. "I don't share men I am seeing with other women. I figured if he wanted her then what we had meant very little to him."

"How long ago was this?" he asked hesitantly.

"About six months ago. I think they were together for a couple of weeks before she became bored." She chuckled softly before she continued, "He had the nerve to call me. He left message after message, asking to talk, but I never answered the phone nor the door when he would come by."

Mason wasn't sure what to say, so he stayed quiet.

"You know what I miss though?' She finally looked back up at him, and he saw the hurt that had taken up residence in her eyes.

"What?" he asked, knowing it had been a rhetorical question.

"My sister. I miss my sister." Silence loomed over them for a moment before the waitress came back to the table with their desserts.

He didn't know just how fragile the earth was around them at that moment, but he chanced another question.

"I thought you said you lived together."

"We do for the moment because I was promised my townhouse would be ready when I moved last month. If it were a few days I would have stayed in a hotel, but when they told me it would be a few weeks, I took Shannon up on her offer. She's on-site for a modeling job, so she isn't there right now anyway."

She must have seen the question in his eyes because she continued, "Shannon was on vacation when she came to visit me. Carl and I were getting pretty serious, or so I thought, and had been talking about moving in together. I'd talked to Shannon about it because I wanted to wait, but it was nice having someone who desired to be with me all of the time. I'm glad I found out the type of person he was before we moved in together." She shrugged. "Anyway, I had been thinking of moving for a while. That just galvanized me into making a decision and making it happen."

"Won't that be awkward if she comes back before your place is ready?" He couldn't imagine how he would feel if one of his half-siblings tried to infringe upon his relationship with Rachael. He probably would have ended up in jail. It was bad enough with Paige, and he barely knew Brandon. It was a good thing none of them really knew each other.

She shrugged. "Yes, at first. We will have to talk some things out, but she's the only sister I have." She stared back at him for a moment before turning her attention to her dessert.

She cut into her chocolate thunder cake and he watched as the hot fudge oozed out from the middle. He glanced at his own strawberry cheesecake before watching her take a bite. The look of pleasure on her face made him consider changing his order. She opened her eyes and caught him staring. He could feel his face getting hot.

"Would you like some? It is divine." She pushed the plate closer to him but he hesitated. She began to slowly pull it back when he decided to grab a forkful. "I see you're a bit of a temptress."

She laughed, this time for real. "I knew you wanted it. I just needed to make it a little more enticing."

"By slowly pulling it out of reach?" he asked skeptically.

"It worked, didn't it?" Her eyes glittered with mirth.

He shook his head. "Yes. I guess it did." He bit into the chocolate confection, and it was all he could do to keep from groaning. His eyes closed briefly because he was on sensory overload. What did they put in that cake?

He opened his eyes to catch her watching with a sly smile on her lips. "Yep." It was the only thing she said before she took another bite.

Trying to be polite, he offered her some of his cheesecake, but she declined. He suddenly wasn't in the mood for strawberry cheesecake either.

As Mason walked Tabitha to her car he briefly pondered whether or not to go in for a kiss. It wasn't technically their first or second date. They'd had lunch in the coffee shop, and the weekend after he got back from the wedding—he would soon have to find another point of reference—he took her on a small tour around the city.

They reached her late model Nissan just as he made up his mind to wait. He believed dinner went well, albeit a little dark in regards to her relationship with her sister.

Shannon turned to him after opening her door. "I hope me sharing about my sister didn't make you have second thoughts about...this...us...dating, us dating." Some of her vulnerability was showing and he found it almost as appealing as her confident side. It was good to know that he wasn't the only one fumbling around in the dark when it came to dating.

He smiled at her and hoped she could read the sincerity in his eyes as they stood under the dim parking lot light. "If we'd met years ago, I could have given you advice on how to pick your family, but I think you're doing a pretty good job with what you've got." Mason said.

She laughed. "You think so, huh?"

He stepped a little closer, changing his mind again. "Well, I can't be completely sure. You only shared bits and pieces about your parents and other siblings. I might need more time with you to fully access your family before I can make a sound judgment."

A small smile played at the side of her mouth and her eyes turned a slightly darker green. She leaned on her open door, bringing her into closer proximity to him. "More time? I might be able to find some time in my schedule to help you research." He watched her glance at his lips, and the warmth in her eyes lit his insides. She wanted him to kiss her. That was good because he so wanted to kiss her. He realized she'd stopped talking when her lips stopped moving. He searched back in his mind to her last words. He needed not to mess this up.

"How generous of you." He responded and was relieved to see her lips rounded into a full smile. He raised his hand to secure a wayward lock of hair behind her ear and heard her breath catch.

"Yes, that's—" She stopped speaking. She seemed to run out of air. She wouldn't need it for the next few seconds anyway. He thought to himself as he lowered his head and brushed his lips across hers, wanting to test out their softness. He brushed them again before applying more pressure because her smell, and the feel of her skin under his fingertips beckoned him to get closer. Instead of dropping his hand from her ear he palmed the lower side of her head to secure her to him. His heart raced in his chest, and he felt excited. When was the last time he was excited about anything? He quickly chased away those thoughts and went back to concentrating on Tabitha's lips moving under his.

What seemed like minutes, though it couldn't have been more than seconds later, Tabitha parted her lips on a sigh, and a tremble went through him at the invitation. Should he or shouldn't he? What came after that? Oh, how he wanted to, but…what was the "but" for? Why was he in his head when he was kissing a beautiful woman?

He slowly lightened the pressure and moved back so their lips separated. He rested his forehead on hers because he was still trying to catch his breath and she wasn't doing much better. He leaned back to look into eyes that had gone from a pale green to a color that rivaled his own. What made him uneasy was the question he saw there.

"You are amazing, Tabitha. That kiss was..." He blanked. "Amazing." He winced. Then to try and rally what was going to the left real quickly he said, "I want to savor this newness. I want to savor this newness with you."

He saw the question that was morphing into vulnerability in her eyes turn into something soft. Something that glowed around her.

"Is that okay?" he asked to make sure he was reading things right.

"That's perfect," she said beaming at him.

He smiled back at her then kissed her on the forehead because it just felt right. He handed her into the car and promised to give her a call the next day. He watched as she maneuvered her car around the posts until she exited, then walked to his car.

What was wrong with him? He just had a near perfect date, kissed the willing woman, but backed off when she made it perfectly clear she would be willing to take it further? He liked her; he knew that. His body knew that, but his mind kept a running dialogue of everything else.

He thought of calling Dr. Seagret, but he didn't think he was willing to try and defend himself against the "I-told-you-so" looks.

He needed to talk to someone. The answer came to him just before he reached his townhouse.

CHAPTER 4

Richard leaned back in his office chair and stared up at the colors on the ceiling reflecting from his watch, while he listened. A small smile came then left almost as quickly. He sat forward, his attention completely transfixed on Mason's last sentence.

"Brandon told you what?"

"Haven't you been listening to me? Brandon asked me to meet him on their wedding day and totally messed with my mind."

Richard wondered if his wife was privy to this information.

"Mason, I'm sorry, but can you really blame him for trying to make sure his wife is taken care of in the event of his death?"

"Yes, because I'm the last person he should have approached with such a ridiculous plan. There was a reason why she chose him over me, and I was close to convincing myself that she was right. I had resolved myself to the fact that Paige and Brandon were together. I was moving on with my life."

"I don't think you need to take this as serious as you are—" Richard began, but was interrupted by Mason's next statement.

"I've met someone."

Richard couldn't have filled the void of the pause that came after that sentence if he wanted to.

"I really like her. I want to see where this will go, but last night when I kissed her goodbye, my mind kept straying."

"Straying to what?" Richard prompted when Mason fell silent again.

"All sorts of things. When was the last time I'd felt that way about a woman? What was proper for a first kiss? Why was I thinking at all with this beautiful woman's fragrance all around me beckoning me closer?"

"Why do you think you were thinking so much? By the way, that's a few questions; how long was that kiss?" Richard asked picking up the pen on his desk and twirling it through his fingers. He'd considered asking Mason why he called him to talk this through, but shrugged it off.

"I don't know. With Rachael it was like being hit over the head with a mallet. I couldn't think if I wanted to. She had that type of power over me. It was…"

Richard grimaced. "Do you mind if we keep the details regarding you and my daughter 'G' rated?"

"Oh, yeah. Right. I was just trying to give you a point of reference. Even with Paige…"

"When did you kiss Paige?" Richard sat forward in his chair, his heart lurching.

"No. I mean I've never kissed Paige. I was trying to say that when I was around her I was enveloped in a warmth that made it hard to focus on anything but her. Her presence was one of those that just came in and consumed you. You know what I mean?"

Richard relaxed a little and rubbed his fingertips across his forehead. "Yes, I know. Rachael may have gotten the red hair, but her mother got the fiery characteristics." His phone buzzed, notifying him of his conference call in twenty minutes. He brought his attention back to the call.

"What do you want me to say, Mason? Everyone is different. Chemistry is different with each person we are with. I'm certainly not telling you to try out that theory, but I'm hoping to reassure you."

"Why do you think I'm thinking so much?"

"Mason, at almost any other time in your life I would just chalk it up to nervousness and lack of experience with dating. At least you better not have had any experience while my daughter was alive."

He meant it as a joke, to lighten the conversation and what he was about to say, but his words were met with silence.

"Mason?"

"I never even thought of cheating on Rachael, especially when she was sick." Mason's voice was strangled. He was making a mess of this.

"I didn't mean to insinuate that you would have ever stepped out on my daughter. I was joking, but obviously it was in poor taste." He heard Mason expel a long breath before he continued.

I think you need some time to go over your feelings about everything. Can you honestly say you are over Paige?

"She's married, Richard. I don't touch married women."

"That isn't the question I asked you, Mason. Feelings don't die just because the person is out of your reach." Richard cast a glance at his computer and brought up the plans he was going to go over in the conference call.

"I really like Tabitha. She makes me want something I thought I wouldn't want again." Mason's voice was quiet.

"What's that?" Richard asked, noting Mason still hadn't answered his question.

"She makes me want to give dating and maybe a relationship a try."

"What did Paige make you want to do then?" Richard asked, confused by Mason's latest admission.

There was another lull on the line.

"Paige made breathing less painful."

Richard let out a long breath, but the sudden weight on his shoulders didn't budge. He rested his elbows on the desk and peeked again at the clock on his phone. "Mason, I don't know what you want me to do."

Mason interrupted him again. "I'm getting on with my life. I've met someone I'm interested in. I just want to know with the information I've given you if I'm destined to hurt her."

"I can't answer that, but if you kiss her and her touch, taste, and smell don't shut off your mind there's a good chance she isn't the one for you." Richard smiled to himself briefly. "Then there's the fact that you were concerned enough to call me, your former wife's father. You know what that tells me?"

There was a slight pause before Mason responded, "What?"

"That you need friends."

"Ha ha ha."

"I thought it was funny," Richard said through a chuckle.

"Seriously, though." Richard nodded to Nancy as she came and handed him a file folder.

"You've only had three dates with this woman. Do you think maybe you're rushing things?"

"No," Mason jumped in. "I just wanted to know if this was common when coming back into the dating world."

Richard shook his head at the man's hasty reply. "Mason, I appreciate you thinking you could get dating advice from me, but it's been longer for me than you. Besides, I think your issue is something completely different." He heard Mason's slow breaths coming over the line.

"What, Richard?"

Richard had to give it to the man. He didn't know if he would have had the courage to ask his former father-in-law anything, but the last few months did give them a chance to get a little closer. He glanced at his watch one last time. Well, no matter how close they were he needed to get off the phone, so he could have a minute or two to get ready for this presentation.

"Honestly, I think you're trying to rush your way into a serious relationship, so that you have a good reason for not coming to Paige's aid if Brandon passes away soon."

"Really? You think I would do that?" Mason's voice sounded strangled and on the edge of disbelief.

"It would cross my mind, especially if I was already seeing someone else. You need to find a happy medium in your relationship with Paige. It can't be all or nothing, especially with a child. If the worst happens, and Brandon doesn't beat this bout with cancer, Paige will need her family and friends and you are counted among them. You will have to work this out. I gave you my answer. Now I have to get off the phone because I have a really important meeting in..." He looked down. "Three minutes."

"All right," Mason said on a sigh.

"I think you need a little more time. There's no need to be in a hurry. It will only cause you to make mistakes." Richard placed his elbows on the desk and wiped his hands down the sides of his face. He hoped Mason really listened to what he was saying otherwise there was a good chance he could not only cause himself more pain, but hurt the woman in the process.

"If this woman is in it for the long haul, she'll understand. You need to see if she's friend material more than dating material anyway. You come with a lot of baggage." There was a long pause over the line, but Richard welcomed it. He would have been disappointed if Mason had come back with a rash statement.

"Understood. Thanks Richard," Mason finally said.

Richard's heart went out to this man who had lost so much. "You aren't just my granddaughter's father, Mason. You're my son. Okay?"

He heard Mason exhale. "Thank you, Richard. Have a good meeting."

"I plan to. Talk to you soon and kiss that soon-to-be teenager for me." He glanced to his left and watched as a bird flew by his window.

"Awww, don't remind me." Mason groaned. "I just started shopping for a shotgun."

"You're late, son," he said chuckling. "Get that done quickly." His desk phone's line lit up. "Bye for now."

"Bye for now."

*   *   *

Richard activated his bluetooth headset as he maneuvered his way through the light afternoon traffic. He was headed toward his apartment in the city where Victoria was waiting. They had plans for dinner, and he was looking forward to seeing her. First, he had to get an update from one of his men, and he only had twenty minutes to do it.

"Good afternoon, Sam. It's been a great day. I'm hoping your news will make it even better," Richard said in greeting to his lead investigator.

"As you know, Mya had little success finding anything else in Colorado Springs with the lead she was given, but she kept eyes on Michael as you asked, even though it was a little harder since you told Victoria you knew about him." Richard shrugged off Sam's reference to him making their job harder knowing it was true, but his wife had made things complicated. He'd shared the fact that he'd known about Michael with his wife. He was hoping she would want to pool their resources, but she neither asked for nor offered any help so he continued to have his men search for any information they could find on Victoria's son Brian, Grace and her craziness, and Paige's biological father since Melanie, aka Grace II wasn't forthcoming with the information.

"Hmmm."

"Well we went back to the beginning like you suggested. All the way back. You said Victoria didn't have any contact with the father after the summer they parted, but I thought I would double back to do a more thorough search."

Richard's pulse jumped at the mention of Victoria's son's father. He didn't know why he always felt so uneasy when the man

35

was brought up. It wasn't as though Victoria had any contact with him. He would have known.

"What'd you find, Sam?"

"Well, the Sable family has a deeper past than what is shown on paper." He paused, and Richard saw the conversation taking longer than his commute.

"Do I need to pull over or do you think this is something you can explain in fifteen minutes?"

"All the paperwork we found is already on its way to you, but I thought you would want to know who the real family is behind Antonio Sable."

"I don't mean to be rude, Sam, but that is what I pay you for."

"Our original background search on the Sable family showed an upper-middle-class family who made a respectable living while slowly getting into the market of event planning. The family as a whole took on the project and they have done well." Richard heard papers being shuffled in the background before Sam continued.

"Since we were concentrating on Victoria's family and anything pertaining to the adoption we might have overlooked something." There was another pause.

"Hold on, Sam." Richard glanced at the exit in front of him. At the last moment he decided to take it even though his normal exit was still another four miles. He pulled into a vacant parking lot and placed the car in park.

"Alright. Since you don't seem to be in a hurry, Sam, I pulled over. You now have ten more minutes than you had before. My wife knows how long it takes me to get home. I figure if you arrange for some flowers to be sent to the house in half an hour while we discuss this business it should appease her curiosity."

"Yes. Consider it done," Sam said without hesitation this time. He got the message that to do so would cost him at least double what he was going to be paying for the flowers. Richard was very calm and slow to rile except when it came to Victoria.

"On paper, the Sable family led us to an entirely made-up family tree. Mya caught the discrepancy back in the line where someone got careless. The real lineage leads to a very very old line with very, very old money." Richard didn't like where this was going. He was hoping that they could completely remove the family from their list. He had no desire to go down that road.

"Two generations from Antonio's father Luca Sable, the family emigrated from Italy and broke off from their ancestors. Marco Sapienti came to America in 1887. He changed his last name to Sable and kept up very little communication with his family. From what Mya was able to surmise, Marco broke a family code. He was betrothed to Galiana Iseppa Bianchi, but instead of marrying her he got on a ship to America." Richard's mind fogged then cleared again. He was once told never to ask how Mya got her data, but Bianchi was as popular in Italy as Smith was in America. He couldn't begin to imagine what thread she found and began to unwind.

"Marco met and married Aldiana Rosanna Esposito a few years after arriving in Manhattan. They had three sons and two daughters. His second son Philip Nicolas Sable was good with numbers and was fortunate to get an apprenticeship in accounting. His job transferred him to Chicago where he met and married Maria Lorraine Damico. They had two boys and two girls. Luca Sable was the eldest and was even better with numbers. He graduated with a degree in business finance and added to the family's wealth, sending them up a few tax brackets. He was working his way up the corporate ladder when he met Helena Rossi, a debutante, who loved socializing. They married and had four sons. Lucas Jr., Antonio, Maximillian, and Dexter. Which brings us to the present." Richard sighed, feeling as though he'd been taken quickly through an American history course.

"Antonio was betrothed to Graciella Bianchi." Alarm bells went off in Richard's head. "Was she part of the original line of Bianchis?"

"Yep. It looks like the families were trying to heal an eighty-year rift because Helena wanted to add clientele to her entertainment planning business and the Bianchi family had all the connections." Richard shook his head at what people would do to get ahead. He wondered if it weren't for the betrothal if Antonio would have married Victoria. He pushed away from that line of thought and refocused on Sam's voice.

"They were supposed to be wed the summer after Victoria became pregnant, but the betrothal was terminated. It seemed like the families were right back where they began, but three years later he and Arrellia, the youngest daughter, met at a conference and hit it off. They were married a year later. Without too much infighting the families accepted the match, and the breach was mended.

Antonio and Arrellia moved to Boston and now have two daughters: Leandra, and Rosanna, and a son by the name of Antonio Jr. They have eight grandchildren: three by each of the girls and two by Antonio Jr."

"Sam, I appreciate the history lesson, but you didn't need to call me with this information. I could have just read it for myself."

"The Sable family has more money than what is seen up front. They have a corporation under the Sapienti name. It seems to be the second layer to their wealth. More importantly the Bianchi and Sables are partners on the papers everyone sees, but the Bianchis and Sapientis are partners behind the scenes. I guess the question is, since they are the same two families why the different names and different partnerships? Mya is looking into that."

Richard exhaled a breath, trying to dispel his irritation. "Sam, you have five more minutes."

"Mya found correspondence between a Luca Sapienti and the Grossenbergs a couple of months before they adopted Brian." Sam paused again, but this time Richard didn't notice. He didn't notice much of anything outside of the rushing sound of blood in his ears and the parking lot light going in and out of focus.

He heard Sam's voice from far away and fought for breath. He rolled down his window and the fresh air helped clear his head and shrink it back to its normal size. "Richard, are you still there?" The sound came back with a whoosh, snapping him out of his stupor.

"I'm here." He leaned his head back and closed his eyes. He had no clue how he was going to tell Victoria.

"Richard, Mya is still gathering information, but so far it looks like Luca only had contact with them before the adoption, but then the person was using a mostly fake name."

"Just continue to give me updates as they come in. I'll go over the hard copies when I get them and tell you if I want you to modify the search."

"Okay. Are you alright? You were quiet there for a moment."

Richard stared up at the ceiling of the car. "Do you know what a stroke feels like?"

"No, why? Do you think you're experiencing one?"

Richard blew out a sigh. "No, just not looking forward to telling my wife that her child's father's family was in communication with his adopted parents."

"You have some time. I suggest you not say anything until you have all of the facts. You know when she finds out she's going to put her people on it, and they will only get in Mya's way. At least wait until Mya has exhausted all of her resources, and you have the information you need to give her as much of the story as possible."

Richard took a few deep breaths and sighed again. "Well, thank you, Sam. Tell Mya I really appreciate the work she's done."

"Will do. Talk to you later."

"Talk to you later," Richard replied then waited for the sound of their call disconnecting." Suddenly he was very tired. He loosened his tie and reclined the seat back. He needed a moment of quiet so he could come to a decision he could live with. He looked at the digital display on his dashboard. Victoria would have to be mollified by the flowers. He was going to be late getting home

CHAPTER 5

Victoria fingered the petals of a larkspur in her bouquet of wildflowers. These were at least a change from other flowers her husband would send her when he was late and wanted to avoid an interrogation. For all of her husband's intellect she didn't understand how he could be so predictable sometimes.

She glanced at the clock on the oven and turned down all of the burners so dinner wouldn't be ruined. By the size of the bouquet it looked like he was going to be at least twenty minutes late. She didn't understand why he wouldn't just call her and tell her he was going to be late. Well, she would be the unpredictable one in this instance. She would act as if nothing was wrong. She would thank him for the flowers and go through the motions of a doting wife. Wouldn't that be something Jesus would do—if he were a female?

She shook her head trying to dispel the insecurity she felt. He could have sent the flowers just because he was thinking of her, and he wanted them to arrive before he got home. They were starting over, and he'd promised things would be different. They'd been in each other's pockets for the last week and a half and Michael hadn't reported anything new in his search for information regarding Grace or Brian. She was pretty sure he wasn't keeping anything from her, but when people trusted one another they asked each other questions and expected the truth. She fingered the new ring he'd given her and took a deep breath. She would ask him point blank, and she hoped for the sake of their new beginning that he would give her the truth.

She poured herself a small glass of wine and walked out onto the balcony to watch the sunset. She laughed at herself as she took a sip. She hadn't watched so many sunrises and sunsets as she had over the last few weeks. Of course, they were different all over the country, but the ones from the farm were always the most beautiful to her. As the last of the colors faded, she went back inside the apartment to check on their dinner.

Victoria was taking the ready-bake apple pie out of the oven when she heard the locks turn in the front door. She kept at her task of preparing everything so it could be transferred to the table. She smelled Richard's cologne just before she felt his arms creep around her waist. He placed soft kisses on the side of her neck. "I thought we were going out to dinner?"

She smirked to herself. "I thought I would surprise you with a home-cooked meal." She bit her tongue on the remark that she was the one that had been surprised and got a little squeeze for her efforts.

"Thank you for the flowers," she said, and his body stiffened slightly before he kissed her head and backed away.

"Your welcome. I was thinking of you and thought you would appreciate them."

She turned with a couple of serving dishes of food in her hands and gestured for him to take them. "You were right. They're gorgeous." She turned back to the stove to retrieve the rest of the food and followed him into the dining room.

Once they were situated with food on their plates, she offered to say grace and noticed the glimmer of surprise in his eyes. He smiled at her and she began. She was still self-conscious about praying out loud, but grace was pretty simple and after thirty seconds of thanks for her husband, the food, and the nourishment it would provide, she closed. Lifting her head with a sheepish smile on her lips she saw that her husband was watching her with a smile of his own.

Victoria searched her mind for a benign conversation topic. "Oh, how did the presentation go for support for the finishing of the orphanage in Uganda?" Richard looked up at her, a look of pleasant surprise on his features.

"It went better than I'd hoped. It was as if they were already primed." His eyes began to gleam, and she was reminded of earlier days in their relationship.

He told her about the company's board he'd been courting since the previous year and how they'd unanimously voted to help fund the digging of two wells within 5 miles of one another, the addition of one story, and one wing to the recently completed orphanage, along with maintenance and pay for a full-time staff of 15 for five years or 10 for seven. She figured the board had given much consideration to the fact that Richard's group had accomplished a great deal of the total project on their own. This orphanage would be able to house up to five hundred children comfortably upon the completion of the additions. The trade school, garden project, and small in-house medical clinic brought food, jobs, and accessibility for better health care to the area. Victoria found that she was just as, if not more so, proud of him for this victory as she had been when he worked for the stock market. She still wouldn't offer to go with him on his next trip, but she did find his philanthropic work intriguing. She reached across the table and squeezed his hand then focused back on her food for the next few minutes.

"What did you do today" Richard asked her as he sat away from the table.

Her mind began going over different scenarios. Should she steer the conversation to the questions she really wanted to ask or should she just do what she could to make it easier for him to open up to her on his own? Her devotional just that morning spoke of a woman who would pray over her nonbelieving husband while he was sleep and did her best to be an example of God's love in his life. It took years, but he did come to the Lord at a moment when she felt her weakest where her faith in God was concerned. The woman said she came to the realization that the timing of her husband's acceptance of God's gift of salvation was what kept her humble. She viewed it as a gift that only God could provide rather than anything she had done through her works. Victoria didn't know if she fully agreed because the woman was obviously praying to God constantly about her husband and should have at least taken responsibility for being obedient, but that wasn't what caught her attention. She wondered if the scripture Matthew 10:16, that was referenced by the woman for her story would be applicable for her situation. Though she didn't consider herself in the company of wolves, she did believe this situation presented itself to be a perfect opportunity for her to be as wise as a serpent but innocent as a dove.

"Victoria." The soft prompting drew her out of her reverie. She refocused on him and remembered she hadn't answered him just as he opened his mouth. She pressed to get in front of his next question.

"Today was quiet." She sipped sparingly from her wine glass. "I spoke to Martha this morning and she assured me the farm was still there." She smiled and winked at him. "The reports on the acres coming into the planting rotation next year arrived, and Harry wasn't too optimistic about it producing a record crop. But what else is new." She said with a wave of her hand. "He hasn't been enthusiastic about a crop in years, yet with each harvest we surpass the previous year's crop." She shifted in her chair and sighed. "He has been on me about wanting to use some experimental chemicals to help enrich the land, since last year." Honestly, she had been giving it more and more thought lately, but she needed more case studies before she would give over such a huge chunk of land to those chemicals. "If their stats keep rising I will give it some serious thought in a year or two." She ended the statement with a shrug.

"I did a little shopping for Vivian and Gladys' birthdays. I found the cutest matching coats. They are a really soft faux fur with animal ears attached to the hoods. I think they'll get a kick out of them." She paused for a moment. "If not, they will at least enjoy the hundred dollar Visa gift cards in the pockets."

Richard chuckled. "Yes. I think you covered the bases with those presents." He went quiet for a moment and stared at her with what she interpreted as admiration. "I think it's really nice of you to include Gladys in your gift giving."

She frowned at him. "They will be together next week. I could hardly send a present to Vivian and not include one for her twin sister. That would be inconsiderate."

"I agree, but it's not like you're Gladys' grandmother. You just met the child for the first time less than a month ago." She watched his face and realized what he was doing.

"I've talked to her on the phone a few times over this last year. Vivian would sometimes call me when she was already on the phone with Gladys. I think she was trying to get me used to the fact that she and her twin were only going to get closer." She shrugged again. "The child is pleasant enough. She is quite intelligent and has an interest in science and chemicals I find unusual for a child her age. She even asked me about some of the pesticides we used on the farm." She watched Richard's brows go up. "Yes, I know. I thought Vivian was exceptional. Looks like she came by it honestly." She thought about her statement only a split second before voicing it. "It makes me even more curious about their grandfather as it would be." She picked up her wineglass again. "Have you heard anything from Paige in that regard?"

Richard shook his head. "She hasn't approached the subject with Mel since the wedding. I think she is trying to keep the fragile truth they established at her wedding." She watched his eyes grow wary. "And she may have asked me if I could do a little digging."

Victoria wasn't sure how she felt about that. "What did you say?"

He looked at her in confusion. "Yes, of course."

"Who did you put on the job?"

"Berry" He replied without hesitation.

She breathed a little easier. "Oh, and how is that going?"

Richard's brows creased slightly. "It's only been a few weeks. He hasn't found much of anything yet. The birth certificate was obviously no help since the Senior Grace had the paperwork doctored to show herself and her husband as Paige's birth parents."

There was small sense of unease that formed at his last statement, but Victoria couldn't credit it to anything other than just hearing the woman's name made her uncomfortable.

"He is going through Mel's school records, any files he can find regarding neighbors she may have been close to, and medical records that aren't sealed, though I don't think he'll have much luck there. It's like that family is shrouded in shadows."

"Why do you think that is?" She said more to herself. "She must be hiding something pretty huge."

Richard nodded slowly seeming far away in thought.

"Speaking of research. Any news on the Senior Grace's background? You know, before her employment at the hospital?" She watched him closely, but only noticed a slight tensing of his hand on his glass. He shook his head as if frustrated and downed the last of his wine. He stood up slowly and collected their plates. He was halfway to the kitchen before she asked her next question.

"So, when are you going to tell me why you were late getting home tonight?"

She watched him slow slightly then continue on to the kitchen. "All you had to do was ask."

She frowned. "Why must I ask, when you weren't where you said you'd be at the time you said you were going to be there?" She raised her voice to insure he heard her. She heard the clanging of the plates against one another as he prepared them for the dishwasher in response to her reply.

She finished her wine and took her glass into the kitchen.

"Richard?" she asked as she handed him her glass.

46

He glanced at her briefly. "I had a phone call that went long. I figured I had a little grace time since we weren't planning on going out to dinner until seven, but you surprised me with dinner."

She leaned her hip against the counter. "Is that why you sent the flowers?"

He leaned over and gave her a chaste kiss. "I gave you the flowers because I know you like fresh flowers, and because I would rather see a smile on your face when I get home instead of a frown."

She touched his nose with the tip of her forefinger. "I know one way to ensure that you get a smile when you come home."

He smirked. "And what is that?"

"Be home when you say you will." She turned and headed for the door, but stopped before exiting.

She allowed her thoughts to be seen in her eyes. "It would have been nice to share the sunset with you." She watched as regret crossed his features before she left to go sit back on the balcony. It was way too beautiful a night to be cooped up in the apartment.

* * *

Victoria woke up to the smell of coffee. She stretched and shifted, her feet skimming across nothing but sheets. She listened intently to see if she could tell where her husband was in the apartment. She heard slippered footsteps on the carpet in the hallway heading toward their bedroom and smiled sleepily.

Her mind went back to the night before and she sighed. Richard had joined her on the balcony and after giving her shoulders and feet a bone-melting massage he picked her up and sat back on the lounger with her resting between his legs. They enjoyed the city lights and activities of the city from the quiet darkness of their lookout. She felt pampered, and cherished, and at peace. They remained there sharing a companionable silence until her yawns came more frequently than she guessed he was able to ignore.

He walked her to the bedroom, and after they got ready for bed and slipped between the sheets, he held her just a breath short of tightly. He wrapped himself around her until she felt cocooned in his heat. With her head on his chest she heard the rumble of his words forming before they came out of his mouth. "I love you so much, Victoria. I would do anything to keep you happy. My life wouldn't be worth half as much without you in it. I would live, and I'm sure I would fulfill my purpose, but you are my reward here on earth." He gave her a squeeze on the last words, and it brought tears to her eyes.

How she loved and adored this man. She'd made the right choice not to question him about his call nor his guarded mood at dinner. She didn't want to know just yet if he would have lied to "keep her happy."

She heard the door to the bedroom creak slightly as it opened. She opened her eyes to see Richard, still in his robe, carrying a tray, so she pulled herself up in bed and gave him a brilliant smile to go with her morning greeting, "Good morning, my love."

Richard placed the tray on her lap. The smell of his cream of wheat and coffee made her mouth water. He leaned down and kissed her lips slowly and softly. "Good morning."

She blinked up at him, warmed by his attention. "What is the reason for all of this?" she asked when he came to the other side of the bed.

"One, I love the fact that you came into the city to join me for the night and day. It tends to get lonely here without you." He gave a small pout, and his face was transformed back into the young man she'd met so many years ago. She couldn't hold back the giggle the action evoked.

"Two, you looked so beautiful this morning with your hair on my pillow, I felt immeasurably blessed, and I thought I would return the favor." She smiled again and sipped her coffee to hide her embarrassment which always happened when he looked at her so irreverently.

"What do you have to do today?" he asked as he took the cup from her and took a sip himself.

She tried to think through the romantic haze he'd weaved around them. "Hmmm, it's a light day. All I can think of is mailing the twins' presents to Paige, so she will have them when they arrive at the end of the week."

"Good, then we will spend the day together," he said handing her back her cup.

"You're not going in to the office today?" She loved the idea of walking around town with Richard. It had been a while since they'd done so in the middle of the week and it sounded decadent.

"Nope. It was going to be a pretty light day since most of the last two weeks were spent in preparation for yesterday's presentation. I emailed Nancy early this morning and asked her to reschedule the few appointments I did have then close the office early."

"Wow. Are you going for boss of the year?" she said, spooning up some of the hot cereal. It didn't matter what temperature it was outside, she was always in the mood for his cream of wheat. He always made it with the perfect balance of sugar and butter. She placed the spoon in her mouth and let the smooth texture lull her through the rest of her senses. She sat back against the pillows with a sigh. "Amazing as usual. Thank you, honey. This was so thoughtful of you."

She glanced up at him and saw that his eyes weren't teasing or quietly content anymore. She placed her spoon back in the bowl. "What is it? What's the look for?"

"It's for my third reason, but finish your breakfast first, and we'll talk." He took a slice of toast from her plate and bit into it.

Curiosity sparked in her mind like a firecracker. She watched him for a moment then asked, "Is it good news or bad news?" Her stomach did a small flip.

Richard cupped her jaw in his hand and stared into her eyes. "It's news. Just news."

She nodded her head. She said, "Okay." Because she couldn't think of anything else.

"Eat, baby," he said as he rubbed his thumb back and forth across her cheek. "We have a big day ahead."

She worked to calm herself. She took a few deep breaths trying to relax the constriction in her throat.

She looked back up at him, imploring him to just tell her. "It's just news, which is, I guess good news since we didn't have any before. Now eat."

"Okay, but can I ask you something?"

"Victoria," Richard said with warning.

"No, not that." She took a bite to appease him. "I just wanted to know… Is this the reason for your delay, yesterday?"

He took a deep breath. "Yes."

"Why didn't you say so, last night?"

He fiddled with the sash on his robe. "I wasn't sure I was going to tell you, yet."

She absorbed his statement while she took another sip of coffee. Its fragrance seemed to dim.

"Would you have told me if I'd asked you point blank?" She didn't look at him as she asked. Her heart was still too exposed.

"I would hope so," he said, resting his head on the headboard.

"You aren't sure?" She finally looked at him because she needed to see the answer in his eyes.

He turned his head toward her. "No. Not a hundred percent at the time."

"Why now?"

"Why didn't you ask me point blank last night?" he asked in response.

"I decided to trust that you would tell me when you were ready," she said without hesitancy.

"And that is why I decided to tell you now rather than later. I wanted you to know that your trust in me would never be in vain."

Victoria watched those beautiful chocolate eyes crinkle slightly at the edges, and she knew he was smirking before she looked down at his lips. She shook her head at his arrogance and went back to eating her breakfast. She knew she was in for a bumpy ride

CHAPTER 6

Paige walked around the apartment trying to see if there was anything she had overlooked in her preparation for Vivian and Gladys' visit. She was so excited she couldn't sit still all week, and poor Brandon had tried, on more than one occasion, to calm her in a few different ways. She smiled to herself as she thought of the way he took her mind off of the twins' visit early this morning. How she loved him.

Life was so different with him in it. She knew that should have been a given, but she really wasn't as prepared as she thought she would be. There were more compromises than she could have imagined. She didn't know how regimented her life was until she tried to conform to Brandon's schedule during their first week at home with one another.

She knew her unease was nothing compared to Brandon's, who after two rounds of comparing pros and cons had given up his apartment. She'd only won that challenge because her place was bigger, and the more open floor plan would allow for an easier adjustment if they should need a change of furniture in the future. She also had two subterranean parking spaces because she had a three-bedroom, two-bath apartment.

Their original plan had been to find a new apartment for the two of them, thus allowing them to start fresh together, but her lease wasn't up for another four months, and they hadn't seen anything they both liked.

Brandon and his brothers had begun moving some of his belongings into her—their—apartment a week before their marriage.

52

The last of his things were moved in while they were on their honeymoon. She wasn't too happy with the thought of people in her space while she wasn't there, but they were family, and she didn't have anything to hide. She just hoped they didn't break anything or put anything heavy, messy, or too ugly next to, or on, her things. She knew it was wrong to feel this way and that she was really going to have to work on being more tolerant to the changes, but until they found a new place, this was going to be a challenge.

Her once spacious-looking place was now somewhat smaller. She'd been taught by her father that everything had a place and furniture could bring peace or chaos to an area. Grace hadn't subscribed to the same outlook. She liked a house to look "lived in" with magazines on the coffee tables and knickknacks not just in the china cabinet but on other surfaces as well. Paige always felt like she was going to knock something over. Her childhood was plagued by dreams of breaking crystal statues and china figurines. She told herself at seven years old she would have a place where children could play with a minimal amount of furniture and no knickknacks.

She let her fingertips glide along the spines of his books on the bookcase he set beside hers against the wall in their office. They actually looked pretty good side by side and with them both being high and narrow they took up less wall space than she originally thought. She moved around the office to his desk, which thankfully wasn't one of those dark wood, heavy monstrosities. It was solid oak with just enough room for his Bibles, a pad of paper, his laptop, and some pens.

The office was made up from the smallest bedroom, but she'd picked this apartment because its bedrooms were spacious. She was thankful they wouldn't feel squished. if they wanted to use the office at the same time. She wondered if she would be able to write, with him so close. Was he one of those who would want to look over her shoulder? Would he now consider her creativity, their creativity? She shivered at the thought and walked out of the room.

She walked down the hall to the bedroom. This space looked untouched for the most part. They had changed out her daintier, white quilt for a neutral-colored duvet. It still matched her furniture, which was left as it was in the room. His chest of drawers was placed at the end of her walk-in closet alongside his suits. What was considered the odd piece of clothing was placed in the office closet. She knew it was inconvenient, but so was the small storage unit they purchased for some of her books, luggage, heavy coats, and his furniture that didn't fit.

She reached out to touch one of the pill bottles on his nightstand when her phone rang. She jumped slightly then scolded herself at her feeling of invading his space in her home. When would she start to feel comfortable again? When would her home feel like a sanctuary again?

She walked around the bed to the ringing cell on her bedside table. After checking the caller I.D. she answered. "Hi, Lady Menagerie." She couldn't help the smile that came to her lips.

"Well, hello yourself, married lady. How's married life treating you?"

"It's good." She paused slightly, trying to decide whether or not to share her challenges. "I think I'm going to like married life."

"You do, do you? Then what's with the hesitation?"

Paige shrugged her shoulder as if Lady Menagerie could see her. "There may be a challenge or two." She hedged.

"Oh Paige, as forthright and eager as you are, you are not perfect." She chuckled during the statement. "How are you feeling about the move?"

Paige looked around her once again. "It's not so bad. Brandon's habits seem to be a lot like mine. He's tidy and has a place for everything. We just need a little more space. I don't see how we would have fit in his place."

"You would have made it work. I still stand by my opinion that you should have moved in with him instead of the other way around."

"Why?"

"Paige, I know this comes as no surprise to you, but you have a hard time giving up control. I think it would have been more beneficial for both of you if he made room for you instead of the other way around."

"But I have more room. It was a practical decision on both of our parts," Paige argued.

"Practical, yes, but not necessarily correct," Lady Menagerie said in response. "How are you really dealing with his things being next to yours?"

Paige went silent. She felt guilty enough having the thoughts she did. She wasn't sure she was ready to voice them. "It's change. All change takes some adjusting."

"Paige, for you adjusting is moving one color of socks to the other side of the drawer. I'm not even sure what you need to do to change your socks to a whole different drawer."

Paige stood up and walked to the living room. She skirted around a box that Brandon was still unpacking and moved to stand in front of the window she was happy she didn't have to give up. "It has been challenging, finding a place for all of his things, but we have both been making some compromises."

"Paige, answer me honestly. How are you handling this?"

"It's not as easy as I thought it would be. I thought we could just make things blend."

"The two of you or him?

"What do you mean?" Paige didn't like where the conversation was going.

"I mean the reason why I think you should have moved in with Brandon instead of the other way around is because he would've made more room for you, as your husband, than you have probably made for him, due to your obsessive tendencies."

Paige started feeling defensive. "I've given up a lot of room for him, and if I'm so obsessive wouldn't it be best that remain in a familiar environment?"

"No, it would have been best if you needed to lean on him and start fresh with him rather than him starting fresh with you."

"We are looking for a place we can move into together. That was the original goal." Paige tried to keep from sounding irritated, but was quickly losing her patience.

"Then why did you fight so hard to have him move in with you?"

"I still had some time left on my lease. I have more space and…" She decided to just go with the full truth. "I feel more comfortable this way. Besides, the girls will be here at the end of the week. I didn't want them to have to stay in a hotel."

"Are you going to let all of your relatives stay with you? You're newly married, so you don't have the benefit of having years of experience with each other to fall back on if questions should arise about either one of your fidelities?"

"Huh?" Paige was totally confused by the left turn the conversation had taken.

"When you are newly married you may want guests, be they family or not, to stay in a hotel. If any type of accusations should come forward, you need to be able to back your spouse up one hundred percent." When Lady Menagerie finished speaking, Paige found herself trying to absorb and deconstruct the sentence without projecting. She couldn't help but ask her own question.

"Is there something going on, Lady Menagerie?" She spoke hesitantly, wondering if she was overstepping her bounds.

"Yes, well, I did call you for a totally different reason than to harp on your decision. I just want to help you get off to the best start possible." She sighed. "Okay, enough of that." Paige heard clapping on the other side of the line.

"While you were away we met with the trustee board and the legal team."

Paige walked over to the couch and sat down. She was on neither board, but if Lady Menagerie was sharing this information with her it had to be very important. "What's going on?"

"There have been allegations brought forth against my husband. A woman claimed he made sexual advances toward her." Lady Menagerie's voice had gone steely.

"What? I don't understand. When was this supposed to have happened? I've only been gone for two weeks. Who is she?" Paige couldn't seem to keep the questions in her head from coming out of her mouth. She was in shock. "What about you and Pastor Lawrence? How are you handling this? How do you feel? She couldn't seem to get her mouth to shut off.

"I think I can answer at least one of those questions if you'd let me," Lady Menagerie responded with a hint of amusement.

Paige was not amused though. How could Lady Menagerie even think about making a joke at a time like this? "Does the membership know?"

"Paige, I'm going to need you to take a few deep breaths and while you are doing that I need you to keep your mouth shut. Can you do that for me?"

Paige nodded, then remembering she was on the phone she answered verbally. "Yes." She could imagine Lady Menagerie nodding her head.

"Good. Now let me start at the beginning."

"In March, Pastor Lawrence started receiving letters threatening to expose him and his alleged behavior toward a former member. At first he didn't tell anyone, not even me. I can tell you, he won't do that again." Lady Menagerie sniffed, and Paige could see the pursed lips and narrow gaze in her eyes."

Paige was sure she didn't want to be in on any part of that conversation.

"Anyway, he sought legal counsel and was advised not to give in to any of the threats as that would make him look guilty."

"Is there proof on either side?" Paige said before cursing her loose tongue.

"No, but since she refuses to give up her claim we decided to get in front of things and speak to the trustee board." There was a pause on the line, but Paige tightened her lips to keep from talking.

"It's been...rough, but I believe my husband, Paige. He told me it was a completely false claim." Lady Menagerie's voice suddenly sounded tired.

"What do you need me to do?" Paige asked, wanting to take that weariness away.

"What? Nothing. I just wanted you to know. You're family." Lady Menagerie ended the sentence more quietly than the last.

"Then why didn't you tell me sooner?"

"Think back to March, Paige. What were you going through in March?" Lady Menagerie asked knowingly.

Paige didn't need to think back. She already knew. Her life had been a whirlwind since the previous September. She couldn't count the highs and lows she'd taken. March had been low. She started feeling guilty. She had been so caught up in her life she hadn't noticed the obvious distress her parents were going through.

"I know you see yourself as a mother figure to me, and you aren't wrong, but I don't want your position in my life to dictate what you let me help you with and what you don't," Paige said tentatively.

"Do you think I kept this from you because I wanted to hide the fact that Major and I were going through a trying time?" Lady Menagerie's voice got tight which warned Paige of her impending temper.

"No. I know you have trials. There is no person on this earth that doesn't, and I don't expect you to always pick the box marked 'Jesus did it this way' because it isn't that simple. I just want you to know that sharing your challenges with me will not send me screaming from the church nor God."

"Oh, baby, I know that. I want to let you know that as your mother figure, mentor, and First Lady, I will not be the one crying on your shoulder, sharing my momentary doubts or giving in to emotionally led outbursts in front of you. I will not deny having them, but my job, on many levels, is to guide and instruct you, by example, on how to walk through them trusting in God."

"Don't you think that if I never see you concerned I might think there was something wrong with me if I became concerned?" Paige asked, her voice impassioned with her need to make her point.

"I would never think or treat you like you were that dense," Lady Menagerie said almost indignant.

"Not dense, Lady Menagerie," Paige said beseechingly. "But fragile, weak, unable to seek the same great God that you sought to receive peace and understanding."

Lady Menagerie was quiet for a moment before she spoke. "It seems I have unintentionally underestimated you."

Paige smiled to herself. "So you won't keep things from me?"

"Oh, sweetie, I may still keep things from you, but the reason will not be because I don't think you can handle it." Lady Menagerie's voice had returned to a benign decibel.

Paige had been taught how to pick her battles, and she felt more than assuaged at how this went so she wouldn't challenge Lady Menagerie's last statement.

"Alright, Lady Menagerie. I'm here for you," she said to solidify their truce.

"I know," Lady Menagerie said on a sigh then changed the subject. "So, are you ready for Gladys and Vivian?"

Paige looked around the living room again. "Yes, because I don't think I can do anything else to make this place more appealing to two teenagers."

"Well, just enjoy them, and they won't have any clue you are close to a nervous breakdown. Children smell fear, you know," Lady Menagerie said with a chuckle.

"Ha ha ha," Paige began, but stopped when she heard the key in the door. "Lady Menagerie, may I share what we talked about with Brandon?"

"Of course. No need to start out keeping things from each other, besides I figured if I told you, you would talk to Brandon.

Paige looked up to see Brandon walking through the door. "We will be praying for you."

"I expect nothing less, and I ask for nothing more," came Lady Menagerie's quick reply.

"Brandon's home. I'll talk to you soon, okay?" Paige said, watching as he placed his briefcase in a kitchen chair. Day three of him ignoring the special hook she'd installed in the hallway closet especially for his piece of luggage. She barely heard Lady Menagerie's response before she hit the "end" button. *God help me.* She whispered under her breath.

"Hi, honey, I'm home," Brandon said smiling at her. "I've always wanted to do that," he shared as he walked toward her.

There it was, she thought. That was the reason she loved this man. The reason why she married him. The simple joy of being able to recite a corny line and have it be relevant to his life made him light up from the inside and he shared that with her by giving her that heart-stopping smile.

"Hi, baby," she responded as she tilted her face for his kiss. He leaned down, touching his lips to hers, then lingered. He pulled back enough to look her in the eyes.

"Hi, sweetie," he whispered. He kissed her again, but this time he pulled her up from the couch and wrapped himself around her as he angled his head, deepening the kiss. When he finally released her lips, she was reeling and fisted the back of his shirt in her hands to keep her steady. When the world came back into focus she saw him grinning at her.

Such a man.

"How was your day?" she asked.

"It was good," he said while leaning in to rub his nose against hers. "I thought I might have to stay overnight to complete enough of the files to be able to see over the stack of them on my desk, but my boss shooed me out." He sat on the couch and pulled her onto his lap. He wrapped his arms around her and squeezed gently as he rubbed his nose under her ear. The feeling turned her insides to liquid, distracting her.

"She said they were happy I was back, but she wasn't taking the blame for the bruise I would be sporting tomorrow if I came home late for dinner."

"Awww, how nice and violent she is," Paige said giggling. She leaned back against his arm.

"I don't know how to tell you this, but I haven't started dinner yet. I was too busy getting ready for the twins' visit."

"I figured as much," he said using his arm to pull her in close enough to kiss her forehead. He breathed in deep then let it out slowly. "Are you alright with all of this?" He gestured with his other hand by sweeping it across the room. "I know you've gotten used to living here on your own, and the adjustment hasn't been as smooth as I thought it would be."

She slid herself back off of his lap and onto the couch between him and the arm of the couch so she could get the distance she needed to let him know it was worse than what he perceived. She took one his hands in both of hers, running her fingers across his knuckles watching as she did so.

"It's been more of a challenge than I thought. I mean, I know I have a few issues with needing to be in control." She took an apprehensive breath, but continued when she got no sound from Brandon. It gave her the courage to look up at him. "But I never thought it would fill so many of my thoughts." She rubbed her hand across her forehead. "I barely got a page written today; I had such a hard time concentrating. I know the girls' visit is a big reason for my anxiety, but I need you to understand that I feel like my whole structure of organization has been shaken."

She'd warred with herself against sharing her inner turmoil. She knew Brandon had so much more on his shoulders, but these feelings weren't going away. In fact, they were getting worse, and she didn't want them putting any more weight on their marriage than they already had.

Brandon pulled her back on his lap, but allowed her a little distance so they could see each other. "Tell me something. When you get up in the middle of the night, what do you do for that hour before you come back to bed?" Paige sucked in a breath. She thought he'd slept through her nightly meandering around the apartment. It was more to sooth her than anything else. She would go through all of the closets rearranging anything that was out of place or sit in the room where the girls were going to be staying and pray while she rearranged the pictures, knickknacks on the furniture, or gifts she'd left in their closet. She took in the concern on his face and decided to give him full disclosure.

"I don't do well with change."

"Baby, I think I've got that," he said with a small quirk of his lips.

"Well, I didn't know it would be quite this bad." She saw a shadow cross his features, and his lips set.

"What do you need?" he asked, his eyes intent.

Her heart flipped. This man who she felt she'd cheated in some way was willing to give more. She bit her lip to keep it from trembling. "You're giving it to me. You're giving me the space to think, but a chance to talk, and I need both. I'm sorry I didn't tell you how bad this could get, but I'm working on it, I promise."

"Paige, I need you to back up because you have just taken this into the stratosphere, and I'm still on earth," he said peering into her eyes. "Now what do you do when you get up in the middle of the night when you think I'm asleep? I know it isn't just praying because you move around too much."

Paige looked up at him with what she knew must be sorrowful eyes. "I, um, look in the closets and cabinets to make sure everything is arranged neatly, then I..." She cleared her throat. "I go into the girls' room and pray and rearrange their room and closet to make sure it is welcoming and they have enough hangers, the exact same amount of space for their clothing, and same amount of things on their desks and furniture." Unable to look at him anymore she stared at her lap and shrugged. "I think I've rearranged their space at least six times—"

"Eight," Brandon said, cutting her off. She looked up at him surprised he'd been so attuned to her, but then he always had been.

"You aren't in this alone. That's what I'm trying to get across to you. Adjustments and compromise are a part of change, and we just made a few big ones. We aren't going to find all the answers overnight. I'm sure we will find out some things about ourselves and about each other we are not particularly proud of, but if we don't communicate we don't stand a chance." He squeezed her gently before continuing, "I need to know what you need from me to help you feel more comfortable."

Paige slowly began to tell him about the feeling she's been dealing with all week in regards to sharing their space. She told him what made it worse and what made it better but most of all she told him what she thought it stemmed from.

"After the girls were born and taken, I told you I went into a deep depression." At Brandon's nod she continued, "What I didn't tell you was that I needed things just-so in my room—my space—in order to function properly. It was really bad at first because it affected my sleeping and eating. I was seeing a therapist." She rolled her eyes. "That didn't really go well. I was so angry and just wanted everyone to leave me alone. I sat there and stared at her the first few times I was there. There was no way she could understand what I was going through. No one could, but at the fourth appointment she sat there and looked at me for the first fifteen minutes, which was more than awkward, then she asked me if I wanted to get back what was stolen from me. That peaked my interest. I was tired of people stealing from me and in a lot of ways I wanted revenge." Brandon began to frown and Paige placed her fingers on his lips to keep him from commenting.

"The therapist was speaking more figuratively, something I didn't catch on to for a whole other session. I wouldn't be able to get my innocence back, but I could get back the confidence, self-esteem, and security he stole. I could decide how much more he took by getting out of bed each day and doing something new for myself each week. I could find moments of happiness that would come against the blackness I felt like I was surrounded in and do it more and more each day until there was more happiness than blackness. She showed me some coping techniques and I still use them when I feel like there are more changes than constants in my life." She rubbed her hands up and down her arms to soothe herself. "Looking at it now, I have to say that it may seem a bit obsessive. After I gave my life to Christ and immersed myself in Him I let go of some of the techniques, but it was so hard getting out of my head these last few weeks I resorted back to a few." The room was silent except for her heart that was now pounding against her breastplate.

"I double check things. I count things to make sure they're, um... even. I moved some of your things into the office closet, not because we didn't have enough room in the bedroom closet, but because I couldn't make them line up with the clothing on the other side of the closet. You have a lot of, um, odd pieces of clothing. You know, like one plaid shirt." He cut her off.

"I don't really care for plaid," he said sheepishly.

"Do you want me to donate it to the church?" she offered, wanting to help in any way.

"No, my mom gave it to me as a gift."

"Oh, okay." She didn't know what else to say, but his little shake brought her eyes back to his, and she saw the small smile of encouragement that gave her the courage to continue. "I, well, like I said, you have a few odd pieces. There's a pair of old, faded, green sweats that don't have a matching top and they didn't really go with anything you had in the drawer so...they're in the closet along with a bronze suit jacket, a tie-dye hoody, a zip-up jacket with some kind of bowling logo on it, a pair of black cowboy boots and a really huge knit sweater." She took a deep breath as if she'd let go of a huge weight.

"Are you alright with them being in that closet?" Brandon asked.

"Yeah. It's fine. I consider that my dark matter space. It's there but not really there until I need to think about it." She half grimaced, half smiled at him. "I'm okay, really I am. I just need a few concessions until I feel a little more accustomed to everything.

Brandon seemed to contemplate something. "Do you think you would have been better off moving into my place?"

"No. It probably would have been worse. I would have felt a lot less comfortable carving out a place for myself than making space for you here."

She saw his jaw tighten then relax. "And when do you think you will feel comfortable enough in your home, that you have made space for me in, to begin to consider it our home, our things, our space?"

"I do, for the most part. I know my words don't always reflect that, but I'm working on it. I know it was a sacrifice for you to give up your place. I know that you may be feeling more like a guest than the priest of this home." She placed the palms of her hands on the sides of his face. "I am just working with some handicaps that set me back a little. I'm sorry I didn't say anything about it before, but I honestly didn't think this was going to be such an issue." She began pressing kisses on his cheeks. "This is our place, our life, but I just need more time to adjust to it." She waited as he watched her with bewilderment.

"How did I not see this?"

"I wasn't hiding it, if that's what you're thinking. I haven't felt the compulsion to do any of these things for years. That is mostly because I have had a pretty strict schedule until last year. It may be the culmination of everything. I just didn't think to look out for any triggers, so I was caught off guard."

"Alright, what do you feel that compels you to rearrange and reorganize things around our home?"

She smiled at him, humbled by his understanding. "I get a little concerned about things being in their right place. It starts out as a small thought, but then I wonder if I let it go, how much more will I let go, and will I be able to get everything back in line in the morning or in a few hours. If I don't do anything, it grows to anxiety. I know it is irrational and only symbolic of how I'm feeling about everything going on around me, but if I can just keep it all in order in this house then I am free to slowly work through everything completely out of my control.

"Like what? What do you feel is out of your control?" She didn't want to go here. She didn't think she could explain how his illness left her feeling helpless. Not hopeless, but still not able to receive what she felt she truly needed which was to know with confidence that her husband would be with her to celebrate not only their first-year anniversary, but many more. She decided to bury it among all the other changes she was dealing with.

"Well, like I said, it's been a year of changes, starting with the funeral, meeting you, finding out Vivian was still alive, the complications from surgery, getting ready for the wedding, learning the latest results in your bout with cancer, finding out Mel was keeping secrets, and still is, about my parentage, and sharing space with a man and his things, even if he is the most delectable man I know."

"You're trying to distract me," Brandon said with a mock frown.

"Is it working?" Paige whispered saucily. She glided her hands down his jaws to his neck and opened the top button of his shirt. She began working on the second button when he stilled her hand with one of his. She looked back into his eyes which were now serious.

"What do you need from me to make you feel secure and comfortable in *our* home?" he asked quietly.

"A little time, a lot of patience and some understanding," she said as honestly as she could.

"Will you tell me if I do anything to trigger a compulsive or obsessive need?" he asked as he ran his hands up and down her back.

She nodded, feeling unexpectedly shy.

His hands slid lower. "So is there anything I can do to keep you from leaving our bed in the middle of the night?" She looked up and to the side as if thinking.

"Hmmm...I'm not sure," she said tapping on her chin.

"I see I will need to refresh your memory," he said repositioning her to straddle him before he stood up. She wound her arms around his neck to keep from falling and nipped at his ear. "Refresh away, my love."

He was halfway down the hall before he spoke again. "Paige."

"Yes?" she whispered in his ear.

"I'm going to be late for dinner." She started giggling, but it was cut short by his deep kiss that lead to another and another.

*   *   *

Paige lay in the dark of the bedroom listening to Brandon's heavy breathing. She glanced over at the clock. It read three thirty a.m. Maybe she could wait it out until Brandon got up and left for work. The impulse to check the girls' room just one more time came over her stronger than the last. She just needed to make sure the clocks were on and the closet light still worked. It would be hard for them to see their clothing if the bulb went out. She decided to slip out, quickly check the light and come back to bed before Brandon was the wiser. She eased one foot off the bed and began to slip the other over when Brandon's arm came to wrap around her waist and pulled her closer to him. "Where are you going?"

"To the bathroom." She wasn't completely lying. He had startled her so bad she now had to go to the bathroom. She would just go and check the light after.

"Go back to sleep. You need to be up early."

The hand around her waist lifted, and she slid out. She walked to the bathroom, took care of business and tiptoed out to check that all the clocks were at the right time and the closet light was bright.

She slipped back in bed and began to breathe evenly when Brandon moved closer and whispered in her ear. "I'm praying for you, baby." He wrapped his arm back around her waist, spooning her from behind then fell back to sleep. Paige lay still until his breathing evened out and began to pray for herself

CHAPTER 7

Brandon stood at the counter in the break room taking deep breaths. He breathed through his nose and out of his mouth because his physician said it would help tamp down on the nausea. Almost one year of chemo, and the only thing that really helped was the anti-nausea medicine, which he had taken nine minutes ago, but he still unconsciously reverted to the deep breathing when bile rose in his throat.

He gripped the rounded formica counter and squeezed as he willed his breakfast to stay down. He needed to get back to work. He had reports stacked higher than his head that needed completing, and he was only going to be able to do a half day as it was because he was going with Paige to pick up the girls.

He swallowed twice and thought about giving visualization a try. He'd come into the break room instead of the men's room because the smell of coffee seemed to help soothe his stomach in prior attacks. He just needed the pills to stay in his stomach long enough to take effect. Perspiration broke out on his upper lip, and he was about to give in and head to the men's bathroom when he heard the faucet turn on, and a wet paper towel was thrust in front of him.

"Place it on the back of your neck," came a familiar female voice. "It might be cool enough to shock your system." He did what he was told. and the chill slowed the rising bile enough for him to get back a small bit of control. He looked over at his boss, embarrassed. "Thanks," he mumbled between pants and then forced himself to breathe more evenly until the overwhelming urge calmed some more.

"Better?" his boss asked with a hopeful note in her voice.

"Better," he said on a sigh.

"Think you can make it to my office?" she asked.

He took the cloth away from his neck and wiped his upper lip. He took another deep breath, thankful that the medication finally seemed to be working. "Yes," he said, straightening and turning to look at Barbara Holden, his director and friend. Her look of understanding calmed his nerves a little and gave him the strength to push back from the counter and follow her down the hall to her office.

"Well, I guess I don't have to ask you how you're doing," Barbara said with a sardonic grin as she closed her door behind him.

Brandon sat in the chair facing her. "I was just playing the waiting game. I should be good now."

"Are you on a more aggressive treatment of chemo and radiation?" Barbara sat down behind her desk.

Brandon had been dreading this particular conversation. His boss had supported and allowed him to work around his chemo and radiation schedule as well as take the needed days to recover. It brought him down to almost zero sick days and a week of vacation when only a year ago he'd accrued the maximum allotted sick/family days and vacation time.

She was especially empathetic because he was one of the few that stepped in and helped keep her cases up-to-date when she was battling breast cancer. He didn't know how she was going to take hearing that chemo and radiation was no longer a viable option for him. He knew she and her women's group prayed for him constantly and hesitated, sharing his last diagnosis with her.

He said a silent prayer, asking God for the right words, so she would receive some type of comfort with his news.

"No. I'm no longer taking chemo or radiation." He took a deep breath and looked her in the eye. "My new regiment of medication is taking some getting used to. I was late taking my anti-nausea medicine today. Sorry for that display in the break room."

His boss waved her hand as if to dismiss his last sentence. "So you are through with your latest cycle. What did the doctor say?" she asked with an expectation that made his heart hurt.

He swallowed. "He said it's out of their hands. The cancer has metastasized and is growing at a rate that has made chemo and radiation ineffective." He watched her brow furrow and a light dim in her eyes. He had to give it to her though. She quickly masked it by pressing her lips together and forcing them into a smile.

"So what do they have you on now?" she asked after a heavy moment of silence.

"Supplements to help bring up my blood cell levels so my body can fight as long as possible. All sorts of medications to help my liver and kidneys continue to function optimally and a blood thinner also to help my liver and kidney purge toxins. I think I'm at five medications to purposely help my body and three more to counteract the side-effects of the five. That plus prayer will give me the time I need."

She smiled at the last statement. "How are you doing mentally?"

Brandon shrugged. "It's a little surreal. I've been through the cycles of chemo and radiation before and nine years later I'm still here. God healed my body before and if He wills it, He will do it again. I can deal with that. Only now it isn't just me. I have a wife I love deeply and would like to spend more time with."

"What are you going to do?" Barbara asked seeming to have collected herself.

Brandon leaned forward placing his hands on the front of her desk. "I'm going to come to work, if you will allow it. Continue working with the men's department at my church and spend time with my gorgeous wife. I need the structure right now until I can wrap my head around everything. I will try and give you at least two weeks if I feel the hours are becoming too much."

"How much time did the doctor say you had?" Barbara asked hesitantly. She played with the pen in her hand, rolling it back and forth between her fingers.

Brandon grimaced, but answered the question the only way he was willing. "I don't think what man says really matters right now. If they feel they've exhausted every bit of knowledge they have to save me, I can't trust their knowledge when it comes to an expiration date. I go when God says I go." He finished the sentence more in determination than resignation.

Barbara nodded her head once in acquiescence. "I'm here, you know." She stood up from her chair to come around her desk. Brandon sensing the meeting was over, stood up and reached his hand to shake hers. She clasped it in both of hers and held it for a beat longer than was professional, but then there wasn't too much about this meeting that was professional. It was two colleagues turned friends in the trying times.

"You know, we should all go out to dinner soon. Troy was just asking about you and outside of the wedding, and what you've told me about Paige, I barely know her," Barbara said matter-of-factly.

"I accept for both of us. How about two weeks from tomorrow? I will double check with Paige, but I'm pretty sure that would be good for us. We have the girls beginning tonight, and Paige is running herself ragged trying to make sure she hasn't forgotten anything."

Barbara watched him carefully. "I think two weeks from tomorrow will be perfect. How is Paige doing?"

Brandon was momentarily at a loss for words. He wasn't completely sure himself. "Paige is remarkably strong in so many ways. She never ceases to amaze me with her ability to surrender herself to God. Whether it's emotional or physical, she has derived great strength in giving over her weaknesses to Him," he said truthfully.

Barbara nodded, a small smile coming to her lips. "I'm so happy you found one another."

Brandon offered her his best rendition of a smile in return. "I have quite a few things to get through before I leave for the day. I'll be taking Paige to the airport to pick up the girls." He walked to the door turning back before exiting. "Thank you, Barbara. I appreciate everything you've done and are doing."

"You would do the same, if not more for me, Brandon. I appreciate the chance to give back to you in any way I can."

Brandon gave her one more glance as he turned to close the door behind him. *Thank you God for keeping my mouth and my emotions in check. It really would have been hard if she'd started crying. I don't know if I would have been able to keep it together.*

He went back to his desk, thankful the medicine had kicked in and vowed to get through at least five of the folders sitting on his desk before he left for the day.

*   *   *

Brandon looked over at Paige ringing her hands in the passenger's seat. He had just pulled into a parking space on the arrival side of the airport. They had a couple of moments yet since both girls had checked their luggage and were waiting for them at the baggage claim.

Brandon took one of Paige's hands and kissed the knuckles. He was always surprised at how soft her skin was. He memorized some of the lines crossing over her knuckles before looking up into her eyes. "I'm with you on this. You aren't just hosting them. We are. They are my family now also, and I want my time with them, so don't even think of monopolizing them during their whole visit."

Paige's lips quirked into a little smile. "Okay."

He could tell she wanted to say more, but she closed her mouth. "Okay." He paused briefly. "How about we seal that agreement with a kiss." He leaned over and pressed his lips against hers slowly. He tipped his head slightly to deepen the kiss hoping to pull her out of her head, but she pulled back. He stayed in her space sharing her breath for a few seconds. "Stay." was all he could say as he stared at her lips.

"Stay?" she repeated.

"Yes. Stay. Stay outside of your head. Here with me."

Her breath hitched, and he leaned back slightly to look into her eyes. "Okay," she said again.

"Promise?" he teased.

"Hmmm, I wonder if it would be more fun if I didn't," she replied saucily.

"Definitely more fun." He leaned in again whispering in her ear, "Please don't promise."

He felt, more than saw, the shiver run through her and did an inner fist pump at causing the reaction. He kissed her earlobe and jaw, slowly moving back toward her lips. He felt her give in just before her phone began to vibrate. His heart was beating fast, but he chuckled and sat back in his seat. He watched as Paige fumbled slightly with her phone before accepting the call. He couldn't help the grin that tipped the side of his mouth.

After a few words Paige glanced at him, her ears flushed a lovely shade of pink. He saw her catch his grin and watched as she shook her head. "Incorrigible."

He took in the fire he lit in her eyes. "No honey, I'm your husband" he said with a wink before exiting the car and coming around to open her door. He wrapped his arm around her shoulders as they walked toward baggage claim and pulled her in close. He took in the moment like a breath and stored it away in his memory so he could write it down later.

*   *   *

Brandon leaned against the doorjamb as he watched Vivian, Gladys, and Paige interact with one another. After stowing their luggage in their bedroom and excitedly moving through their closet of new clothes they came back out into the common areas to see what had changed since the last time they'd been there. Paige answered all of their questions with patience and almost as much excitement. He loved seeing the glow of triumph on her face and his heart warmed even more toward the girls as they expressed their gratefulness and pleasure at almost all of Paige's efforts to make their stay as comfortable as possible.

Brandon hooked up his video game console in the living room earlier in the week, but asked them if they wanted him to move it to their room. They both agreed that keeping it in the living room would be best so they could have a family game night. It didn't take long for their excitement and overall happiness to become contagious. He couldn't have thought of a better remedy for Paige and all of the challenges she was still battling. He whispered a prayer of thanks before he left the females on the couch talking over one another as they filled in the blanks of the schedule Paige laid out before them for the week.

He was tired and knew that they could get lost in the details for hours. He would set his alarm and get a couple of hours of much needed sleep before they took the girls to dinner. Trying to keep watch over Paige the last few nights had been exhausting. The thought reminded him of the meeting he'd scheduled with Pastor Lawrence the next day. He would take advantage of the time Paige and the girls would spend shopping. It meant another short day, but since it was only by an hour, he wasn't too worried. The last thing he heard as he laid his head on the pillow gave him a peace he'd been seeking since his wedding day. It was the sound of his wife's unbridled laughter. Everything would be fine. She would be alright.

*   *   *

"So, how is married life?" Pastor Lawrence asked as he lowered his long frame into the chair across from Brandon's and placed his ankle on his knee.

Brandon couldn't help the smile that came to his lips, but before he could answer, his pastor did so for him.

"That good, huh?"

Brandon merely shrugged knowing any answer would only incite more teasing.

Pastor Lawrence reached forward and grabbed a bottle of water off the cart between them. Brandon watched as he uncapped it and took a swallow. It took a few seconds before he realized Pastor Lawrence was giving him time to open up the conversation he'd scheduled the meeting for.

He repositioned himself in his seat and worked hard to find a starting place. After a few more seconds of silence went by Pastor Lawrence set his bottle aside, folded his hands raised a brow at Brandon.

"I know I called this meeting," Brandon said hurriedly. "I'm just not sure where to begin."

"Start with what's bothering you the most then we will branch out from there."

"Did you know Paige struggles with a compulsive disorder?" Brandon blurted then winced at the way it sounded. Pastor Lawrence lowered his leg, but his face went blank.

"No I didn't. Did she tell you this and if not what makes you think so?"

"After I addressed my concern about certain behaviors she was exhibiting, she admitted that after the birth of her children she was diagnosed with obsessive-compulsive disorder. With talk therapy and medication she was able to gain some sense of control. By the time she came here it was well under control. She said constantly reading her Bible and her relationship with God were a huge help in quieting the panic-inducing thoughts."

"What's changed?" Pastor Lawrence asked, his brows furrowing.

Brandon swallowed back the incredulous chuckle. "What hasn't changed for her over the last year?" He paused then began counting his points off on his fingers. "She eulogizes her cousin's funeral and a few months later becomes a living organ donor, which didn't go as smoothly as it should have." He leaned forward slightly. "She finds out the young woman she's giving one of her kidneys to is the biological daughter she was told was stillborn. If that isn't enough, she is told the woman she's only known as her sister, is her mother, and a week before our wedding we find out that chemo and radiation are no longer viable treatments for the cancer that is now spreading through my body." Brandon stopped to catch his breath. He told himself he would try to make this plea for his wife with more facts than emotion.

"Is she seeing anyone? Is she getting counseling?"

"Besides your wife? No."

"Is she against counseling?"

"I don't know. We haven't talked about it yet. It's been a little busy with the honeymoon, move, and now with her daughters staying for the week. I will approach that subject with her, but I came here today to talk to you about what will happen when..." Brandon mentally regrouped. "If I die sooner rather than later." He straightened in his seat. "I know you are Paige's extended family, and you have known her much longer than I have, but I need the assurance that no matter what she tells you, you will not let her live alone the first couple of months after my death."

Brandon saw Pastor Lawrence's jaw tighten and knew he was fighting an impulse. Brandon jumped back in. "I know you will be there for her as long as you think she needs you and then longer than that, but I would feel better knowing that she wouldn't go home to an empty house for at least a few months after I pass."

"Do you think she might harm herself?" Pastor Lawrence's face was a mask of concern now.

"Not really. She has her daughters to think of. I just don't want to give her time to curl into herself."

"What makes you think she won't come to us?"

"Because she won't want to put more on you than you have on yourself now, and if it isn't resolved before I go she won't come to you."

Brandon watched the clenching of his pastor's jaw quicken. "I didn't say this to upset you or make you angry," he said, misunderstanding his pastor's reaction.

"I'm not angry at you, Brandon. I'm frustrated with this situation. It's a waste of my time, a waste of money and resources, and every day I wake up to find that it has disrupted or damaged another piece of the relationships I have built with people." His exasperation was apparent, and Brandon's heart went out to the man.

When Paige shared with him what Lady Menagerie had told her about the sexual harassment claim against Pastor Lawrence he waited for the punch line, then upon understanding that it wasn't a joke he found it nearly impossible that anyone would believe such a claim. He'd never seen Pastor Lawrence flirt with anyone besides his wife, let alone touch someone inappropriately. He held to his strict rule of keeping his office door slightly ajar when meeting one-on-one with women, and he was quick to refer any woman to his wife or the women's department if he thought they were using their counseling time as a ruse to make advances.

"What happened, Pastor Lawrence? If you don't mind talking about it. Why did she do this?"

Pastor Lawrence watched him for a moment, seeming to gauge him. He finally let out a breath and leaned forward while rubbing his forehead with his thumb and forefinger. He began speaking slowly, as though he was reluctant to revisit the root of the problem.

"Marilyn Shuster assisted Tanya Blasen with the children's ministry about three years ago. She had a heart for children ages five through eight. They seemed to blossom under her direction in Sunday school. Beyond that, she was a very peculiar woman. Outside of Sunday and Wednesdays no one had contact with her. She didn't strike me as a weekend Christian, but I know she turned down offers to attend more than a few social functions."

He paused for a moment. "One day she comes to my office for an appointment. She was having some problems with her ex-husband and needed some advice. After she told me the issue, I asked her a few questions and had to let her know that she was in the wrong." Pastor Lawrence smiled wryly. "She didn't take it very well." He shifted back in his seat.

"She continued to help out, but she was skittish around me for a while. A month or two went by and she made another appointment. Since things seemed to have gone back to normal, I had no reservations about meeting with her again. I actually thought she wanted to give me some follow-up news. Boy, was I wrong." He smoothed out his pant leg.

"She asked me for advice on a whole different matter, and when I asked her if she'd taken my last advice to heart, she balked." Pastor Lawrence shrugged his shoulders. "My thought was, if she didn't want to take my advice the first time, why would she come back for more?"

Brandon, having several siblings that would at any time accept or reject his advice, kept quiet.

"I listened, and once again asked her a few questions before giving her some wisdom backed by Scripture. She thanked and hugged me, and I thought we were back on track, but once again for the next couple of weeks she shied away from me in public and continued to keep to herself." Pastor Lawrence began chuckling.

"You know I even brought her name up to Lady Menagerie one day, and she decided to invite her personally to a couple of events. Ms. Shuster begged off, and the next time she made an appointment with me she told me she didn't appreciate the charity. Even after I denied it, she claimed she knew I told my wife to befriend her and didn't want the false acts of kindness. I decided right then that I wouldn't be taking any more appointments with her." Brandon watched him go back to his initial posture with one ankle over the other knee.

"I told Pam to refer her to one of the elders for appointments in the future and just kept an eye on her through Tanya and other leadership. Pam let me know she accepted appointments with other elders a couple of times then stopped making appointments. A few months later she and Tanya had a difference of opinion in regards to certain lesson plans being appropriate for the children in the age group she taught, and she stopped helping with the children's ministry. Five months after that she left the church."

"Wow." Was all Brandon could say. His mind was full of questions he didn't know if he had the right to ask, but Pastor Lawrence continued so he remained silent.

"In early February I received a letter from Ms. Shuster. She stated that I should work on my counseling skills." I was surprised to hear from her, but brushed it off as negative mail. Two weeks later I received a similar note, but this was about my poor skills in picking leaders. This went on a few more times, and I told Pam to document when I received a piece of mail from Ms. Shuster. The last two just had questions." He paused as though he were trying to recall the letters.

"The first one said. *Did you tell your wife about our meetings?* The next one said *You should follow some of your own advice."* Pastor Lawrence quirked his mouth. "You better believe I showed my wife those letters."

"What did she think?" Brandon asked before he realized he was talking.

"She read them all then told me to call our lawyer because the woman didn't sound like she was done." He smiled briefly. "She was right too. The next correspondence came in the form of a notice that she was suing me for sexual harassment. I was floored. I hugged the woman like three times total in the two and a half years she was with us. I never completely closed my door when we were meeting, and Pam even had to interrupt once." He shook his head still seeming to be baffled by it all."

"What's next?" Brandon asked. Shaken by what was happening to his friend.

Pastor Lawrence shrugged, portraying an air of nonchalance, but Brandon could see he was having a hard time.

"My lawyer says she doesn't have a case, but it's going to take a moment to make this all go away because her lawyers are purposely slow to respond."

"What does that mean for you?"

Pastor Lawrence was quiet for a long moment.

"The longer this goes on the more my name gets dragged through the mud."

Both men were quiet for many moments. Pastor Lawrence visibly shook himself and seemed to refocus his attention on Brandon.

"Alright. From the earlier part of this conversation I get the feeling you are preparing Paige to live without you."

Brandon began feeling the unease roll up his spine. "It would be irresponsible for me to do less," he replied.

"Just be careful of how much energy you expend toward her moments after you're gone. Make sure it doesn't outweigh the energy you spend on making beautiful memories with her while you're alive."

Brandon absorbed his words which sounded so close to the ones God had given him many times in prayer. He waited for the lecture that would accompany those words, but after a few moments of them quietly watching each other he realized none was forthcoming.

Pastor Lawrence cracked a smile. "I still love it when I surprise people." He shook his head as he stood up. "God's message is perfect on its own. I can't make it any plainer." He waited until Brandon stood up as well before he continued, "Are you hungry? I'm hungry. Let's go have a bite. Besides I think you need some more male conversation before you go back home to three females."

Brandon chuckled. He checked his watch and shrugged. He had an hour or two to spare.

*   *   *

For Brandon the week went by in a little bit of a blur. Each day seemed long on its own, but he was surprised to wake up on Friday with just an overall feeling of pleasant tiredness from the week at work and with the girls. They found a way to insert their birthday celebration into almost every activity they did, especially meals in restaurants. Brandon didn't believe he'd had to pay for either of the twin's dinners once. Vivian would pour on the charm and Gladys would act shy one night and then they would reverse the roles. They were both hilarious and a little scary. He felt for any young man that fell for either one of them—not that they had to worry about that for many years. Mason and Marc would make sure of that.

He tried not to be so obvious about watching Paige that week because he didn't want to alert Vivian to any issues he and Paige were having, but he'd felt Vivian's hawk-like gaze on him more than what was comfortable.

The last day of their visit Paige was called in to meet with, Carmen, her agent. Gladys jumped at the chance to go, but Vivian asked to remain behind so she could read a little and lounge around until they came back. Paige promised both Brandon and Vivian she and Gladys would be back in a couple of hours, so they could go out to lunch together. Brandon watched as Vivian waved them off, went into the bedroom she shared with Gladys to get a book and came out to sit on the living room couch.

Brandon sat in his chair in the corner of the living room leisurely reading the sports section of the paper. There was just something comforting and nostalgic about having the physical paper in his hands and since he rarely had time to do so, he only read it on Saturdays and Sundays.

"We never had a discussion on what to call you," came Vivian's voice from across the room. Brandon looked up, sure confusion was written across his face. "What to call me?"

"Since you married Mati. I mean at first we called you Elder Brandon...and that was only courteousness." She crossed the legs that were already laying on the couch. "But now that she is Mati and you are married to her you are a family member. When I talked to Gladys about it she was also unsure." Brandon waited for Vivian to take a breath, thus giving him the signal that his opinion was being solicited, but it didn't come. If she didn't seem so serious he would have smiled.

"You're not our uncle. Not really." She emphasized the last part. "Technically, you are more like a stepfather." She wrinkled her nose. "But that sounds so distant." He only nodded because he knew she wasn't finished.

She played with her bookmark for a moment then looked up. "Would it be considered wrong if Gladys and I called you 'our Brandon'? I know it isn't clever or as smooth as Mati, but after talking about it for a while, Gladys and I feel the same. We think of you as our Brandon." She stopped and looked at him expectantly. He knew it was finally his turn to speak, but his heart was in his throat and it had cut off just enough air supply to cause his eyes to burn. He swallowed convulsively for a moment and folded up his paper to stall a little longer.

"Our Brandon will do just fine." He didn't trust himself to say anymore.

Vivian watched him for a moment, her radiant smile dimming slowly.

Brandon thought the previous conversation left him a little off-kilter, but it was nothing like the question she hit him with next.

"Do you believe you're going to die?"

His whole body recoiled at the question. She probably saw him go visibly still, but his insides were roiling. He shifted uncomfortably in his chair. "Um, I don't know if we should be talking about this," he hedged.

"Do you want me to talk to someone else about this?" she asked innocently, and he was struck dumb by the simplicity of what she asked. Of course, there was no one else to ask. She was getting her answer straight from him. He tried to clean up his faux pas.

"No. I just meant I didn't think we should talk about this alone. Maybe your mom should be with us." He was drowning and hoped she would throw him out a lifeline.

"I think it would be better if this conversation remained between the two of us," Vivian said, cocking her head to the side as if posing her statement as a question.

Idly, he wondered how she learned to do that.

"Can we? Please."

"Yes we can," he responded with a deep breath.

"So?' she prompted.

He felt completely off guard and couldn't remember the question that started the conversation. "So, what?"

She watched him for a second before blinking twice. "Do you believe you're going to die?"

He wasn't ready to answer that question. He had actually asked himself that question a few times, but didn't have an answer, or he didn't want to answer.

"I see you are having trouble with that question," she said, putting her book aside and turning herself on the couch so she could place her feet on the ground. I'm going to ask you in another way."

This girl would make a fantastically scary psychologist, he thought to himself as he deep breathed. Breathing deep was supposed to work when you were in pain, right? This whole conversation felt like...well he couldn't think of anything as painful as this conversation.

He glanced down at his watch. Had it really only been ten minutes?

Not knowing whether the question would be easier he nodded his head in acquiescence hoping he could at least answer it.

"Have you started preparing Mati for your death?"

This question was no less heartbreaking, but at least he could answer it because his action had already spoken for him. "Yes, I have," he said in a quiet voice.

She nodded in acceptance of his answer then she speared him with her gaze. "So there is a part of you that knows you're dying," she stated.

Scratch that. She should would be a great investigative reporter. "We are all going to die, Vivian," he said, but Vivian interrupted him by waving her hand like she had with her sister and Paige.

"I'm not talking about in the distant future or in general. I think you know that." She had the nerve to look at him like she was disappointed in him.

He didn't believe he'd had a more grown-up conversation with someone more than half his age. "Okay." He took a deep breath then continued, "Yes, I have been preparing Paige in case I die sooner rather than later."

She looked at him for a moment biting her lower lip as if wondering whether or not she should ask him the next question.

His mind screamed "No! No more questions. But his mouth gave a different answer.

"Do you have another question for me Vivian?"

She nodded. "Have you been preparing yourself to die?"

He was momentarily stunned. It took a certain amount of boldness to ask these questions, and he was finding out it took even more courage to answer them. He went back to deep breathing. "Sometimes yes and other times I try to avoid it."

Vivian sat there staring over his shoulder as if trying to absorb his last answer. "So, it isn't always on your mind," she said with hopefulness in her voice.

"No. Not all the time." She nodded at his answer, seemingly appeased by his reply.

"Good. I'm glad it isn't on your mind all the time. It wouldn't leave a lot of room for living," she said it so matter-of-factly, he wasn't sure he heard her correctly, but when all she did was stare back at him he just nodded and resigned himself to the fact that she just might be there by divine appointment.

"I need to tell you something," Vivian said with all seriousness. Her voice was a little more than a whisper, but he felt as if "the hammer" was about to come down.

"Okay," he said hesitantly.

"Don't allow fear to lessen the power from your testimony." Brandon blinked at Vivian, then blinked again. It was so close to what God had told him a few months ago he couldn't deny who originally scripted the message. Goosebumps broke out along his arms, and his mouth went completely dry. Once he regained his composure, he asked her the question that had been rolling around in his head since the conversation began.

"Did you set it up so you could speak to me alone?" He watched as her eyebrows furrowed in confusion.

"No. I don't have Mati's agent's number. I couldn't have set it up."

"When Paige said she needed to see her agent, did you stay knowing we would have this conversation?"

"I didn't *know,*" she said emphasizing the last word. "I just figured if God gave me a message for you, He would also provide the opportunity for me to tell it to you in person. When Mati said she had to go to the meeting this morning I thought it would be the perfect time?" She finished the last sentence with a shrug.

"Does He do this often with you? Give you messages for people?" He was intrigued.

"Hmm, not often. Just when it is really important." She picked her book up and rotated herself so she was stretched out on the couch again. He assumed that since she'd delivered her message she was going to relax until Paige and her sister returned.

He envied her trust and faith in God. He felt so far away from that child who could hear with such clarity, there was no need for second guessing. The thought gave him an idea.

"What if that wasn't the right message?" he asked Vivian, studying her intently.

"Why wouldn't it be? God told me. He doesn't lie," she said adamantly.

"How do you know the message came from God?" He watched as she gave him a quizzical look.

Such knowing.

"I don't understand what you're really asking, but I know your message came from God because I know His voice. You don't believe me?" The distress that took over her features made him rush to assuage her.

"Yes, of course I believe you. I just revel in your open acceptance and faith in God." He was surprised when his words had the opposite effect.

She looked disillusioned. "But you're an elder. Don't you hear it when God talks to you?"

He thought about it for a moment. Pure honesty was his best bet with this child. "I hear from God; just lately there have been so many thoughts in my head His voice comes in amid a lot of interference."

Vivian started nodding her head, and her expression lightened. "I understand that. Sometimes His voice is clearer when the word is for someone besides me or my dad."

"Your dad?" He watched as her face crumpled, and the pain he saw in her eyes had him out of his chair and on the couch trying to comfort her in a heartbeat.

"He's in so much pain, and I want him to be happy so badly I wonder if I actually hear God say he will be alright or if I'm making it up, myself."

He shushed her and rocked her softly, just as he'd done for his youngest sister when she would have a bad dream and run to his bed when they were young.

"You will learn one day to separate your wants from God's will, but until then I will make an agreement with you. I will listen for what God will say about you and your dad, and you continue to listen to what God will say about me."

She looked up at him with hope shining in her eyes. "Really? You'd do that?"

"Sure. I would be getting just as much out of the deal as you."

"But—" She broke off suddenly, and he suspected he knew why. He would have let it stand if his curiosity didn't get the best of him.

"But?" he prompted. She seemed reluctant at first but finally gave in.

"He loves Mati too."

"Ah, yes. But Mati...Paige married me, so I have no reason not to keep up my end of the deal."

She seemed to consider his words for a moment then complied. "Okay."

"Okay." He hugged her once more then shook her slightly. He got up off the couch and resumed his place in his chair.

"Our Brandon," she said it so quickly it came out sounding like Au-branden.

"Yes?" he responded with a smile as he reached for his paper.

"Paige chose right." She smiled at him.

He smiled back trying not to reveal just how profoundly her words   affected   him.

CHAPTER 8

Mason turned his blinker on as he maneuvered his vehicle through the afternoon traffic. When he first got on the parkway he was almost relieved to see the mass of traffic which would keep his mind on the cars around him instead of what happened the last time he'd picked up his daughter from the airport.

After changing lanes again he allowed his mind to wander back to the previous week which, if he were honest with himself, was one of the best he'd experienced in a long time. It felt wrong to feel that way when his daughter had nothing to do with his new-found happiness, but it didn't lessen the feeling in any way.

He'd talked with Richard regarding his developing feelings for Tabitha and the thoughts that continued to come unbidden during the most passionate moment they'd had so far. He'd even shared parts of his conversation with Brandon on his and Paige's wedding day. The silence on the other side of the line was more of an answer than the one Richard was able to voice. Richard didn't think it was right for Brandon to ask what he did. He didn't feel it was fair to place that type of responsibility on Mason or to expect Mason to hold on to emotions that would essentially keep him chained to Paige.

Richard's advice for him regarding Tabitha wasn't too much more positive. He insisted that Mason deal with his feelings for Paige and make sure that the relationship he was culminating with Tabitha wasn't part of a plan to exorcise Paige from his mind and heart. He told him that it never worked as well as people would hope, and it usually ended in hurt feelings and regret.

Mason considered Richard's words and ran through some of his earlier thoughts regarding Tabitha. He wouldn't deny that some of his initial thoughts surrounding Tabitha were sprinkled with the hope that she could help occupy those places in his mind that liked straying to Paige and the time they'd spent together. He would just work harder to keep Tabitha with her light green eyes, fragrant, mass of curly, brown hair, soft lips and witty sense of humor at the front of his mind.

After seeing his daughter off at security and waiting until she called him just before boarding, he returned home to a quiet house and waited until she called him right after her plane landed in Atlanta, where she and Gladys would meet then take a plane to LAX. If he'd known how much the wait would wear on his nerves he would have made sure he didn't go straight home. He would have planned an outing with Tabitha that would have taken at least six hours, but he'd already asked her to go out with him the following day.

By the time his phone rang with Vivian's name lit up almost eight hours later, he knew he had sprouted a few gray hairs. Thankfully she'd waited and called him once she arrived at Paige's home, so he didn't have to worry about her car ride from the airport to the house, though he didn't share this with him. After a brief conversation and a promise from her to call each morning and evening he let her go.

Mason moved through the house feeling caged. It was too late to call Tabitha for a dinner date, and he chided himself on his poor planning. He knew if he stayed home he would be courting disaster so he took his coat out of the hall closet, picked up his keys from the bowl on the kitchen counter and walked out the door.

He purposefully turned the opposite direction of the bar. It didn't matter that the place served food until eleven p.m., he didn't need the temptation. He walked to a small diner a few blocks away and took his time ordering and eating his meal. By the time he got home it was late enough for him to go to bed.

Once he was situated and had turned off all the lights, he arranged himself in bed, so he could watch television while talking to Tabitha if she returned his text letting him know she was home after the long day she'd told him she might have, the night before.

Mason flipped channels until his phone vibrated on the covers. He read Tabitha's returned text and smiled before dialing her number. She always had a funny reply to the most mundane questions he would pose. He decided to put more effort into his greetings. Today's was:

Hello Ms. T. I know your day was busy, but I hope it was productive and treated you well. I will say "Good evening" if you want to talk, but I will say "Good night" if you are too tired.

Today was very productive, but I must confess that a conversation with you would probably take it from good to great.

Waiting...

"Hi Mason." Her soft voice surrounded him, making him want to wrap his arms around her soft body and breathe in her fragrance. He took in a deep breath imagining her smell.

"Ms. T." He'd gone back to using the name on her card as a form of endearment. He heard her intake of breath.

"Are you alright?"

"Yes. I just got in my bed. It's warm and soft, and the combination of your words and voice are giving me material for my dreams tonight."

He was surprised she voiced such intimate thoughts, but he was happy she had.

"Mmmm. Well I hope by the time we get off the phone you will have even more material.

"Me too," she said softly before changing the subject. "Did your daughter get to her destination safely?"

92

"Yes. She called me a couple of hours ago letting me know she and her sister Gladys had arrived safely at their mother's home."

"How are you doing?" Her voice was hesitant as if she didn't know if her asking would make it worse.

"I'm doing alright. I'm going to miss her a lot this week. She hasn't spent more than a day or two away since last summer when she visited her grandmother on her ranch. That was tough."

"From some of the pictures you showed me from the wedding, she seems like a very mature young lady. I noticed that she held herself like you in some of the pictures. She quirks her brow and lips like you when you are thinking of something ironic. She's just a little more transparent with it than you are. I like that. It shows that you two spend quite a bit of time together."

Mason didn't know what to say to that. He doubted she knew the gift she had just bestowed upon him. He had idly looked for those telltale signs himself, but had only come away with his wife's smile, her mischievous gleam, and of course the unapologetic love for God. Vivian even shared her demonstrative form of storytelling. It warmed his heart whenever she had some exciting experience to share with him. Her hands would go flying, and he was sure people could understand her just from her movements from yards away.

"Mason?" Her voice brought him back to their conversation.

"I didn't know. Thank you for that. I'll have to keep that in mind the next time I look at pictures of us." He worked hard to keep the emotion light in voice. "So you said in your text that it was a very productive day...?" he prompted, so she could talk and he could get his emotions under control. He didn't want to come across as a simpering man who couldn't contain himself when given a compliment.

"I actually got a job today. I got a call back from a woman who just bought a condo. She needs a place that will allow for her to entertain business types and a young women's group." The excitement in her voice reverberated through the phone.

"That's great. I know your feet didn't touch the ground for a few hours today,", he replied, genuinely pleased for her.

"What do you mean?" They still haven't touched the ground." She let go of a small giggle and it caused him to smile. He placed his arm behind his head in an attempt to make himself more comfortable while he got to know this intriguing woman who could make his future just a little bit brighter.

The Saturday morning came faster since he'd been on the phone with Tabitha late into the night. His choice in the Chicago Architectural Boat Tour seemed to win him some points where Tabitha was concerned. Her excitement was palpable. He could practically feel the electricity in the air of his car after he picked her up and told her where they were going.

Once on the boat he quietly filled in any gaps and gave background information missed by the tour guide by leaning in close and whispering in her ear. The smile in her eyes and on her lips reminded him of something he'd missed since his wife's passing. The companionship he shared with Tabitha in that moment began to fill in a deep crevasse in his psyche and ego. It was nice to have been able to elicit such a response from her.

After the tour he took her to his second-favorite restaurant. His first was the one he'd taken Paige to, and it was still too soon to subject himself to that. Richard's words came at him while he was driving them both across town, but he pushed the words back until he could no longer hear his former father-in-law's voice. He felt a pang of guilt for soliciting the man's advice only to ignore it, but he was tired of being sad. He was going to do what his daughter had suggested and seek out happiness. Tabitha made him happy.

Mason's arms lingered around Tabitha's waist, and his forehead touched hers as he worked to catch his breath. Kissing this woman left him feeling like he'd run a mile. He wondered if he did it more often would he recover quicker then start to build up a type of endurance that would keep their kisses from rendering him breathless. He mentally shook himself because that would actually take some of the fun away from kissing Tabitha.

"May I see you tomorrow?" he asked, wanting another opportunity to be in her space.

She leaned away from him and looked up into his eyes. "I'm going to church tomorrow. It's my ministry day to advertise some of our upcoming events, so I will be there for at least two, maybe three services. Afterward I'll be going to a planning meeting for some of those events. So I don't think so… unless." She let it hang in the air for a moment as she bit her bottom lip. His stomach bottomed out.

"Tomorrow's Sunday. I don't know what I was thinking. Maybe after that kiss I wasn't thinking."

He smiled down at her briefly. "I have a work thing to go to." It was more like a department picnic he was planning on skipping since Vivian was out of town. It hadn't occurred to him to invite Tabitha. Things were too new.

He plastered a sheepish smile on his lips and moved away from her so she could unlock her door. He saw the confusion that crossed over her features and hoped to escape before she was able to form any questions.

"Go ahead and get inside." He took a step back. "It's getting cold out and I don't want you catching anything." He leaned back in and gave her forehead a quick kiss then backed off again and waited for her to go inside.

Just before she closed the door behind her he leaned in the doorway. "I'll give you a call later in the afternoon tomorrow, okay?" She nodded giving him a ghost of a smile before closing the door.

He stood there for a moment wanting to kick himself for his response to finding out she was a churchgoer. Not only a churchgoer, but a participant. She was part of a ministry. He wondered why it hadn't come up in their conversations sooner. As he made his way down the stairs he considered briefly the irony of being attracted to yet another woman who believed in God.

He spent the night going over his conversation with Tabitha. He enjoyed her company, but he needed to make it absolutely clear that he wasn't interested in going to church with her at any time. She was an intelligent woman so that meant telling her about his childhood. It wasn't a conversation he was looking forward to, but better to have it sooner rather than later.

He woke up to the sun in his eyes and his iPad alerting him to a call. He shifted in bed so he could reach the tablet and enter his security code. He opened a bleary eye and saw that his daughter was hailing him on Skype. He answered the call but didn't enable the video on his side.

"Dad, Daaaad." He heard his daughter's cheerful voice come in loud and clear right before her image took over the screen.

"Yes, honey." He glanced down at the time. "Good morning."

"Good morning," she responded. "I wanted to call you before we went to church because Mati said it was going to be a long day. I think Lady Menagerie has something planned for us after church for our birthday, so I don't know if I'll get to talk to you later."

"That's fine, honey. I was just getting ready to find myself something to eat." He lied.

"Really 'cause you sound like I woke you up and you didn't engage your side of the video," she said, giggling.

"Smarty-pants. Maybe I'm taking advantage of your absence and walking around the house in my underwear."

"Ugh." She laughed, then he heard more giggling in the background just before Gladys walked into view."

"You see I was right to keep my video disengaged. I certainly don't want to share any bare chest shots with Gladys. It might faze the poor girl. Hello Gladys," he said smiling.

"Hi, Mr. Jenson." Gladys gave a small wave and backed out of range.

"Naaa Dad, I think the word you're looking for is traumatize." She snorted.

"No. I think the word I'm really looking for is grounded. You know like what you will be when you come home."

"Sorry, Daddy," Vivian said, but it was just shy of being sincere.

"Hmph," he replied, showing he wasn't appeased, but continued before she could try harder.

"Are you having a good time so far?"

"It's been a blast. Mati and Uncle Brandon have been keeping us busy. She showed me the schedule she made for us, and I might need to sleep for two days when I come." Since she'd engaged her side, he could see the excitement on her face and was happy she was so giddy.

"Good. Please tell Paige I said, 'Thank you,' again." He rolled over on the bed and made himself more comfortable. He prided himself on remembering to tell Vivian to share his gratitude with Paige. He didn't want her to think he held any reservations regarding Vivian wanting to stay with her and her sister for the week, even though he did.

"I will, Dad. So what have you been doing while I've been gone?"

"Not too much. I went out to look at a few buildings." He watched his daughter roll her eyes. He knew it would bore her and easily allowed for the conversation to swing back to her. "Tell me what you did."

Vivian went on to share some of the events from the day before. He watched the animation on her face and couldn't help but smile. He got up and dressed in a fresh T-shirt and pajama pants and padded into the living room while she was talking, so he could let her see him before they ended the call.

The rest of the day was spent with him cleaning the townhouse. He considered attending the picnic he'd mentioned to Tabitha the night before, but they were really only bearable when Vivian came with him. He played his music a little louder than usual and decided to go after the less desirable job like deep cleaning the bathrooms, changing the air filters, and washing down the back patio and balcony off of his room. He made sure he stayed too busy to think about calling Tabitha. He wasn't sure he was ready for the conversation they needed to have.

Most of Monday came and went with him putting in extra time at work. He was content with the amount of progress he'd made on his latest project and didn't want to stop until he reached a clear ending place.

He checked his phone a couple of times, but excluding a few texts and photos from Vivian, there was nothing. He shrugged it off at first but as the day went on, it wore on him. He wanted to know what she thought of his hasty departure and if it was a "red flag" for her.

Once he got home and prepared and ate his TV dinner, he sat back on the couch and flipped through channels until he found a documentary on Egyptian architecture. He picked up his cell phone off the coffee table and took a deep breath. He penned a text to Tabitha to see if she was up for a phone call. It was cowardly, but he gave himself points for reaching out to her.

Fifteen minutes later his phone alerted to an incoming text. He took his time picking up the phone. He didn't know which response he was hesitant to see more—a rejection or acceptance. When he finally looked at his text he saw that Tabitha had responded positively to a talk.

"Good evening." Her voice was pleasant enough.

"Good evening," he responded, hoping his voice didn't relay his anxiousness. "How was your day?"

"Mmm. It was alright. It was busy. How about yourself?"

"It was productive," he said, forcing his voice to lighten. Then just got fed up with himself. "Look. I want to apologize for my behavior on Saturday night. It had very little to do with you and a great deal to do with my past."

"Do you want to talk about it?"

No reference to how he acted Saturday night nor the fact that he hadn't called her until now. She was being easy on him and he didn't deserve it.

He leaned forward running his thumbs back and forth across his forehead. He'd avoided thinking about this and thus wasn't remotely eager to talk about it out loud, but first he needed an answer to a question that had been hopping around in his mind for most of the last three days.

"Can I ask you a question first?"

"Sure," she responded quickly, but he heard a tinge of apprehension in her voice.

"Why didn't you tell me sooner that you were a member of a church? Well, not even just a member of a church, but a participant."

He heard the sigh she let out, but it was only followed by silence for a few moments.

"I can't say for sure," she said softly. "I thought about it a few times, but there never seemed to be a good time."

"I don't understand," he started out saying more to himself than her. The relationship Rachael, Vivian, and Paige had with God was written all over them. It was imprinted upon everything they did and said. Their very mannerisms seemed to exude love for God, and he had to admit, His people. The other side of the coin was his late father and the ministry he'd led. The self-absorbed, two-faced, fork-tongued man who had single handedly led his mother and himself to the poorhouse with his death. The lies still filled his throat with bile, and the embers that had somewhat cooled over the last few months burned anew.

"Well, from one of our first conversations you seemed to have an aversion to God. I wanted to get to know you, hoping I was misreading your voice, when you talked about your daughter's interest in her church and the fact that you called it her church. I didn't want to come off like one of those overbearing Christian fanatics that lay their religion on you like a yoke around your neck. I don't wear my Christianity on my sleeve or feel I need to share my beliefs everywhere I go. It is a more private thing between me and God."

Mason was almost ashamed to ask the question, but was suddenly very curious. "Then how do you evangelize. How do you share your faith with people?"

"I usually wait for them to ask me. It's happened a few times, and we have had some very interesting conversations."

Mason shook his head slightly wondering if they were talking about the same thing. Did he want to clarify? Would it lead him to the quicksand he felt this conversation could become? He found that his curiosity was getting the better of him. He wanted to know where she stood. Not that it really mattered. It wasn't as if he would accompany her to church or have long, drawn-out theological debates with her, but even as he thought it, he couldn't squelch that prying voice in the back of his mind.

"Are we talking about the same thing? Does it ever lead to you praying for them?"

There was a pregnant silence on the other side of the line.

"I'm not really comfortable praying out loud," she said with a hint of wariness.

"Oh," he said, because he didn't know what else to say to that admission. He didn't know what to think of her.

"What's with the questions? I thought you were an atheist?" she asked. If he didn't know better he would have thought it was a barb. He kept his response as bland as possible so she wouldn't think he was retaliating in any way.

"I'm not actually an atheist. My father was a pastor and traveling preacher of a small church. I was raised in my early years to believe in God. I know He's up in heaven just as sure as Satan is in hell." He paused to take a breath, hearing the note of derision in his voice. "You can say we had a parting of ways when I hit my teens."

"A what? What happened?" she asked immediately. Then began to backpedal. "If you don't mind telling me."

"My father died of a heart attack," he said, pausing to get the rest of his thoughts in order.

"And you're angry at God for taking your father while you were young?" she asked, and he almost laughed at her assumption.

"No. It wasn't that my father died. It's what he did to my family when he did."

"Oh," she said, and he heard it—the misguided understanding.

"My father was a polygamist. He had another family: a wife, children. He had other sons. He would go on 'speaking engagements' and go be with his other family—his first family. So when he died my mother had nothing but me to hold on to."

He tried to reign in the feelings, but he'd opened the proverbial spigot and figured he would let it pour out just a little bit longer before he shut it off. "You can call it what you'd like, but I'm not too excited about worshipping a God who would employ and allow such a man to represent Him. There is a problem there, and though others choose to ignore it and speak of His grace and mercy for those who 'hit and miss' but still wish to represent him; I can't. I can't because the liars, cheaters, and false prophets who misrepresent Him destroy people's lives when they should be saving them."

"What about Jacob, Joseph, son of Jacob, King David, Peter, Paul..." she began, but he interrupted her.

"If you're trying to make a case for Him, you're not doing a very good job. Jacob cheated his brother out of his birthright and a blessing that was to go from father to first son. He had God's favor long before and for some time after Jacob stole his brother's livelihood. Joseph was a zealous arrogant, snot-nosed brat who ended up in prison. At least he did some time which is more than I can say for David who even as a king, and God's beloved, set his eyes on a married woman, slept with her, and brought her husband off of the battle field to cover up the fact that someone else had gotten her pregnant. When he wouldn't sleep with his wife, David had him killed then took her for himself.

Who did you say next?" The fire of indignation was fueling his argument. "Oh yeah, Peter was a barbarian even after walking with Jesus and Paul, and if it weren't for the life-changing incident on the road to Damascus, he would have continued to persecute and kill Jews."

"My point exactly. If Paul could have a life-changing experience with God and turn his life around, why shouldn't the others."

"It's not even remotely the same. Paul killed before he had an encounter with God. The other men wreaked havoc after their encounter with God. What hope is there for men who do whatever they want even after they have come into the understanding of God? The ones that steal, kill, and destroy people's lives under the guise of serving God? And what kind of God continues to allow it?" His impassioned question met utter silence.

"Wow. Um." Her voice sounded hoarse. "I'm not judging. Really, I'm not. I just don't think that's a healthy line of thought. You don't feel... well... uncomfortable thinking like this? Stupid question, Tabitha," she said answering herself.

He could hear her anxiety level rising.

"He wouldn't have said the things he did if he was uncomfortable." She kept talking to herself.

To Mason the words in her last statement ran together so quickly it almost sounded as if she were mumbling. Finally, she took a deep breath. He kept quiet, knowing he could have very well just placed this budding relationship in a guillotine and let the blade fly with his diatribe.

"I don't know what to say Mason. I love God. I might not be an evangelist or have any ambition to become a missionary, but I love God and what you just said scares me and makes me afraid for you."

"I think you just expressed yourself very well," he said not working too hard to keep the sarcasm out of his tone. He shook himself. He wasn't ready to throw in the towel just yet.

"Look Tabitha, I am not a killer; I don't steal; I'm not a pedophile; I never cheated on my wife, and since her death the only real female in my life has been my daughter. I don't smoke; I don't do drugs; I may have an occasional drink, but when I do I'm at home, or I walk from the bar. I have a job I love; I pay my taxes and give to charities. I help my female neighbors with their groceries if they need help and have been known to host an all-girl sleepover. I'm an upstanding citizen, and I like you. I'm not a bad person. I just don't hold God's judgment or favoritism in high regard."

The line was quiet for a moment. He heard the weariness in her voice before she got to the end of her sentence. "It's been a long day, Mason. I just can't give this the type of reflection it needs right now. I'm going to talk to you later, okay?"

"Yep," he said, but he knew it was over. Her voice was flat with resignation. He knew he should have just kept his opinion to himself. Hadn't he learned anything from the Paige fiasco? "Have a good night," he said, knowing he was really saying, "Have a nice life."

"Mason?"

"Yes."

"I'm really sorry about the pain and suffering you and your mother went through."

"Thank you, Tabitha." Her compassion hurt worse than her rush to get away from him. He didn't want to consider what he was losing. Not yet.

"Goodnight Mason."

"Goodnight Tabitha." He waited until he heard the click of her phone line then hit end.

He tossed the phone back on the coffee table and leaned back on the couch. He stared unseeingly at the now cold, forgotten TV dinner and blew out his breath in disgust. He wanted to cuss, but figured there was already more than enough negative energy in the air. He picked up the remnants of his dinner and got up from the couch. He walked into the kitchen and tossed it into the garbage. He glanced at the clock but shook off the thought of going to the bar. He turned off the lights, locked the doors and walked to his bedroom trying to keep any thoughts of the past hour at bay. He would deal with the thoughts and emotions the next day between working on his job's assignments and his daily call from Vivian.

Tuesday ran into Wednesday with him ignoring the tug on his heart and immediately shutting down any stray thoughts of Tabitha. His early morning call with Vivian bolstered his morale and gave him a few hours of peace. He almost asked her to call him again that afternoon, but knew it would only set off warning bells in her perceptive mind.

Wednesday evening he gave himself a small reward for his diligence toward keeping himself from indulging in any wayward thoughts of Tabitha. He went by the grocery store on his way home and bought two quarts of ice cream, hot fudge, caramel sauce, and a bottle of maraschino cherries. He relished in the decadent feeling of rebellion as he placed all of the ingredients for his sundae in a serving bowl and sat on the couch to consume his dinner/dessert.

Thursday seemed to be going much like Wednesday until his phone rang as he was leaving work. He engaged his Bluetooth without look away from the line of cars in front of him waiting to leave the parking lot.

"Hi Mason," Tabitha greeted, and his mind went momentarily blank at the sound of her voice.

"Mason?" Her prompt shook him from his stupor.

"Uh, yeah."

"I was just wondering how you were?"

"I'm fine," he responded after a few moments. He'd never expected to hear from her again so he was having a hard time engaging. The car behind him honked, and he realized there were at least five car lengths between him and the driver in front of him. He sped forward concentrating on the brake lights in front of him.

"Is this a bad time?" Her voice was hesitant. It was, but he wasn't going to share that with her.

"I'm just leaving work."

"Oh." Her response gave him no place to go and he was relieved that she continued.

"I was wondering if you could meet me at Myrtle's coffee shop." Was it a good sign that she wanted to meet him where they first had lunch?

"When?"

"Right now, if it's possible." Her voice sounded odd to him.

"Are you alright? You're not hurt or anything?"

"No. Just very tired. Can you meet me?"

"Sure. I'll be there in twenty minutes." He looked both ways as he pulled out of the lot, turning in the opposite direction from his home.

"Thank you, Mason," she said quietly before disconnecting with him.

His brow furrowed in confusion, and he went back over the conversation in his mind. The life and vitality he'd come to associate with her voice was gone. Had their separation affected her as much as it may have him if he'd allowed himself to feel?

He continued to contemplate the last question as he inched through the congested streets toward the coffee shop.

He walked through the door to Myrtle's, glancing around until his eyes rested on hers. They were red and slightly puffy even with the noticeable amount of makeup she'd used to conceal them. He forced his gait to slow, but lengthened his stride so as not to give away his anxiousness to reach her. When he arrived at the table he had to keep himself from leaning forward to press a kiss on her cheek. It was awkward to say the least. He settled himself in the chair opposite of her never taking his eyes from hers.

"Hi," she said through a wan smile. He mirrored her actions.

"Hi."

"Would you like something to eat or drink?"

He noticed then that she was rolling a mug between her palms. A telltale sign of her nervousness.

"Sure." He was about to get up, but saw her lift a finger to hail someone behind the counter.

"I didn't know they served you at your table unless it was an entrée," he said in wonder.

"That's true, but since it's pretty quiet I asked if she wouldn't mind taking your order from here. It's more efficient that way."

The hope that lingered in his heart died a quick death. She meant for this to be quick.

When Sarah came to their table he hastily gave his order and returned his attention to Tabitha who was looking at him with curiosity. He suddenly wanted to be anywhere but here. He knew he'd been rude, but he would make it up with a generous tip.

"So what did you want to talk to me about?" He schooled his features so as not to give away his inner turmoil.

"I hadn't heard from you and I wanted to see you."

"Why?" he responded before he could catch himself."

"Because I wanted to see your face when we talked about Monday night."

"Forgive me for sounding like a parrot, but why?"

The hurt that crossed her face had him cursing under his breath. "I mean I thought you said everything you were going to say to me that night. I thought your good night was really a goodbye."

She looked down at her mug hiding her reaction behind the curtain of her hair.

Sarah placed his cup in front of him, and he gave her a smile to help apologize for his earlier behavior.

"I told you I needed to think." She looked at him. "I thought you knew me well enough by now to know that I don't mince words."

He sat back in his chair to add to the space between them. "We still have a lot to learn about each other as evidenced by the conversations this week." He took a deep breath and allowed himself to feel the painful void her absence from his life had formed over the forty-eight hours. He splayed his hands on the table to anchor himself as the wave of feelings washed over him. It was too soon.

"I wanted you to join me here because it reminded me of our first meeting. The lightness and newness of something that has brought me many hours of happiness. You make me happy, Mason. I enjoy our conversations and your dry humor. You are intelligent, sensitive, and attentive. You listen to me whether we are face-to-face or on the phone. When I'm with you, I feel special. I feel cherished. I don't want to give that up." Her eyes were imploring and though a small voice warned him that there was something slightly off about her admission, a huge part of him just thankful.

"And what about my feelings about God? That hasn't changed, Tabitha." It was best that they dealt with this first. If it was a deal breaker, he could still walk away.

She took a deep breath. "If you can deal with the fact that I'm a participating member of my church, and every now and then I won't be available because I have commitments to them, then I'm alright with it. I don't have any misguided goals to change you, but if by being around me you have a desire to come to church with me one day, I won't fight you." She hitched her shoulder and quirked her lips in a saucy smile. He just watched her for a moment. He didn't have the heart to point out that he'd been married for more than ten years to a devout lover of God, and she hadn't been able to tempt him into changing his mind.

She reached across the table and squeezed his hand.

"Are you sure?" He gave her one more chance to walk away.

"Yes," she said nodding her head.

He reached forward running his fingers along her cheek and watched her eyes close as she leaned into his touch. He shook off the feeling that he was leading a lamb to slaughter. She was an adult. She knew her feelings and like she said, she didn't mince words. They'd not gotten to the place where they were whispering words of forever, but he liked to think that maybe they could get there.

Mason didn't consider himself a playboy. He liked stability and the thought of being with one woman for the rest of his life, but the woman's life he'd first chosen to spend his life with ended much sooner than he ever thought possible. Maybe it was good that they found this out about one another. It would slow things down a little and he would be more cautious about his feelings where Tabitha was concerned.

Though he did a good job of ignoring his feelings regarding their agreement to put some space between them for a while, he knew it was only a matter a time before he would have to face them, and he wasn't looking forward to the pain. He had to consider the fact that this may not work, that Tabitha may change her mind and decide that she didn't want to risk her heart to a man who found the being she worshipped, distasteful.

"Mason?" Her voice pulled him from his thoughts. "Yes?" He took in her features, and the uncertain smile that tipped the edges of her lips tugged at his heart.

"You just went somewhere else. Are you having second thoughts?" Her normal confident tone had been absent for most of their conversation today and he knew in some way he was to blame for that, but instead of giving her superficial assurance, he decided to tell the truth.

"I'm having second, third, fourth, fifth, and more thoughts on us. Pick a number and I think I have a thought for it regarding us, but ones I'm deciding to follow are the ones that whisper proceed with caution."

"Caution?" Tabitha tipped her head slightly. "How cautious?"

"Well, I have to admit that I pursued you heavily. I didn't consider the possibility that if you gave me a chance that we wouldn't last. I had to face that option this week and it hurt." His gaze never wavered from hers, but he shrugged with his next statement. "I'm just enlisting my right to protect myself. We've been seeing each other a little more than a month, but the way our talk affected me on Monday let me know that I was more emotionally invested than I was aware of."

He could still see the strain of hurt in her eyes, but she smiled ruefully. "I understand. I had to build a couple of reinforcements myself."

"Really." He was a little surprised since the perpetuation of their relationship had been in her hands.

She looked at him accusingly. "I had some thoughts of my own, Mason. I had to ask myself some hard questions and see if the benefits outweighed the risk. I had to find a couple of ways to lower that risk so that even though the benefits shifted the scale in our favor, I still wanted added protection." She looked down watching as she twisted a napkin in her hands.

"Do you mind telling me what some of those reinforcements are?" Once the question was out of his mouth, he regretted it. He didn't really want her to answer. He wasn't sure he wanted to know and judging by the expression clouding her face, she didn't want to share. "You know what? Don't answer that." He reached forward taking her hands in his one. "It was an automatic reaction."

He felt more than saw her relax and used that to his favor.

"I'm glad you called me to meet you here. It was a gracious gesture and I want to return it by taking you to dinner."

She looked adorably baffled. "You didn't want to get something here?"

He leaned close to her to avoid being overheard and just to be in her space. "The food here is great, but I'm thinking of somewhere a little darker and more intimate." He watched her blink twice and could tell she was thinking too much. "There's a restaurant I wanted to take you to this week, and now that I have the opportunity I don't want to waste it." He leaned even closer. "Besides, I'm dying to kiss and make up with you which means I want to hold you close and reassure myself with the feeling of you. I can't do that, one, if you don't get up and two, in this environment."

She gave him his answer when she gifted him with her first full smile of the evening. "Okay, but could I go home and change first?" He followed her gaze to her T-shirt and slacks. "If you'd like, but I wasn't kidding about that kiss." He leered at her playfully and watched her attempt to ignore the blush climbing up her neck. She slowly turned her mug and brought it closer then looked at him beneath her lashes.

"You will have to wait until I finish my coffee." He caught a glimpse of a smile right before she hid it behind the cup. She made him wait ten minutes while she slowly finished her coffee. He was going to have to build more reinforcements.

Friday evening he took her out again because he knew with Vivian coming home the next day it would be awhile before they would get the chance to spend so much time together. This restaurant was a lot brighter than the one from the night before, but the high-topped, oversized booths supplied just as much privacy for the diners. He'd discovered it one weekend when Vivian attended an ice-cream birthday party there. They'd come back for lunch once and gorged themselves on burgers, fries, and malted shakes.

He moved into a booth right behind her instead of taking he seat across from her. At first she looked startled, but after taking in the size of the booth, laughed at him. "You planned this."

"Of course I did," he admitted, cheerfully opening the menu for them.

"I take it you've been here before."

"Yes. Vivian and I came here over a year ago. Their burgers are great and their shakes are better."

"Nice," she said, looking over the menu. "Do you want to share a shake?"

He winced. He didn't even want to look at ice cream for a couple of weeks after Wednesday's sundae binge. "Naaa. I'm just going to have a burger and fries with a soda." She looked at him sideways, but didn't say anything. Though the food was as good as he'd said, his real reason for choosing this restaurant was so that he could have an excuse to be close to her during the evening. He was going to miss seeing her almost daily, but if Vivian caught wind of Tabitha he'd never hear the end of it, and he wasn't ready for them to meet yet.

They spent the rest of the evening touching from hip to knee as they ate their food. It was a sweet kind of torture he stored in his memory to pull up when he was missing the feeling of her.

*   *   *

He sat in the airport's cell phone parking lot waiting for Vivian to let him know she'd claimed her baggage. He told himself for the hundredth time that everything was going to be fine and they would reach the house without incident. His phone rang, cutting off the thoughts before they could turn dark. "Hi Daddy, I'm ready." Vivian's cheerful voice filled the car.

"I'll be right there. Did you have a nice flight?" He put the car in gear and pulled out of the parking lot.

"Yes, I got upgraded to first class and got a free lunch. Those seats are so much nicer than the ones in coach." He didn't point out to her that was some of the reasoning behind paying the exorbitant price of a first-class ticket.

"That's wonderful, hon. Looks like the airline gave you a birthday present as well," he said, taking the entrance to the arrival side of the terminal. He heard her giggle and he assumed from the rise in the background noise level that she was now near the curb. She went on about the niceness of the stewardess and the free pair of headphones she was going to sport for a while.

He slowed as he approached her airline service area and directed the car to the curb just before he caught sight of the mass of brown curls sticking out of a messy bun attached to a beautiful, now teenage, girl. His beautiful teenage girl who was growing up faster than he liked.

He placed the car in park and got out to embrace her in a hug he was happy she didn't pull away from after a few seconds. His light was back home, in his arms. He gave her a squeeze before letting her go and planted a kiss on her forehead. "I missed you, honey." He took in her pale gray eyes, round nose, cherubic lips, and pointy chin.

"I missed you too, Daddy," she said smiling brightly up at him. He placed her in the car and attended to her luggage. He had to apply more strength to haul the larger one into the trunk. "How much did you buy while you were out there?" he asked when he was back behind the wheel.

"I only bought a couple of souvenirs for you. Mati and Gran got the rest for our birthdays. I almost had a whole wardrobe in the closet Gladys and I shared. I only brought back what Gran gave me. That way I'll already have stuff at Mati's when I go back to visit.

"Oh, and when will this be?"

He saw her shrug out of the corner of his eye and relaxed. "I don't know, but hopefully before the end of the year," she said while she scanned the street in front of them. "Speaking of Gran. Have you talked to her lately?

Puzzled by her change of subject, he glanced at her quickly. Her expression was too innocent. "No. Have you?"

"No." She sighed. "That's what I mean. I called her a few hours after I arrived at Mati's house to thank her for the presents and we had a good talk. She called me, or us...as in Gladys and I, on Tuesday which was cool. I figured she would call me again on Thursday or Friday, but she didn't. I was going to call her, but I forgot, especially after getting through Mati's crazy, long itinerary." He chanced a quick glance and saw her roll her eyes before she turned to her window.

Mason felt the urge to defend Paige. "You know she's going through quite a bit right now. It's bound to make her act a little different.

Vivian sighed. "I know Dad. I'm not saying I didn't have fun. It was a blast, especially with Gladys being there, but it was like Mati was trying to schedule every single activity there was to do in Los Angeles. It was all I could do to get to my bed before I passed out each night. Gladys was the same way."

Part of him was reluctant to ask, but he did so anyway. "How's Brandon doing?"

"He's doing really well. I didn't know what to expect with him being so ill, but he is doing really good. He didn't go to everything with us because sometimes he had to work, but he tried to be with us in the evenings and Friday afternoon." She paused briefly. "He's a good man. He loves Mati a great deal." He listened to the change in her voice and knew her next words were important, at least to her. "But as much as he loves Mati, he loves God more. I think it really helps." She let the sentence fade and he found himself reluctantly wondering what she wasn't saying.

"I have the feeling there's more to your story, Vivian. Why do you think it helps that he loves God more than Paige?"

Vivian took a deep breath. "Brandon loves Mati and loves his life with her, but because he loves God more, he has hope. He has something, someone to look forward to seeing. I'm not saying that he hopes he dies because he is really open to being healed miraculously or by any new treatment. It just makes being around him better somehow." She turned to him. "Is that bad?"

Mason shrugged. "You may not want to say that to him or around Paige, but I guess it's good that he isn't depressed.

Vivian was quiet for a moment. Then perked up. "What was I saying before we got to all of this? Oh yeah, so since I didn't get a chance to call Gran on Friday I called her while I was waiting for my luggage to come down. Papa Richard answered the phone and said Gran wasn't going to be able to talk to me for a few days."

"Really." Mason couldn't begin to imagine what would keep Victoria from talking to his daughter. Maybe he would give Richard a call later to get an idea of what was going on. "You think she might be sick?"

"If she was, I think Papa would have just said so." He could feel her eyes on him.

"I don't know, hon. I'll give him a call when we get home. Okay?"

"Okay." She sat back appeased.

Since he took the streets home it cost him fifteen minutes driving time. Vivian began reporting on some of the events and places she visited and he tried to concentrate on the road while paying enough attention to her conversation to participate in a timely matter. As he pulled up to their townhome and placed the car in park, Vivian became quiet. He looked at her curiously. "All talked out?"

She looked back at him. Her sober eyes drawing his undivided attention. "No. I was just trying to keep you occupied until we got to the house." She had known about his apprehension. He didn't think he was being that obvious.

"How'd you know?"

"Because I was scared too, so I figured if I talked about all the fun I had and made you listen we would make it here with no sweat. And see we made it here safely and you didn't have a stroke." She teased him.

"I'll show you stroke." He reached for her, but she quickly released her seatbelt and scrambled out the door.

Later that evening Mason chose to call Richard from his bedroom just in case whatever was going on with Victoria needed to stay between them.

When Richard answered he knew it wasn't good.

CHAPTER 9

Victoria was seeing red. The more she thought about it, the angrier she got. She wouldn't be surprised if smoke was coming out of her ears. "The gall of that family." She caught herself pacing and sat back at the kitchen table. She glanced at Richard, but he was sitting across from her in the same position with the same stoic expression he had when they first got the call from his top investigator.

"Why are you just sitting there watching me? Don't you have anything to say?"

She watched as Richard leaned back and stretched his legs out in front of him. His lack of anger infuriated her. "I am upset and angry on your behalf, but me ranting and raving is not going to calm you down before your blood pressure reaches a tipping point."

She threw up her hands in exasperation. "What do you think I should do, Richard?"

He leaned forward and took her hands in his. "Pray, baby. I think you should pray."

"Pray. Really. What am I going to pray? It's not like God didn't already know what was happening. Why didn't He already give me what I needed to get through this? Better yet, why didn't He intervene?"

"I think everything that has happened in your life has helped to shape you into the woman you are. There were many different variables and decisions that could have reshaped your past. Quite a few of them could have kept us from ever meeting. Then Rachael wouldn't have been born. I have wondered in my darker hours if you'd have kept Brian, would you have taken a chance with me."

116

"I would like to think that I wouldn't have been so bitter that I would have been able to notice your genuine adoration for me." She smirked.

"But if not. There would have been no us and no Rachael."

"Are you asking me which of my children I would pick?"

"No, I'm telling you that because of God you don't have to. You had them both for the amount of time you were supposed to have them."

"I'm wondering if your son died, if you would say the same."

Richard stared at her looking dumbfounded for a moment then spoke with quiet deliberation. "I have three sons buried in our garden."

The dawning of what she'd said came too late and she was desperately sorry for her callous words.

"I'm sorry, baby." She looked him in the eye hoping he would see the genuine regret in hers. She rubbed her forehead with the pads of her fingers and took a deep breath to calm herself. "I really don't feel that way. I'm so angry, my words just got away from me." She watched the quiet heat recede from his chocolate-brown orbs and relaxed a little.

"I don't know what to do with this anger, Richard. I can barely believe what Mya found is true. If I didn't know her to be the competent, super-sleuthing investigator she is I would ask you if she double-checked her findings." She stood up and started pacing again.

"Once Antonio was surrounded by his family it was as if neither I nor my child existed." She turned to face Richard, her anger from moments before morphing into hurt. "They set it up. They made it nearly impossible for me to keep my child then turned around and placed this couple in front of me with everything I wanted my child to have instilled in him." Her fists clenched in sync with her jaw. "They set me up and took my baby. What kind of monsters are they?" She watched as Richard got up and walked to her.

"Vickie," he began with warning. "You need to consider your blood pressure."

"Blood pressure. My blood pressure is just fine." She furrowed her brows even as he reached out and tried to smooth the lines between them with his thumbs.

"It won't be if you keep this up." He led her back to the table and sat her on his lap. "Look, we don't have all of the facts. Maybe Antonio had a change of heart. Maybe after breaking off his engagement he wasn't allowed or just couldn't contact you, but still wanted to make sure the child was taken care of. It could have been that he wasn't aware of what his grandfather was doing until after the adoption took place." He ran his hand up and down her back in a soothing gesture.

"Mya was only able to go back as far as Brian's fifth birthday with regards to any communication and money trail leading to Antonio Sable's early accounts. He could have been as much in the dark as you until then." Victoria considered it for a moment, and the steam began to cool before the next thought came to her.

"Fine, maybe he didn't find out what his grandfather was doing until Brian was five, but the data shows that he gave the Grossenbergs money until Brian was fourteen. The payments stopped after Brian's death. He knew my son was dead and he didn't try to reach me or anything. It's been twenty-seven years." Her voice began to rise but she couldn't help it. "Twenty-seven years my child has been gone and I just found out about it this year. This year!" She banged her fist on the tabletop, and her husband took it in his hand and kissed the still-smarting edge.

"I know, Vickie. I know." She could hear his voice go soft and knew he was trying to calm her, but her anger was keeping her from crying so she dug her claws in deep. The pain cut almost as deep as when she found out about Brian's hundred and forty-five-day stay in the psyche ward. She never considered herself a naïve woman, even in college, but it was still hard to reconcile the Antonio she knew with this devious and conniving man who would practically steal her child out from under her. She would give Mya a week before she approached Antonio herself to get the answers she desired.

A few months before, she would have plotted a way to cause him and his family the type of pain she'd recently been through. She told herself, now she just wanted answers. Before she finished the thought she backtracked. No. There may still be some pain. She would ask for God's forgiveness after she finished indulging in thoughts of the family's demise.

His tight squeeze pulled her from her plotting and she rearranged her features to hide her thoughts. "What are you devising in that ever-working mind of yours?"

"What do you mean?" she asked as innocently as possible while fidgeting with his mug.

"Vickie. I know you. And though the process of you becoming a new creature in Him has begun, it is still very new and one you haven't fully committed yourself to."

She turned to him truly offended. "Why would you say that?" He sighed, and she could see him working out his next statement carefully, so she interrupted him. "Don't try and sugarcoat it now. The damage is done."

"Richard leaned away from her, but tightened his hold so she couldn't get away. "Have you paused to think that Antonio may have done this because he cared about you?"

Victoria laughed, but Richard cut her off.

"I know it was a long time ago, but was there anything Antonio did while you were together in college that would have given you a clue to what he would do when you two parted? Were there quiet phone conversations with his family or odd behavior?

Victoria went through the now hazy memories of her time with Antonio. She tried to remember the good times they shared,

119

unmarred by the betrayal she felt that summer. "I can't think of anything. He seemed really happy with us being together and didn't initially balk at having a child.

"There is a good chance that his family convinced him to let you go, but he only agreed if they made sure your child was taken care of."

"But then why wouldn't he have contacted me at the time of Brian's death?"

"What would be the reason?" Richard asked. "Your child was dead. If he had any contact with the family besides just giving them money he would have known that you had no idea where Brian was. After all that time it would have been cruel to approach you just to let you know that your son was deceased."

Victoria gave what he was saying some thought. It was hard to get around her emotions, but she considered what she would do if she were in his position. It was difficult because she was used to telling people who told her she couldn't do something, to go to hell. She had basically told her family the same thing after she gave up her precious son. She nodded her understanding at Richard's scenario.

"Don't just nod. Tell me what you're thinking?" Richard prodded.

"I think I can wrap my head around what you're saying. I can even imagine the type of family that has a say about every big decision in your life. It doesn't keep me from feeling cheated though." Her gaze turned intense as she looked him in the eye. "He had what I didn't get. He had the option of being in Brian's life. He got to watch him grow, even if it was from afar." She let the tears go. "He got that."

"Oh, baby." Richard brought one of his hands up to her shoulder, wrapping his arm around her back so that she was fully enveloped by him. She placed her face in the crook of his neck and let him rock her slowly. She took in his spicy scent and let the movement calm her for a few minutes.

Once the tears began to recede she took a deep breath and sought the strength she'd more recently found in his arms. She felt the tension flow into his body at her movement.

"Are you going to approach him?"

She lifted her head to look at him. "I don't know." She could see his eyes roaming along her face and wondered just how badly she had ruined her makeup.

"I know this might seem like an odd thing to say at this moment." He swiped the remnant of her tears from her cheeks. "But you are extremely beautiful to me. Trusting me with your true emotions is a gift I treasure, but the strength it takes for you to show your weakness in this area makes me admire you."

She stared at him, incredulous. He continued to amaze and surprise her even after thirty-three years of marriage. She closed her eyes and thanked God for helping her to come to her senses before she completely ruined her relationship with this man.

"I know what you're doing," she said trying to move out of his embrace.

"What?" he asked, looking the picture of confusion. "You're trying to take my mind off of this very important subject." She saw a flicker of a smile touch his lips before it disappeared.

"Can't I tell my wife how beautiful I think she is without her suspecting that I have ulterior motives?"

"I'm sure you could if you were a better actor, but the sentiment wasn't lost." She kissed him on the nose. "I think you're beautiful too."

She pressed her lips together wondering how she should approach this last sentence. "I want to say one more thing, then we can drop this discussion for the rest of the evening."

Richard looked bemused. "Rest of the evening. How magnanimous of you."

Victoria wanted to roll her eyes, but wanted to continue the discussion, so she just stared at him.

"Alright." He held up one finger. "One more thing."

"I was also wondering, why now?" She saw his perplexed look and hurried forward.

"I hired men to try to find Brian the moment the Grossenberg family moved. Nothing." She sliced her hand through the air to emphasis her point. She pointed at him. "You have also had men investigating the Sable family and trying to find Brian for many years now, but neither set came up with anything about Brian until earlier this year and now Mya's contacts have miraculously come across proof that Luca and Antonio Sable had contact with the Grossenbergs. Don't you think that's rather odd?"

She noticed Richard staring at her. "This is why I love you, woman." He hugged her to him quickly. "I was too concerned about how you were going to take all of this information, and I admit I was a little afraid when you started yelling and pacing, but you never fail to get to the crux of what's going on."

She placed her hands on his shoulders. "How do you think we should go about getting that answer?"

He looked at her for a moment, and she could tell he was trying to decide whether or not to share his idea. He blinked and she got her answer before he spoke.

"Maybe we should consider what you were thinking about doing earlier." She didn't want to get her hopes up if he misread her earlier thoughts.

"And what is that?"

"Maybe we should pay Antonio Sable a quiet visit," he said, but she could hear the hesitation in his voice. Still, it wasn't enough to keep her excitement from rising.

"You think so?"

"Yes, but I also get the feeling I'm going to regret it."

"No you won't." She kissed him on the cheek.

"Really, how do you know?"

"Because…" She kissed his forehead. "It will…" She kissed his ear. "Make me." She kissed his neck. "Very." She kissed his lips. "Very." She turned her body in his lap. "Very happy." She kissed him again, but deeper.

*   *   *

A week later with an address and reliable schedule of Antonio Sable's work calendar in hand, Victoria walked up the steps to the building that housed Sable Management Industries. As vice president, she knew Antonio wouldn't have a great deal of time, but once he recognized her, she knew he would be reluctant to leave her alone on his company's immediate floor of offices. She was absolutely sure that if Antonio was able to find Brian, he had been keeping up with her and her family. Normally she would be incensed by the violation of her privacy, but today it would work in her favor.

She walked through the lobby to the guard at the oversized, round desk situated in front of the elevators. In the log, she signed in her name and what company she was going to. She smiled at the guard and pretended to read the directory for Sable's company on the twenty-fifth floor.

After a swift ride she stepped out onto plush gray carpet and made her way to the main reception desk in the middle of the receiving area. As she approached, the young woman with a severely cut hairstyle and aqua-blue eyes looked up to greet her.

"May I help you?"

"Yes, I'm here to see Mr. Antonio Sable."

"Your name please?"

"Mrs. Victoria Branchett."

Victoria didn't see any recognition in the woman's eyes before she smiled and picked up the receiver.

"Hello, Ms. Ryan, I have a Mrs. Victoria Branchett here to see Mr. Sable." She was quiet as she listened to the woman. "Very good." She hung up the phone then pointed to the black leather sofas to the left of her desk. "Ms. Ryan will be right out to escort you to Mr. Sable's office."

Victoria nodded to the woman in thanks and made her way to a sofa. She didn't trust herself to speak lest she give away her surprise in being received so quickly. She didn't like the feeling that she was being led right to where Antonio wanted her. She sent Richard a quick text to reassure him all was well. He hadn't been happy with her plan to see Antonio alone first, but she convinced him that Antonio might feel less threatened if only one of them approached him. Besides, Richard was parked on the street and could be upstairs with only a moment's notice.

A middle-aged woman turned the corner from what must have been the executive wing. She approached Victoria with a cool reserve and the confidence of an executive that had been her position for a long time. Her suit was impeccably made which told Victoria, Antonio Sable paid his employees well.

"Mrs. Branchett?" the woman asked, stopping a few feet away. Victoria nodded, and the woman continued forward to shake her hand. "I'm Paulette Ryan, Mr. Sable's executive assistant. I will take you to Mr. Sable, now. The easy acceptance made her feel uncomfortable, and she couldn't help but ask, "Does he take walk-ins often?"

Ms. Ryan glanced at her briefly and smiled. "No. Mr. Sable is a very busy man."

Victoria didn't like her answer one bit and the smile would have freaked out a weaker woman, but Victoria reminded herself that she was here to get answers and Antonio Sable had them.

They walked down a long, wide corridor with office doors on both sides. As they neared the end, Ms. Ryan slowed and stopped. She knocked on a door two down from the end, and the sound of a male voice caused Victoria's mouth to go dry with momentary dread. She clenched her fists around the handle of her purse to keep herself from rubbing her damp palms on her expensive black linen suite. The door opened, and she squared her shoulders before stepping into the room.

The first thing she saw was the Cincinnati skyline that lay beyond the office floor-to-ceiling windows. It was a spectacular view. The second thing she noticed was the man sitting behind the huge desk placed in the middle of the room. He made a formidable vision, but then she remembered the last time she'd seen him and any admiration she felt disintegrated.

She walked closer and Antonio Sable stood and moved from around the table. As he moved closer she tried to shake the feeling of familiarity that caught her off guard. She schooled her features and met him mid-stride. She took in the perfect cut of his suit and what seemed to be a lean physique beneath it. Antonio's thick, dark brown hair, now graying at the edges, with wisps of the same gray running through the low-cut style only served to set off the bonze tone of his skin. She wondered briefly if it still curled once it reached a certain length. He had grown into his features, and his younger narrow jaw had squared somewhat. He was still a beautiful specimen of a man, but their history tainted his looks.

"Victoria," he said, taking her hand in both of his. He scanned her face, making her feel slightly uncomfortable with his intensity. "It's been a long time."

"Yes it has," she said pulling her hand out of his grasp.

He smiled sadly then gestured to a set of chairs to the right of his desk. She led the way and made herself comfortable. She laid her purse on her lap then looked up to find him watching her.

"How have you been?" He unbuttoned his suit jacket, folded his hands and crossed his long legs.

"Good, and yourself?" she asked more out of politeness than an invite to conversation.

125

"Life has been good to me." She nodded slightly and surreptitiously glanced at his left ring finger which was adorned with a thick platinum band with an embedded diamond.

"I was surprised your husband didn't come with you." The absence of judgment in his eyes kept the anger at a simmer. She considered lying, but figured there was no need.

"He's down in the car. I wanted to meet with you alone first."

His lips lifted in a small smile, but the sadness in his eyes remained. "Still the deeply independent woman." He unfolded his legs and leaned slightly toward her. "Will you please call your husband to join us? I would rather not start out this new association with more mistrust than there already is." When she didn't move, his smile thinned and his eyes became imploring. "Please." In that moment, he looked more like the Antonio she knew in college than the successful businessman of a Fortune 500 accounting firm. She was sorely tempted to deny him.

She stared back at him for a moment longer, then pulled her cell phone out of her pocket and pressed a button. As it dialed she looked back at Antonio whose smile had returned broadly.

"What?"

"I liked that you were prepared to call for help and that you consider your husband that help." She didn't know what to make of this stranger with her old lover's face, but she was willing to overlook the latter so she wouldn't miss anything.

"Victoria, are you alright?" She could hear the concern in Richard's voice.

"Yes, will you come up, please?" She kept her voice calm so as not to give away her feelings to either man.

"I'll be right there. Do you want me to stay on the line?" She heard the car door shut on his side.

"No need. It was more Antonio's request than mine." She could imagine Richard pausing during the momentary silence.

"Anything else?" He was all business now.

"I was greeted and welcomed as if I were expected." She smiled briefly at Antonio to make it seem like less of a message and more of a reassuring word to her husband.

"I'll let Sam know and be on my way." The line disconnected before she could say anything else.

"Would you like something to drink while we wait?" Antonio gestured toward a small refrigerator in the corner.

"I'll wait until Richard comes in."

Antonio leaned back, and she watched him consider his next words before speaking. "I understand if you have a hard time believing this, but I never meant to hurt you. I do apologize for the way things transpired between us."

"You make it sound like a business deal gone wrong."

"No, that's just my way of keeping the years between us."

Victoria couldn't keep the sarcasm out of her voice. "Life has a way of doing that all on its own."

He nodded his head choosing to ignore the drollness behind the remark. "True, but seeing you takes me back to a time when anything was possible. I had a life's worth of decisions in front of me beginning with one."

Victoria felt her chin lift in defense. She knew she was playing with fire, but she was intrigued. "Are you telling me if you had to do it all again you would do it differently?" She watched him intently, hoping to get an unfettered answer from him before her husband walked in.

"Are you happy, Victoria?" She was startled by the openness in his gaze and his posture that spoke of the importance of her answer. She paused for a moment, tempted to hold back the answer, but she was curious at what he would say.

"Yes. I'm happy."

He leaned back in his chair again. "Then no, I wouldn't change a thing." Her breath caught at his candor. What was he getting at? She opened her mouth to ask just that, but there was a knock on the door and she saw the mask slide in place right before he gave the person permission to enter.

She looked away as Richard stepped over the threshold. Her husband cut his own striking figure. She took pride in her husband's appearance. He had dressed for the occasion as well. She wondered if he knew he would find himself face-to-face with Antonio.

Her gaze shifted to Antonio as he stood and approached Richard to shake his hand. She tried hard not to compare the two men with their bronze and mocha complexions. Richard had a couple of inches on Antonio but Antonio's physique looked lethal even in his suit.

As the men parted, she saw Ms. Ryan bring a chair over from the other side of the room. Antonio gestured to the new chair placed next to hers. Richard bent down and kissed her forehead before sitting, but took her hand once he was settled.

She saw Antonio smile slightly at Richard's possessive display. He seemed amused.

Victoria turned fully to Antonio giving him her undivided attention.

Antonio returned to his preferred sitting position. "I believe you know by now that I was expecting you. Maybe not today, but soon." Victoria didn't move.

"The reason why I was expecting you was because I have been placing information where your people could find it. Not easily, mind you." He looked at Richard. "Your girl, Mya, is very skilled."

Victoria went hot then cold. For him to admit to that so quickly, made it the least of their concerns. What was the real reason why he led them to him? She really hated being the last one to know something.

"We have a mutual associate. But before I get to her, I want to apologize to you, Victoria, for not making you aware of the whereabouts of our son when I found out what my father had done. I thought..." He looked down for a moment then back to her. "I thought there was more time."

"But why do it in the first place?" Victoria couldn't have kept from voicing the thought if she wanted to.

Antonio's mouth thinned. "Family is very important to us. No child conceived inside or outside of marriage with Sable blood is raised without knowing their heritage."

"Family?" Victoria bit her tongue before giving anymore of her feelings away.

"I know it may be hard to understand, but I did what I thought was best at the time."

"Abandoning me and our child was best?" Victoria felt Richard's hand tighten around hers and took a deep breath to calm her anger.

"I told my father about you as soon as I got home."

"But..." Victoria tried to interrupt but Antonio raised a hand.

"I know what my parents told you at my engagement party, but they did know. It was part of the agreement I made with them."

Victoria didn't like this feeling. She wasn't in control of the rate in which this information was coming, and so she wasn't able to guard her motions. *Please Lord, help me with what I'm about to discover. Please, don't let it hurt too much.* She felt Richard's hand squeeze hers again and she looked at him and squeezed back. He nodded slightly and they turned back to Antonio.

"I knew the family rule about children. It was pounded into us as children, then teenagers. I thought it would cause them to have to take you and our child into the family. But their need for an alliance was more important to them and I was the pawn." His eyes went cloudy for a moment and Victoria could see that he was revisiting the past.

"Were you engaged when we...when we were together?" She could have kicked herself for stumbling over the sentence. She was giving away too much.

"At birth. We were engaged at birth. I saw her maybe a half-dozen times before that night." He kept eye contact with her.

"Initially I refused to go forward with the engagement, but they threatened to destroy your academic career then your parent's livelihood. I told them I would marry you and go away, but they told me just how far their reach went, and I knew if I stayed in your life they would destroy not only ours, but your family's."

Victoria was momentarily stunned to find out that he'd fought for her. She mentally shook away the haze.

"The data Mya recovered noted that you didn't marry the girl you were engaged to."

Antonio quirked a smile. "That was because of you." He nodded at her. "When you showed up during the party she was embarrassed to say the least. She adamantly refused to marry me. I was downright relieved, but it didn't change my parent's minds about you or our child."

"I didn't know it. I promise you I didn't." He implored Victoria to believe him. "My father kept tabs on you and Brian without my knowledge. I didn't know anything about the Grossenbergs nor their arrangement. I only found out about Brian and the Grossenbergs by accident. I was in my second year in our family business. My parents had taken a second honeymoon and I was asked to file some bills of sale. There were medical records in with some of my father's other bills. I was about to file them with the rest of the medical bills when I caught sight of the names. I did some research and found out my father was paying for Brian's medical bills and sending the Grossenbergs money.

I confronted my father, and he told me the same thing he told me as a child. No Sable child would grow up without knowing their lineage.

"Did you know I was looking for him?"

"Not right away." He looked a little uncomfortable.

"Did you find out while he was still alive?" She held her breath, hoping it would numb the pain.

"Yes."

The initial sound of the word felt like a slap in the face, but the pain began to ebb a few seconds later.

"Are you okay?" Richard's voice pulled her away from her self-examination.

"Yes." She was surprised to find her answer was true. He saw it in her eyes and smiled at her.

Thank you Lord. Maybe she was finally starting to heal.

"I didn't think it was prudent at the time and I was proven right."

"How was it right for you not to inform me of my child's whereabouts?"

"Like I said earlier, we have a mutual acquaintance and she is all kinds of evil." Antonio unfolded his legs. "Would either of you like something to drink. I have soft to hard drinks. Believe me you will want something."

Victoria felt dread bubbling up in her stomach. "I'll have water." She didn't want to delay things any more than they were dragging out now. "I'll have water as well if it comes in a bottle," Richard said.

Antonio came back from the refrigerator with three bottles of water and handed them theirs.

He sat back down and took a long pull from his bottle.

"I'm talking about Brenda Gorman, aka Grace Morganson."

Victoria was happy she hadn't taken a sip yet because it would have ended up on the carpet.

"Brenda, I mean Grace used to work for my father. She was one of his top accountants until she started selling secrets to some of our competitors. One such competitor was under investigation for racketeering and she ended up as a witness. My father fired her and had to separate himself and our business from her in such a way that she would never work for any company in the state nor its surrounding states again. It didn't really matter because she ended up in witness protection so her time in that profession was over." He leaned forward resting his elbows on his knees.

"She held a grudge though and blamed the family in some convoluted way. She sent my father letters threatening our family code. He didn't know what type of revenge she was planning until it was too late.

The dread was spreading through Victoria's core. "What did she do?"

"Brenda was also my father's personal accountant. She knew about Brian and the money my father was sending the Grossenbergs. Originally he thought she was going to start a scandal around the family, but when things remained quiet we thought they were only threats.

Brenda found the Grossenbergs even after my dad convinced them to move. She, her husband, and her daughter Grace Melanie Morganson moved a street over from them."

Victoria wanted to place the cold water bottle in her hands, on her forehead to cool her sudden temperature. She could feel her stomach roiling. She felt perspiration break out on her upper lip and took some deep breaths.

"Brenda's husband was in the military at the time so some of their records were considered classified. She and her family befriended the Grossenbergs and the two children became close. Under Brenda's manipulation they became very close; too close for a twelve-year-old and a thirteen-year-old."

Victoria raised her hand in surrender. She couldn't seem to wrap her mind around what he was saying anymore. It was all jumbled together and she couldn't get a full breath.

"Victoria, breathe." Richard was kneeling in front of her with his hands on either side of her face. His face went in and out of focus, but he shook her firmly. She watched his eyes then looked at his lips.

"Breathe deep and slowly, Victoria." He unscrewed the cap of her bottle of water and placed it to her lips. "Drink Victoria." She took a sip, but it went down the wrong pipe and she coughed, inhaling in between. The extra oxygen cleared her head and the darkness at the edges began to recede. She continued to breathe heavily until she could feel her heartbeat return to normal.

"Will she be all right?" Antonio was no longer across from them but at his desk. "Do I need to call someone?"

Richard raised his hand to stay Antonio's movements. "She's all right. It's just a bit overwhelming, and she is having a hard time piecing everything together. Just give us a moment."

Richard's hands came back to her cheeks. "How're you doing?"

"Better," she said quietly, now embarrassed by the display of weakness.

"Do you want to go back to the hotel?" He released her face and took her hands.

"No. I want to know everything." She put as much conviction in her voice as she could.

"Sure?" She saw the love in his eyes and smiled.

"Sure."

"Alright, Mr. Sable, she wants to go on."

Antonio came back and sat across from them. "Where was I?" he murmured more to himself than anyone.

"The children were twelve and thirteen years old."

"Yes. Well, the girl ended up getting pregnant as Brenda planned." That got both Victoria's and Richard's attention.

"Pregnant?" they both said in unison.

Antonio nodded. "But she had the girl hide the pregnancy. Brian and his family didn't know and so we didn't know." He rubbed his forehead with his fingers. "What follows isn't going to be pleasant to hear."

"And a psycho woman convincing two children to have sex as early as twelve and thirteen wasn't hard to hear?" Victoria said, tapping into her anger. Antonio just stared at her.

"Brenda worked at the State General Hospital in Colorado as an accountant in billing." She felt Richard's hand clamp down on hers like a vice, but he let go when she made a sound of surprise. She looked at him, but he kept his attention directed at Antonio.

"Grace Melanie went against her mother's wishes and went to see Brian in her eighth month. They planned to run away because they couldn't tell who to trust, Mel went into labor. The Grossenbergs said that Brian was incensed and couldn't be appeased. He told them Brenda was going to steal his baby. That night they had to sedate him and in the morning Brenda and Melanie were gone. Some of the furniture was still in the house, but it looked empty. Melanie's father was on deployment so he was of no use." Victoria started deep breathing again. She knew what was coming and the fire of anger in her was roaring.

"Brian didn't handle things well. He fell into depression. His parents were worried he was going to do himself harm so they took him to the hospital to be seen by a psychologist who recommended he stay for a few days. It was supposed to be seventy-two hours but medical records got switched somehow and he ended up in the mental ward of the hospital for four and a half months. When he got out it was even worse. He asked his parents repeatedly about Grace Melanie, but they had no answers for him."

"Why?" Victoria asked, anger evident in her voice. "Why was he in that place so long? Why didn't you get him out?"

Antonio stared at her. "Because Brenda had the medical records switched. By the time the Grossenbergs told us what was going on, Brian was in there for almost two weeks. It took some time to even find him. Brenda had paid some people off to keep him hidden and moved. We got him out as soon as he was healthy enough to go home."

Victoria was disgusted and angry. It was unbelievable that one woman could cause so much damage. Then another thought came in crystal clear.

"Did the girl have the baby?" she whispered.

Antonio nodded.

"Do you know what the child's name was?" Victoria asked, fighting to remember to breathe.

"Grace Melanie had a baby girl. The original birth certificate has Grace Melanie Morganson as the mother and Brian Antonio Grossenberg as the father. Brenda had it replaced and sealed with a new one with her as the mother and her husband as the father, when they adopted her." Antonio took a deep breath and it seemed to go on forever though she already knew the truth.

"The child's original name was Briar-Rose Paige Morganson, after the father and grandmother. Brenda changed it to Paige Rosen Morganson, for obvious reasons." Antonio leaned in close to Victoria as she tried hard to focus. "

"We have a granddaughter, Victoria."

CHAPTER 10

Richard was glad he was sitting because a small wind could have blown him over at that moment. Paige Morganson was Victoria's granddaughter. He found pulling his gaze away from Antonio an almost impossible task. The word flabbergasted came to mind. He continued to sit there holding Victoria's hand trying to absorb all of the information they'd received so far. He looked over at Victoria and saw that her jaw had gone slack and her eyes were glazed over. Her pallor had turned a sickly gray and he knew he didn't look much better.

He needed to get color back into her cheeks. "Mr. Sable, I think we will take you up on your offer for something stronger." Victoria's head whipped toward his and she opened her mouth. "Could you get my wife two fingers of whatever you have in your liquor cabinet?" he asked without taking his eye off of her. Her mouth closed and he gave her a rueful smile.

"And for you?" Antonio asked as he made his way to his bar.

"Coke, if you have one," Richard replied and watched as Antonio threw him a glance.

"I'm driving." He said. before understanding came into his eyes. Antonio said nothing when he returned with their drinks.

He watched as Victoria sipped at hers, but when she would have put it down he guided it back to her lips.

After a few minutes he was happy to see some color return to Victoria's cheeks. He went back to thinking about some of the ramifications of this news as he turned his attention back to Antonio.

Two questions pushed through his thoughts. He remembered something from months ago when he stumbled across the information regarding Melanie Grace. "Paige told me Melanie Grace is only ten years older than her.

Antonio shook his head to the negative. From what I know Melanie was twelve at the time she gave birth even though she was enrolled in school two grades behind."

Richard looked at Victoria who was already watching him. *More lies.* He would have to let that go for the present.

"Why now? You could have shared this information with us at any time. Why now?"

"Because now it's relevant."

Richard felt the words bounce off of Victoria and felt for her hand again. He was surprised at her reserve. Maybe it was the shock that kept her silently seated next to him.

"Please explain."

Antonio looked back and forth between him and Victoria, and he prepared himself for another blow.

"Though she may have had some interaction with the two of you, you were never Brenda's target. The Sable family and all of its heirs were."

"You two came into this because Victoria called in a few favors to have her daughter adopt one of Briar..." He cleared his throat. "I mean Paige's twins."

"How long have you been watching my wife?" Richard tried to keep the emotion out of his voice, but knew he failed when Antonio's eyes fired briefly.

"I have kept up with some of her accomplishments. Nothing that wasn't already public knowledge. I was curious as to why she swung the adoption her way if she didn't know about Paige." He paused and looked at Richard to see if his answer sufficed before continuing. "She definitely had Brenda hot under the collar. Brenda wanted to use Vivian as a pawn in her scheme against the Sable family. If her plan had worked she would have had a very valuable bargaining chip."

"Explain." Richard knew he was speaking for both himself and Victoria with the one word, but honestly he didn't know how much more he could absorb before reaching capacity. Judging by Victoria's reaction, she was closer than he was.

Richard watched as Antonio looked at Victoria closely and out of the corner of his eye Richard saw her give him an almost imperceptible nod.

"When Paige gave birth to Vivian and Gladys, Brenda had a nurse switch Vivian with a child who was stillborn. Neither the mother nor the child made it through the labor. She told Paige her child died and made sure the child was placed in the system for adoption. She had a couple set up, waiting to adopt the child, and it would have gone smoothly if Victoria hadn't stepped in."

"Why?" Victoria's voice was small.

"Why what?" Antonio asked almost as quietly. Richard didn't like the intimate picture that formed, but just squeezed Victoria's hand slightly.

"Why didn't she do or say anything?"

"Who?"

"Brenda. Why did she wait until Vivian was six before she contacted me?"

"Your name wasn't in the records, Victoria. Your daughter and son-in-law's were. You may want to ask him if they were contacted by her. Brenda didn't know about you until you started researching the dead mother's medical history and found out that she couldn't be Vivian's mother. I think she was feeling you out when she blackmailed you."

"You knew about that? That wasn't public record." Victoria sounded like she was choking on her words.

"No." He shook his head. "Brenda has been under surveillance by one of my firms for a very long time."

Victoria shook her head. "I still don't get it. You have had many opportunities to step in and say something—anything. Why now?"

"You were completely separated from the Sable family until Paige donated one of her kidneys to Vivian and found out she was her daughter."

Richard could tell Victoria also realized he hadn't answered the question when she leaned forward.

"Why now, Antonio?" Her voice had regained its depth.

"I want to meet my granddaughter and great-granddaughters. I believe it's time we meet." Antonio sat back to cross his legs again, but Richard could read the position now. It was one he used to look nonchalant when the subject meant more to him than he wished to convey.

"You want me to introduce you," Victoria said in disbelief. Richard knew the slightly airy timber in her voice meant she was on the verge of going off. He decided it would be a good time to step in.

"You could have started this ball rolling a long time ago. I think there's more to this."

Antonio watched him for a moment. "Vivian's need for a kidney came about due to a car accident. In a blink of an eye I could have lost one of my greatgrandchildren and I'd never met her. In the hospital, Paige didn't get away from the operating table unscathed, and once again I was faced with losing another family member without ever meeting them."

"Did you meet Brian?" Her voice lost its edge.

Richard couldn't imagine the emotional turmoil she was going through. He was reeling, and he was somewhat removed from this except for his concern for his wife. He wanted to pick her up and take them far away from this man who seemed to be holding all of the strings in regards to their family, but no matter how he or

Victoria reacted, he had the feeling that Antonio was now in their lives for a long time to come.

Antonio's eyes shuttered, but he nodded to the positive. "Yes. When he was six."

Richard gaged her reaction and the visible way she swallowed told him a great deal. That had rocked her. "Was he happy?" Her voice was strong, but the sheen in her eyes told him how much this conversation was costing her.

"Yes, Stella, he was." Antonio said then caught himself. Victoria visibly blanched.

"Excuse me, Richard. I meant no disrespect." He looked genuinely apologetic.

Richard nodded in acknowledgment. "I think if we stay with English we won't have to worry about Italian endearments." Antonio nodded back.

"Did you tell him who you were?" Victoria continued with her line of questioning.

Richard took notice of Antonio's pause, but the man's answer gave nothing away. "No, I did not tell him."

The air around him grew cool and he glanced over at Victoria. "What aren't you telling us, Antonio?"

Antonio looked a little reluctant, but breathed in and out deeply. "Brenda became a very wealthy woman playing organizations and people against each other. She hasn't contacted any of the former companies even though the organization she testified against is no longer a threat. She has, however aligned herself with some of the elitists in the New England area and has been spreading rumors about my wife's business. In the event-planning industry, word-of-mouth referrals are important. Brenda has done just enough damage for my wife's family to see it affect their profits. It isn't substantial, but I'm sure Brenda isn't going to be satisfied until it is irreparably damaged.

"Okay, I'm going to point the spotlight on the elephant in the room. Your family is Italian and from some of the records you leaked to us..." She raised her fingers in air quotes. "You have very old money and older ties. She is one person. Why don't you just call in a hit and get rid of her."

"Victoria." Richard couldn't keep the dismay out of his voice.

She looked at him. "You didn't think about it?"

"No," he said, appalled.

Victoria shrugged. "I obviously have some more praying to do."

"Are you being serious?" Richard could barely believe what she was saying.

"Yes." She looked back at him. "Look at all the damage she has caused these families, and still causing. She needs to die."

"Even so. It isn't your choice. It isn't any man's choice," he said, sickened at even having this conversation with her.

"Well, knowing God, He will leave her here long enough for her to get saved and ask for forgiveness," she said in disgust.

"He left you here, Victoria." Richard watched her press her lips together as color rose up her neck, but she couldn't hold it in.

"Are you comparing her with me?" She practically hissed.

"No!" He nearly yelled then tempered his voice. "No I wouldn't think of comparing you to her. I'm considering some of your actions against Paige before you received Jesus in your heart and her reaction to you."

Guilt danced in her eyes before she schooled her features and looked back at Antonio.

"It's a moot point," Antonio began.

"Why, what does she have on your family that no one has killed this woman?" Victoria

"I don't know." Antonio said, looking convincing so she let it go.

"What do you want from us?"

141

"Like I said, I want to meet my granddaughter and great-granddaughters." Antonio leaned forward in his chair placing his elbows on his knees.

"I'm not sure this is the best time." Victoria hedged.

"But she got married recently, right? Isn't she happy with her new husband?" Antonio asked.

How did he find out his information? Richard wondered.

Antonio must have seen the perplexed look on his face because he answered him. "It's a public record. I have an application that will alert me if her name comes up." He turned back to Victoria. "Is there something going on with Paige's marriage?"

"No." Victoria waved her hand. "Brandon is very good to her. Her twins even visited them for a week for their birthday."

It was Antonio's turn to look confused, but Richard could see he mistook Victoria's reluctance.

"Mr. Sable, Paige's husband is ill."

"Oh, I'm sorry to hear that. Is it serious?"

"He is fighting cancer," Victoria said. Her voice revealing her emotions on the subject.

"Maybe there's something I can do…" Antonio positioned himself to get up.

"The doctors have done everything they know to do. It's in God's hands," Victoria said, interrupting him.

Antonio sat back down and stared at Victoria for a moment. "Don't you think she should be surrounded by family?"

"They are determined to have as normal a life together for as long as they can. They are enjoying each other as any other newlywed couple would."

Antonio seemed to ponder this. "Well, maybe I could still meet her."

"Paige didn't find out until earlier this year that this Brenda person was her grandmother and Melanie was her mother. She didn't handle it well and with Melanie not willing to reveal Paige's father's real name, their relationship has suffered."

"Why wouldn't she tell Paige who her father was?" Antonio asked.

"We think Grace... uh... Brenda has something on her so she can't say anything," Victoria responded.

Antonio seemed to consider that but Richard couldn't shake the notion that there was something he wasn't sharing.

"I just think it would be a lot to place on Paige at this time," Victoria stated firmly, but Antonio didn't look convinced.

"I'm not saying that family isn't important, but if you've waited this long what is another few months?"

"What if I want to meet this fellow my granddaughter married?"

Richard watched his wife go quiet. She looked at Antonio as one would look at a bug under a microscope.

"How would we explain you? Hey Paige, not only am I your grandmother, but here's your long-lost grandfather who has been patiently waiting in the wings of your life."

"That may work without the sarcasm," Antonio stated dryly. "Are you saying you won't tell Paige you're her grandmother, when you get home?"

"I don't know what I'm going to do with any of the news you gave us today. I'm still trying to wrap my mind around most of it, including the fact that you've known and met our son and still refused to share the information with me until now."

Antonio looked disheartened by her last response. Richard wanted to tell the man to get used to it if he was going to deal with Victoria in the future.

Victoria shook her head slowly. "I don't think Paige and Melanie's relationship can survive any more surprises at the moment and Paige will need her mother."

143

Antonio sighed. Richard fought back a smile. He'd seen that beaten expression before, in the mirror.

"Where do we go from here? Will you help me meet Vivian and Gladys?"

"I'm very protective of my granddaughter."

"I have no doubt of that after meeting with you today," Antonio replied.

Richard covered his chuckle with a cough, drawing Victoria's attention, but he looked away.

After a moment Victoria nodded her head. "Give me a few days to contact Vivian's father. I will also have to contact Melanie and ask her if she wants Gladys to meet you."

Antonio didn't speak, but nodded his agreement before getting up, thus signaling that their meeting was over. "Is there anything else?"

"I don't know. Have you shared everything with us?" Victoria asked, but ignored his hint by remaining seated.

"What else should there be?" Antonio's eyebrow raised, and Richard leaned back to enjoy the standoff.

"Don't give me that look, Antonio. You're the one holding all of the information. I would be foolish to think you shared everything, but I'm not sure I can take any more." Richard saw her mind whirling and almost felt sorry for Antonio. Almost.

A now composed Victoria made a big show of opening her purse, taking out a card, and closing it again. She picked up her bottle of water and took a slow drink before she spoke again.

"Where is Brian buried?"

Richard who had been watching Victoria, shifted his gaze to Antonio who was having a hard time keeping the surprise off his face. Richard found that odd, since it was a perfectly reasonable question.

"Our family has a plot of land. Brian has a grave there," he said, looking a little uneasy.

"Did you see his body after… after he died?" Victoria asked, pushing through the sentence.

"No. News didn't reach us right away. He was already in the cemetery by the time I learned of what happened," he said quietly.

"Why? Where were you?"

"My wife was having some complications with her pregnancy. It was a very challenging week. I refused to leave her side." His posture shouted his reluctance to go into either subject further.

"So you had the casket dug up and moved?" Richard knew Victoria was asking her questions in a more purposeful manner.

Antonio paused and looked at him quickly before answering the question. "No. He had been cremated."

Victoria gasped, and Richard stood up to move behind her. He rubbed her arms hoping it would console her. He felt her take a few deep breaths before she continued.

"Did you see the medical examiner's report?" she asked.

"Yes," he answered slowly.

"Did you see pictures?"

"Yes, of different body parts. Not on the whole," Antonio answered.

Richard watched the volley and wondered who was leading whom.

"Did you move the urn?"

"Yes, I had it moved to our family plot after Lilith Grossenberg passed away this year. She requested that we let her keep her son's remains in their family's mausoleum until after she passed."

"That wasn't odd to you?" Victoria was getting frustrated.

"The woman's fourteen-year-old child committed suicide. There is no measure for normal behavior after that."

"You know why I studied law in college?"

"Besides the fact that your parents wanted you to?" Antonio asked with amusement.

Since Richard couldn't see Victoria's face he imagined from Antonio's reaction, her look was one that could freeze a drink in Hawaii in August.

"It was because I was a great researcher, and the reason I was so good was because I asked the right questions." He saw Antonio pale ever so slightly.

"Did you have the remains tested?" she asked Antonio squarely.

Antonio walked back to his chair and sat down. "Yes."

Richard moved back to his own chair so he could gage Victoria's expressions.

"And what were the results?"

"Inconclusive. The sample we already had of Brian's DNA was tainted." Antonio looked down at his hands as he rubbed them together.

"Was that the sample your father had taken when he tested to make sure Brian was yours?" The edge in her voice could cut diamonds.

Antonio didn't respond.

Victoria looked at Antonio for one calculating moment. "Where's my son? You son of a…"

"Victoria!" Richard interrupted her as he got up to step in front of his wife just in case she had a mind to go after Antonio.

"Baby, calm down."

"Why?" She didn't take her eyes off of Antonio. "He was going to let us walk out of here without telling us that my son may still be alive."

Richard turned to Antonio. "You might want to put a little more space between the two of you until she calms down." Antonio looked at him in surprise then got out of his seat and walked behind his desk.

Richard felt Victoria get up and turned back to her. She winked at him and he was momentarily stunned. She wasn't incensed, she was scheming. He placed his hands on the sides of her face and spoke quietly. "You will be the death of me one day."

"I hope not. We still have too much life to live and I want to introduce you to my son." The light in her eyes pulled him in and he would have kissed her, but he had to play a part.

"Where's my son, Antonio?" Her voice went back to steel.

"I don't know," Antonio replied, agitated.

Victoria peered around Richard. "What do you mean you don't know?"

"Almost everyone who would know is dead, except Paige and Grace Melanie," Antonio said.

They had finally arrived at the reason why Antonio had led them here. Richard moved out of Victoria's way. Antonio was now on his own.

Victoria walked around him toward the desk. "You're a real piece of work." She placed her hands on her hips, and Richard didn't know whether to cheer or pray so he stayed silent.

"What makes you think you can treat people this way? All you had to do was be truthful from the beginning and let me share a part of my child's life. I would have been grateful even if it was just pictures from time to time." She sucked her teeth in disgust.

"If I hadn't asked you the right questions would you have shared what you were really up to?"

"Eventually," he said solemnly.

"I don't believe you," Victoria spat.

Richard saw a glimpse of pain pass through his eyes before he wiped his features clear of any emotion. He didn't outwardly respond to her statement.

"I'll contact Mason and Melanie to see if they will allow you to meet their girls, but I'll keep to my earlier decision. I will not tell Paige about you until I think it will benefit her and her family." Victoria turned toward the door.

"What's to keep the girls and Grace Melanie from telling her about me," Antonio called out to stop her.

Victoria stopped. "If Melanie wants to tell her about you, which I doubt, she can." She looked at Antonio over her shoulder. "But if we tell the girls that withholding the information of your existence from Paige is one of the conditions of meeting you, they will make their decision upon that condition and you will respect their choice."

Antonio nodded.

"I'll be in touch, Antonio." Victoria turned back around and Richard made sure he was at the door before she was so he could facilitate her flawless exit. He would have to ask forgiveness for his thoughts later.

He dipped his chin at Antonio right before he followed her through the door.

*   *   *

They were halfway to the hotel before Victoria spoke. "My son might be alive." Her whisper was barely audible and he understood her fear of hoping too loud. He reached over and squeezed her knee.

"When did you figure it out?" he asked referring to her knowing Brian was alive.

"He didn't share his plan for stopping Brenda. Instead he started flinging hash about how much he wanted to meet his granddaughter and great-granddaughters." She turned her body toward him.

"If you had a woman who was threatening your family and their livelihood wouldn't your first priority be to get rid of the threat?"

"Yes," he responded even though he knew she meant it to be rhetorical.

"And why would he test Brian's remains unless he questioned his death." She said.

He nodded, thinking the exact same thing.

"I think he's trying to get to Melanie. I think he believes she might know where those files are." She went quiet for a moment. "And where Brian is."

"What do you need?" he asked, not taking his eyes off of the road.

"I need any information you can find on Antonio Sable and his immediate family. I don't trust that he shared everything with us."

"I'll call Sam when we get to the room," he replied easily.

She shifted in her seat to look out the window. "I also think we should take a trip to Atlanta. The talk we need to have with Melanie can't be done over the phone."

He agreed with her and was glad that the morning hadn't taken a huge toll on her. She was much stronger than he was. His thoughts were still reeling. He would need a few days to sort it all out.

"How are you feeling, Victoria?"

She turned back to him and he was finally graced with the smile he'd been looking for. "Slightly overwhelmed, but..." She paused for a moment to think about it. "Hopeful," she said. "Very hopeful." She covered his hand with hers and turned back to the passenger side window.

Thank you God. You are so awesome. I don't mind your ways being mysterious especially when you force what is being done in darkness into the light. Thank you for bringing peace to my wife. I praise your name, Lord. You are my God, and I am your child.

He continued to silently praise and pray to the Lord as he drove.

CHAPTER 11

Paige turned the volume up on the contemporary Christian song and began to sing along as she made her way through afternoon traffic heading away from the Wilshire District. Normally the forty-five-minute drive from her agent's office tested her patience, but not even the fifteen-mile trek driven at a speed of twenty miles an hour could put a damper on her happiness at this moment.

She would be in New York sitting in front of one of the most prestigious publishing companies this time next week to go over the final revision of her contract. She had to hand it to Carmen; she had more than earned her paycheck this time. She had negotiated and haggled like the girl from the Bronx she claimed, when she wanted to show off her O.G. status. Not only had Carmen gotten Paige out of her contract with her former publisher with two less books, she got the new company to help pay any early termination fees she couldn't talk them out of.

It was nothing short of a miracle. She was sure God had softened their hearts since their last conversation made Paige feel more like an indentured servant than a bestselling author. She'd tried to work within their parameters, but the two nonfiction works to every fictional novel was stifling her creativity. She loved the voice she'd found in Women's fiction and Young Adult fiction and was excited at the prospect.

The money wouldn't only place Paige in another tax bracket, it would give her latest work the exposure she was hoping for while affording her the freedom to try out yet another genre. The young adult story that had almost been writing itself in her mind since she'd been interacting with Vivian and Gladys was going to be birthed with a silver spoon in its mouth. The story of a young boy unashamed of his faith and the new girl in town suffering from an undiagnosed bipolar disorder, came to her as she and her daughters were praying one morning. It took evangelizing, immovable faith, and boldness to another level. Her fingers were already itching to get to her laptop.

She touched the hands-free button on her steering wheel and instructed her device to call Brandon. She couldn't wait to tell him the news. They would celebrate tonight. If he was feeling up to it they could go out. If not, she would order takeout from their favorite Thai restaurant. She listened as the phone rang and then went to voicemail. "Honey, it's been a fantastic day just like you said. Carmen didn't even have to pull out the big guns and the company capitulated. There's nothing else keeping me from signing the new contract once they finalize it this weekend. They want to meet in person, but I'll tell you more about that when I get home. When you get this give me a call. I was thinking we could get takeout, watch something boring, and make out like teenagers on the couch. Call me. I'm so excited." She ended her last sentence on a squeal before disconnecting the call. She was riding so high she didn't think anything could bring her down.

*   *   *

The last month and a half with Brandon had felt like a fairy tale. She was extremely blessed. After the girls left the house and she slept off the emotional high, she noticed the quietness of the house and Brandon. She took a day to thoroughly clean the house and make a special dinner for Brandon. When he got home she met him at the door with a warm hug and deep kiss. She looked at him. Really looked at him. It was exactly what she thought. He was tired and trying to hide it. She knew having the girls come for a while was going to take a lot out of her, but she didn't realize how much of an affect it would have on him. She took his attaché case and pushed him toward the bedroom so he could change into more comfortable clothes while she placed dinner on the table.

She had forgone an elaborate meal for lighter fare since it had been hot that day. The air-conditioning had kept the apartment cool, but he had been in and out of the elements all day. It was time to nurture her husband.

By the time he returned from the bedroom he looked somewhat less haggard. There was soft jazz playing from the speakers in the living room and the lights were dimmed in all areas except around their table. She moved slowly around the table until they both had everything they needed in front of them, then sat down opposite him. When he hadn't said anything she looked up expectantly, and her breath caught the love that had shown from his eyes.

"You're alright." His voice was barely louder than a whisper. She didn't really know how to respond since it sounded like it could have been a question, but it didn't have the normal inflection at the end. Right then she knew that it wasn't so much the girls visit directly that had placed a toll on him. It had been her reaction to everything. He had been worried about her when he should have been using his energy to fight the disease.

"I'm alright," she said smiling to reassure him. The visible relief in his eyes and shoulders almost broke her heart. Obviously, the obsessive urges she'd not been able to deny over the last few weeks had scared him. This was a wake-up call she never thought she would get. She was so used to being in her head she failed to realize the shift from being concerned to being obsessive until Brandon said something, but where she thought she could handle it herself at the time, she saw in his eyes her failure to cope with her compulsive behavior in a healthy way.

"I'm going to give my therapist a call tomorrow and see if she can see me sooner than our normal monthly session. Though the girls are back home, and I consider their celebratory week a success, it came with too many sacrifices. I'm sorry it took me so long to really understand how much this was affecting you." She watched the expression shift in his eyes.

"Are you doing and telling me this because you love me or because you are afraid I'm too frail to deal with you being human?"

She was slightly taken aback by his words, but tried to see things from his eyes. She took a moment to consider her true motives, and the conclusion she came up with in that quick moment was one she could live with. "Both. I love you so I want to you happy and healthy. I want you happy and healthy so we can have more wonderful times together. I want more wonderful times with you because they make me happy." She looked at her plate as if contemplating her last words. "Wow. I guess I'm being selfish." She looked back at him and watched as he worked to keep the smile off his lips. "You have a selfish wife."

She took in his gaze and twitching lips until he got up and came around to her side of the table. He took her hands and pulled her up so he could sit in her chair and place her in his lap. "I think I'll let it go this time, but not to the point where you are overlooking your own health." She had been staring at his shirt collar so wasn't surprised when she felt his fingertip under her chin. "We are in this together. We give to each other, we pray for each other and lift up each other." He wrapped his arms around her and squeezed. "When one of us is struggling the other steps up their nurturing, comfort, encouragement, and anything else the other person needs more of. I got to do that for you and it was and will continue to be an honor." He paused and she met his eyes again. "You are my wife. You are my best friend. I love you. Not just the pretty parts or the intelligent parts—not even just the very attractive parts," He squeezed her again. "But the cracked parts, the over-critical parts, even the snoring parts." She leaned back.

"I don't snore," she denied, affronted.

He began patting her back. "Keep telling yourself that, honey."

She just stared at him without a thought of what to say.

"Before we get totally off my point. I want to let you know that I know what you're doing and I love you for it. It was a long hot day and I'm happy to be home being pampered, but after we eat this beautiful meal you've prepared, I want some cuddling time on the couch then some more cuddling time in bed." She shivered and scrambled off his lap. Then stood to look down at him. When he didn't move she placed her hands on her hips.

"What are you waiting for?" she asked saucily. "Go eat your food. We have some cuddling to do."

He laughed and got up. "I also love your adorably bossy ways."

It was the beginning of a wonderful month and a half, filled with a level of communication and intimacy she'd never imagined. She'd met with her therapist and was trying a new anti-anxiety medication which left her feeling a little woozy at first, but made the distant future a little less daunting and thoughts of the upcoming meeting with her publisher easier to stomach, thus the recent very successful meetings.

*   *   *

She realized she had made a lot of progress in her drive home, but still hadn't heard from Brandon. She tried calling him again, but was met with the same results. She cut off the impulse to worry and focused on getting through the last few minutes of her drive.

She was pulling into the subterranean parking lot when her phone lit up. Since reception was horrible at best in the garage she checked the caller ID. Not recognizing the number she continued forward letting the call go to voicemail. She would check her voicemail when she got in the apartment.

She reached the door to the apartment without incident, but as she slid her key in the lock she heard something behind her. She quickly grasped the pepper spray at the end of her keyring and whipped around prepared to surprise the interloper. The surprise was on her.

"Melanie?" she screeched more out of shock than the annoyance that was filtering in. "What are you doing sneaking up on me, and what are you doing in Los Angeles?"

"I need to talk to you."

"You couldn't have called me?" Paige said as she turned back to unlock and open the door.

"No," Melanie said, her tone wavering between exasperation and anxiousness causing Paige to turn and study her.

"What's going on? Is Gladys okay? Marc?" She froze, reluctant to say the next name that popped in her head. "Is Grace up to something?"

After getting a headshake to the negative to all her guesses she walked into the apartment and laid her keys down and walked into the living room.

"Are you in a hurry? I need to check my phone. I haven't been able to get in touch with Brandon in a while."

"No. I'm good. I'm sorry for coming with no notice. Go ahead and do what you need to."

Perplexed, Paige took out her phone and gestured for Melanie to make herself at home before she went to her bedroom for a moment of peace. Sure enough there was message on her phone. She engaged her voicemail and sat on the bed as she waited for it to begin. The woman identified herself as a nurse from the hospital Brandon frequented. Paige was immediately on alert. Brandon was fine, he had just become dizzy and disoriented at work and was currently receiving a cocktail of liquid and medications that would deal with the dehydration. Paige quickly walked to her desk and wrote down the number the woman started reciting. She disconnected the line and dialed the number.

The information station transferred her to the nurse's station in the emergency wing where Brandon was being attended to. She assured Paige that Brandon was alright, but he had another hour of observation and liquids to receive. She said as soon as he was lucid he started asking for them to call her because he couldn't remember where he'd left his phone.

She assured the woman she would be on her way and hung up.

She quickly changed into something she would be comfortable sitting in for a while and walked out into the living room where she stopped short. She'd forgotten about Mel.

"Um, Brandon is in the hospital. They say it isn't serious, but I need to go." She began walking toward the kitchen to get a water bottle and fruit. She looked over as Mel walked into the doorway. "Do you want to stay here? You must be tired, and I don't know when I'll be back." She screwed on the cap and waited a few seconds for an answer. Mel was visibly trying to control her emotions. The sadness at the edges of her eyes made Paige bristle. "You'd better be able to compose yourself better than that, or you can't come with me or stay here, which is what I presumed you wished to do since you brought an overnight bag with you. This is Brandon and my haven. We aren't going to walk on eggshells because you're already mourning something that is still very much alive." Mel shook her head and made one swipe at the tears. She gave Paige a watery smile. "You are the strongest woman I know," Mel said.

Paige pointed her finger at her mother. "None of that Saint Paige stuff either. My strength only reflects my love for my husband." She took a deep breath. "So if you can follow those two rules we should be fine. The nurse said he will be at least another hour. Do you want to come or stay?"

"You got another water bottle?" Mel nodded her head toward the container in Paige's hand.

Paige shook her head in an amused quirk lifting the left side of her lips. "You never could answer a question straight on." She saw Mel stiffen and instantly regretted her flippant remark.

She turned back and got another bottle and filled it with water while Mel went back into the living room. She hadn't really had to deal with the stumbling blocks in their relationship since the wedding. Even though they'd had some time to talk and build a fragile bridge filling in the gap the betrayal and lies Mel had surrounded Paige with caused, Paige had relentlessly pushed the thoughts of reconciliation aside. That would have taken a great deal more energy than she was willing to give as of late. She knew deep down that the lack of attention given to their relationship would make it harder to get back to the place they were before. The pain of it was still too sharp. For years Mel had been the only person Paige could lean on. She was the only one who Paige could pour her heart out to and trust it would be safely held in secrecy.

Whatever Grace had over Mel was stronger than that trust and Paige still grieved the loss. Seeing Mel at her door only magnified that loss at this moment when she could have used someone to speak her feelings and fears to.

"I'm ready." Mel's voice pulled her from her thoughts. She pasted a smile on her face and handed her the bottle.

"Can I ask you how many times you've done this?" Paige looked at her confused. Mel swallowed. "Gone to the hospital for Brandon like this." She finished lamely.

Paige knew she should feel bad for making such conversation so uncomfortable to Mel, but she shook the thought off. She looked Mel square in the eye. "I have quite a few more to go before I catch up to the same number of hours he waited by my bedside a year ago."

Mel looked like she wanted to say something else but was hesitating. Paige sighed in impatience at herself. "Sorry Mel. I don't mean to make it this hard. It just is right now. My emotions are all over the place. What do you want to say?"

Mel placed a hand on her shoulder and Paige tried not to flinch, but she couldn't keep herself from stiffening. "Do you think you owe him for being there for you when you were in the hospital? And I only ask that because of your last statement." Mel raised her hands in surrender. Paige forced her lips to soften from their hard line.

"No, I owe him as a wife who loves him to be by his side. I was just making a comparison with my last statement. This is the only time he has gone into the emergency while we have been married. It's been hot and he got dehydrated." Paige said it as though that was all there was to the situation.

She watched as Mel took a deep breath. "Then let's be on our way," she said as she walked toward the door. Paige stared after her briefly and prayed for fortification.

They were halfway to the hospital before Paige remembered what Mel said when she met her at the door.

"You said you needed to talk to me," she prompted without taking her eyes away from the road.

She heard Mel clear her throat. "If it's alright, I'd like to wait until I can speak to both you and Brandon." Paige took her eyes off the road to take a fleeting glance at Mel. Seeing no guile in the brief assessment, she just shrugged.

"Okay." She didn't say anything else until they entered the hospital.

Paige was given directions to the wing where Brandon was receiving treatment. When she reached the nurses station of the emergency area she calmly stated her husband's name and her relationship to him. When the woman directed her to the curtained cubical, Mel told her she would wait in the waiting area they'd just passed. Giving her a cursory nod, she turned toward the last sectioned-off portion of the room and tried to keep herself from running.

Her first glance at Brandon nearly sent her to her knees she was so relieved. He was sitting up reading a magazine with an I.V.

connected to a tube running to the vein in his left arm. He looked up when he heard the curtain being moved aside. She caught the rueful smile that tilted his lips right before she rushed to embrace him in a light hug.

"Sorry, baby. I think I left my phone at work," he whispered in her ear.

She couldn't help the shudder that ran through her as she held onto the last string of her composure. "You're okay. You're okay." She inhaled slowly taking in his scent, allowing it to calm her.

"I'm okay. It was just a small bout of dehydration. I didn't take into consideration the heat lately. I'll do better," he promised in her ear.

She let his voice and words sooth her.

When she finally moved back she'd gotten in control of the burning in the back of her eyes. She searched his and saw the sheepish smile that made him look more like a little boy whose hand was caught in the cookie jar than a man who'd been brought to the emergency for severe dehydration. She laughed because she couldn't do anything else at the moment.

Brandon's hand slipped up to the nape of her neck. "I'm still a little thirsty." He pulled her face toward him. She placed her hands on his chest to stop her advancement, and glancing to his right she picked up the cup of water from the side table. She placed it to his lips. "Here you go."

"Wow baby, you just ruined a perfectly romantic moment." She made a show of looking around them. "Yes, I can see that now. You hooked up to this sexy I.V. sitting in this comfy, single chair-bed." She pushed on the mattress as if to test its softness. "In this room with a very sturdy curtain between us and the rest of the emergency room." She smiled mischievously. "Yes, I see it now. I'm sorry, honey; I'll make it up to you later." She moved in to kiss his cheek, but yelped when his hand came down hard on her backside. She moved out of his reach, rubbing her injured behind. She pouted at him and was about to give him a piece of her mind, but the sound of the curtain rings sliding along the rail caught her attention.

A slight woman about ten years older than them with a cocoa-colored complexion, in a long white coat, stood there smiling. She looked around Paige at Brandon. "I take it this is your Paige."

Brandon nodded. "Dr. Nadirie, this is my wife, Paige Tatum." Paige couldn't help but smile. She loved hearing him introduce her to people.

She turned to shake the doctor's hand. "Nice to meet you," Paige said politely.

"You as well." The doctor relinquished her hand and walked over to look at Brandon's I.V. bag.

"It's good to know that you are able to deny the advances of this extremely handsome man when he tries to tempt you into a compromising position in the middle of an emergency room." The woman's lips barely lifted as she delivered the dry statement, but the twinkle in her eye had Paige's cheeks warming and her ears going up in flames.

She looked up at Brandon to gage his reaction, and he too was having a hard time keeping the flush from his cheeks.

"Well it looks like you are definitely feeling better and your tests came back looking pretty positive. I will let you go after this bag is through if you promise to go home and stay in bed for the next twenty-four hours to give your body a chance to rest." She pointed at Brandon then Paige and back to Brandon. "Rest. Strictly rest for the next twenty-four hours. The crestfallen look on his face almost had her laughing again, but she took his hand and rubbed her thumb along his knuckles. "Well I guess it's for the best. Melanie showed up at the apartment just before I got the call from the nurse."

"Mel?" He looked perplexed. "Did you know she was coming?"

Paige shook her head. "She surprised me in the hall. I almost pepper sprayed her."

She could see he wanted to ask her more, but turned his attention back to his doctor. She looked at both of them expectantly for a second then clapped her hands together and walked over to type something into the computer in the corner. "Alright. You should be good to go." She turned back to Brandon when she was done. "I want to see you at the end of next week for a follow-up" She turned her eyes to Paige. "Nice to meet you, Paige."

"You too, Dr. Nadirie." She watched as the woman sent a stern look Brandon's way before exiting their space.

"You're in so much trouble." She teased him. He looked a little embarrassed, but shrugged it off. She looked at him, and the amusement left his face. "Why do you think she's here?"

"I have no idea and that troubles me. I totally didn't see this coming. But whatever it is. She said she wanted to talk to the both of us."

"Oh, this really can't be good. Do you know if Marc is with her?"

"I didn't even ask, but she had an overnight bag with her so I'm thinking she's by herself." She looked at him. He let go of her hand and rubbed her arm.

"Well whatever it is we will approach it as we do everything else: together." He smiled reassuringly at her, but she could see the concern he couldn't hide.

"Together," she echoed him.

It wasn't until they were in the car headed to the house that she remembered the good news she'd been wanting to share with him. The two of them were alone in the car with Mel following behind them in his car which they'd picked up along with his phone from his job. The after-hours security guard had heard about Brandon being taken to the hospital and was happy he seemed to be doing better. Paige wondered if Brandon had met a person he didn't like or didn't like him, outside of Victoria, of course. But she knew that was only because he was concerned about her. He made a couple of calls to reassure his boss and a coworker who'd called the ambulance when he'd become disoriented at the end of the workday. She considered it fortunate that he'd stayed just a little later than usual otherwise he could have found himself in the middle of afternoon traffic without help.

Brandon placed his phone to the side. "That's fantastic! I'm sorry I ruined your celebration," he said.

She shrugged. "We can celebrate once Mel leaves."

"Let me make the arrangements. I have an idea that I think you will like." His voice deepened.

She glanced at him. "Hmmm."

"Hmmm, what?" he asked. She could see from the corner of her eye, he was watching her.

"I've been around you long enough to know what you're thinking when your voice dips like that."

"What?" he asked, daring her to spell out what she was accusing him of.

"Whatever arrangements..." She drew out the word. "You are making, do they have something to do with a bed at some point during our celebration?"

He was silent for a moment. "Maybe."

She smiled then quickly rearranged her features and glanced at him.

Reading her thoughts correctly, he exclaimed. "I can't help it if I find my wife incredibly attractive!"

Paige reached over and squeezed his knee. "I don't want you to help it," she said. She let out a breath and made the turn onto their street. She pulled into the garage and parked. She waited for Mel to maneuver Brandon's car into the slot next to hers. She looked over at her husband and smiled wryly at him.

He seemed to read her thoughts because he pulled her close. "I don't care who sees. I want to kiss my wife." He leaned in and took her lips in a soul-stirring kiss and didn't pull away until they were swollen. She watched him take in her hazy gaze and wet, puffy lips. He smiled smugly. "Yes, that'll do."

She would have said something sly and witty, but her thoughts had been wiped clean. She smiled back and looked beyond him to see that Mel had exited his car and was leaning against the passenger side door away from them. She met his eyes again. "I love you, Brandon."

His smile shifted into an expression of such tenderness her breath caught. He brought his hand up to cup her cheek. "I love you too, Paige. Very, very much." He touched his lips to hers, this time with a gentleness that relayed his words. She felt as if she were drowning in the feel and smell of him. She turned slightly so she could rub her cheek against his and catch her breath.

"Come on, let's see what Mel wants. I think we've both earned some cuddle time." She pulled back and saw the gleam in his eyes. "Cuddle." She pointed her finger at him much like his doctor had. Just cuddling." She thought about it for a moment. "And maybe a little making out." He smiled.

He turned to his door and released the locks then glanced back at her. "Come on. What are you waiting for?" She laughed out loud at his antics then opened her door to exit and followed him.

They walked slowly through the building to the elevators because though Brandon would deny it, his normal long, unhurried strides were now sluggish. Paige wanted to put him to bed before she and Mel had their talk, but Mel had been adamant that they all talk together.

Once they were in the house settled in, she put a light meal together since it was later than their normal dining time. They ate in silence after all of the small talk had been exhausted. Paige saw Brandon waning and asked Mel to join her in the kitchen. Once there she placed their dishes in the sink and asked if they could talk in the morning. Mel looked disappointed, but couldn't deny Brandon's haggard look. She checked her watch. "Sure, we can talk in the morning. I know it's been a long day. I originally had a flight going back tomorrow morning. I will change it to the afternoon."

Paige gave her a brief but grateful smile and turned back toward the sink. She felt Mel move in beside her and looked over. "You don't have to help. I'm sure you're tired after your trip and tonight," Paige said as she filled the sink with water.

Mel laid her hand on Paige's arm, pain shooting through her eyes at Paige's flinch. "Sorry," she said as she removed her hand.

"No, I'm sorry. I just." Paige stopped and started again. "It's just hard." Paige blew out her breath.

The silence in the kitchen was deafening, but Mel didn't leave her side. They finished the dishes and wished each other a good night. Brandon was sitting on the couch with a book it was obvious he wasn't reading since his eyes were closed. When she whispered his name his eyes opened with a snap.

She smiled softly, "Come on, baby." She took the book out of his hand and laid it on the coffee table. Let's go to bed." She shifted aside so he could get up.

He looked confused then looked at his watch. "You didn't talk?"

She shook her head. "It's been a very long day. She agreed we should do it in the morning when we are all fresh."

He looked at her for a moment. "Are you sure?" He pushed to his feet and took her hands in his.

"Yes. Come on," she said, leading the way to their sanctuary.

Twenty minutes later they were both on the edge of sleep as they lay on their pillows talking in the dark of the room.

"Congratulations again on your victory today," Brandon spoke in hushed tones. "I'm very proud of you," he continued, one hand tucked under his pillow, the other lazily rubbing her hand that lay between them.

"Thank you. That means a lot to me."

"You remember the dreams I told you I started having when I found you?" he asked quietly.

She wondered what prompted this conversation. "Yes."

"It was true you know," he said, his eyes scanning her face. The whites of his eyes reflecting the light of the moon shining through the blinds. Normally she would doubt his ability to see her, but the nightlight she'd bought before the girls' visit was still in the wall on the opposite side of the bed.

She looked at him for a moment before answering. She loved these moments they shared when they weren't comatose before their heads hit the pillows. It felt as if they were the only two people in the world. She considered it their haven that no one could penetrate.

"What was true?" She snuggled against her pillow.

"I started to breathe again when I met you." He ran his fingers between hers and squeezed.

Her breath caught at his words, but her mind raced. "Again?" she whispered.

He looked momentarily startled at her one-word question but recovered quickly. "After my first bout with cancer I contented myself to sit on the sidelines. I was afraid if I embraced life or fully engaged myself in some of the pleasures of this world I wouldn't be able to let go. I systematically distanced myself from my family, friends, well, not Dominy. He was like gum on my shoe. He couldn't be shaken." Brandon smiled briefly. "Though I love my job, I let some of the adventures go, resigning myself to staying grounded."

He breathed in slowly and exhaled the same. "Then I met you. You with your zest for life, crazy, wonderful imagination and a heart bigger than I'd ever seen in a person. You literally weep for those who mourn, and you laugh with abandonment for those who rejoice." She heard him swallow.

"You taught me how to breathe deep and take life in. You taught me that I was reacting to fear rather than just being pragmatic." He shifted closer and she could feel his breath against her lips and chin. "I've lived more in this past year than I have in the last eight."

The warmth running through Paige at his words turned cold. "Why are you telling me this now? What are you really saying?"

Brandon gave her a sad smile. "Baby, I'm saying 'Thank you.'"

"Nothing more?" She couldn't stop the fear from fluttering around her heart like butterflies.

"This is not my eloquent way of saying goodbye, if that's what you're asking." He lifted up and kissed her cheek. "We have some time yet," he said before laying back down.

"I want more," she replied impulsively.

His lips pressed together, but everything she needed to know was in his eyes. He felt it as well.

"Whatever Mel has to tell us in the morning…" She placed a finger on his lips.

"Not here. Not now. Just you and me. The rest of the world has no business here," she said with determination.

He nodded gently. Then kissed her finger before removing it. "You know the last full day the girls were here Vivian stayed behind because she wanted to talk with me."

"Really?" She shouldn't have been surprised. Vivian was as intuitive as she was intelligent, and the child was very intelligent.

"She told me you made the right choice when you chose me." She could tell he was having a hard time keeping the smug look off his face. She let her features go slack.

"Wow. That's huge, considering who her father is."

"Yeah," he replied, but looked uncertain. "Why would you say that?"

She barely checked the impulse to roll her eyes.

"He's her father. She wants to see him happy."

"Yes. I was thinking the same thing. I was just making sure we were on the same wavelength."

"We are." She smiled at him, taking in the beauty of him. She loved looking at him. His dark brown eyes were so expressive. She sometimes knew what he was going to say before he said it. She watched as his blinks became longer, and he began forcing his eyes to stay open.

She placed her hand against his cheek. "Go to sleep, Brandon. You're so tired."

The regret in his eyes floored her. "I'll be here when you wake up."

He didn't say anything, but continued to fight sleep so she reassured him using his own words. "We have some time yet."

"I don't want to waste it sleeping," he said sounding like a pouting child. She found it so adorable she kissed his cheek again.

"Go to sleep and get the rest you need. Dream about me and I'll dream about you."

"I don't need to dream about you." She could see him give in to the weariness. On one sigh he said, "I have you." Then he was asleep.

She watched over him through most of the night as she had many times before. She watched his chest rise and fall and listened to his even breathing. She brought his hand to her cheek and took in its warmth. He may have started breathing when they met, but she'd given him her heart. The only difference between them was when he stopped breathing he would take her heart with him.

CHAPTER 12

He lay there watching her sleep as he had done many times before, only this morning the smell of the dew was stronger, the colors around the sun were more vibrant, the bed was softer, and his wife was even more beautiful than the night before. She still had dark circles under eyes. They were less prominent in the early morning light, but bespoke of a tiredness that sleep couldn't cure. He cut off the thoughts before they could lead him to a place where he fought with himself on his decision to stay in her life. He took in her mussed hair and the tendrils framing her face. He wanted to reach out and touch her face, but from previous mornings knew she was a light sleeper, and he wanted to insure she slept as long as possible.

He glanced beyond her at the clock on her bedside table. He'd slept nine hours which wasn't a lot considering his ordeal the day before, but he wanted to make sure his eyes were the first thing Paige saw when she woke up. He wanted to pray with her before the thoughts and concerns of the day swept in. He wanted to reassure and encourage her with a Word from God before she heard one from her mother, Melanie.

He continued to stare at her as she breathed in slowly and exhaled the same. Her lips lifted in a small smile and his heart fluttered. Was she dreaming about him? Her eyelids fluttered and he was met with her golden gaze. He watched as sleep began to slip from her and she fought to hold on until her eyes cleared. The small smile turned wide before she became self-conscious and hid her mouth behind her covers as she whispered, "Good morning."

"Good morning," he replied. Trying not to smile at the adorable picture she made. "How are you feeling?"

"I should be asking you that question," she said.

He shrugged. "It works the same," he said then pointedly waited for her answer.

"A little groggy, but good. Boy would I love to stay in bed with you today. I think I could use a good twenty-four hours of rest myself.

"We can go back to bed after Mel leaves. We can order takeout, let a movie watch us and call it an early night."

He saw her eyes squeeze together in a yawn. "That sounds perfect." She was quiet for a second. "Is it wrong to work out a plan to get to bed when you haven't left it yet?"

"It's only wrong if you deny it," he said placating her. She nodded in agreement.

"How are you feeling?" she asked coming back full circle.

Like a dog with a bone. He sighed. "I'm tired, but I can't sleep anymore. I'll just take a nap later in the day."

He saw the concern darken her eyes. "I'm telling you the truth so take that look off your face."

She sighed. "What time is it?"

He grinned at her. She would never turn over to look at the clock on her side. Instead she would ask him and he would answer without fail.

"It's eight thirty-nine a.m. Why don't you ever look over at the clock yourself?"

"Why should I when you can see it perfectly?"

"How do you know I'm giving you the right time?" he asked, staring at her face.

"I trust you," she replied back matter-of-factly.

He was taken aback by her quick admission—how instinctive her reply was.

"Yeah?" he asked.

He watched as she froze then stared at him for a moment. "Yeah. You act like you didn't know."

He shrugged wishing he could brush it off, but this meant the world to him. "You're so independent and headstrong. I mean that in the best possible way," he added just in case she misunderstood his compliment. "I just thought after earlier this year it would take longer for you to trust me as fully as you do." he added another preface. "I wouldn't purposely give you any reason not to trust me with everything you hold dear, but it doesn't mean you have to," he finished, wondering if she could understand his convoluted statements.

She reached out and cupped his jaw with the palm of her hand. "I wouldn't have married you if I didn't trust you." He could see her eyes seek out the realization in his. She was waiting for him to grasp what she was saying and he was finally there. "I trust that you trust God," she continued on, "I trust you to surrender to His will and love him too much to want to grieve Him." She smiled, and he realized that she wasn't hiding behind her blanket. "I trust that you will seek Him if you don't know what is best for me or your other loved ones, and you will hear and obey Him."

His gaze scanned her face and hair, shoulders and neck. When she stopped speaking he looked back up to meet her eyes. "Are you listening to me?"

"Yes. You have my undivided attention. I'm just taking in all of you. I want to make sure I don't miss any part of you in this moment because I want to take this memory with me." He didn't have to tell her where. She knew where and from the moisture collecting in her eyes she also knew just how important this moment was to him.

He moved through the sheets to her and embraced her. He whispered in her ear. "Thank you, baby." He felt her squeeze him tighter.

"You have ruined me." Her muffled statement sent his heart racing. He leaned back, but she buried her head in his chest.

"What? Why would you say that?"

Shifted her face to his neck. "You say and do the best things for me. There isn't a day that goes by that you don't touch my heart in some way. I think we've actively loved more during our time in this relationship than most people do in a lifetime."

Brandon didn't want to ruin the beautiful moment, but a rogue thought had him working hard to hold back laughter. When Paige looked up at him curiously he lost the battle.

"I always considered Dominy to be the 'Don Juan' of our duo. Wouldn't he be surprised to learn that you have made a poet out of me."

"I didn't bring out anything that wasn't already there. I had thought you were terribly romantic since you flew to Chicago to see me in the hospital. I still remember what you said."

He leaned back. "No you don't."

She looked at him, her eyes sobering. "Yes I do."

"Remind me," he said, pushing back and coming up on his elbow to watch her.

She giggled. "Seriously?"

"Seriously," he said determined not to let her out of proving her word. Honestly, he had no doubt she remembered word for word. He just wanted to hear her repeat his words that bittersweet day.

She cleared her voice and lowered it an octave—lower than his own. When she began to speak he broke into laughter but fought for control when she immediately stopped.

"My voice isn't that low," he protested.

"It is when you get emotional. Your voice always dips when you feel something deeply," she said with confidence.

"Mmm." He told himself he would give it more consideration later. "Okay. Sorry I interrupted you. Go ahead."

She looked reluctant, but he started pushing at her arm with three fingers. He continued to press, moving lower toward her waist.

She shied away and put up her hands in surrender. "Okay. Don't tickle me. I'll do it."

He leaned back and waited.

She cleared her throat again and proceeded with the too-low voice. "Come on, baby. I am going to have to leave soon." She repeated, word for word, what he'd said at her bedside almost a year ago, never taking her eyes away from his. When she was done he was slightly shaken, but hid it under a sheepish smile.

He shrugged. "I was concerned."

She laughed. "You were smitten. Mel said so."

He pretended to think about it then haggled with her. "I was concerned and I might have felt protective of you."

She sat up as if that would give her leverage. "You really liked me and decided to see for yourself how I was so you could get close enough to put your hat in the ring when I was recovered enough for you to ask out."

He opened his mouth to deny it, but couldn't. "I came, yes, because I wanted to see how you were, for myself, but once I'd met Vivian and Mason I just wanted you to know that you had people in Los Angeles who cared for you."

He watched her take in his words. Her eyes softened briefly before they narrowed.

"I'm calling your bluff, Brandon. You were smitten."

He gave up and chuckled. "Yeah, you're right. I was smitten."

"You should be happy I didn't label you as a stalker," she said turning to get out of the bed.

"You wouldn't have done that. Not a 'sweet and sour' man," he said, bringing her words back up to her. "Admit it. There was some interest on your side as well."

"I will admit no such thing," she said walking toward the en suite bathroom.

He got out of bed intent on intercepting her. "Lady Menagerie knew what you thought of me."

"Lady Menagerie would deny it." She sped up realizing his intent. She broke out into a run, reaching the bathroom door with just enough time to close it in front of him. He could hear her laughter on the other side.

*   *   *

Brandon sat next to Paige holding her hand, but he wasn't sure if it was more for her comfort or his.

"This really isn't the best time, Mel," he heard Paige say after a long pause. Her reluctance was obvious, but regretful.

"This isn't a light request, Paige," Mel said firmly. "I really need you to do this for me." Mel sat on the edge of the couch across from them looking poised to stand again.

"And you can't tell me why?" Paige asked still sounding as confounded as Brandon.

Mel splayed her hands out in a pleading gesture. "I can't just yet, but I will. I promise."

Brandon felt Paige's hand spasm in his just before she asked Mel the next question. "Are you in trouble again?" He looked at Paige in confusion.

Melanie was momentarily still before she tried to play off her surprise. "Why would you ask me such a question?"

"Because of your request," Paige said as though it should have been obvious.

"No, I mean what would make you ask me if I were in trouble *again*?"

Paige sucked her teeth and Brandon was surprised by her reaction. What had he missed? It was as if he'd stepped in the middle of a story.

"Just because I was young doesn't mean I was deaf. I heard Dad and Grace talk every now and then when he wasn't happy with something she did. Then there were the times when we would go for

173

vacations and there would be extra men around us. They were never too close, but they were there until Marc."

Brandon looked back at Melanie expectantly. This family seemed to have more secrets than the Freemansonry.

Melanie closed her eyes briefly and took a deep breath. "It's really complicated, but I promise I will tell you everything once I get back."

"Back from where?" Paige asked before Brandon could.

"I can't tell you yet."

"So let me get this straight. You want Brandon and me to take in Gladys for an indefinite amount of time because you don't want to take her with you to the undisclosed place you are going to with Marc."

Melanie only nodded in the affirmative.

Paige threw up her hands and stood up to start pacing beyond the couch. "You know what Brandon and I are up against. Do you really think a child should be subjected to that, and do you think it's fair to Brandon?"

Brandon didn't want to be the main reason for Paige's reluctance to keep Gladys for the rest of the summer, but he knew better than anyone that the type of transition he was about to go through wasn't one he wanted a child of thirteen to witness.

"Why?"

He was briefly stunned by the quiet, yet stern voice. He was about to plead his case when an essence of a memory came upon him of him asking God for a dignified shift from this body to his next.

You're saying your answer is "Yes"? You will give me a quiet and peaceful graduation from this life to life eternal?

The overwhelming peace that enveloped him rocked him, making him sway slightly. The rush of relief he felt on behalf of Paige was almost heady. She wouldn't have to endure watching him waste completely away until he was a mere shell of himself. It had

174

been the one prayer he had raised before the Lord over and over again and God had just answered him.

"It'll be alright, Paige." He watched as she turned mid-stride and took in the look on his face. She came back to sit next to him.

"How can you say that?" She looked perplexed.

"Because I know it will be," he said with all the surety he could muster.

"I already have one cryptic conversation going on here." She raised her hand, pointing at her mother. "I'm not sure I can take another right now.

He considered how to let her know that he'd been negotiating his death with God and could only come up with a straightforward approach.

"I prayed that my transition wouldn't drag on, that I wouldn't waste away in a bed. If I were going to be healed I would be healed without a great deal of bodily degeneration. If it was His will to have me transition from this earth that He would leave my body relatively intact and the memories we created throughout our marriage wouldn't be overshadowed by what this disease did to my body."

The room was so quiet he was sure neither Melanie nor his Paige were breathing. He went on with a small shrug. "I figure if I'm going to live this life to its fullest, I should pray for the ability to leave the same way."

He watched Paige blink a few times as if she were trying to understand what he was saying. He saw it hit her with its full force and she shivered before her eyes filled with tears. He reached for her, but she shook her head and visibility struggled to compose herself.

"Which..." Her voice caught and she started over again. "Which one is it?"

He gave her a sad smile. "I get the dignity."

Her eyes closed for a moment. He watched as the tears continued to flow down her cheeks and around her trembling lips. He moved to take her in his arms, but she placed a staying hand on his chest. She took a deep breath, but when she opened her eyes, the look of resignation in them tore through his soul. It wasn't meant to be like this. He knew this wasn't the time, but he would have to convince her not to harp on what she was losing, but what they'd gained together. He stretched around her hand and kissed her forehead.

"It will be alright. You'll see."

He looked over at Mel to find her eyes filled with a heavy sheen. "I'm not sure I can console you both at the same time, Mel." He watched as she sniffed and straightened her shoulders. He nodded his gratitude. "When should we be prepared to receive her?"

"Brandon, we haven't talked about this?" Paige hissed.

He looked at her. "We are now and we will later. I'm just asking questions." He turned back to Mel.

"The end of the summer. She's going to be with Vivian for a few weeks at Victoria's farm."

"Really? When did that come about? The girls didn't say anything about it when they were here for their birthday," Paige said sounding dejected.

"Victoria called a couple of days ago and offered to have Gladys join Vivian starting next week," Mel said quietly.

"Wait, you said the end of the summer. Are you wanting Gladys to attend school out here? Isn't that a big deal? All of her friends are in Atlanta." Paige became more agitated with each sentence.

"It can't be helped. It's something I need to do and timing is of the essence. I've put it off too long as it is," Mel said, then winced as if she'd said too much.

"Will she be staying here for the entire school year?" Paige asked.

"I don't think so, but I can't say for sure," Mel said swallowing hard.

Brandon could see that this was harder for her than she was letting on. Whatever it was that could possibly take her away from her daughter for months had to be very important.

He sat there with Paige contemplating the ramifications of this decision. He knew this would be more responsibility for Paige and a possible trigger, but now that she was in therapy, that threat was on a smaller scale. Gladys was a very independent child, but the new city and environment would make her vulnerable and insecure. Her being here would be a guarantee to him that Paige wouldn't be fully alone even after his family departed and that wouldn't be for weeks after he passed. He'd had his mother promise him not to leave Paige alone, not to mention Dominy and Robin who would be visiting the next week with the newest addition to their family. Dominique Brayden Harteman had a big name to live up to but knowing his father, he would have no problem being shown how to fill in those shoes.

He hadn't realized just how much he'd missed Dominy until he watched the girls interact with each other, and he was reminded of the ease in his relationship with Dominy at that age. He'd pushed their visit back a couple of times, not just so Robin and the baby could join him, but so that he could delay the conversation he would have with Dominy. No matter what Dominy wished, this wasn't going to be like before and it was time Dominy started getting prepared for the inevitable.

"So what were you wanting to come away with from this meeting?" Paige asked Mel, pulling him away from his thoughts.

"I just wanted to talk to you about the possibility of you taking Gladys for a while and get a tentative answer or at least get you to start a conversation about it between yourselves," Mel said while rubbing her palms together.

"Not a 'Yes'?" Paige asked.

Mel blew out a breath. "No offense, Paige, but it took twelve years just to get you to tell Gladys that you were her mother. I know you don't jump into anything which is why I'm giving you a couple of weeks to think it over. I have to go, Paige, and taking Gladys with me is not an option. If you won't take her there are only two other options."

Paige visibly stiffened. "You would consider leaving Gladys with that, that woman." Paige sounded like she was having a hard time getting the words out through her teeth.

Mel shrugged. "It wouldn't be my first choice. You, her mother, are my first choice and that is why I'm here."

Paige seemed to think about that and Brandon knew Mel had just played her trump card. Paige wouldn't let Grace take care of Gladys if she could.

Paige barely opened her mouth. "I will give you your answer within two weeks."

Mel nodded her head accepting Paige's offer.

Two hours later Paige closed the door on Mel's receding form and turned to stare at Brandon. He opened his mouth, but she raised a hand. "I just need a little time." She turned toward the bedrooms and he watched silently as she slowly walked down the hall.

He walked over to the kitchen counter and reached for a piece of paper and pen. He left the note telling her where he was going on the table by the door.

*   *   *

Brandon sat in the car for a few minutes having second thoughts about his hasty exit from his apartment and uninvited visit to his pastor's house. He debated whether or not to call from the street where he was parked, but figured it was too late to be courteous now. All the drapes were pulled back from the windows which meant that at least one of them was home. Since they parked their cars in the garage he couldn't tell exactly who was home.

He finally got out of the car and walked up to the door. He could hear voices growing louder as he drew closer. He could hear his pastor's voice, and lifted his fist to knock when he made out a few words that caused him to pause.

"Because it's my name. My name that I have fought for many years to make reputable and safe for those who have questions about God and their salvation. I can go places other preachers can't because of my name. People trust me because of my name. I can't continue to let them defame my character and slander my name." The passionate rant caused Brandon to lower his hand. This didn't seem like the right time to approach Pastor Lawrence with his questions.

"Your name? If I said your name who would be healed? If I said your name who would be delivered? If I challenged demons in your name would they listen? Would they or anyone else bow at the sound of your name? What tongues will confess if I say your name? Before this is all over everyone will know who the real liar is. If members leave before everything is resolved then they weren't meant to stay. The ones that stay are the ones that are planted and meant to serve the Lord with and through this ministry. You've done nothing wrong. You know this. I know this and God knows this. Let Him continue to fight this battle for you because He will make sure there is no doubt after all is said and done."

Brandon felt his feet planted to the spot, unable to move at the sound of Lady Menagerie's voice, wishing he could unhear what he had just heard.

"I just need some fresh air." He heard right before the front door opened. Pastor Lawrence came up short and Brandon could see Lady Menagerie beyond him standing at the foot of the stairs before Pastor Lawrence quickly shut the door and gestured for him to follow him.

179

Brandon turned on his heel and walked back the way he'd come only a minute before. He unlocked the car with his key fob and rounded the vehicle as his pastor got into the passenger's seat.

"Good timing, Elder Tatum," Pastor Lawrence said as Brandon slipped into the driver's seat. "I needed to get out of that house, but I wasn't happy about having to take one of our cars. I'm just tired of all of the drama and attention they bring these days."

"I'm sorry to hear your situation isn't getting better," Brandon said as he turned the key in the ignition.

He felt more than saw Pastor Lawrence look over at him as he clicked his seat belt into place.

"How much did you hear?"

Brandon shrugged slightly. "Enough to know that I'm very blessed to have Paige as a wife, though I understand what Lady Menagerie was trying to do." He smiled sheepishly over at his pastor. "Sorry, I didn't know whether to knock or walk away when I heard you talking near the door. I already wrestled with whether or not to come to the door without calling first."

"And yet you did both. You must really need to talk."

"Well, it can wait. You have more important things to deal with," Brandon said hastily.

"Nonsense, I know you aren't given into dramatics, so for you to show up on my doorstep unannounced it has to be very important. Let's head toward Santa Monica Beach," Pastor Lawrence said as Brandon made a U-Turn in the middle of the street.

Thirty minutes later Brandon pulled into a parking space near the Santa Monica Pier, and the two men got out to walk closer to the sand.

"So you say you got your 'Yes' from God in regards to you dying with what you consider dignity," the pastor said slowly, replaying some of their conversation from the ride to the pier.

Brandon merely nodded.

"What makes you think you would handle your last days with less dignity than you have handled most of this situation?" Pastor Lawrence placed his hands in his pockets and they made their way slowly to the boardwalk.

"I needed to know that my last days with Paige wouldn't be overwhelming for her. I didn't want her spending all of her time taking care of me and becoming more of my nurse than my wife. I also didn't want the memories we've been creating over the last year to be lost in the grief and pain of the last days as she witnessed my body slowly shutting down."

Pastor Lawrence was quiet for a moment. "I think you fail to realize that there is a process in all things, even in transitioning. Are you sure you aren't cheating your wife of some time with you where she can learn from your surrender in everything, even control—no matter how minute it may be—over how you die?"

Brandon thought about his words for a moment and couldn't deny that this was the very reason why he had gone straight to his pastor. Brandon knew his pastor would understand his prayer, but was trusting him to show him any consequences of his decision that he'd not considered.

"Every chance the Lord gives me to share with her what He reveals to me about my life and death, I will. I will do it while I'm on this earth and after."

Pastor Lawrence stopped to look at him. "What do you mean? You're not thinking of haunting her, are you?" The last of the sentence was said with his disarming smile.

Brandon smiled back briefly. "I keep a journal for her and a couple of other things so she won't have to go through the first few months without my voice-in words, at least. It's not my wish to leave her alone, no matter what my surrendering looks like. My mother and sister Marjorie will stay with her, now along with Gladys."

"What? Why Gladys?" Pastor Lawrence asked resuming their walk.

Brandon went on to tell him about the visit and talk he and Paige had with Melanie.

"And she wouldn't tell you why or when she would be back to pick up her child?" Pastor asked sounding dumbfounded.

"I know it sounds odd, but I'm so grateful that Paige will have someone else to think about, I was more than happy to oblige. Paige told her she would think about it for a couple of weeks, but I know she will concede because the other option for Gladys really isn't one as far as she is concerned.

Pastor Lawrence glanced over in question.

"Melanie threatened to leave Gladys with Grace."

Pastor Lawrence grimaced.

"Exactly," said Brandon, as he watched for his reaction.

"She has us, you know," Pastor Lawrence said after they'd walked in silence for a while.

Brandon looked out over the water, watching the waves break as they met the sand. He let out a long breath. "I know. I never doubted that—but..." He changed his mind about the direction he was taking the conversation.

"But..." Pastor Lawrence prompted.

"No buts. I'm sorry I even started to say anything," Brandon said, letting out a long breath.

"Well you did, so why don't you continue."

"It's really none of my business, and despite the fact that you are going through something really challenging, I know you will still be there for her."

Pastor Lawrence nodded, but didn't immediately respond.

They walked for a while longer in silence allowing the activities of others to distract them.

Brandon, lost in his thoughts of Paige and his immediate family, was surprised to hear Pastor Lawrence speaking behind him.

He turned to find him sitting on a particularly large dune, his long, jean-clad legs bent at the knees. Brandon retreated a few steps and sat down beside him.

He followed Pastor Lawrence's line of sight to the seagulls hovering over what looked to be some seaweed over the water.

"When Paige first arrived at our church, she reminded me of a wounded animal. She had already accepted Jesus in her life and was diligent with her studies. She was available and willing to help with several of our ministries. Lady Menagerie at one time took her aside and told her to go home. We could tell she was searching for approval, but was going about it the wrong way. We see it pretty often where young men and women who have been abused or are carrying a huge measure of guilt feel the need to serve and assuage their guilt with works. For some, once they feel like they have served their penance or can look in the mirror again you don't see them anymore. The same with those who give into temptation and feel they have failed past the point of redemption.

With Paige, though, it was something more. You could see the joy on her face when she was serving and worshipping, but you could see the fragility in her eyes, like it was her lifeline. When Lady Menagerie sent her home that day she looked... lost. When I called her in to talk to her, soon after she told me pieces of her life, but as you recall I didn't even get all of the story until the day she met you." He smiled ruefully.

"Since the things we discussed are confidential I will just tell you that there was something in her that struck a chord in my heart. I thought that if my daughter Dana had gone through half of what she did I would be sick as a parent. I would consider myself a failure if my child looked at her lot in life as Paige did at that time." He blew out a deep breath then turned his head to look at Brandon.

"She's come a very long way. I wouldn't have agreed to elevate her to the place of an elder if she wasn't ready. I just think everything she has gone through in the last year will eventually catch up to her. I'm surprised it hasn't yet—the obsessive and compulsive tendencies notwithstanding." He placed his elbows on his knees and ran his hands over his hair.

Brandon was surprised to hear those words come from Pastor Lawrence, but then they all were very close. "Did she have many issues with it before?"

Pastor Lawrence's brows furrowed in concentration. "It wasn't so obvious when she first started attending Skylight Temple. Her behavior just came off as very quiet and slightly peculiar. She was very good at following instructions and was willing to help in any project, big or small. She just did it with more precision and in even numbers. I'd seen the traits before, but she was good at covering them. Every now and then I would see her counting her steps or stop in the middle of a task and recount her steps from the beginning no matter how many there were. That was in the beginning though. As she became more comfortable with us and developed a deeper relationship with the Lord the less I saw her rely on a count or a routine." He glanced over at Brandon.

"I know she's gone through a lot and with someone other than Paige I would almost expect them to fall back on an old habit or crutch. With Paige, it's concerning. She knows we are still there despite the stupidity that's going on in our lives right now, but I don't see the peace she used to carry like a banner around her. As I'm sure you know, she is still in good attendance. She hasn't missed a service or Bible study, but there seems to be a desperation behind it. Maybe she's trying to escape from all of her trials or she's hoping her continued obedience will guarantee her something she desperately wants to keep." Pastor Lawrence looked him squarely in the eye and he felt a shiver run down his back.

She seemed to be doing better, especially with the addition of her sessions with her therapist. Well, better until today when he'd callously shared his conversation regarding being given the gift of dying with dignity.

"I might have shared with her what I told you earlier about God answering my prayer regarding my death.

Pastor Lawrence looked at him so quickly he thought the man would have gotten whiplash.

"What did she say?"

Brandon shrugged, feeling even worse now than he did when Paige had walked away from him this afternoon. "She said she wanted to be alone and walked to our bedroom."

Pastor Lawrence stared at him for a moment. "And you left her alone?"

Brandon hesitated for a moment but held his ground. "Yes. I thought it best to give her what she wanted at the moment. Besides, I needed to talk it out, myself."

"I can't imagine what you are going through right now, and to see and hear how you're handling this is inspiring. You are a true witness of God's love and grace."

"I don't know," Brandon said turning away from him. "Sometimes it doesn't feel like I have any other choice." He raised his hand against Pastor Lawrence's interruption. "I know that if I give it enough thought I could come away with a few ideas of how to act out and they would all be justified, but I'm resigned to the fact that I only have a little while left. If I were to be completely honest, in some ways I've been preparing myself since my last bout with cancer." He sent a ghost of a smile Pastor Lawrence's way.

"If it weren't for Paige I would be absolutely ready to go, but also if it weren't for Paige I wouldn't truly be able to appreciate what I'm leaving behind. It's a bit of a conundrum."

"No Brandon, it's life, and since you're walking it with Him you get to experience it with the fullness in which it was meant to be lived."

Brandon nodded his agreement but didn't trust himself to say anything else. They sat in companionable silence for a while, then

Brandon, tired of being the main topic of their conversations, turned to Pastor Lawrence. "So what is this about your name?"

The pastor looked over at him in puzzlement for a moment then smiled sheepishly. "Just something I thought I couldn't live without up until a half hour ago, but since then I've come to understand that there are more important things that I should be concerned with."

"Like what?"

"Like the glory God would like to get out of this situation." He paused briefly. "Just like what He's been getting from your life."

Brandon felt the man's praise all the way to his toes, but only smiled slowly and nodded again.

After lunch and an update on the woman trying to wreck Pastor Lawrence's name, Brandon went back home to the woman he would fight to have even another breath with.

*   *   *

Brandon entered the apartment slowly, not quite sure what he would find. It was so quiet, at first he didn't think Paige was home. He set his bag down even as he reminded himself to take it back to the bedroom with him after he checked for her presence.

He looked in the living room and was getting ready to pass the kitchen when he caught sight of her sitting at the table looking at him. Her eyes were slightly swollen, but that wasn't a surprise.

"You left," she said despondently as she looked back down at her hands folded on the table.

"I wasn't equipped to handle the conversation at that moment. I would have made it worse. I needed reinforcements," he said slowly as he sat across from her.

He watched as she lifted a brow though she didn't look up at him.

"Did you get them? The reinforcements?" she asked with a sigh.

"I think so." He reached for her hands. "I want to apologize for sharing my conversation with God the way I did with you. I don't, however, apologize for telling you because I feel it's important to me to have you to continue to walk alongside me in this."

She sat there watching him rub his thumbs along her knuckles. He didn't want to interrupt her thoughts or add any more pressure than he already had, so he remained quiet. He would wait for her for however long it took.

The sun had dipped under the horizon encasing the kitchen in darkness when she finally spoke. "What do we do now?" Her voice was rough as though she'd just awoken from a long sleep. She didn't look up.

"We trust God as we always have and we squeeze as much life out of each day as we possibly can." He tried to will her to look at him.

He watched her breathing change slightly. "I'm afraid to go back." She looked up then and he was rocked by the look of desolation in her eyes. "I've done everything I've been taught. I've been obedient..." She stopped abruptly, but he didn't urge her on. He was almost afraid to hear where this line of thought was taking her.

"I know works don't guarantee anything, but shouldn't obedience mean something? Shouldn't my love and adoration of Him mean something?" She opened her mouth but seemed to change her mind as she looked back down at their hands and closed it.

He reached out and cupped her jaw to direct her eyes back to his. "Maybe it should mean that you can see beyond just what you or I want. Maybe it should mean asking Him what He wants you to learn or do in this situation. But I know that it definitely means that instead of turning your back on Him you can turn to Him for comfort and allow Him to prove to you that this too will be alright."

Paige placed her hand on the hand still cupping her jaw. "I don't want you to die."

Looking into her eyes at that moment he couldn't think of anything that would ease her pain and it frustrated him. He hated feeling this helplessness.

You don't have anything to say to that?" she asked, her eyes growing bright.

"What do you want me to say?"

"How about you not wanting to die, either. How about you wanting to fight to the end to stay. Stay with me," she said fervently.

"You don't know what you're asking, Paige." He pulled his hands away.

"And you are giving up too easily." Her pained expression turned into a sneer. "Well, I guess you can afford to be magnanimous. You're the one that's going on to glory. You get to be with Him and all I get is to experience life after you."

"Wow, Paige. That's an interesting way to project your selfishness. Tell your husband, who loves you so much he would rather leave you with memories of our life together when he is relatively healthy, that he is selfishly choosing death rather than a long life with you.

"I'm not giving up. I want to live *with* you instead of becoming a prisoner of this decaying body and just be cared for *by* you." He watched to see if what he was saying registered with her.

"If I don't get more time, I want the time I have with you to be quality time. That was my prayer. You can understand that, right?"

Paige stared at him as if he hadn't spoken, then whispered. "I need you to pray in agreement with me that God heals you."

"I will pray that God's perfect will be done. If they are the same then I am in agreement with you."

Paige stared at him for a few more seconds then stood up and walked out of the kitchen.

Brandon took a deep breath and let it out slowly. He checked his watch. He would give her a half an hour to pout, then he would find her for round two. No matter how much she pushed he would not allow her to place distance between them now, that they would regret   later.

CHAPTER 13

Mason hung up the phone. His mind was stuck on the last words Richard had spoken. "We'll see you and our great-granddaughter next weekend."

Mason had only whispered a perfunctory, "Okay." Then hung up the phone.

Not that he would allow it to change anything, but what were the odds that Vivian was actually related by blood to Victoria? The whole thing was so surreal. He understood Victoria's and Richard's reasons for not involving Paige just yet, but he couldn't help feeling guilty. She'd been through so much over the past year, and from what Vivian had shared from her birthday week, her suffering wasn't over.

He'd agreed to accompany his daughter to Richard and Victoria's where Gladys would join her sister for a few weeks on the farm. He was curious to meet the man who had bested Victoria for so long.

Richard had explained to him that Antonio Sable, Victoria's college boyfriend claimed to have planted some of the information Victoria and Richard's investigators had found on Melanie, Grace, and Paige earlier in the year. He also presented them with the new information though wasn't too clear on where he'd gotten it. He didn't know much about the man except that he was vice president of a financial company with very old contacts and very powerful clients.

He'd given his permission for Vivian to meet her great-grandfather if he was present during introductions. Despite

Victoria's assurance, he wasn't going to allow any man he didn't know to talk to, let alone spend time with his daughter.

He would have to postpone his weekend getaway with Tabitha. She would be disappointed. Heck, he was disappointed. He'd been looking forward to spending some uninterrupted time with her. He thought the small town just outside of Chicago was perfect for sightseeing and experiencing life on a nineteenth-century style farm in the Midwest. It would pain him to call the romantic-looking B&B he'd found on the internet and cancel his reservation, but there would be plenty of time once he got back from Oklahoma, if everything went well.

Rachael had a brother. How many times had she told him how much she'd wished for siblings, someone to play with, though Brian would have been some years older. He shook his head at all of the secrets that were being exposed. He couldn't help but wonder how this would change their family dynamic. The lines that bound him to Victoria and Richard were growing in quantity and thickness. His world was getting smaller by the day, and he was beginning to feel the strain of walking the narrow line of perfect father, son in-law, and friend.

The only relationship that seemed to be unencumbered by secrets was with a woman, who, though vastly different in looks, reminded him of Paige when she spoke of her faith. He'd never told her outright not to speak of God, but he hadn't encouraged it either, and after their initial conversation about her relationship with her church she'd seemed hesitant to bring it up.

He smiled ruefully to himself. Paige wouldn't have hesitated. She wore her love and adoration for God like a second skin, whereas Tabitha seemed to wear hers like an extremely beautiful, but slightly uncomfortable garment.

He groaned. There it was. The same conviction that separated him and Paige caused him to admire Paige for her loyalty and refusal to consider Him as anything less than good. Mason ground

191

his teeth at the mere thought that God could be all good. It was inconceivable that a being who not only created but led a man such as his father in his faith and home lives could be good. Could a being be both sovereign and good? Could he have a master plan and in that master plan still have the best outcome planned for the lives of everyone? He shook his head as if to clear the thought, because as usual the train of thought was going someplace he didn't think he wanted to go.

He refocused on his immediate surroundings, checking to make sure no one had lay witness to his moments of deep contemplation, let alone the conversation that just tilted his world on its axis. Seeing no one, he plugged his phone into his car charger and made sure he didn't have any texts nor emails he needed to answer before he got on the road. He was happy he'd made the decision to take Richard's call before he left the parking lot. The revelations he'd received from that one conversation were enough to distract his attention enough to cause a few fender benders.

He concentrated on getting home in one piece and tried pushing aside the conversation he would have with his daughter after dinner.

* * *

"Dad?"

The voice came from far away, pulling him away from his thoughts of Paige, again. He looked up to see his daughter watching him from across the dinner table.

"I'm sorry. What was it, honey?"

He watched the look on his daughter's face morph from exasperation into concern as she continued to look at him.

"Are you okay, Daddy? You've been distracted since I got home from Mirabelle's."

He took a deep breath and pushed his plate forward on the table. *No time like the present.*

"I have something to tell you. It's very important, and it may even seem a little exciting to you, but I need you to keep the information to yourself for a while. Do you think you can do that?"

Vivian stared at him for a moment. "Keep it to myself or not share it with certain people?" she asked and he couldn't tell whether she was being very insightful or testing her boundaries.

"Uh... For now, let's say you should keep it to yourself," he replied, feeling a little off-kilter.

She nodded at him with a look of expectation.

He forced himself not to fiddle with his hands or spend too much time trying to form the right sentences. He'd spent the last few hours contemplating how he would begin with Vivian and he still had nothing.

"Richard called me today." He paused, but when she silently continued to stare at him from across the table, he continued, "He told me that when you and Gladys come to visit next weekend he and Victoria would like to introduce you to your great-grandfather."

He watched as the expressions flitted across her face. When her features settled on confusion he knew he'd started wrong.

"My great-grandfather? Richard's father?" She looked deeply perplexed.

He cleared his throat as if it would help clear his thoughts. "No..." His voice lifted at the end of the drawn-out word.

"Well if Gram, uh, Victoria and Richard are my grandparents and Victoria's parents died before I was born then who is my great-grandfather?"

Mason sat back for a moment to reconsider his approach. "Well, as you know, Victoria and Richard are your adoptive grandparents because they are your mother's parents, but biologically Victoria is your great-grandmother, and your great-grandfather is a man she had a child with long before she met Granddad Richard." He let out a long breath, both out of relief of not losing his train of thought and getting the information off of his chest.

He watched Vivian as she worked through the information. Her eyes widened. "If Victoria is my great-grandmother, then who's my grandmother?"

He hesitated for a moment. "Melanie, Paige's mother."

Vivian's eyes widened farther, if that were possible. "Melanie is Gram, uh, er, great-grandmother Victoria's daughter?"

Mason realized his mistake immediately. "No. Victoria had a son. He's your grandfather. He's Paige's biological father."

"Oh my goodness," Vivian said, her words barely above a whisper. "Victoria is Mati's grandmother? We're all related by blood?" The last was said with a squeal.

"Yes." Was all he could get out before she bombarded him with more questions.

"Does Mati know? Is my grandfather going to be there too? Do you know who he is? What did Victoria say now that she knows she's Mati's grandmother?" She would have continued if he hadn't cut her off when she took in a deep breath.

"Paige doesn't know, and you can't share this with her just yet."

Some of the excitement left her face. "Why not?"

He rubbed his forehead with his thumb and forefinger. *Why not? Why not.* "Paige is going through a lot right now with her husband and can't come to the farm. Richard and Victoria want to tell her in person and thought it would be better to wait." *Please don't ask why. Please... His silent plea was cut off.*

"Why?" Vivian cocked her head to the side. "Why wouldn't they want to tell her now so she would have more help? Besides his family, she's all alone. I think it would be good if her family was there for her."

Mason loved his daughter's mind and heart. She was so logical and loving. Everything seemed to so clear to her.

"Unfortunately, it isn't that simple. They aren't sure if this will be news that will help or hurt Paige." He saw the gears turning in her young mind.

"Mati doesn't like secrets, Daddy," Vivian said solemnly.

"No." It was the only word he could force past his throat.

"Does Gladys know?"

He sighed, grateful for the momentary reprieve. "If she doesn't already, she will soon."

"May I call her?"

His heart went out to his little girl. He couldn't imagine how hard it would be to have to keep a secret from someone as close as she was to Gladys.

He compromised. "How about you give it a day, just in case."

Her chin went up, and he braced himself for an argument. "Tomorrow," she said firmly.

He nodded his head.

She stared at him a few moments before her bottom lip began to tremble. "Mati isn't doing well. You should tell her, she whispered fervently.

He stared back at her without blinking. "It's not my place."

"It is if you love her," she responded without pause.

He felt the words like a punch to the gut and it made him angry. He knew she wouldn't take the news regarding Paige well, but he wouldn't allow her to judge him. He took a deep breath hoping the influx of oxygen would cool his ire. She was hurting and lashing out.

"I understand that this must be a shock for you, but watch yourself."

Her expression turned petulant, and for a moment he was afraid he would have to deliver the ultimatum Richard and Victoria set forth, but her expression shifted to reluctant curiosity.

"Where is Mati's dad?" She spoke the words quietly.

He wondered if she was as afraid of the answer as she sounded. He closed his eyes twice as long as it took to blink. When he opened them he looked into her silver ones. "I don't know."

"Is he dead?" she whispered.

"I don't know." He swallowed.

Tears filled her eyes, but she sniffed them back. She looked down at her forgotten meal then back at him.

"Tomorrow," she said resolutely.

Instead of nodding he pushed his chair back from the table to make room for her and opened his arms signaling for her to come over for a hug. She got up and walked around to him, wrapping her thin arms around his neck and began sobbing. He pulled her onto his lap and rocked her as he did when she was younger. This he could do for her.

*   *   *

Mason lay in bed long after turning off the lamp in his exhausted daughter's room. He hadn't handled the beginning of their conversation well, nor the middle, if he was honest, but Vivian had let him comfort her and considering the friction between them lately he considered it a win.

He called Tabitha and broke the news to her about canceling their weekend. Although she sounded disappointed there was a note of relief in her voice. He wasn't sure how to take her reaction and told her so.

"I'm sorry, Mason. I know I sound indecisive, but I do really want to spend more time with you." She sighed. "I like you, Mason. I like our conversations, and um… kisses." She cleared her throat. "I guess I'm feeling a little nervous about what comes with going away together.

"There's nothing that has to come with going away together that wasn't included in our dates, because it isn't my intention to push you into anything you aren't ready for. Why didn't you say something last week when we saw each other?"

The line was quiet for a moment. "What I'm about to say is really embarrassing, so please don't laugh."

She sounded earnest so he promised. "When I'm with you, I can hardly think straight. You have this way about you. You're so confident and assertive that you intimidate me a little." She let out a little strangled laugh. "Not to mention that you are extremely handsome, and your kisses take my breath away.

There was no way he could keep from quietly preening at her compliments.

She went on. "You're funny and charming and your love for your daughter lets me know you are a wonderful man." The next pause let him know a huge "but" was coming.

"It's hard to wrap my mind around the fact that such a good man could have such disdain for God."

Mason tried not to let her words rub him the wrong way. She did say she thought he was a good man. "There are plenty of good men, or people for that matter, who don't give God the credit for their moral standing."

He heard her exhale long and slow. "I know. I just wanted to give you a reason for my hesitancy."

He had to respect her for sharing her opinion. It was good to know where they stood. She was wrong, and her tunnel vision made him wonder if the delay in their getaway wasn't a good thing.

"Okay," he said because he could tell that she was waiting for a response.

"Okay?" she repeated.

"Yes, okay. You told me how you feel, and I'm responding to let you know I heard you," he said without the emotion he felt a few seconds before.

"What do you think about my opinion?" she asked.

"Tabitha," he started out reluctantly.

"Mason, please," she said interrupting him.

"I don't believe a man needs God to be good or kind. I don't believe a man or woman can only be kind if they go to church and pray to God. I know for a fact that God didn't make man to be robots so they could love Him. He gave us free will. We have a choice. A choice to follow Him or not. A choice to be kind or not. A choice to be honest and truthful or not. I'm not kind, respectful, or love and care for my daughter because I am told to do so by some book or through any type of prompting. I do so because I want and choose to." He went quiet because he'd been speaking for a moment without a sound from her.

"What if you and I get closer and you choose to end what we have? I'm not seeing any assurances."

And here was the real root of their situation. She was feeling insecure about them. "Then we spend more time together in situations that allow you to feel more secure in my feelings for you."

"Okay." She breathed.

"Okay?" he asked, repeating her use of the one-word question.

"Yes. I'm good with your answer." He could hear the relief in her voice.

"Good to know," he replied with a lightness he didn't completely feel. This was their second conversation about God and his lack of reverence of Him. He had a feeling it wouldn't be the last.

"How is Vivian doing?" Tabitha asked.

He'd shared with her why their weekend had to be postponed. That he needed to accompany his daughter to her grandparent's home so he could supervise her visit with her newly discovered great-grandfather.

Tabitha seemed intrigued by the story of his daughter's lineage, and he didn't mind answering her questions regarding Victoria and

Richard. He even tried not to feel uncomfortable about some of the questions she had about Paige, but he started deflecting the conversation when she asked about Paige's lineage. He didn't feel it was his information to share, and the likelihood of Tabitha and Paige meeting, let alone becoming acquaintances, was almost nonexistent.

They spoke a little longer, and he let her know that he would call her during his trip if they didn't have time to see each other before.

Once they hung up, his thoughts went back to the upcoming week and his daughter. He was apprehensive about her meeting her great-grandfather and what the man's true motivation was. From what Richard had said, Antonio had a great deal of data on Melanie, Paige, and Vivian. More than wanting to know where the man was getting his information, Mason wanted to know how long he'd had it and why he chose to come forward now? Richard seemed to think he was after some answers to his son's whereabouts.

Mason wondered again if he was making the right choice by allowing his daughter to meet her great-grandfather. He knew both Richard and Victoria were wary, which kept him on edge. Then a thought came to him that threatened any sleep he was going to get that night.

Since Richard and Victoria wanted to hold off on telling Paige of her grandfather's existence, she wouldn't be allowed to make a decision on whether Vivian should meet her great-grandfather. It sat wrong with him. He knew she was going through a lot, but from their short time together it was clear that she cherished family, and the knowledge of a paternal grandfather might help her more than harm her.

He groaned and rolled on his side. His bedroom had a nice view of the Chicago skyline in the distance but it was lost on him. He would be angry if Victoria introduced Vivian to a man with unclear motives. It didn't matter whether he was her great-grandfather or the president of the United States.

For what had to be the thousandth time, he wished Rachael was there to help him decide on what to do.

The sky was turning from black to purple with the impending sunrise before he decided to give Paige a call to gauge her ability to accept   another   shift   in   her   reality.

CHAPTER 14

Paige walked down the hall feeling a little harried. She ran her hand across her forehead as she passed through the living room to the door. She was on deadline with her new book and hoped to get in another chapter before taking a break for a few hours. Brandon wasn't due home for a couple of hours, and she'd finally broken through her writer's block, and the thoughts were flowing.

She knew it had a great deal to do with her conversation with Brandon earlier in the week after he'd given her a moment to retreat to her prayer closet and rant and rave at God for the unfairness of their situation. She wanted more than just answers. She wanted a "Yes," and she had no reservations in saying so to God. She was desperate. She would have promised anything if the Lord had asked her for a compromise in exchange for Brandon's health, but He was just as quiet as He had been since she'd begun praying for Brandon's healing.

Brandon had walked into her office and lifted her off the floor where she'd been crying and carried her into the living room where he sat down on the couch with her in his lap and just held and rocked her. He didn't whisper a word of comfort nor encouragement. He just swayed back and forth with his arms wrapped tightly around her until she stopped crying. He dried her tears with his thumbs and kissed her heated face until it cooled.

He laid her head on his shoulder and spoke softly. "I need you to listen to me without interrupting me for a moment." She tried not to stiffen, but she was afraid of what he would say. She couldn't help how she felt.

"Do you know what drew me to you besides your beautiful eyes, your abandoned laugh, and the way you filled out your skirts?"

The last was news to her and she tried to raise her head, but he kept his hand on it to keep her still.

"Don't be shocked. I was never a choir boy, and I'm definitely not a saint. You are a beautiful woman, and I am proud to be your husband. What drew me to you was your indisputable and unapologetic belief in God. You were unwavering in your speech and actions and you embraced life."

It dawned on her that he was speaking about all of those attributes in the past tense. True he was speaking of what drew him to her, but she couldn't help thinking he was going somewhere with it. Somewhere she wasn't sure she wanted to go.

"I have tried to put myself in your shoes from the moment I was told the chemo and radiation treatments weren't working. I gave you every opportunity to step away and protect your heart, but I was wrong because you already loved me as much as I loved you and that is for a lifetime." He removed his hand, allowing her to raise her head and look at him.

"I stayed, for us. I asked you to marry me, for us." He cupped her head in his hands, holding her gaze. "I will fight for us, but I need you to fight too." She opened her mouth, but he placed his fingers on her lips and gave her a look that reminded her of her promise to stay quiet.

"I need you to remind yourself of who you are. You are a child of the King of kings and Lord of lords. You have started to live in fear and you have no reason to. Your Father is not a God of fear, but of power, love, and a sound mind. If you would allow Him to comfort you instead of continuously pleading your case, blaming Him for your pain, or trying to negotiate with something that isn't yours to bargain with in the first place, you'll get the peace you seek." He cupped her right jaw in his hand and quietly watched her for a moment, letting her absorb his words before continuing.

"In all that has happened I believe you've lost focus on the big picture." She watched the dark richness of his eyes warm even more as he stared into hers. "I know you realize that the death of this body is not the enemy to life itself, but you're acting as if cancer or me separated from you on this earth is the enemy. The one and only true enemy is the one that tricks you into embracing the fear, becoming distracted with thoughts that cloud your mind, and falling back on dangerous habits. The fear is a weapon used to steal time, memories, and victorious testimony from us." He stroked her face as if the caress would take some of the sting away from his words.

They both knew that her recent obsessive-compulsive tendencies were triggered by his diagnosis and other issues in her life that were out of her control, but where her relationship and constant conversation with God helped a great deal of years before, it was now almost nonexistent. Their dialogue had become more of a monologue, and she struggled to push all the drama of her life aside so she could concentrate on Him one hundred percent.

"In no way is this a judgment because there are moments that I am gripped by fear of the unknown, but I have asked God for certain things, and I believe He will give them to me. I need you to remember what it was like when you first came to God. I need you to remember the pain and anger you surrendered to Him and the scriptures He gave you to quiet some of the storm in you." He placed his forehead against hers, and she could feel the breath from his words brush her lips. "I need your strength, baby." His voice broke and the lump in her throat burst, and the tears she'd been holding back silently streamed down her cheeks.

"You will be the deciding factor in how easy or hard this time is. I know it doesn't seem fair with everything else going on, but I'm asking more from you. I need the Paige that gave herself over for young women who were struggling with understanding their self-worth, the Paige who stepped in to donate an organ to a young girl she never met, the Paige who held fast to God's promise for her and fought her way back from the edge of life with a will stronger than any warrior I know. I need the Paige who embraced a child and family she thought had died and led a woman back to God with gentle firmness and by being an example of His love." He pulled her in closer and touched his lips to hers.

She could taste the salt of her tears mingled with his, and her heart cried out for the strength he was seeking in her. She couldn't let him down. If nothing else, she had to get out of the fog of her mind and truly be there for him. She held him tighter and let the warmth of him soothe her.

He pulled back only enough to speak again. "My life is His. I surrendered it to Him the day I dedicated my life to Him. I believe you did the same. He will not dishonor that. He wants to get glory from it, and I choose to do what is needed to see He gets it." He squeezed her gently then pulled his handkerchief from his pocket and began wiping her tears. "I'm not trying to martyr myself as you have been thinking. I'm just not living in denial. If it's His perfect will to heal me here I will embrace it completely.

"Meanwhile, I want to live every day to the fullest with you, but I can't do it if you are constantly trying to rewrite our history or fight against a future we have no control over. We only have control of how we live today." She took the handkerchief, turned it over, and wiped his face. He squeezed her to him again and held her close.

There was nothing he said that wasn't true. There were parts of her that wanted to rise up and tell him all of the ways he was falling short, but there was a bigger part of her that wanted to be that woman he talked about.

"When you married me, you promised to love and cherish me, and I vowed to do the same. Whether we are arguing, making love, or somewhere in between, I cherish you and each and every moment we have together. I want as many moments as you'll give me, but you can't do that unless you are living in the present with me." She struggled briefly, but gave in to the pleading in his voice. She knew she would regret it even more if she let their moments pass by without grasping and holding on to some for herself.

"I love you, Paige. You make me feel like I did things right." The intense light in his eyes made her feel shy and extremely blessed at the same time. She remained quiet as she tried to process everything he said. She was tempted to go back to her prayer closet and lay prostrate until she got a word from God that she could embrace and hold close.

"One thing I'd rather not have are more of these bittersweet moments. I'm starting to feel like I'm in the middle of a really sappy and angsty love story where the heartbreak overshadows the happy ending." She took his earnest expression and her breath caught. "We are living our happily ever after right now."

She laid her head on his shoulder and took a shuddering breath. She placed a hand on his chest and felt the strength of his heartbeat. She could do this for him. She could dig in and seek God for His strength. She could ask Him to help her battle the voices in her head, again. Pride be darned. She'd have to seek God as she did when she first asked Him into her heart. Paige swallowed back the tears and surrendered, knowing as she did she would have to let go of her shroud of anger and sense of control.

They sat in that position quietly sharing warmth and a view of the sunset for many minutes before he pulled away enough to look at her. His eyes skimmed her face, pausing at her lips. "Guess what some of my favorite moments are." Her giggle turned into a laugh when he began lightly running his hands across her rib cage. "Do you promise to live in the moment with me?" She squirmed in his arms trying to get away from his fingers.

"I can't hear you," he said, running his hands up her sides again. She stopped their ascension by squeezing her arms to her sides and began poking and squeezing any place she could reach to tickle him in return. It became a strategic match of quickness on her part and strength on his until they were both laughing uncontrollably on the couch. They ended up side by side trying to catch their breaths. He placed his hand in hers and looked at her.

"Do you promise me more of these moments?"

"Yeah, I promise," she answered without hesitation, and she meant it.

They spent Sunday morning in church since both of them decided to resume their duties, then joined the other elders in a special Sunday brunch. They spent the rest of the afternoon at home napping and reading out loud to each other from a book Brandon had picked up regarding a man's pursuit of Jesus from the moment of birth and the North Star appeared. Paige thought it was a beautiful illustration of man's pursuit of a relationship with God. She listened to the rumble in Brandon's chest as he spoke. He had become one of her favorite pillows.

The next couple of days they took walks around their favorite lake after he got home from work, or went to the movies and tried out new restaurants.

He was right, and the peace that came with concentrating on their present was a catalyst for breaking through her writing block two days later.

It also gave her the help she needed when Grace called her out of the blue the day before.

She'd been carrying a load of clean towels to the bedroom to fold when she saw her phone light up. The number said unknown, but she picked it up thinking it was a ministry call.

"Paige?"

The voice on the other end of the line made her wish she was the type of person that could hang up on people.

"Grace."

"I trust you are well."

"Yes. And yourself?" she asked, placing the phone between her shoulder and ear and picking up a towel to give her hands something to do.

"As well as can be expected with the children I have."

She didn't want to go there. She really didn't want to go there with this woman.

"Sorry you feel that way." *Good. That was a good comeback. It wasn't leading or open-ended.*

"Humph." Was all she got in return.

She folded one towel then another before her mother spoke again. "You know I was hurt not to receive an invitation to your wedding."

"Yeah, sorry about that. I wasn't quite sure where to send it. By the way, congratulations on your marriage. How is your husband?"

"He's good: handsome, virile, healthy. And yours?"

Paige closed her eyes and held her breath for a count of five before responding. "He is wonderful. Everything I could ask for in a husband," she said then clamped her mouth shut.

"Oh, I'm sure not everything..." Grace let the sentence fade, the innuendo clear.

Paige moved to her bedroom window hoping the scenery would help calm her. "Grace, was there a reason, other than wanting to get caught up, that you called?"

The silence was not enough to warn her regarding Grace's next comment, but she'd learned never to let her guard down where the woman was concerned.

"Have you talked to your sister lately?"

"You mean my mother, Mel? Uh, no."

"When was the last time you spoke to her?"

"I'm not sure. Maybe a few weeks ago."

"Did she say where she was going?"

"No."

"Are you sure?"

"Yes."

"Who has Gladys?"

"What do you mean? Isn't Gladys with Mel?" Paige knew Gladys was with Mel for at least a few more days before she was put on a plane to join Vivian at Victoria and Richard's.

There was another long pause before Grace spoke again. "I'm sorry to have interrupted you. We should stay in touch," Grace said as if it were decided, and it touched the wrong nerve with Paige.

"No. These little chats are more than enough. Goodbye Grace."

"Goodbye, Paige." Paige could hear the smile in her voice before the line went dead and could have kicked herself for allowing herself to be baited.

She took a deep breath and walked back to the mound of towels. "Well, that didn't go too bad," she said to the empty bedroom.

*   *   *

Paige tried to push down the impatience as she approached the door, but all thoughts fled as she got a peek at who stood on the other side. Suddenly she couldn't open it fast enough.

On the other side of the threshold stood Dominy, Robin, and their son Dominique whom they'd already started calling Nicky.

She let out a short squeal then stepped forward to hug Dominy, then Robin, and the baby. "I'm so glad to see you guys. What time did you arrive? Why didn't you call? I could have picked you up."

She motioned for them both to come inside and ushered them over to the couch.

"We wanted to surprise Brandon by showing up a few days early. He didn't sound like himself, and I was little concerned," Dominy admitted sheepishly.

Robin gave Paige a look that said Dominy was missing his friend, and she couldn't keep him away any longer.

Paige wanted to laugh, but hid her smile behind her outraised arms. She wiggled her fingers letting Robin know that it was well past time that she be acquainted with her Godson. She leaned forward, taking the round baby boy with huge brown eyes and a tuft of curly black hair from his mother's hands.

He was solid and slightly heavier than he looked. She glanced up at Robin who pointed at Dominy. "Nicky has Dominy trained well. Nicky opens his mouth and Dominy places a bottle in it."

Paige giggled, and the sound drew the baby's eyes from his mother to her. Nicky silently watched her as he gummed his lip. Paige watched as he stared at her, and her heart tripped over in her chest. His olive complexion matched his father's, and the solemn expression in his gaze matched his mom's.

"He's one of the most beautiful babies that I have ever seen," she said and was gifted with a gummy smile. "Oh, yes. I'm in love."

Nicky reached out, grabbing her bottom lip. It was slightly painful, so she disengaged his fingers with her hand and blew raspberries into his palm which made him squeal.

"So, I guess Brandon isn't home yet," Dominy said leaning back on the couch.

Paige glanced at the wall clock to confirm the time. Brandon wouldn't be home for another two hours. I was going to start dinner in another hour but we can go out to dinner to celebrate you bringing this new love into my life," she said looking at Nicky's small fingers while she gently bounced him on her lap.

"You're welcome," Dominy said.

She looked up at Dominy at the same time his wife did.

"What?" Dominy asked, looking from her to his wife. "Didn't you mean how I convinced Brandon to pursue you?"

Robin rolled her eyes, and Paige brought Nicky in for a hug so she could inhale his baby smell and hide her smile.

"I think Paige was talking about Nicky," Robin said, turning to her husband.

He shrugged. "Then you're welcome, again."

Paige laughed and Robin groaned. "Don't encourage him, Paige. He will just keep going," Robin said, griping good naturedly.

Paige tried to stifle the giggle that came forth at the faces Dominy was making as Robin talked to her, but snickered despite her efforts.

"He's making faces, isn't he," Robin said without taking her eyes off of Paige.

The shift in Dominy's expression was comical. He placed his finger on his lips in a "quite" motion, then brought his hands together in a position of prayer.

"Um." She adored Dominy, and though she would be the first to admit that Robin was perfect for him, she was much more serious. "I didn't offer you two something to drink. My manners must be slipping." She shifted Nicky in her arms, preparing to stand. "We have water, milk, orange juice, and apple juice. We may have some apple juice left."

Robin waved her hand. "I'm good."

"Me too," Dominy said. "So Brandon is working a full day. He must be doing good, huh?"

"Yes. He's felt good enough to put in full hours this whole week."

Dominy nodded his pleasure. "That's good. He isn't overdoing it?"

"No. I don't believe so, but you can ask him when he gets here," Paige said and waited for Dominy's response.

His mouth turned down. "Naw, I better not. He thinks I'm too overbearing as it is."

"Ahhhh, baby, that's because you are," Robin said reaching over to pat him on the knee.

She turned back to Paige. "I thought after we had Nicky most of his overprotectiveness would have shifted to our son. Nope. Dominy has more than enough concern and worry for everyone."

Dominy shrugged unapologetically.

"Dominy told me the girls came down for your birthdays. Did you have a good time?" Robin asked her, and she was happy for the change of subject.

They talked about the girls' week-long trip and discussed one event after another until Paige heard the lock turn in the door. She'd handed Nicky back to his mother an hour before when he started fussing. Robin had given him a bottle and placed him in the carrier they'd brought up with them, for a nap.

Paige got up and met Brandon at the door, obscuring his view. "You have a surprise," she said taking in his slightly disheveled appearance. He looked like he'd had a long day. She hoped his surprise guests would help revive him a little.

"Really?" Brandon's eyes grew warm as he looked down at her. He drew her in for a hug. "I don't need any surprises. Your beautiful smile and embrace are more than enough." He squeezed her a little tighter then leaned back to kiss her. He felt good, and the kiss went a long way to reassuring her that he was indeed feeling well.

"I taught him that move." She heard stage whispered from the living room and Brandon's lips left hers. He looked down at her in confusion.

"Surprise," she announced as she stepped back and opened the door wider.

He looked over her shoulder and she watched as his eyes lit up in pleasure. She loved seeing that expression of pure joy on his face. She logged it in her memory as he bent down and gave her a quick peck before moving forward to embrace his friend in a hug.

She shook her head at herself as she watched her husband's reunion with his friends. And she had been perturbed about losing some   writing   time.

CHAPTER 15

Brandon was having a rough day. He couldn't remember the last time he was so tired from doing nothing. The paperwork had dragged on and on. He'd gone through at least fifteen client folders and still had another fifteen to go before he was caught up. It seemed never-ending, and all he wanted to do was go home, kiss his wife, eat something, and pass out on her lap while pretending to watch whatever was on television.

He was trying to make up for some of his time lost before he had to go part time. He knew his boss was prepared for him to make the switch any day now, but he didn't want to take advantage of the situation. He would work full days until he couldn't.

He liked his job most days, but there had been nothing to break up the monotony of data entry and double-checking facts. He called Paige during his lunch hour and was happy to hear that she was writing again. It cut their conversation short because she'd broken through whatever had been blocking her writing, but after seeing her struggle and worry about not meeting her deadline he was fine with letting her go for the moment.

When five o'clock finally rolled around, he heaved a sigh of relief and locked up his desk and office. He slowly made his way to his car and breathed another sigh when he was inside. This was his time. He wasn't at work or at home. He was able to get into a quiet place and think or not. Today he didn't want to think about anything. He'd been thinking way too much lately, and he wanted to take his own advice and live in the quiet of the moment.

Dominy and his family were coming in a little over a week. He missed his friend and was looking forward to the levity he always brought with him, but soon after their visit, Gladys would come and stay for an indeterminable amount of time. Then his parents and family threatened to come as early as the end of October for the upcoming holidays. He had precious few days alone with Paige, and he was feeling more and more possessive of that time as the days went by.

He would never share these feelings with her. They were best left unsaid. She wouldn't understand the bittersweetness of it all; that sometimes knowing your number of days were shorter than most made you appreciate them more.

He took a few more minutes for himself after pulling into the underground parking. He thanked God for seeing him home safely.

He dragged himself out of the car and took the elevator up to their floor. When he got to their door he imagined a perfect night with his wife and slipped the key in the lock. He was pleasantly surprised when she met him at the door whispering something about a surprise. He told her what his heart felt at that moment and hugged her as close as he could and focused on the feel and smell of her so he could use it to combat the pain when or if it came.

He leaned back and watched her eyes light up as they always did when she was excited about something. He meant to give her a short peck, but she held on and he wasn't about to deny himself.

The sound of a male's voice startled him out of their kiss, and he looked down at Paige as recognition came to him. *Dominy.*

"Surprise," his wife said with a brilliant smile as she stood back and opened the door to reveal Dominy, his wife, and new son. The joy that came over him wiped out any thoughts of tiredness when his best friend came forward to embrace him in a hug.

Brandon sat on the love seat with his arm around Paige's shoulder, feeling content as he caught up with his friends on the last few months. He breathed in and out slowly, taking in Dominy,

Robin, and Nicky asleep in his car seat. He didn't know how many times he'd dreamed about spending time with his best friends and his wife, but this was better than them all. Paige was now completely integrated in his life. There was no memory in the last year and a half that didn't have her in it.

He ignored the pang in his chest at the sight of Robin lifting a restless Nicky out of his car seat. The boy was the spitting image of Dominy with his dark hair and brown eyes. Over the last few months there wasn't one conversation he'd had with Dominy where Nicky wasn't mentioned. Dominy was such a proud father, and Brandon considered it a timely blessing.

Dominy refused to consider, let alone talk about Brandon's illness. Brandon wanted to use part of their visit to try and convince Dominy that he needed to prepare for Brandon's inevitable transition.

Robin calmed the fussing baby and came over, holding him out to Brandon. As the youngest of seven, Brandon was used to being handed over babies and toddlers. He took the cuddly, warm baby in his hands and adjusted him on his lap so that Robin and Dominy were still in his sight. He took in the feel of him and was caught by the somber look in the child's eyes as he stared up at him.

He pushed back thoughts of what he would miss with Paige. He kissed Nicky's head and took in his baby smell. There was nothing like it in the world. It was warm sweetness, milk, and baby powder. Nicky wrapped his chubby finger around Brandon's forefinger when he caressed the boy's chubby cheek. He watched the child with rapt fascination as Nicky tried to direct the digit to his mouth.

Brandon pulled his finger out the boy's grasp but distracted him with a simple form of peek-a-boo where he covered and uncovered Nicky's eyes with his hand. The third time Nicky gurgled and laughed his way into his godfather's heart.

"And he's a goner." Brandon looked up at Robin's voice to see his wife, Dominy, and Robin watching him play with Nicky.

"I love watching the moment Nicky wiggles his way into a person's heart," Robin said smiling. "It's the laugh," she said addressing both himself and Paige. "The first time he laughed was in the grocery store. The person behind me had this teacup poodle in her purse. The dog stuck his head out of the small opening and was licking Nicky's leg. At first I was appalled and afraid he would frighten Nicky but when my baby let out that gurgling laugh it was as if everyone in the store stopped." She looked adoringly at her son. "It's so innocent and abandoned."

Brandon remembered the first time he heard Paige's laugh and glanced over at her. The look of longing in her eyes caught him off guard, but she blinked it away so quickly he thought he had imagined it.

"Paige's laugh affected me much the same way," he said without taking his eyes off her hers. "I was afraid I would get caught staring at her from across the table at the Chinese restaurant by one of   the   Elders."

.   He watched as Paige's eyes widened. "We had just met," she said, surprised.

"You have no clue the power of your laugh," he said sincerely and stared as she smiled at him shyly, the tips of her ears growing red in embarrassment.

Dominy cleared his throat and he took his time glancing over at him. "Yes."

"Are we going for dinner soon, or are you going to make moony eyes at your wife all night?"

Brandon wanted to wipe the mischievous grin off of his face.

"We're going to dinner, so I can feed my wife and make moony eyes at her from across the table," he said while standing. He handed a cooing Nicky to Robin and helped his wife off of the couch.

He took in her comfy writing clothes which made her look closer to nineteen than twenty-seven. He kissed her cheek because he loved her smell. It was warm peaches, and Egyptian musk, and her. "You think you might need a jacket?" he whispered in her ear. He felt her look down.

"Yep. Are you comfortable in your work clothes?" she asked, moving back a couple of inches and looking up at him.

"Nope." He took her arm and glanced back at Dominy.

"We're going to change clothes and be right with you."

"Okay."

He walked with her to their bedroom and closed the door. "I need two minutes. Just two minutes to hold you," he said before wrapping his arms around her and taking a deep breath. He marveled in the fact that he could cross his arms around her back, she was so slight, but her will was stronger than anyone he knew. "It feels like I've been waiting forever to get you back in my arms." He allowed himself to bask in the moment.

He leaned back slightly and kissed her lips, just wanting to feel the texture of them beneath his. It took him back to their first kiss, and he held her closer for a minute longer.

"We need to get ready. I don't want the reason we came back here together to be too obvious."

He didn't tell her that Dominy knew exactly why they went to change so quickly. Dominy's whole marriage was one big honeymoon. Anytime he could get Robin to himself he was in her space.

Reluctantly he let her go and they changed into warm and comfortable clothing.

*   *   *

They decided on an early dinner at a nearby family restaurant that made it easy for Robin to feed Nicky.

"Brandon told me that Melanie came to see the two of you," Dominy said by way of conversation during dinner. The waitress had just taken their orders, and they were watching Nicky play with the mobile hanging over the top of his booster seat.

"Yes, she did," Paige replied.

"He also said she wants to leave Gladys with you."

"Yes. That too," Paige said before taking a sip of her water.

Brandon felt her unease and was about to interrupt their conversation when Dominy asked his next question.

"That gives me hope," Dominy said quietly.

Paige took a sip of her water then gave him a brilliant smile.

His wife was an actress. Brandon thought to himself.

"So, why do you think she's doing this? Do you think she's in trouble?" Dominy asked, watching Paige closely.

"I don't really know. She wouldn't say." Paige shrugged, "But she needs our help, so we're going to give it to her. Besides..." Paige smiled at him. "I choose to concentrate on Gladys and giving her what she needs for now."

Brandon hugged her to him out of pride and a need to comfort her. That was his Paige: strong, resourceful, compassionate, and nurturing. He kissed her temple and grinned at Dominy.

He watched the furrow between his friend's brows smooth out a little, but he recognized the gleam in his eyes. Dominy wouldn't let this go for long.

"Are you two thinking of how long you'll wait to give Nicky here a little brother or sister?"

Dominy's eyes glazed over slightly, and Robin squinted but she answered, "It will be a few years if ever. I want to give my organs time to move back into place, lose some of this baby weight, and give Dominy a chance to forget what he saw in the delivery room." She finished with a laugh.

Brandon glanced back to Dominy whose eyes were now completely unfocused and couldn't hold in the laugh. It began as a deep chuckle as he tried to hold it back but after it escaped his mouth he stopped trying and let it out in a deep guffaw. He caught Paige's eye and saw her laughing right along with him.

After that the conversation switched to less intense topics, but every so often Brandon would glance over and see questions in Dominy's eyes.

"I'm taking the family out touring tomorrow, but you and I have an appointment on a basketball court on Saturday morning. You up for it?" Dominy asked after giving him and Paige a brief hug in the parking lot after dinner. The two families were going their separate ways for the evening.

"Are you up for me wiping the court with you?"

. Dominy chuckled. "See. I invite you to a fun and slightly competitive game of ball, and you're talking about wiping the floor with me. You've gotten violent all of a sudden."

"There's never anything slightly competitive about your invitations to play basketball." Brandon deadpanned.

Dominy shrugged playfully. "Challenge taken."

Brandon shook his head and went over to kiss and hug Robin and Nicky goodbye. "Make sure he doesn't wear himself out tomorrow, Robin. I don't want him to blame his loss on tiredness when we play on Saturday.

Robin nodded her agreement while moving to hug Paige goodbye.

"Want to have a spa day Saturday? I have the feeling these two will play for a while?" Brandon heard Paige ask Robin.

"Oh my gosh. I don't know the last time I had a spa day, but do they have a daycare for babies as young as Nicky?"

"I know a couple of girls that will come by the apartment, so we don't have to worry about a babysitter or daycare. I found them when I was still rehabilitating from the surgery last year."

"Perfect. I'll come with Dom in the morning. I'll bring breakfast, and we can have a day of it," Robin said sounding more enthusiastic about the idea as she spoke.

"That sounds great! I'll see what time the girls have available and give you a call." Paige hugged Robin again and nuzzled Nicky.

Brandon moved closer to take Paige's arm and escort her to their car before she started talking to Robin again. He was happy the two women got along so well for being newly acquainted, but they were alike in so many ways he was sure they would all be out there for another hour if it were up to them.

He waved as his friends piled in their car and handed Paige in his.

They were halfway home before he spoke, "I'm happy you and Robin are going to get to spend some time together."

Paige grabbed and squeezed his hand. "She's a riot. I love all the faces she makes when Dominy is trying to be funny, but when he holds Nicky or just shares about his day or their family she looks at him like he hung the moon."

"Dom adores her, and I think if he could, he'd hang some stars just for her," Brandon said, slowing at a light. "I'd do the same for you." He looked over at her illuminated by the light of the red light.

She smiled at him with her heart in her eyes. "I know. It's one of the reasons I married you. You make me feel like a queen."

"Then I'm doing my job." He brought her hand up to kiss it as the light turned and he pulled forward. "Because you are my queen."

"Yes I am," Paige responded before placing his hand to her cheek. "And you are my..." Her profession was cut short by the loud ring of his cell phone resting between them.

"Sorry. Could you see who that is?" he asked without taking his focus from the road.

"It's Mason," she said with a note of confusion in her voice. "Why is he calling you?"

"Well if you answer it, you might just find out," he said jokingly.

"Ha ha. Two hours with Dominy and you already have jokes," she said as she pressed the button to accept the call.

"Hi Mason."

"Uh, Hi Paige." Mason's voice came over the car speaker.

"Brandon and I are in the car on the way home so I answered. He's here though."

"Mason. How's it going?" Brandon rang out.

He heard Mason expel a breath before continuing. "I'm good, you two. How's everything going for you?"

"Good," Brandon said, taking over the conversation. "We're just coming back from dinner. Dominy, Robin, and the baby are in town for a couple of weeks so we were catching up," Brandon explained.

"Oh, I didn't want to interrupt."

"Mason, why are you so skittish? We're the only two in the car." Brandon glanced over at Paige.

"Is Vivian and the family alright?" Paige asked, a small frown coming to her face.

"Yes, yes. Vivian is doing very well," Mason said, but Brandon didn't miss the fact that he didn't mention the rest of the family.

"What's going on, Mason? You can talk to us."

"Well, I'm glad you two are doing good. I have some news I think Paige would like to hear, but I could be wrong."

Brandon glanced at Paige again. Her grip on his hand had tightened but her face was calm. "Do you want to know?" He glanced at the road and back to her. She nodded though she looked hesitant.

"Okay, Mason. Paige would like to know," Brandon responded for her.

"Richard called me earlier this week."

It was Brandon's turn to take a breath. The last time Mason received a call from Richard he told Paige the woman she'd known as a sister for her entire life was her mother.

"Okay. What did he say?" Paige asked before he could open his mouth.

"Victoria and Richard went to Cincinnati a couple of weeks ago. They were called there for a meeting with Victoria's son's father."

"Victoria had a son with another man? How's Richard taking this?" Paige asked while looking at Brandon.

He glanced her way for a quick moment letting her know he was listening.

"No. This was Victoria's ex from college. She had a son by him but was urged to give him up," Mason began. "Oh yes," Paige inserted, sounding a little relieved. "I think she recently found out that he died when he was young. She was torn up about it. Victoria talked to me about it briefly."

There was a short pause after her statement. "Um, yeah," Mason said haltingly. "I didn't know she shared that with you," he said before going quiet again.

Brandon pulled the car into their subterranean garage, and they sat there listening to Mason breathe.

"Mason?" Brandon prompted.

"Yes. Sorry. I was taking in what you just said, Paige."

"It's okay. Why do you think I would want to hear about Victoria's ex, Mason?"

"Maaaan." The word was said in exasperation.

"Mason?" Brandon asked, not at all happy with the amount of apprehension that one drawn-out word gave him. He looked over at Paige.

"Antonio Sable, Victoria's ex, told Victoria and Richard that he's your grandfather."

"What?!" His exclamation was echoed by Paige even though they were staring at each other.

"Sorry, Paige, I didn't know about their son. From the way Richard talked about everyone, I thought he was alive."

"Mason, I'm going to need you to go back and give me the details. How do you know what this man said is true, and if it is,

221

why did it take so long for him to come forth? Why didn't Richard and Victoria say anything to me?" Paige opened her mouth to say more but Brandon shook her hand which was still held fast in his.

"Victoria and Richard thought it would be best, with everything you're dealing with, if they waited to tell you. They are also wary regarding her ex's sudden appearance with so much knowledge of everyone. They were hoping to get more information before sharing this with you."

Brandon watched the light come into her eyes. "Wait. Are you telling me that Victoria Branchett is my grandmother?"

"Yes." Mason's voice was clear.

Brandon could feel Paige's hand shake, and he let go so he could slide his arm around her shoulder.

"And they weren't going to tell me?" she asked quietly.

"Yes, they were. She just doesn't fully trust Antonio's motives because he seemed interested in meeting you and Mel."

"Well, how dare he want to get to know his granddaughter or granddaughter's mother." Paige's voice grew loud in the car, and Brandon squeezed her shoulder to comfort her the only way he could.

"They didn't tell you because Antonio might also be looking for your father," Mason said in a rush.

The words seemed to take the wind out of Paige. She slumped against Brandon.

"Mason. We've arrived, but we are in the garage. Let me get Paige upstairs, and we will call you back."

"Um. Okay. I didn't mean to upset you, Paige. I thought you should know."

"No one is blaming you, Mason. I for one appreciate you telling us. Let me call you right back," Brandon said, pulling away from Paige so he could unlock the doors.

"Okay." The phone line disconnected and Brandon took in Paige's pallor.

"Come on. Let's go upstairs. You look like you could use some apple juice."

Paige gave him a wan smile. "Or something stronger."

"Tsk, tsk, tsk. What would your pastors say?" Brandon asked, teasing her.

"Bourbon or vodka?" she replied saucily.

"That's my girl." He smiled at her before getting out of the car and walking around to her side.

Ten minutes later Paige was hydrated to Brandon's satisfaction. Her caramel-colored complexion had lost the gray pallor and her hands were warmer, but when Brandon sat next to her on the couch he continued to rub them. He wasn't sure whether it was more for his benefit or hers, and he didn't really care. He never knew a family with so many unraveling secrets. If it weren't for her recent strides toward accepting the reality of their future and Dominy's visit he might have encouraged her to wait to receive any more news from Mason.

"Do you want to call him back now or later?" Her look of vulnerability nearly broke his heart.

"It'll be alright. He might have jumped the gun, but I think Mason had a very good reason for sharing this information despite what Victoria and Richard said, and I also think Victoria and Richard have good reason for wanting to wait. Maybe they were trying to protect you."

Paige frowned at him. "Protect me from what?"

Brandon shrugged. "If this Antonio is anything like Victoria— maybe from him?" He knew he was grasping at straws, but he would do anything to erase that look of abandonment from her eyes.

"I don't understand why they wouldn't have called me themselves? Did she not think I would be happy to discover I had more living relatives, especially from my biological dad's side?

"Baby, I think there is a lot more going on here than the fact that you are related to Victoria. From what little Mason has told us so far, this Antonio Sable man has known this information for a while, but he's looking for something or someone. If you're up to it let's go ahead and give Mason a call back so that we can get the whole story." She took a deep breath and nodded her head. Brandon hugged her to him, squeezing gently. Then he took out his phone and dialed Mason back.

"I'm really sorry if I caused Paige distress," Mason began when the call was connected. "It was the last thing I wanted, but I felt she had the right to know."

"I understand Mason. It's just a shock." Brandon was quick to try and ease Mason's guilt. He just wanted to get the whole story. "So let's start from the beginning."

Brandon placed the phone on the coffee table so that he and Paige could listen, and his hands would be free to hold her if there were any more shocking revelations.

Mason started going over what Richard had told him almost a week ago. He told them how selective Antonio was with the information he shared, only giving over more details when Victoria asked certain questions.

From what Brandon was able to surmise, Antonio Sable's family separated Antonio and Victoria but set up the adoption for their son without Antonio's knowledge. Antonio found paperwork and tracked down the child's whereabouts, even interacting with him from time to time until Brian disappeared completely and was thought to be dead.

"Wait, Mason, are you saying they think my dad is alive and this man may have a lead on his whereabouts?

"I'm not sure. Richard said they were only able to get minimal information from Antonio, and he didn't seem too certain."

Paige looked up at Brandon with a new light in her eyes. "My dad might be alive."

"There's another reason why I believe you have a right to know, Paige," Mason said interrupting her.

"Vivian and Gladys will be staying at Victoria's during the time Antonio wants to visit. As her biological mother I thought you should have a say as to whether or not Vivian and Gladys should have any interaction with Antonio Sable.

Brandon felt the tension flow through Paige and could practically hear what was going on in her mind.

"Richard told me Antonio showed a great deal of interest in meeting you and Melanie but was also grateful Victoria was allowing him to visit with his great-granddaughters. He said Victoria believes Antonio has an ulterior motive and really wants to get to you or Melanie."

Paige leaned away from Brandon. "Do you think that's why Melanie left?" She turned back toward the phone.

"Mason, do you know if Victoria and Richard have talked to Melanie?"

"I'm not sure."

"Okay, thank you Mason. I know it was hard breaking Richard's confidence, but I appreciate you telling me. It means a lot."

"You're welcome. I want you to know that I'll be there to supervise Antonio's visit with Vivian."

"Thank you, Mason," Brandon said. "Have a good night."

"You too. Good night, Paige and Brandon," Mason replied then hung up the phone.

Brandon watched Paige as she stretched then got up off the couch.

She was halfway out of the room when he spoke, "You do remember that little meeting you have with Carmen and your new publisher in New York on Monday."

Paige looked at him over her shoulder. Yes. I do."

"Will you be coming back here before you go to Victoria's to meet your grandfather, or will you be going straight from New York?"

She gave him a mischievous smile. "I have to make a couple of calls, but I'll let you know." She winked at him and continued out of the room.

Brandon didn't even get off the couch. He just nodded to himself and checked his phone to see what the weather would be like during the next week in Oklahoma City.

CHAPTER 16

Victoria stood at the window of one of the two guest rooms her great-grandchildren would be staying in while visiting her and Richard. She couldn't help comparing this summer with the previous one. So much had changed. She remembered when she would start preparing for Vivian's summer visits in the spring. She would plan their schedule to the day, and more times than not Vivian would disappear early in the morning only to be found wrist or elbow deep in soil, hay, or muck by the time they were due to leave the farm for the day. It didn't matter how much Victoria cajoled, chastised, or threatened, Vivian could not be put off from spending time with the animals on the farm.

She wondered why it never occurred to her to question Vivian's love for the place. She figured it was the contrast between the loud, bustling city and the quietness of the farm. She never considered that it would be in Vivian's biological makeup to be predisposed to being drawn to the farm as she was. Rachael didn't want anything to do with farm life once she left for college. She wanted a more convenient life.

It wasn't like she didn't already have most of the modern conveniences outside of sharing an acre of land with two other families in tract housing or by sharing a wall. Victoria wouldn't be able to go back to that life after living so long on her farm. For one she wouldn't know what to do with herself. Farm life started early and ended way past sundown with paperwork.

The early years were hard even though she wasn't one crop away from bankruptcy like most other farmers in her region, but for a young woman who was used to being pampered, the budgeting and prioritizing was hard. Her grandparents had left her a beautiful and thriving legacy, but to make it the success she knew they'd been hoping for, took many hours in the fields and paying tribute to bureaucrats, agricultural chemists, and geologists. There were two fields they wanted to cultivate but one wasn't in the irrigation line. She knew her grandfather had once dreamed of building a bigger bunkhouse and new stables on that area but only after consulting with a man who described himself as an agricultural architect rather than a farm mapper or planner.

He took pictures and tested the land for two weeks before he came back to her with a plan that would help them efficiently yield the best crops. They had to give up one forty-acre zone or field a year and plant the crop designated for that field until they'd cycled through them all. What they reaped in return was up to five bushels more per acre in their wheat, corn, and sorghum fields and a greater weight in green beans, squash, and melons.

Inside of three years they'd more than doubled their profits, and Victoria was able to get more help. They'd renovated and added on to the main house, preparing for the large family Victoria had wanted. They'd also raised a new barn on the opposite side of the main house, added a bunkhouse, otherwise known as "the little hotel," at the north border of their land. It was only half a mile from the main house, but it was far enough to give the workers breathing room.

Victoria's foreman, Nathan Isles, was a godsend, though she would never admit it to his face. He kept the men in line, the zones planting and harvesting times scheduled to a tee, and updated the calendar for the vet's vaccinating and servicing the few heads of cattle, goats, and horses.

She didn't know what had prompted him to come to her farm early that late-fall morning thirty-five years ago, but she did her best to make it hard for him to leave. She snooped and found out that he came to their farm newly widowed. His wife and two children had been killed when a tornado touched down on their town while he was helping his mother who'd recently had a stroke. She wouldn't learn until later that he was so distraught he sold the land as it was, along with his belongings, after his family's funerals. He moved in with his mother until she died two months later from another massive stroke and stayed in town until he'd settled her estate. Nathan showed up on Branchett Farms three months and two thousand wayward miles later. He'd been to three other farms in the area, but Victoria often considered it her good fortune that Nathan showed up when he did.

Twenty years ago she caught him and her housekeeper, Martha, speaking in hushed tones as they crossed through her garden and under her window. She knew eavesdropping on what seemed to be a pretty intense conversation was wrong, but once she realized that the fervency in their voices wasn't derived from anger, but from passion, she moved away. She did catch enough to know that Nathan felt deeply for Martha, but never intended to marry again. He said he wasn't meant to have a family, and it had taken almost fifteen years to come to peace with that.

Victoria had forced herself to step back from the window then and go back to what she had been doing prior to hearing their voices. She remembered mentioning something about it to Richard that evening, because she was afraid of losing her foreman, housekeeper, or both. Richard gave a few noncommittal grunts to her request that he say something to Nathan, making her think it was a lost cause.

A month later Martha, who was just a few years younger than what her own mother would have been had she lived, approached her shyly offering Victoria an invitation to her wedding. Victoria was so elated she was sure she startled the woman with her hug, but the surprise didn't last long, and with a little coaxing Victoria had the entire story of Nathan and Martha's courtship.

The farm that she ran full time and Richard ran part-time, when he was deep into investing and now worked with her when he wasn't building for orphans in Uganda, was a family of people from different walks of life who stayed and grew with the farm or passed through. Victoria knew she kept her distance most of the time, but there was very little she wasn't aware of when it came to her farm and the people on it. She often wondered, if she paid more attention to her immediate family would she have been able to avoid the last ten years of heartache, and could she have gotten her daughter the help she needed to save her life.

There were many thoughts that assailed her since she'd given her life to Christ. She wished more than she liked that she had just a few more minutes with her Rachael to tell her all of the things she hadn't been willing to do those last months. Her pride seemed so trivial next to her relationship with her daughter now, but before her thoughts started laying into her she would remember the moments when Victoria knew she did right by Rachael and showed her daughter love to the best of her ability. Instead of feeling boastful about those moments she felt humbled just to have them and thanked God for reminding her of them.

She promised herself she would do better by her grand... great-grandchild. It was going to take some getting used to. She didn't consider herself to be old enough to be a great-grandmother. She shook her head from that line of thought and glanced around at the more modern decorations of the room. She hoped Vivian would enjoy both the subtle and big changes. Teens could be unpredictable, but since her Vivian had never given into tantrums or drama of any kind, Victoria figured she would enjoy them.

Victoria knew everything there was about farm life, but learned from her daughter that farm life may not be every child's dream. When Vivian came to visit Victoria made sure there was a variety of outings to museums, fairs, markets, historical landmarks, and preservations, so Vivian wouldn't grow bored or restless. Restless children were hard to deal with. Their attention was easily swayed in the wrong direction, and it wouldn't do to send Vivian home with anything more than a cut or bruise.

This summer Gladys would be in attendance, and though Victoria had witnessed nothing but a quiet maturity and intelligence from the child, she was not naïve enough to think it was Gladys' everyday behavior. The twins had grown so close so quickly she knew they could easily entertain themselves in almost any situation, but she also knew they could get into mischief twice as quickly.

She made room in the daily schedule for them to spend time on the farm. She knew Vivian would want to show Gladys all of her favorite places, animals, and chores. This year, Richard would join them for an early lunch each day before they all left the farm for most of the day. Victoria was looking forward to spending more leisure time with Richard and watching as the girls explored and discovered new places. It was one of her favorite things to do in the summer after the big harvest when Rachael was young.

She got lost in the memories of all the energy they put into making the farm as big as it was. The muscle and sweat she invested into the land, so she could prove her parents wrong and try to get out of the earth what she couldn't seem to get out of her body.

Tomorrow her great-granddaughters would arrive to newly decorated rooms in their favorite colors—part of an extension of her birthday gift. They would have only a few outfits each in their closets because she didn't want to be accused of spoiling them, and a set of books ranging from children's Christian fiction to young adult mysteries on their bookshelves. She knew they adored the tablets their mother had given them for Christmas, but Victoria just couldn't imagine reading from those things. It was one of the last pieces of electronic equipment she held out on. Books were for holding, sniffing, and listening to when you turned their pages.

The last two weeks seemed to fly by in the wake of their trip to Cincinnati. It didn't help that their trip after that to Atlanta was made in vain. Richard made several attempts to contact Melanie, but without Paige's help it was fruitless, and as much as he tried, Victoria was determined to leave Paige out of this latest chapter of drama for as long as possible. Paige had enough on her plate.

Victoria didn't mind the extra trip. It gave her a chance to absorb some of the things Antonio had said about Brenda aka Grace. It was hard to consider that the woman had been such a pivotal part of their lives for so long. What kind of psychosis caused the irrational thinking behind her plots and schemes? The woman was certifiable and obviously very dangerous. That thought caused her to ask Richard for help.

"Do you have a man or two that can keep an eye on Paige and Brandon for a couple of months?" Victoria asked over breakfast at a cute B&B Richard's secretary had found for them during their hour and a half flight to Atlanta.

Richard took a sip from the coffee cup in his hand, laying it down carefully on its saucer before looking at her. "Do you think there's just cause?" His gaze was unwavering.

She wet her lips in anticipation of a debate. "No, but Antonio's words gave me a very bad gut feeling."

"Do you really think Grace, uh, Brenda would do Paige harm after all of this time?"

Victoria stopped herself from shrugging. "She might if what Antonio told us pushes her into a corner, and now that we have been brought into this bazaar form of family hide-and-seek."

"What if Paige notices she's being followed?" Richard asked before taking a bite of his eggs.

"Then your men aren't as good as I think they are." She smiled playfully at him and was rewarded with one of his roguish grins.

"You would have made a great lawyer," he said, not for the first time.

She sat back taking her own cup in hand and sipping at its contents. Happy he wouldn't fight her on this. "Yep."

"I have two men already scheduled to fly out as soon as I get word of Brenda's whereabouts. She can't move too much now that she's married again."

"Not if he's helping her," Victoria said, voicing the first thought that came to mind.

"Your mind is a little scary, baby."

She gave him a mock pout. "I thought me making a great lawyer meant I had a brilliant mind."

"Brilliant, devious, cynical, but wonderful now that you are using your powers for good instead of evil.

She balled up her napkin and threw it at him.

"I'm kidding, baby," he said, swatting away the paper. "Mostly," he mumbled softly as he reached behind him for his phone on a side table.

"I heard that," she said, giving him a stern look.

"I know," he said, unphased by her admission.

"Do you really think my mind is scary?" she asked genuinely curious.

"Yes I do," he said with more than a little admiration in his voice.

"Thank you, baby." She smiled at him, watching as he tried to keep his lips from twitching.

"You're welcome."

They spent two more nights in Atlanta and arrived to a package at their home the next morning. One of Richard's investigators had been very busy.

Without unpacking Victoria walked with Richard to her office. She watched as Richard opened the letter-sized, gold envelope with her opener. He withdrew two sheets of paper. The first one read. "MELANIE IS IN THE WIND."

Richard let out a long breath before shuffling the papers. The second sheet made Victoria want to swear. It was a list of moves Melanie had made over the last month. She'd resigned from her job, closed up the house, and sent Gladys to stay at a school friend's house until she flew to Oklahoma. Unlike Melanie, Marc was on sabbatical and would be for another six months.

The copy of a receipt for a ticket to Los Angeles made Victoria's spine tingle and she had to fight the temptation to call Paige to see what, if anything, Melanie had told her.

Why was Melanie running and was the timing a coincidence or had she been tipped off? If she was tipped off, then by who and why? What or who was Melanie hiding? Was she running from, or running to, someone?

There were too many questions buzzing around in her mind for her to make head or tails of this puzzle. She'd run over in her mind their meeting with Antonio both on fast forward and super slow, and though she couldn't put her finger on it, there was something off. There were too many pieces that didn't easily fit together if she questioned the timing and Antonio's motivation.

This all went from bad to worse, and she wanted to make sure more than ever that Paige was protected.

She made a few inquiries into Melanie's last few months and still came up with nothing. Maybe she and Richard had been focusing on this family from the wrong angle. Instead of placing Brenda in the middle of the web of lies, they needed to place Melanie there to see what threads led from her.

Regardless of the fact that she'd kept her true relation to Paige a secret, Melanie never posed a threat. She still didn't, but she was definitely hiding something, and Victoria would bet half her farm it had to do with Brian.

*   *   *

With a heavy sigh Victoria came out of her reverie and turned full circle taking one last glance around the room. The staff had done a great job. There was nothing out of place anywhere in the house and she needed it to stay that way at least until both Antonio and Mason had finished their visits.

The thought of Antonio Sable visiting their home made her stomach roil. Victoria knew she and her husband had a thriving industry. Good investments, new technology, and a huge network helped them do more than just keep their heads above water. She hated that it mattered to her what he would think, but Antonio was the last part of her past that reminded her of the gullible and naïve girl who looked for approval through her rose-colored glasses.

When Antonio Sable stepped foot on Branchett Farms she'd make sure he saw a successful business. A business she and her husband expanded on and took to another level in the industry.

She stepped out of the room on her way to the bedroom across the hall when she heard her name.

She turned to see Richard striding toward her. The look on his face made her frown.

"Hi." She looked at her watch to double-check that she wasn't late for their dinner date. She knew she could lose track of time when she was on a mission.

"You did say four o'clock for Paul and Mary's right?" Victoria took in the guilt he wasn't able to mask before reaching her side.

"What's wrong?" Goose bumps broke out on her arms.

"Is it…"

Richard lifted his hand to stop her. "The health and status of our family is the same today as it was yesterday.

She took a deep breath to calm herself. "Okay. Good," she said on the exhale. "Then I can handle just about anything else."

"I just got off the phone with Mason."

"Okay. Vivian is still coming tomorrow, right? I didn't receive any status changes from the travel agency," Victoria said, feeling a flutter in her belly. She touched her forehead. Not sure why, but it gave her hand something to do.

"Mason called Brandon and told him and Paige about our meeting with Antonio Sable." The look of defeat on his face made her want to smooth away the lines creasing his forehead.

She took another deep breath. "Okay," she said feeling a bone-deep weariness. For once she wanted things to go smoothly.

The shock she saw cross his face might have made her laugh if she wasn't now worried about Paige.

"I was expecting you to yell or at least say, "I told you so," Richard said, reminding her of a young boy as he slipped his hands into his pockets.

She looked up at him and gave him a half-hearted "I told you so."

He looked crestfallen at her pittance of a response. "Honey, I'm really sorry. I thought Mason would understand the need for silence in this situation. He cares for Paige just as much as we do."

"I know you did," Victoria said, just wanting to step away from it all for a moment. "Call Brandon, and let him know they are invited to join the twins if they'd like. Do you think Paul will be back with the corporate jet by Tuesday or Wednesday? We can send it to pick them up instead of placing Brandon in more harm's way on a commercial plane."

"I'll ask." He looked at her strangely. "Are you sure you don't want to yell even a little bit?"

Victoria gave him a wan smile. "No use crying over spilled milk. That's what Vivian says."

"Huh. Smart kid," Richard said, still looking at her strangely.

"Yeah. Some even say her great-grandmother is brilliant," Victoria said with as much energy as she could muster. "And stop looking at me like that, Richard. I know in the past I've acted less like a child of God and more like…" She gestured with her hand. "Well, you know." She rubbed her head again. "It's just every time I get close to having the family I've always wanted, something or someone comes in and snatches them away."

Richard frowned in concern. "Are you alright? You have been doing a great deal lately."

"No more than I would for our galas. I'm just a little tired. I'll be fine." She reached up to caress his cheek. "I'm just a little tired. I'm going to lie down before dinner."

Richard caught her hand as she moved to turn away.

"I have a couple of calls to make, but I will come in and check on you in a little while. Do you want to cancel our dinner with Paul and   Mary?"

She smiled up at him. "No. I enjoy their company. It will be nice to get away for a few hours."

"Okay," he said, bringing her hand to his lips and kissing the knuckles.

She offered up one more smile and turned to walk to their rooms.

Once she stepped inside their bedroom suite she changed into a robe and lay down hoping to escape for a few minutes, but sleep didn't come. She was still laying there listening to the many different sounds of machinery and animals when Richard walked in. Though her eyes were closed she felt his presence immediately. It was like a shift of energy in the air when he was near.

She felt the bed dip behind her and the warmth of him was at her back. His arm came around her waist And she caught a whiff of his cologne. She took a deep breath to drown herself in the scent of him.

"It'll all work out, Vicki. You'll see. Just believe that God has a bigger plan for all of us," he whispered before kissing her neck.

.   "I'm trying, baby," she whispered back.

Richard pulled her closer and ran his nose along the back of her neck as he did some nights before going to sleep. "Try to get some sleep. I'll stay right here holding you tight, and when it's time to get up I'll wake you." He rubbed her arm and held her close until sleep finally overtook her.

Victoria knew she was quieter than usual on the way to Mary and Paul Ambross' house. If she didn't already know, the quick glances Richard kept giving her would have given her a clue. She had tried to convince him that she was fine, but her odd reaction to news he believed should have had her seeing red, had him concerned.

Not her.

Victoria knew exactly how she felt. She felt defeated. She didn't even know how to begin to convince Paige that her reason for keeping the news from Paige was for her benefit. She was at a loss at what to say and couldn't blame Paige for jumping to conclusions. She tried to talk herself out of assuming Paige would be hurt and angry, but knew that she herself would be no matter what else she was going through.

Victoria took a deep breath and let it out slowly. She had made the wrong choice to keep Paige's lineage from her. She felt it deep in her bones, but the impulse to keep Paige out of harm's way, no matter who or what posed as harmful, could not be tamped down. Now she would have to deal with the consequences. "Sorry, my love. I was just trying to keep you safe," she whispered on a sigh as she looked out of the passenger side window.

They were coming up the driveway to their friend's home.

After putting the car in park Richard turned to her taking her hand. He brought it up to his lips for a soft, lingering kiss. He didn't say one word to her, just let his eyes relay his feelings and desire to comfort her.

At the door they exchanged the customary greetings and hugs with Mary and Paul. Mary took her aside and looked at her intensely. Richard catching her gaze over Mary's head, smirked and allowed Paul to lead him off to another space in the house before dinner.

"I know you *will* mind me telling you this, but please understand it comes from a place of love. You don't look good,"

Mary said, concern written across her face as she took Victoria's hands. "I told you I would help you with the preparations for your granddaughter's visit. Why haven't you called me?" Mary went on without giving Victoria a chance to respond. "You're looking pale and a bit bedraggled."

Victoria wanted to be offended. The anger behind feeling affronted would be more welcomed than this feeling of defeat. There were only a few things in life she was unable to overcome with sheer will. Granted, they were huge things, very important things, but nevertheless they were few.

"I'm fine, Mary. The staff took care of most of the preparations. They are excellent at their jobs. I just have a lot on my mind," Victoria said, taking her hands back and wiping the dampness off on her slacks.

Mary looked at her skeptically but did not comment on her response.

Instead she took one of her hands again and led her toward the kitchen. "Well then, I won't have to feel guilty about recruiting you to help me finish dinner." She glanced back quickly at Victoria as she pulled her through the huge living room.

The woman was so touchy-feely. Victoria thought to herself.

"Paul and I got home late only to find that the outdoor kitchen is still not finished." Mary stepped back and slipped her arm in the crook of Victoria's elbow. It was all Victoria could do to keep from rolling her eyes.

Mary and Paul had been renovating one or another part of their house over the last couple of years. Even though Mary complained about how much time it was taking, Victoria knew she adored seeing the end results of each renovation project.

"What will you do when you have renovated each and every corner of this house?" Victoria asked, catching a glimpse of the sunroom off the dining room they'd just walked through. Victoria knew that her and Richard's house was big as houses went, in

Oklahoma, but her square footage was split between three floors. Most of this home was on the first level and it made it seem to go on forever.

"I don't know," Mary said, waving her hand. "I might have Paul design a gazebo at the end of our property so I can go down there to get away from him whenever we have an argument, or I just want to be alone."

Victoria nodded her head, but she knew that Paul wouldn't let Mary out of his sight for more than thirty minutes at a time if they were both home. He doted on his wife, and his eyes still sparkled every time she walked into a room. It made Victoria even happier that she and Richard had been able to resolve the heaviest of their issues. She wouldn't have been able to be around this couple if she were facing a divorce. Their presence would have reminded her of everything she'd lost.

"Earth to Victoria."

Victoria turned and focused on Mary's face. "I'm sorry, were you talking?" She noticed they'd finally made it to the kitchen.

Mary shook her head slightly. "No, because then I would have been wasting my breath. Do you wanna share what had you so captivated?" Victoria continued to look at Mary, wondering if she should share her thoughts.

"No," she said as she disengaged her arm from Mary's and walked over to the island in the middle of the kitchen. It included several feet of countertop space and a sink.

"Well, if that's all you have say—'no.' I thought our friendship might warrant a little bit more explanation. Like… 'I'm sorry, Mary, I just can't talk about it right now. Or… maybe later, Mary. Or… Mary I know you wanna help, and you're so intelligent and full of wisdom that you probably would help, but I'm just not ready to receive that assistance at this time." Victoria worked to keep her lips from twitching as she started to chop the lettuce. "First of all, I don't use the word 'wanna.'"

Mary turned to her and hissed. She actually opened her mouth baring her teeth and hissed. Victoria was so taken aback she giggled before she could cover her mouth. "Did you just hiss at me?"

Mary smiled brightly. "Yes." There was no forthcoming explanation, and Victoria blinked trying to assess the situation. Meanwhile, Mary went on as if she hadn't just freaked out Victoria.

"Look Victoria, I don't like to see you hurting. I knew something was wrong the moment you walked in the door." After stirring a pot a couple of more times, she replaced the lid and moved closer to Victoria.

"Are you nervous about your granddaughter visiting? Isn't it much the same as last year?" Mary's hands started moving as they usually did when she became passionate about a conversation. "True, her twin sister is going to be accompanying her, but I thought you liked Gladys?

Victoria glanced at Mary as she finished the last of her chopping and began mixing the salad fixings. "Gladys is a beautiful child just like Vivian. I'm excited about her coming to visit, and I'm always happy to have my granddaughter come to see me. If I had my way, their visit wouldn't stop at the end of the summer."

Mary moved away to turn off all of the burners and spoon the side dishes into serving bowls.

Victoria didn't know why but decided to elaborate. "There's much more going on, but it's a long story, and I came here tonight to get away from all of that."

Mary shrugged. "Fair enough." She began placing the bowls and plates on the dinner table then came back to stand in front of Victoria. "You know, if you ever need to talk to someone, I will be there to listen to you."

Victoria was touched by the sincerity in Mary's eyes. "Yes I do."

"Good," Mary said, stepping forward and into Victoria's space.

Victoria allowed Mary to embrace her and couldn't help but reciprocate when after a few seconds Mary hadn't released her but had squeezed her harder.

"Look at this, Richard," Victoria heard Paul say. "We kindly get out of their way so they can finish dinner, and what do we find when we come into the kitchen? A hug fest."

Victoria pulled away from Mary slightly embarrassed to be caught accepting comfort from someone. She felt her cheeks heat but refused to avoid her husband's eyes when he walked up to her. She saw curiosity in the depths of his chocolate brown eyes but more than that she saw relief and pride. She wanted to know why walking in on her being hugged by someone would bring him pride? Richard moved closer to her as Mary moved back to the stove.

He kissed her temple but made no mention of what he'd walked in on. "Dinner smells delicious. I can barely talk, my mouth is watering so much." He turned to Mary, placing his arm around Victoria as he used to do when he would take her out to eat at their favorite little diner. She smiled to herself enjoying the warmth and feeling of protection.

Dinner was pleasant with Richard and Paul monopolizing the conversation with plans to visit the newly completed orphanage in Uganda in two months. She and Mary discussed some of the preparations she'd made to the house for her summer guests, and the new crops in line for the northeast field.

Victoria promised to share a few tulip bulbs from her garden with Mary as they waked around Mary's garden after dinner. Paul and Richard decided to take the opportunity after dinner to solidify a few plans regarding an event their foundation was hosting with a well-known foundation that funded the construction of wells in Uganda.

Victoria could see the outline of a design in the newly planted flowers and thought Mary could get at least one good bloom before winter. The thought came unbidden, and she spoke before she could stop herself. "Come by next week to see the changes I've made to my garden. With everyone coming in over the next week, you and Paul should come by at the end of the week for dinner."

Mary stopped and turned to Victoria. "Are you sure? I don't want to intrude on family time."

"I might need a friendly face by the time the end of next week comes," Victoria said, hoping she was wrong.

Mary shrugged. "You don't have to ask me twice. I've been waiting weeks for another invitation to see your garden."

Victoria, surprised by Mary's comment, winced. "Why didn't you say something?"

"Uh, that would have defeated the purpose," Mary said, walking forward again.

Victoria let the comment go since it wasn't one of her most intelligent moments.

They were on their way back to the house when Mary spoke again, "So should I consider that an open invitation?"

Victoria glanced at her then turned away to hide her smile. "No."

"Well, I never," Mary said in mock affront, placing her hand on her heart.

Victoria turned back and frowned at Mary. "Are you sure because I'm thinking you definitely have." She finished with a mischievous grin.

Mary opened her mouth continuing to play along. "How dare you speak to me like that." She lifted her chin and looked down her nose at Victoria who was trying hard not to burst out in laughter.

"I'm someone important," Mary went on.

Victoria couldn't keep her lips from twitching, her sweet Mary looked so ridiculous. "Really. Important to whom?"

"Why, to you, of course," Mary said, lowering her chin.

"Touché, Mary. Touché," Victoria responded, then before overthinking it she turned and gave Mary a quick hug. "Thank you for dinner and the conversation."

She turned away after catching the surprised look on Mary's face. "I'll see you next week." She waved over her shoulder before going back inside the house to look for Richard.

CHAPTER 17

Richard watched his wife go through her evening ritual as he pretended to read his manual. It brought him a measure of comfort watching her remove the thin layer of makeup and go through the process of cleaning her pores and applying moisturizer. It was much like the mask she would take off once she stepped on their land. He was happy that she had a place where she felt safe enough to lower her defenses. He just hoped she would still feel that way when the rest of their visitors came later in the week.

He wished she felt just as comfortable in other places because more people could then see the beautiful woman she was on the inside. They could witness the woman he'd married so long ago and again last year.

"You're staring, Richard." He focused on his wife's eyes through the mirror.

"I can't help it, and I've stopped trying."

Though she lowered her eyes the telltale twitch of her lips told him she was pleased by his reply. He continued to watch her until she picked up her brush. He slipped out of bed and sat on the bench at its foot.

"Bring your chair over here," he said, leaning back against the footboard. He watched as her eyes flew up to meet his with question. He didn't say anything else or change his expression. It had been a moment, but he used to brush her hair often before they went to bed. The consistent motion soothed his mind and relaxed her. She hesitated a moment longer, and he forced himself to patiently wait for her to come to him.

245

He didn't lose eye contact with her until she stood up from her chair. She turned with the brush in one hand and dragging the chair in the other across the carpet until she was standing in front of him. He didn't realize he was holding his breath until she handed him the brush. He let it out slowly as he positioned the chair between his legs and she sat down with her back to him. He ran his hand over her hair before running the brush through the waves. The repetitive movement didn't fail to slow his heart rate, and when his wife's shoulders sagged he smiled to himself.

"So, how do you think our girls liked their first day?" he asked, keeping his voice quiet so as not to disrupt the peaceful atmosphere.

"I think they loved it if their screams and giggles were any hint," Victoria said, leaning into his touch, a sure sign that she was relaxing.

He recalled the squeals and other loud expressions of surprise and delight the twins made as they discovered the additions to their wardrobes and other additions to their rooms. He knew Vivian would have taken in the changes as quietly as she could if she were alone, but twins seemed do everything in stereo. Either that or he was really starting to get old.

"True," he agreed trying to keep his face straight even though she could see him. "I'm sorry Mason couldn't take us up on our offer to stay in one of the guest bedrooms."

"Wouldn't, Richard. He wouldn't take us up on our invitation," Victoria said without give in her voice. It paid him no mind. He didn't have the same relationship with Mason or defensiveness where he was concerned.

"I think it was as I said," he said, running his fingertips along her scalp. "It's been three years and there are a lot of memories here that he hasn't confronted. Yes, I think his choice to stay at a hotel has to do with your strained relationship," he said nodding his head as he massaged her scalp. "But it also has to do with the fact that he hasn't been here since Rachael became ill. I think it's just too much for him to try to deal with this week when his focus needs to be on his child's reaction and interaction with Antonio."

Victoria just shrugged in response which surprised him. Richard expected her to argue her point further, but he would take the reprieve and hope what he'd said sunk in to some degree. He went back to concentrating on her hair and scalp. He loved how the curls at the ends wrapped around his fingers as if they were trying to hold on to his touch. He knew it was fanciful but there was very little that he didn't love about this woman.

"I talked to Brandon this morning. It looks like we'll have a full house. He and Paige will be accompanied by his friend Dominy, and Dominy's wife and little boy. They won't be arriving until Thursday because Paige had a meeting with her new publisher in New York today. She flies home tomorrow and they all will be prepared to leave Thursday morning." He felt her stiffen a little at the mention of Brandon's name, but as he continued to work the brush through her hair she melted back into him. By the time he'd finished going over his granddaughter's itinerary Victoria was languidly leaning on him.

"You think..." she started slowly and faded off. "Do you think she'll still be mad at me?"

He frowned at the question wondering if she was too sleepy to make sense. "Do I think who will still be mad at you?"

"Paige," Victoria answered.

"I don't think she was ever mad at you. She's just hurt," he said, running the brush along the fine hairs near the nape of her neck and saw, more than felt, the shiver that overtook her.

Victoria didn't respond to his reply so he kept going. "Paige is a great deal stronger than you give her credit for."

"It's not that I don't think her strong. She's one of the strongest women I know."

"Then why the coddling?"

"I didn't want to put anything more on her," Victoria said sounding clipped and more alert.

"I think there was more to it. Do you regret finding out that you two are related?"

Victoria turned to look him in the eyes. "No. I'm happy with the discovery. I just…" Victoria reached for the brush and Richard pulled it out of her reach.

"You just what?" he asked, looking at her face fall.

"What if she isn't pleased about having me as a relative."

Richard was stunned for a moment that insecurity would be behind Victoria's hesitation to share the news with Paige. "Why wouldn't she be pleased? Paige seems to love family. Look how she embraced Vivian."

"That's different. Vivian is her daughter and they have a lot in common."

"True," he said, turning his wife back around so he could continue his slow ministrations. "But there is one person you all have in common now," he said.

"Me and how overbearing I can be?" Victoria said with a level of self-deprecation he was unaccustomed to hearing from her.

He patted her on the head with the back of the brush to shock her out of her melancholy mood. "No, and stop it. You are being hard on yourself." He watched as she rubbed the spot where he'd lightly thumped her. "I mean God. You have God in common." When her shoulders slumped, he tried again.

"If Paige could know you for only a few days and see the beauty God and myself see in you, how much more beauty do you think she would see in you then?"

Victoria turned to him again. "So you don't think she would be too disappointed in having me as a grandmother?"

"Really? You see who she has now for a grandmother. I think you are definitely a few steps up on the food chain."

The sound of Victoria's throaty laugh lightened his heart, and he leaned in to kiss her forehead.

"That wasn't very nice, Richard," she said, sounding as if she were trying to subdue her laughter.

"I call them like I see them, Victoria." He watched as she went quiet for a few moments.

"You really think she'll be okay with the fact that we are related?"

"Yes. I do," he said, lifting her chin with his forefinger and looking into her penny-colored eyes. "I'm afraid you still owe her an apology for not letting her know right away.

"Yes, I know." She took a deep breath. "Vivian seemed excited that the three of us are related by blood."

"That's because Vivian is wise for her age and has discernment. She is also sensitive and seems to know exactly what makes people happy." He pulled back to take in Victoria's whole face. "You ever notice how spot on she is?"

He could tell his comment caught her attention. Her eyes went glassy as if she were remembering something.

"What are you thinking?" he asked.

Her eyes came back into focus and she gave a small smile. "Just recalling something Vivian once said. "Rachael was still alive and everyone was here for Christmas. I think Vivian was eight. It was Christmas Eve and getting close to the time when Vivian would have to go to bed." Victoria sat sideways in her chair so she could look at him more comfortably. "I could see her starting to get restless, and I offered to take her to bed and read *The Night Before Christmas* to her." She chuckled, and he felt his lips tip at the edges in answer to the sound.

"She had so many questions about the story. What were sugar plums? Why did they have mice? It didn't take long for me to realize that Rachael had never read the book to her. I felt a moment of pain at what I thought of as a family ritual coming to an end."

She paused for a moment, and Richard just waited for her to continue.

"I asked her what Rachael read to her, and she said they read the story of Jesus' birth since it was his birthday they were celebrating. I asked her if it was Jesus' birthday, why did we give each other presents and not Him." Victoria looked Richard in the eyes. "Do you know what she said to me?"

Richard smiled but shook his head instead of voicing his "no."

"She said that we give Him the present of letting Him into our hearts and listening to Him, so we can also give Him the gift of sharing His story with others when they are ready. We could give Him a gift everyday if we wanted to." I was a little surprised that she had been able to grasp that concept at such a young age. I figured Rachael had been reading and talking to her about Jesus' birthday and the gift of Him since she was first able to remember."

He saw her eyes go unfocused and allowed her the moment to lose herself in her thought.

"About a year later I mentioned the conversation I had with Vivian to Rachael because we were talking about them coming to visit again. I told her how Vivian had answered my question, and I was confused when she went quiet. I asked her what was wrong. She told me nothing was wrong, but as much as she wanted to take credit for teaching Vivian the part about giving Jesus the gift of sharing His story with others, she couldn't. Vivian had a special relationship with God, and she had no problem talking about it to people."

He saw a sheen over take Victoria's eyes before she averted her gaze. "I was so angry and filled with bitterness toward God and His people I couldn't see just how special my children were. I think that's another reason why I'm hesitant about seeing Paige's reaction. I wasn't exactly grandmotherly toward her when we met." She took a deep breath, letting it out slowly.

"The day of her wedding I kind of tried to talk her out of marrying Brandon." Richard's mood dipped. He ran her words back through his mind hoping he'd heard her wrong. When the same words came back to him he asked her to confirm what she'd said.

"I went up to her room and had a small last-minute chat with her. I wanted to make sure she understood what she was getting into." She went on quickly when she saw his frown deepened. "I'd received some information about Brandon's health, and I wanted to make sure she was going into it with her eyes open."

Richard knew Victoria too well to believe that she would leave it at that. She was opinionated and had no qualms in sharing said opinion and backing it up with advice. "Were you just gaging her knowledge of the situation she was stepping into on her wedding day or trying to discourage her from marrying Brandon because you found out information they hadn't shared with anyone else?" Richard saw that she felt bad enough to look ashamed. He wanted to shake his head, but it would do nothing to help her through her doubt.

"How did she take it?" he asked trying to keep his voice level.

"Not well," Victoria said, running her fingers across her forehead. A sure sign of distress. "As you see, she completely ignored me and married him." She gave him a wan smile.

"Why'd you do it?" he asked already knowing. "Why did you wait until the day of her wedding to try to talk her out of marrying Brandon?"

She was quiet for a moment then heaved a sigh. "At first I couldn't get a hold of her but that isn't the whole reason. I think I knew she would go through with it no matter what I said, but I felt the need to warn her. To let her know that the road she was choosing wasn't going to be easy. That watching someone you love die is harder than it sounds. I wanted to give her an out."

"You were trying to protect her in your own psychotic way," he said only half serious.

She looked up at him startled by his words and stared at him until he gave her a small grin. Then she shoved him. "I almost thought you were serious."

"I almost was," he said with a small snort. "There aren't too many sane people who will do that right before a person is supposed to get married? Most people. Well let's not talk about most people." He waved his hand in a dismissive gesture. "I would consider it inappropriate," he said needing to get the words off of his chest. "She obviously had given it some thought. She was marrying the man already knowing he was battling cancer. She'd made up her mind the moment she forgave Brandon for trying to decide her future with him for her."

"Yes." Victoria's head came up in the wilful way he was used to seeing. "She said something like that."

"Well, good for her," he said more to himself than to her. "I think if Paige can forgive you for your interference in her relationship with Brandon, she will forgive you for being insecure. But you may have to promise her that you'll stop trying to make life-altering decisions for her."

Victoria's shoulder's sagged farther, and he wanted to wrap his arms around her and send the world away, but Antonio would arrive sometime the next day and Paige a couple of days after that. There was no more time to waste.

"I know this hasn't been an easy road for you. It hasn't been for most of the people in our family, but one thing I am sure of is that we persevere. Now that you are on God's side and not just your own the road may be no less bumpy, but your faith is, in a way, your shock absorber. If you let the Holy Spirit guide you, you'll be amazed at how many potholes and wrong turns you can avoid.

"Okay, enough with the road analogy. I get it." She stood up and placed her hands on his thighs so she could lean into him. He watched as her eyes volleyed back and forth between his. He wasn't sure what she was looking for, but he had his own agenda as he inhaled her fresh scent of soap and moisturizer then lifted a hand to smooth a stray strand of hair away from her face.

"I wish you could see yourself as I do." He didn't mean for his words to sound as forlorn as they did, but it was such a tragedy to watch his wife who, to his knowledge, could accomplish anything she put her mind to, doubt her value in the eyes of her family.

He placed his hand on her forearms to steady her as he made enough room to stand. "Let's check on the girls then come back here for some pillow talk." He helped her don her robe.

"Pillow talk?" she asked

"Yes. A little discussion of what we will and won't share tomorrow and then if you aren't too tired we can do a little discussing of other things," he said, leading her to the door of their room.

"Like what?" she asked, but by the tone in her voice he could tell she knew exactly what he was suggesting.

"Well." He exhaled in exaggeration. "If you must know, let me give you a hint." He leaned down and kissed her with a small display of the love he felt for her. When he pulled back his ego took no small pride in acknowledging the dazed look in her eyes.

When the look cleared he nodded his head. "Mmmm-hmmm," he murmured and flashed her a wicked grin.

Victoria let out a giggle. "You are incorrigible."

"No, I just love my wife," he said sincerely.

Victoria flashed him a soft smile, and he led her out of the room.

Richard stared up at he ceiling with Victoria's warmth snuggled up next to him. She'd fallen asleep with her head on his shoulder but had since moved back to her pillow. Her legs, however, were still intertwined with his. The position which usually helped lull him to sleep did little to coax the sandman this night. His mind was restless, bouncing back and forth between his last interaction with

Antonio and what was to come. There was a niggling thought that wouldn't leave him alone, and he knew better than to force it.

He waited quietly for the pieces to come together as he mentally sifted through the files he had on Melanie, Grace, Paige, Brian, and Antonio. So much had happened since Vivian's accident. It was as if a dam of information and coincidental situations came forth. The timing was... convenient.

He nearly sat up in bed. The timing was too convenient. He started sifting through their conversation with Antonio trying to think of facts that he and Victoria had unwittingly given to him and information he gave them that could have been derived from medical records or files that he gained access to due to his influence with the right people.

It came to him in a rush that made him happy he was laying down. Antonio was on a fact-finding mission, and he and Victoria were providing him with almost everything he wanted regarding Paige and Vivian.

He continued to go through the information in his head feeling both energized and at ease.

He wished he hadn't dismissed his first gut feeling. He considered for a moment that only some of the information he'd received over the last year was planted or doctored and that he and Victoria were being manipulated and tricked into sharing information with Antonio. It seemed plausible given the timing.

With all of the information Antonio told them he had on the family, Richard couldn't understand why the man would alert them of his previous fact-finding mission. He could have confronted Paige and Melanie himself. Sure, it looked and sounded commendable that Antonio would come to them first regarding their grandchildren, but Richard wasn't buying it. Men in Antonio's position always seemed to have hidden agendas.

It didn't matter whether or not Antonio could be trusted, Richard wouldn't be sharing any information with him. He would warn the girls to be kind and welcoming to their great-grandfather but maybe not be too open.

Sleep finally came upon Richard in the early morning and he welcomed it. It was going to be a long day if he was right in his new assessment of the situation.

Late the next morning Richard watched the luxury car come up the long drive from his perch on top of Mayven, his black bay stallion. He slowly walked Mayven back to the barn and dismounted. Richard preferred to cool him down with a brush and a rub himself but wanted to be next to Victoria when Antonio's car made it to the house.

After a few strokes and cooing he handed the reins over to Martin and strode back to the house to alert Victoria of their guest's arrival. He was happy he chose to exercise Mayven that morning. The concentration needed to take the horse through its paces was just what he needed to get his mind off the introductions that were to take place.

It also gave him a chance to build a strategy around the requests he'd made to both Victoria and his great-granddaughters.

"We won't be rude, but we don't know him, and from what I'm gathering neither do you all. I wish the title meant that we could trust him, but from what everyone has said, we can't," she finished with a shrug. Richard looked over to Vivian and her shrug mimicked her sister's.

"I'm proud of how mature the two of you are, but I'm sorry you have been exposed to the parts of life that have given you both so much wisdom at such a young age."

"My mom used to say, wisdom is a friend and a tool. She'll let you know when to lean on her," Vivian said, looking at him.

Richard shook his head as he came out of the memory of that conversation. Those girls were something special. He knew in his heart that they would come away from all of this relatively unaffected, but he would do whatever he could to keep what ill effects were derived from this meeting at a minimum.

The first person he came upon when entering his house was Mason who had arrived earlier that morning from the hotel he was staying in almost twenty miles away.

"How're you doing this morning?" he asked after giving Mason a half hug.

"As good as can be expected with what we're facing today. Victoria told me you had some new concerns about Antonio Sable. I thought I would wait for you to see what you might need from me." Richard couldn't help lifting an eyebrow at Mason's comment. Victoria had spoken to him in a civilized way? Wonders never cease.

"Antonio should be driving up any second," he said looking out of the window. "Just know that I no longer believe he is everything he says he is, and that he might be using us to gain facts instead of what he said he wanted to do."

Richard had to give it to Mason. He barely blinked at Richard's admission.

"Sure. I'll just take your lead," Mason said, placing his hands in his pants pocket. "Have you talked to Paige about this new development?"

"No. I'll give them a call tonight when she's back in Los Angeles. She had a meeting with a new publishing company in New York, yesterday. I'd rather not call her until I see how today goes."

Mason nodded but didn't respond. Richard would have followed his statement with a question about how Mason would deal with Paige and Brandon's presence, but there was the sound of a car rolling over the cobblestone-lined circular drive. Knowing his wife liked to make an entrance, he didn't call for her before opening the front door and walking out with Mason on his heels.

He watched as the black luxury sedan made the turn and stopped at the bottom of the steps. The driver got of the car giving him a small nod of the head and moved to open the back door. Antonio Sable, dressed in a pair of casual, brown slacks, a white shirt, and a lightweight tan jacket, alighted from the car and glanced around before meeting Richard's gaze.

Richard pasted what he hoped was a smile of welcome on his face and walked down the stairs to shake Antonio's hand while the driver went around to the back of the car to retrieve the man's luggage.

"How was your trip?" he asked.

"Uneventful which is always good," Antonio said, returning his handshake then turning to Mason who had slowly made his way down the steps.

"Antonio Sable, this is Mason Jenson, Vivian's father," Richard said, making the introductions.

"It's good to meet you, Mason."

"Hello," Mason said in return. The lack of his mutual greeting wasn't lost on Richard.

"Is that all you have?" Richard asked, gesturing to Antonio's one piece of luggage.

"Yes. With all the travel I do I've learned how to pack light," he said, picking up the medium-sized suitcase the driver had left at his side. "But then you know what I mean since you travel quite a bit, yourself."

"Yes. That's true," Richard said, leading the way back up the stairs. It was too early to start analyzing every single comment that came out of the man's mouth. Anyone with a calendar could see he traveled a great deal as a philanthropist.

"I'll show you to your room so you can freshen up. Lunch will be in a half hour," he said briefly glancing over his shoulder at Antonio. "Nathan will come to get you so you don't get lost."

There. He thought he handled that well. It was welcoming and to the point. It might have been the fact that they were on his turf, but Antonio didn't look as threatening as he remembered.

"Thank you," Antonio said as Richard opened the door to the grand entryway. "I watched as the car made it's way through the drive. You have a beautiful property here. It looks like you have been quite successful."

Richard sent Antonio a wan smile. "Thank you. I'll let Victoria know what you said. She almost single-handedly brought this place into the twenty-first century," Richard said with pride.

"She was always a remarkable girl," Antonio said amicably. Richard clenched his teeth and took a deep breath to keep his voice level.

"Yes. Victoria is an incredible *woman.*" He nodded and led Antonio up the stairs to the guest room Victoria had chosen for him.

Once they were in the room Richard looked around to see if there might be anything he could do, but he knew Victoria had taken care of all the details and double-checked everything in this room, especially knowing Antonio would be staying in it. She'd picked the one overlooking the front of the house and the west fields.

Richard had always wondered how Victoria knew what would give their guests the most picturesque views when she was out in the fields or making plans for the landscape. The rooms on the other side of the house had views of the garden and the southeast field which were full of color most of the year.

"Well, if you need anything, press the intercom button on your phone and someone will answer." Antonio's gaze followed Richard's hand gesture.

"Impressive," Antonio noted.

Richard shrugged. "It's a big house. That is more out of efficiency especially when we have visitors."

"Thank you very much, Richard. I appreciate you opening your home to me," Antonio said, looking one hundred percent sincere.

"You're welcome. I'll see you in a half an hour." Richard nodded before walking back out of the room.

If he didn't distrust the man so much, he might like him. Antonio seemed appreciative and wholly complimentary regarding his accommodations and their home. Richard tried to shrug off the seemingly innocent comment about Victoria when he and Antonio made their way downstairs.

Mason met him at the bottom. "I've changed my mind," Mason whispered as they continued on to the sunroom where Victoria told him she would be entertaining the girls.

"About what?"

"I would like to take you up on your offer to stay here on the farm," Mason commented, leaning close as they walked.

Richard paused, turning to look at Mason closely. "What about your aversion for sleeping under my roof?"

Mason cast him a disparaging look. "My daughter overrides any feelings I have about this house, past and present included."

Richard nodded. "Very well." He resumed walking, all the while smiling to himself about the bet he'd won against his wife. "If you check out of your hotel and get your things after dinner, I'll make sure your room is ready."

As he stepped into the sunroom his wife looked up at him expectantly. He could tell she was nervous and tried to answer the question in her eyes with his smile. He walked behind the couch she and their great-granddaughters were sitting on and placed a kiss on her head. He caught sight of the photo album on her lap. It was of Rachael when she was either seven or eight. Her two front teeth had slightly outgrown the rest, and her flaming-red hair was in two French braids with a part down the middle of her scalp. His heart gave a small lurch. She was such a beautiful child.

He looked up to see that Mason had taken the seat across from them and was relieved.

He thought the girls were engrossed in the pictures when Vivian spoke up. "Has our guest arrived?" He peered down at her upturned face. She was playing possum.

259

"Yes. He is getting settled in and will be down for lunch in about twenty minutes."

"Was he nice?" she asked, not taking her eyes from his.

He thought about it for a second. "Yes, he was. He was very nice."

"Mmm," she murmured before returning her attention to the album.

He was about to ask her what she meant when Gladys began talking without lifting her head from the book. "Vivian has been talking about him almost nonstop. She wondered if he would be snobbish, nice, or real."

"Snobbish or nice aren't real?"

"If he was real he would have taken the time when you two were alone and confessed why he was really here."

"But you don't know if what I said was the absolute truth. It is just a conclusion I made after going over some files because of a feeling I had." He came around the couch to sit on the love seat closest to Vivian and she looked over at him.

"I trust your instincts. Besides, you wouldn't have said anything to Gladys and me if you didn't think it was important."

She had him there. He glanced at Mason who was sporting a proud grin.

"Come on, girls. Go get freshened up before lunch. I barely noticed it, but I don't think you two would want to meet your great-grandfather smelling like the horses whose stable you helped Malcolm clean this morning." Richard saw Vivian send her father a conspiratorial look, and he shook his head to the negative almost imperceptibly. She took a deep breath and waited for Gladys to get up from the couch as well and they left the room.

"So, what was he like?" Victoria asked the moment the twins' footsteps couldn't be heard anymore.

"He's about he same as he was in his office. Courteous, reserved, and observant," he said, leaning back.

260

Victoria looked over at Mason who looked back at her warily. "What did you think?"

Richard answered for him. "Martha will need to make up the green room. Mason will be taking us up on our offer."

He watched Victoria glance between the two of them, her eyes wide. "That bad?"

"No, I just would feel better if Vivian or Gladys could reach me as quickly as they wanted." He rubbed his forehead for a moment before continuing, "Vivian has been very sensitive lately. I think Paige and Brandon's situation is affecting her."

"It's affecting us all," Victoria replied.

Before Mason could respond, Richard jumped in.

"I believe Mason meant that the bond between Vivian and Paige is strong especially since they pray together almost every morning."

"Paige was a little busy last week. They only talked a couple of times. Vivian's afraid she's pulling away."

"No. I'm sure that isn't the reason. Paige is just under a lot of stress right now," Victoria said sounding defensive.

Richard saw Mason's expression change and knew the few moments of comradery was in jeopardy. He opened his mouth hoping what would come out could delay or even stop Mason but he was too late.

"If you would defend Paige so quickly when it comes to how she feels about her family, why would you purposely keep information about her family from her?"

Richard wanted to groan and place his hands over his eyes to keep from seeing what would happen next.

"Mr. Jenson." He heard his wife begin and knew he had to shut it down.

"Mason," he started over the sound of his wife's voice. "I will not sit here and let you accuse my wife of malicious intent."

Mason turned to him. "Really? You were the one who told me she wanted to keep what Antonio shared with you two a secret."

Richard took a deep breath wishing he'd left good enough alone. "First of all, young man, I took you into my confidence, which by the way, means either keep what I was telling you to yourself or only share it with whom I consent to. Secondly, the reason I told you anything was because I wanted to respect your position as Vivian's father." He turned to his wife whose eyes he'd been avoiding. "A parent has the right to know what type of environment his or her child is entering into." He looked back at Mason a little tired after his tirade.

Richard threw up his hands. "Lunch is in about fifteen minutes." He glanced at his watch.

"You two need to get a handle on your anger and resentment before you come to the table otherwise Sable can use it against us if he is looking for any weaknesses," he said as he got up and pointed at them. "Talk about it. No. Better yet. Pray about it. Whatever you decide to do, for Vivian and Gladys' sakes, come to the table ready to conduct yourselves like a caring family."

Richard walked out of the room hoping to gain back a modicum of the peace he would need to get through the rest of the afternoon.

As Richard looked around the lunch table at his family and Antonio he prayed he was wrong about the man's ulterior motives. After everything they'd gone through and were still going through he wanted his family to heal and eventually be whole. They didn't need an outsider with ties to Brenda aka Grace to cause any more havoc.

He silently observed Antonio's reactions and interactions with his great-granddaughters and Mason, who seemed to be behaving himself. He glanced at his wife and her stare caught his eyes. He saw uncertainty and what he could only interpret as an apologetic look in her eyes. He gave her a small smile as a piece offering.

This was his family. They were his treasure, and he would use every bit of his influence and money to keep them safe, but he hoped his walk with God would show him an even better way.

CHAPTER 18

Melanie fought the temptation to look over her shoulder again. She even tried to flatten her hands against her purse to keep from wringing them together. She took a deep breath letting it out slowly and would have taken another if Marc's hand on hers didn't draw her attention from the paranoia that had been gripping her since they got off the bus in La Junta, Colorado.

She hadn't been this close to Colorado Springs since she'd been spirited away twenty-seven years ago. If she could have avoided it for another twenty-seven years she would have, but in order to get the peace she wanted for herself and her family she'd had to go back where it all started.

She pushed the pain of missing her girls to the back of her mind. They were as safe as they could be together.

Marc squeezed her hand, bringing her out of her reverie. "Mel, you have to calm down. We lost your mother's men in Pittsburgh." His warm brown eyes bore into hers, imploring her to relax. "I told you I could take care of this for you." He leaned in to continue but Melanie placed a hand to his lips.

"I have to take care of this. I'm the only one that can make this right."

"No, you're not. There are people who have been trained for this."

She stared at him, knowing she was being unfair, but she was responsible for a great deal of what was going on, and she needed to end it.

"They don't know all of the details, and I'm not willing to risk telling any one person, everything." She touched his chest. "I'm sorry. I know you want to keep me safe and far away from all of this. I also know what you are risking by coming with me," she said, lifting a hand to his cheek. "I love and adore you. You've been with me from the beginning, so I recognize that I wouldn't have been able to persuade you to stay behind nor could I slip away from you. You must realize that if I didn't come here, this whole situation would end up on our proverbial doorstep."

"I know someone needs to intervene, but it doesn't necessarily have to be you," Marc responded while leaning his cheek into her hand. "I wish you'd trust me with this."

"I do trust you, more than anyone. I am just trying to keep the fallout from all of this to a minimum."

Marc let out a long-suffering sigh. "What do you want me to do?"

"Just continue to be here with me." She gazed at him feeling an overwhelming surge of warmth and love. He had been with her through thick and thin. Theirs was not a typical relationship. When she'd first noticed him she had no clue he was protecting her. Though she was attracted to him she was too afraid to even consider having a normal life.

"Besides you've done more than enough. When you get a chance, please tell Freeman thank you for the heads-up. I'm sorry I tried to talk you out of continuing to use surveillance on Antonio. It looks like it finally paid off." She smiled softly at him wishing she could find another way to show him her gratitude, but she didn't want to bring any attention to them. "I can't imagine what I would have done if Victoria and Richard turned up on our doorstep with questions." She shook her head. "That woman is relentless just like her investigators." She sat up straighter. "Maybe when this is all over I should send Freeman a fruit basket. Do you think he likes mangos?"

Marc chuckled. "You don't need to send him anything. It's his job to watch Antonio, his family, and his businesses for anything out of the norm. Victoria and Richard's visit was anything but normal, and it probably made Freeman's week to have something to report." He turned fully to her.

"You knew this was inevitable. The old man's rule wouldn't stand forever. That's why he put some contingencies in place."

"It was a messy business—your mother paying off the nurse to switch Paige's child like that. To this day I don't know what she was thinking."

Melanie blew out a deep breath. She knew exactly what her mother was doing. It didn't matter that they were running from modern-day Italian mobs. Her mother was determined to make the Sable family pay for their patriarch's offense toward her.

She was bent on single-handedly scattering that family to different edges of the earth all because she was considered good enough to bed, but not good enough to marry. Melanie had gotten the whole sordid story from Marc before they were married. She remembered being homeschooled until her family had moved to Colorado Springs. The restrictions were stifling at times, but she hadn't known any other life.

It wasn't just Grace's plan to separate them; she wanted to destroy them. Marc told her that it was Grace's attempt on Brian's life that had gotten her kicked out of witness protection. If it weren't for Luca Sable, Melanie's life would have been cut short by one of the owners of the organizations Grace dared to testify against. She had a lot of things to thank the old man for, but just as much to blame him for, so she figured they were just about even.

You don't have to thank me, Melanie. It's my job to keep you safe, but it's my purpose in life to keep you happy whether you like the way I do it or not.

The engine of the bus they'd been sitting in finally turned over. They were about to make their way to Colorado Springs. The place where she gained and lost so much.

"Rest. I've got you." Marc slid his arm behind her shoulder and pressed her head into his shoulder. "You've been up for almost thirty-six hours." She saw the concern in his eyes and wished she could comfort him, but it wouldn't last. They had way too much work to do before she could be comforted.

She let her body go slack against him, closed her eyes, and tried to rest. It was the only thing she could give him right now.

There was no sound but it didn't strike her as odd until she reached the white-picket fence. Her hand reached for the latch and the gate opened soundlessly. The grass in the small front yard was overgrown, sweeping at her knees in a timeless hello.

She walked up to the door and found it ajar. Pushing it open she expected a creak, but once again was met with silence. The atmosphere of the house came alive as she moved throughout the interior of the house. By the time she reached the kitchen she half expected to see her mother at the sink which was odd since she never remembered seeing her mother in the kitchen.

She looked out the window at the house next door. The gray clouds that had been hovering over the whole town now seemed to have landed over its roof. The once beige paint was now a dirty brown, and she forced herself to look away.

Moving on toward the back of the house she took note of the couch in the living room. Something was wrong. That was the old couch. The one she and her dad used to watch television from when he wasn't deployed. The feeling of foreboding flooded her senses and she couldn't get a full breath. She raced out of the room and up the stairs to her room and came to a dead stop in the doorway. Air filled her lungs as she took in the crib next to her bed. If the crib was here so was her baby. She hadn't waited too long to come back.

She took one step then another until she could just look over the edge of the crib. That's when it occurred to her that she could hear a rustling sound accompanied by gurgling. She took one more step, bringing herself close enough to peer over the side. She held her breath before scanning the inside of the crib and was gripped with horror when all that lay on the mattress was a blue blanket. She opened her mouth to scream but was jostled awake.

She sat up disoriented and was relieved to see Marc staring at her. She sat back in her seat, laid her head on the rest and turned her head toward her guardian and husband.

"You were sleeping well until that last minute. Do you want to talk about it?"

She shook her head only able to catch faint snatches of her dream but she didn't need it in clear focus. She'd had it off and on for over twenty-six years, and it took a little piece of her soul every time. "Just more of the same." She looked beyond him and out the window.

"Where are we?"

"About twenty minutes outside of Colorado Springs," he replied.

"What time is it?"

"Eleven thirty. I called a hotel near the bus stop and booked us a room… if we get there first," he added when she opened her mouth.

"Sorry. I know you know better than I do how to stay under the radar. I'm just wrung out. Did you sleep?"

"No, baby. I told you I would watch over you. I'll get some rest at the hotel. Hopefully, they'll have an all-night restaurant nearby and we can get something to eat before we go to bed for the night."

Melanie nodded her agreement and watched beyond him as the darkness of the rural area they were traveling through gave way to city lights. How many times had she seen this view as a child. It was a new and exciting place. A fresh start with her dad's new military position and the chance for new friends—well, friends, period. Just before hitting town the car veered off the main road and they rode some distance on a street that looked all too familiar. Why was it that the closer you got to military bases the more the landscape looked the same? With her eyes glued to the window she noted the change in terrain from tall grass and dense foliage to gravel and asphalt then concrete. To an impressionable eleven-year-old who adored her father and everything he stood for it was a dream come true to finally move into base housing where she and her mother would be closer to him. It would be months before she realized the distance between her father and his family had more to do with her mother than geography.

A month after their arrival she was enrolled in the grade school for that area and with much trepidation and anxious anticipation she attended her first day of school in a grade she was secretly two years too old for and met Brian Grossenberg who would be both her best friend and greatest heartache.

Melanie had begged her mother after the two years of homeschooling to enroll her in her true grade, but her mom told her there were some subjects Melanie just didn't perform to Grace's satisfaction. She didn't want to rely on the tests and thought it better if Melanie repeat them, but Grace did concede to hiding Melanie's true age, so she wouldn't be teased as she was before being homeschooled.

Most of the children were military brats with one or both parents serving, so she didn't worry about being the only child who may not have a parent participate in the parent career days or attend a recital. Melanie's insecurity didn't stem from what she saw in the mirror. Her mother constantly complimented her on her thick, dark hair with loose curls and almost gold-colored eyes that slanted up on the sides. Her cocoa-colored complexion matched her mother's who told her their coloring made it easy for them to stay young looking if they took care of their skin. Her insecurity came from the fact that she was starting to develop though she wasn't big for her age. She would do anything possible to keep it a secret, even wear layers.

The third week of school Melanie began riding the school bus because her mother took a job at the general hospital. She couldn't remember being more frightened than the moment she walked up the stairs and looked down the rows of seats filled with other kids. She moved forward, hoping someone would take pity on her and make room. Her face burned brighter the closer she came to the end of the bus but to her extreme relief a quiet-looking boy with dark, knowing eyes and incredibly long lashes made room for her. She smiled and offered a whispered thanks and he accepted it just as quietly. They were a few streets away when she asked him why he made room for her. He told her he'd been in the same position a few weeks before and didn't care for it much. She had a feeling the shrug he added to his admission was for her benefit and she relaxed.

"My name is Grace Melanie, but everyone calls me Melanie or Mel for short," she offered shyly.

He held out his hand. "My name's Brian." He stared at her for a moment while they shook hands. "Nice to meet you, Grace Melanie," he said then he smiled and stole a small piece of her heart.

Melanie came back to the present with the sound of the bus coming to a screeching halt. She refocused on Marc and smiled wanly.

"Good or bad?" he asked as he usually did when she spaced out.

"Good," she replied somberly.

She didn't see him move but felt the pad of his thumb rub against the underside of her chin to her jaw. His touch plus the tender look in his eyes made hers burn with unshed tears.

"Don't forget that I'm here with you," Marc said gazing into her eyes.

Unable to speak around the lump in her throat, Melanie nodded and touched her forehead to his.

Their room was sparse, but it was clean. The dinner Marc was able to round up came from an all-night diner. She tried to leave as little as possible on her plate but just being in this city ratcheted up her anxiety level, making it hard for her to build an appetite for anything. After showering she crawled into bed next to Marc, happy not to be moving, and immediately fell asleep.

Tuesday afternoon, Grace Melanie Miller walked into a small bank on the outskirts of Colorado Springs and submitted the requisite form of identification and filled out the information needed to gain access to a safety deposit box that had been set up just in case of the situation she was in.

Since the ID she carried stated that she was single, Marc grudgingly stayed out front in the car. Melanie was led downstairs to a small vault with an even smaller room filled with lockboxes. She didn't know they still had rooms like this.

She was led to a corner cubicle by the attendant and left there with the box for privacy. Melanie sat down because her knees wouldn't hold her anymore. She had to wait until her hands stopped shaking before she could open the lid. Once she opened it she could never go back. The information contained would not only make her vulnerable to her mother and those with more greed than love in their hearts, it could put the lives of the people she loved most in jeopardy as well.

She took one last deep breath, opened the box and pulled out the contents that would bring her face-to-face with her past.

CHAPTER 19

It was the first time in a while that she felt like a writer. She knew there was no one right way to feel, but the way the words were flowing reminded her of how she would pound out books last year and it was refreshing. Even the quick trip to New York with Carmen to sign the documents for her new contract yesterday didn't deserve all of the credit though it left a lasting impression.

Her hotel room had been opulent, and the hotel restaurant was the first four-star restaurant she'd been to since her book-signing tour the previous year. She was surprised that she hadn't missed it, but when she thought about it she had gained so much more.

She spoke to Brandon as she got ready for bed. She'd called him when she landed but he texted her that he was in the middle of a meeting. When he called back she was at dinner. She missed him. It wasn't so much the hours that had gone by without seeing him as it was the realization of the distance that spanned between them.

"Hi beautiful. How's it going?" his deep voice rang through the phone speaker.

"Great. I'm crawling into this huge, comfortable-looking bed with a very full belly wishing you were here to curl up with."

"You always say stuff like that when we are miles apart, or there is no way for me to get away from work." His previous seductive tone turned into a pout."

"Did you really forget last Monday night?" she asked and listened as the other end of the line went quiet for a moment. She started counting down from five. When she hit two he responded.

"Was that the picnic in the living room or the sundaes for dinner?"

"So much for making memories. You can't even remember the day."

"I might not be able to remember the day, but I do remember each night very well," his voice pitched low and so did her stomach.

"I rest my case," she said saucily. "You just proved yourself wrong. but just to keep you from pouting, how about we have another picnic when I get home?"

"Definitely. I'll buy the ice cream and syrup on the way home tomorrow."

She laughed at his antics. "Hey now. You don't want me too tired to fly on Wednesday."

Brandon interrupted her. "We're flying, and we are going on Thursday in Richard's company's jet."

Paige wasn't sure if she heard him right. "What?"

"I returned Richard's call this morning. He let me know that Victoria asked him to send the jet so I could come with you."

Paige didn't know how to feel. She didn't like being beholden to Victoria with the way she felt about her, but she did want Brandon with her when she met this man.

"Do you want to go?" she asked, not completely sure which way she wanted him to answer.

"Yes. I told him Dominy and his family were visiting, and he told me they had more than enough room for all of us, so you have a buffer in Dominy and Nicky."

"Oh, okay," she responded just to have something to say.

"You don't sound okay. Did you change your mind?"

"No. I still want to go, but it's hard to confront someone the way I want to when you use their transportation."

"Yes, but it also shows that Victoria isn't trying to avoid you and may not have kept the information about Antonio from you for the reason you believe."

She felt even more of her anger dissipate where Victoria was concerned. If Brandon kept it up, she would have no anger left to fuel her rant when she saw the meddling woman.

It didn't take speaking to her psychologist for her to know that it was hurt fueling her anger, but she felt more comfortable with the latter around Victoria. She couldn't trust her not to take advantage of that weakness.

"Paige. You still there?"

"Yes." She couldn't think of anything else to say. She knew what she was supposed to feel right now; what would have been the right thing to say to make herself look good, but she was so tired of being the "good" one. The one that always sought to do and say the right thing. She found peace in it, but right now the thought of surrendering over the anger she so wanted to purge by taking a piece out of Victoria did not bring her peace. It only brought her pain and she was tired of the pain.

"What do you think? Would you rather me not go?" he asked quietly.

The uncertainty in his voice caused her to wince. This was so messed up. She wanted to growl.

"I need you with me." She sat on the edge of the bed looking at the phone in her hands. "When's our flight?" She didn't even try to sound happy. It was what it was.

"Paige. We don't have to go at all. You don't need to accept anything from her, but I know you want answers, and I personally believe the air needs to be cleared. I'll support you either way."

Seriously. She thought. Exhaling through some of the frustration. *The man was ridiculously wonderful.* He was so much more than she could have imagined. She closed her eyes and took a deep breath working to get her emotions under control.

"No. Let's all take the jet. It will make things easier all around. I'm sure Nicky will be more comfortable too," she said raising the inflections in her voice.

"Are you sure?"

"Yes. I'm sure." She changed the subject. "Have you eaten yet? I left some makings for tacos in the meat drawer of the fridge."

"I found it. Paige, if..." She cut him off.

"Baby, you know, the flight really has my internal clock off-kilter. Carmen and I stuffed ourselves on high-priced food, compliments of my new publishing company. I'm really tired. I just wanted to call you before I went to bed. Call Richard back. Let him know that we will take his offer."

"I want to let you know that I'm aware of what you're doing, but I really want to ride in a private jet, so I'll make that call as you so sweetly requested, and I'll let you get some sleep."

She wasn't sure her smile was from relief at realizing that he would let it go or his attempt to make her laugh. At the end it didn't really matter. She might actually go to sleep with a smile on her face.

"Sweet dreams, baby," she said through her smile.

"Oh, Lady Menagerie left a message for you. She wants you to call her. I think she tried to call you on your cell. Have you checked your messages?"

"No, but I guess I will now. When was the last time you spoke to Pastor Lawrence?" she asked as she turned down her bed.

"Maybe a couple of weeks ago. It was the night after Melanie left. I told you I went by their place to talk to Pastor Lawrence."

. "Yes. I remember. Okay. I'll give her a call." She slipped between the sheets and sighed.

Brandon's laugh came through the receiver. "I love you. Sleep well."

"I will. You do the same. I'll call you before I board my flight tomorrow."

"Okay, Good night," Brandon replied before disconnecting their call.

Paige put her phone on the bedside table and slipped lower beneath the covers. She sighed again and settled in for a very comfortable sleep.

Carmen smiled over at her in the elevator on the way up to the company's floor. She was impeccably outfitted in a beige-and-black, lightweight suit with a pencil skirt and pristine pumps. Paige was happy she'd chosen an olive-green, brushed-cotton dress from the choices she'd brought with her. One, it was opposite the beige dress she'd also packed, and two, it felt light and airy. It would not do to sweat through her clothing today.

"You are worth every red cent they want to give you and more," Carmen said with a firmness Paige had grown to expect when she wanted Paige to see things as she did.

"You have worked very hard to get here. Now is not the time to forget the time and sacrifices you have made. Most of the negotiations are done and this should be an hour of signing paperwork, but if they try to retract anything let me speak because other than God and your husband I know your book-writing worth, and it is very valuable." Carmen straightened her jacket as she glanced at the illuminating lights flashing behind the numbers.

"You don't think I know my writing value?" Paige asked, wondering if she should be offended.

"I believe you have an overall understanding of your writing value when it comes to its impact on your readers though you have a small blind spot because you are an author who is very hard on yourself.

I, on the other hand, can see how great you are from a more objective point of view and I know how to translate that into a dollar amount."

Paige smiled and nodded at her. Carmen was definitely feeling herself this morning. "Let me know where to give my review for your great work."

"No need. You gave it to me when you gave me a raise and a bonus," Carmen said with a wink.

"When did I do that?" Paige asked, wondering if she missed something.

"You did when you agreed to sign with this company for almost twenty percent more income."

"Huh." Was all Paige could think of to say before the elevator dinged and the doors opened.

The conference room was luxurious with its mahogany table and like finishes around the room. They had treated her as though what came from her hands was spun gold and she had a hard time keeping her feet on the ground. She tried to remind herself that she was as good as what she delivered to them on any given day.

The group waiting for them at the highly polished conference table were all smiles. There was small talk and no shortage of compliments on Paige's talent with words. If Carmen's smile was anything to go by, the numbers on the contract she was reading were in order. An hour and a half later Paige had signed her name more times than she could count and was now the new owner of a contract to write seven books, two of which drafts were already written. It was Carmen's idea, and Paige was grateful for her foresight. It took the stress out of meeting her first deadline which was in three months.

She'd also discussed self-publishing with Carmen under a pen name the following year but wondered if she was taking on more than she could handle.

Throughout the ride down to the lobby, and in the car back to the hotel Paige worked to wrap her mind around what the company was willing to advance her and give her in royalties. It was so much more money than she'd ever been paid for writing, but God had promised her that if she wrote for Him, He would reward her. She'd worked hard to do her part, and it looked like He was once again keeping His word.

"Congratulations, Mrs. Tatum. You are now a woman who has entered a whole other tax bracket. You might need to buy something to keep from owing a mint," Carmen said as Paige brought her luggage to the door for the bellhop.

"When I get home I'm going to get really pricey takeout and have a picnic on the living room floor," Paige said thinking back to her conversation with Brandon the night before.

"I was thinking more along the lines of a new car or a house, but I guess dinner is a good start." Carmen laughed. "You married people sure are weird," she said as they walked down the hall.

Paige turned to her. "You should give it a try."

They walked through the lobby and were waiting at the door for the town car before Carmen responded, "I might give it a try."

Paige looked at her surprised by her words.

"Someday, when I find the right guy," Carmen continued with a small grin.

Paige bumped shoulders with her. "And you will."

"You think he'll be worth it?" Carmen asked as their car pulled up to the curve.

"Definitely," Paige said smiling as she walked out to meet their car. Then thought about her answer most of the way home.

"Paige," Lady Menagerie's voice came through the phone line making her heartbeat quicken.

"Hi, Lady Menagerie. How are you?"

"I was going to ask you the same question."

"I'm fine."

"Mmmm. Well I at least would have told you the truth."

Paige got up from her desk chair and began pacing.

"Can we talk? Do you have time for breakfast?" Lady Menagerie asked.

"Yes. Um…" She tried to silence her mind from over analyzing the request so she could think of a good time for them to meet. "I'm available all morning. This afternoon I have to start packing because Brandon and I are going to Oklahoma."

"So you decided to go," Lady Menagerie said softly.

Paige was surprised by her response, but it didn't last. "You talked to Brandon."

"Yes. Last night. I'd left messages for you, but I called again when I thought you'd be home. Brandon answered, and we had a nice chat. How about I pick you up at eight thirty."

That was Lady Menagerie; she didn't spend a lot of time on small talk, Paige thought.

"Okay," Paige said, sitting back down at her desk because the anxious energy was suddenly gone.

"I'll see you in an hour."

"Yes. I'll be ready."

When the call ended Paige got back up and left her office to get ready. She almost ran into Brandon as she entered their bedroom. He was dressed for the office.

"Good morning, again," he said, holding her to him.

"Hmm," she responded as she took a deep whiff of his cologne.

"I'm going into work early so I can get off early," he said as he shifted their positions.

"Lady Menagerie just called and invited me to breakfast. I should be home before noon, so I can start packing our bags."

"Like I told you last night. I can help pack when I get home." He rubbed her back through her robe.

She thought again of how much she loved his affectionate side.

"I didn't know Lady Menagerie called back the night before last," she said when he let her go.

He looked into her eyes for a moment. She knew he was assessing her mood. He finally shrugged and ran his fingers along her hairline.

"I must have had something better to say and do when you got home last night." The smirk on his lips brought back memories of how he'd welcomed her home and how they'd celebrated her new publishing contract.

Despite the heat lighting up the tips of her ears she played along. "Really? I'm a little fuzzy on the details. Do you think you could give me a refresher?"

Brandon hooked his fingers in the belt of her robe and pulled her to him. He planted kisses along the column of her neck until he reached her ear. He took a nip of her earlobe and breathed into her ear as he held her close. Her head went reeling with the feelings he was evoking.

"That will have to do for now because I have to go to work, and I can't sit there day dreaming." He moved away and she felt bereft. She tamped down the feeling, letting it join the thousands of others and smiled softly up at him. She straightened his tie and brushed at an imaginary piece of lint from his lapel to delay their separation a few seconds more.

"You okay?" he asked, his brows drawing together.

"Yes." She blinked to mask her feelings. "Just missing you already."

"Awww. 'You're such a romantic. You're good for my ego." He gave her a chaste kiss and walked past her.

"You're going to be the end of that romantic," she whispered so he couldn't hear her. Then she walked to the bath to get dressed.

The first thing Paige thought as she got in Lady Menagerie's car was that her first lady looked good but tired. The woman was almost always impeccably dressed whether she was wearing jeans and a flowing blouse or her Sunday best. Today was no different, but her makeup couldn't disguise the dark circles under her eyes or the obvious weight loss.

Paige reached over and enveloped Lady Menagerie in a hug. Lady Menagerie hugged her back tightly reminding Paige of her first year at Skylight Temple when she'd received hugs from the pastor and his wife a couple of times during every visit. Not used to being hugged it took some getting used to because they wouldn't stop.

"Come on. Let's get going before we steam up the windows. Lord knows we don't need to give people any more to talk about."

Paige didn't laugh, but was happy Lady Menagerie hadn't lost her sense of humor.

Very little was said on the short drive to the restaurant. Paige considered asking Lady Menagerie about Pastor Lawrence but didn't want to take any of her attention away from the road.

They were seated in a diner with high-back booths with water glasses at the tips of their paper placemats and laminated menus in their hands before Lady Menagerie began.

You know I'm not one for small talk so I'm going to come out and say it. I hope what I say doesn't offend you because everything I'm about to tell you is out of love and concern.

Paige's defenses went up, but she tried hard to smile and keep her mind open. This wasn't the first time Lady Menagerie had started a conversation with that lead-in when it came to their deeper discussions.

The waitress came back and took their orders just as Lady Menagerie opened her mouth to continue, but instead turned to the waitress and delivered her order as if she were speaking to an extremely important person. Paige wondered not for the first time if Lady Menagerie always addressed people like that or learned it once she'd become a church leader.

"Okay Paige, what's going on?" Lady Menagerie began once they were alone again. She placed her folded hands on the table

"I know it's been a little over a month since we've talked but you don't look like the woman I remember. You don't hold yourself like the Paige I've come to know."

Paige was taken aback by her opening words. What was she really saying?

"Did you forget what you were like when you first came to Skylight? I haven't. You've come a very long way, and we both know the time you spend with God shows quickly. You aren't one of those who can easily hide their emotions, though I see you're trying.

"How do you claim to know this?" Paige asked, giving up all pretense of not being offended. "You haven't been around." Paige knew that statement made her sound like an insolent child and she backtracked to explain her answer. "I mean no disrespect regarding that statement because I can't imagine what It's been like for you. This whole lawsuit business is crazy and that anyone would believe Pastor Lawrence capable of such behavior is beyond my comprehension.

Thank you for that, Paige. You are truly like a daughter to me, and I'm sorry it's been so long since we've talked, but I trusted that your relationship with God would see you through some of this time. It looks like I still have plenty to learn."

"Just how long did you talk to Brandon last night?"

Lady Menagerie frowned. "Not long. A few minutes maybe? We talked mostly about him, his job, and the things that mean the most to him which includes you. He's a little concerned, and I believe he has every right.

Paige's anger ignited, and she tasted betrayal instead of the bite of spinach and bacon omelet she'd just put in her mouth. What they were going through was extremely personal. She wondered if he'd shared her latest breakdown.

"Before you get quiet on me and think we were talking about you behind your back, you can relax. When I said Brandon mentioned you, I meant he told me you just found out some startling information about your parentage and were going out of town tomorrow.

"Is that all?"

"That's all he said about you last night, but I recently learned from my husband that Brandon came to see him two weeks ago, and he was pretty distraught. That was my true motivation for wanting to meet with you. Learning what I did last night just made this meeting more urgent."

Paige relaxed after staring at Lady Menagerie for a moment. Her eyes teared up with the relief she felt, but she blinked them back. She nodded in acquiescence and continued eating even though most of her appetite had fled.

"So back to my interrogation," Lady Menagerie said with a teasing smile. Paige knew better than to let her guard down, but she never left with worse feelings than when they started. Wrung out maybe, but better for having talked to her mentor.

"You look like you've lost focus." Paige was startled by how similar her words were to the ones Brandon used when describing her a few days ago.

"I don't believe it's so much focus as I'm waiting," Paige said quietly so that her response didn't come off sounding defensive.

"Waiting for what?" Lady Menagerie asked with her fork arrested halfway to her mouth.

"Waiting for God to move on my behalf," Paige responded feeling a little embarrassed at hearing her thoughts outside of her head. She sounded egotistical, but she had learned to be completely honest with Lady Menagerie otherwise the woman would slowly pull it from her then chastise her for making her do so.

"And what does that look like to you?" Lady Menagerie set her fork back on her plate without taking the bite.

"It looks like Brandon being healed," Paige said giving up on her breakfast for the moment.

Lady Menagerie took a deep breath and spread her left hand out on the table. They both watched as she straightened her ring.

"And what if the move God makes isn't in healing Brandon here on earth but giving him a complete healing by transitioning him from earth to heaven?"

Paige didn't want to answer that question. She knew it would bring up a whole new discussion that she did not feel ready to have.

"Paige, I'm waiting for an answer," Lady Menagerie said in her no-nonsense voice, but Paige was far from being intimidated. She was actually more irritated that they were having this talk after the fact. Why didn't Lady Menagerie stop her when she found out Brandon was sick. Yes, she did warn her, but she should have been more adamant. Paige knew it wasn't fair to put the blame on her first lady, but someone she would have listened to should have pulled her aside and told her she wouldn't be strong enough for this.

"And so am I." Paige knew she sounded disrespectful, and she didn't like the hurt that flashed across Lady Menagerie's eyes but it was so hard. She was holding on with everything she had.

Lady Menagerie just looked at her for a moment. Paige knew she was assessing her and the situation. She was about to apologize when her mentor leaned forward and spoke.

"Baby, you're gonna have to let go. God can't do His work if you refuse to step out of the way and let His perfect will be done." She took one of Paige's hands. "You have to find a way to receive what I'm about to tell you." Lady Menagerie took a deep breath. "God is not punishing you. He isn't trying to teach you a lesson or doing any other type of thing that would cause you to feel like Brandon's cancer is a personal offense against you."

Paige nodded. This she knew. "I know it isn't personal, but is this what I waited for, what I prayed for?" The emotions she'd been pressing down for so long bubbled up to the surface.

"Is this really what I get? I've been obedient and sacrificed so much."

"We've been here before, Paige. You sound like a person who thinks their works should then qualify for a smooth life and it doesn't. If it did then my husband, one of the most loving and Godly obedient men I know, would have been in the pulpit a few days ago instead of home worshiping God because some woman wanted revenge for being denied."

Paige blinked. It was the first time Lady Menagerie showed any anger by the lawsuit brought against her husband. She squeezed her mentor's hand.

"Sorry. I promise we will talk about that situation later." She sat up and repositioned herself. "Back to you. You seem to be looking for some fairness gage and there isn't one."

Paige hated where she was going and jumped in. "I believe in Him. I love Him. I'm not going to deny that I desired to have a husband, but I would have lived my life without this type of love. I only listened to prophecies about my husband with half an ear, but He told me Brandon was mine and I was his."

"No honey, Brandon is God's, just as you are God's." Lady Menagerie reached for her other hand. "He is on loan to you just as you are on loan to him until it's time to be reunite with God in heaven.

"But we don't have a lot of time together."

"You know better than most that it's not the time that is important but the quality, the love, and what is done in that time period that's important." Lady Menagerie pulled her stern face back in place.

"I need you to get this because you seem to be in a cycle of profound self-pity and it will ruin the chance you have to use this to minister to those who can't get out of their heads. Even more, you will miss precious moments you have with Brandon."

"I understand that. I do. We have wonderful times together. We have a lot of love that we've put into these last few months but it only makes me want more."

"But as of right now, you're not going to get more," Lady Menagerie said with a softness in her eyes but a firm voice.

"I'm not ready to be a widow," Paige said quietly.

"Honey, I can be a widow tomorrow or you could be a widow tomorrow without it having anything to do with Brandon's cancer." Lady Menagerie let her hands go and briefly pointed her finger at Paige. "You accepted this. You chose to marry him. And when you delivered your vows in front of God and Brandon, you said you would love and accept Brandon for better or for worse." She raised her hands.

"Yes, Brandon dying is definitely worse but you made a covenant. You made a vow." Lady Menagerie enunciated the sentence slowly. "You promised God and essentially you told Him that you were willing to take not only the wonderful love and memories but the hard times and any health challenges. With that one sentence you told God that the life you were stepping into with Brandon was worth the heartache you'd have when the two of you were parted from one another.

"When I say you've lost focus, that's what I mean. You've lost focus on your promise. You've lost focus on what Brandon is in your life. He is a gift as you are a gift to him, but he is not the be-all and end-all. Will it hurt? Yes. Will God be there to comfort you if you allow him to? Yes.

"I need you to ask yourself something. If it were you with cancer or an illness that was taking you away from Brandon, would you be railing against God? If you were the one who was going to leave this world for the unknown." She closed her eyes and waved her hands. "Yes. I know you would be going to heaven and going to be with God for eternity, but there aren't too many people who have made that journey and come back to share. If you were the one dying what would you need from Brandon, right now? What would you give Brandon, right now? What would you want to make sure you left with Brandon to fortify him?

"You have been incredibly selfish in this and I get it. I really get it. But at some point you are going to have to remember what

God has promised you, what He has taught you and what He has given you, and you need to step up and act like the woman of God I know you to be."

*   *   *

Lady Menagerie's words were still resonating in Paige's mind when she, Brandon, Dominy, and his family boarded the luxury jet. Though Paige did her fair share of traveling, she had never flown in such comfort. She avoided the thoughts that would have her believing in the possibility of four-generation family trips.

She glanced over at Brandon as they buckled their seat belts. She smiled as he closed his eyes and reclined back in his brown leather chair, heaving a great sigh. "It feels like I've been working up to this moment for years instead of days. I can finally sit still for more than two hours while being conscious if I want and I'm going to take advantage of it." He shifted until he looked even more comfortable and promptly fell asleep, proven by the light snore that came from him less than a minute later.

"So much for being conscious," Paige said under her breath before turning to see Dominy and Robin making sure Nicky's chair was strapped in properly and buckling themselves in for takeoff.

They had just leveled off when Dominy spoke to her across the aisle. "He's been very tired lately." Paige read the underlying meaning to Dominy's words in his expression. She wished she could give him comfort without confirming the decline of Brandon's health. Instead she nodded.

"Did you get the chance to talk to Brandon while I was out of town?"

"Not really. We couldn't seem to get more than a few minutes together, but I think this trip will give us a few opportunities," Dominy said. "I know I have asked you a few times, but if you

287

change your mind about Robin, Nicky, and I staying at the farm, please let me know."

"You are family, Dominy. You're actually doing me a favor by staying. Victoria is more apt to be on her best behavior if there are semi-strangers and a baby present." She sent him a wry smile.

Dominy pressed his palm to his chest in mock pain. "So, you're just using me?"

"No," Paige said with as much sincerity as she could muster.

"I'm using your wife and child." She looked over at Robin and winked.

Dominy feigned a bluster. "Well…"

Paige interrupted him by raising her hand. "Please don't tell me that you have never been so offended because we all know you have."

Robin giggled and Nicky giggled in return.

Dominy frowned at Robin and Nicky before looking back at Paige.

"I was actually going to say 'Well, that hurts,' but now I feel betrayed," he said in a pout.

Paige watched as Robin sat back quietly taking in his antics. When he continued to pout she sucked her teeth. "Oh, come here, you big baby." Nicky gurgled and kicked his feet.

Dominy unbuckled himself, kneeled in front of Robin and rested his cheek on her knee facing Paige.

Robin looked at her and rolled her eyes. Meanwhile, Dominy wiggled his brows at her. A laugh escaped from Paige's lips, and she glanced back at Brandon to make sure she didn't wake him up. When she looked back at Brandon's friends, who were now her own, Dominy had sobered and Robin was running her hand through his hair in a soothing motion.

Paige watched them for a few moments before turning to look across Brandon's deep sleeping form, out the window. The puffy clouds sat perfectly on the section of the sky they were flying by. It looked so peaceful outside as if nothing could disrupt the harmony of the blues and whites surrounding the brightness of the sun. She remembered the first few years after she'd given her life to Christ she would picture this in her mind when she imagined heaven. It had been replaced with different descriptions of heaven in the Bible, but as she continued to look out the window she felt closer to God than she had in a while.

Lady Menagerie's words came back to her but His voice came through clearly. *You are my loves that I've loaned to the world. Just as you will always hold pieces of him in your heart he will do the same of you when he reunites with me. The love you two create is by designed divine providence. Daughter will never be alone.*

Paige stayed as still as possible so as not to draw attention to herself. She didn't wipe at the tears streaming down her cheeks or sniff. She just ran the sound and words over and over in her mind, and when she was done she tucked them safe in her heart so she could pull them out for comfort any time she needed.

Brandon woke up ten minutes outside of Oklahoma looking refreshed. He yawned and stretched then turned to her, smiling lazily. He reached out and took her hand bringing it to his lips. "I just had the most pleasant dream," he said with a groggy voice.

She said nothing, but took in his unlined forehead, thick eyebrows, curled lashes and coffee-brown eyes. She let her eyes lower to the straight bridge of his nose and wide nostrils, but they paused when they met his full, naturally outlined lips. How many times had she daydreamed about his kisses, both before they were together and after they were married?

"Stop that. There are children present."

Her eyes snapped up to his and saw the teasing glint there.

"Just one before we land to fortify me?" she asked quietly.

She watched his eyes turn liquid as he righted his chair and leaned toward her, reach out and take hold of the back of her head.

He pulled her to him and time slowed then stopped as he pressed his lips to hers.

Paige took little notice of the man standing outside of baggage claim holding a sign with her name on it. She didn't let go of Brandon's hand until she had to climb into the luxury sports utility vehicle. Once they were all situated she laid her head on his shoulder and just took in the warmth and smell of him until the car turned into the long drive to the Branchett farm. Brandon rubbed her arm, and she lifted her head to show him she was awake.

As the car came to stop in front of the steps of the Branchett's house she heard Dominy let out a low whistle. She took a deep breath and exhaled slowly. "Yep," she replied. Her voice holding no emotion.

The front door opened, and she was more than relieved to see Vivian and Gladys step out on the porch. Her heart lightened, and she didn't hesitate when it was her turn to alight from the vehicle. When they spotted her they ran down the steps only as young girls could and didn't stop until she was enfolded in two pairs of arms. They were tall enough that their loose, silky curls rubbed her cheeks and she reveled in the feeling.

"You two are a sight for sore eyes." She took in their individual fragrances. "Is it me or have the two of you grown taller in the last month?"

Gladys leaned back so she could look in Paige's eyes then said nonchalantly, "It's you." Paige laughed and pressed her daughter's head back to her face.

A discreet cough came from her left. Paige opened her eyes to see Brandon. "What?" she asked.

"You can't get all the love."

"We have plenty more left," Vivian said, peeking around her shoulder at Brandon.

290

He opened his arms. "I'm waiting for mine." Vivian looked up in Paige's eyes and declared in a stage whisper. "We'll give you more later, Mati."

Paige reluctantly let them go and turned to see if Robin or Dominy needed help with Nicky hoping to delay the inevitable but all too soon she heard Victoria's voice as she instructed everyone to leave their bags to the driver, and come inside out of the coolness of the late afternoon.

Paige turned back toward the house but armed herself with Brandon's hand and Vivian's arm around her waist. She'd lost Gladys to a slightly fussy Nicky. She didn't raise her eyes to the porch until she absolutely had to, but once she did she refused to lower her chin. She saw Victoria and Richard standing next to Mason and considered the picture they made until she reached the top step, and Richard reached out to hug her.

"Hi Paige. Have a good trip?" She felt more than heard him. When he loosened his hold, she responded, "Yes. Thank you so much for sending your jet for us. I don't know about everyone else, but I think it'll be a moment before I take another commercial flight. I'm going to hold on to the feeling of sitting in a moving living room."

Richard's smile grew wider. "I feel the same way. I'm glad you enjoyed it."

She was passed to Mason as Richard turned to Brandon.

"Hey, lady," he said, hugging her briefly.

"Hi. I see you're still alive," she whispered.

"There are bigger fish in these waters," he replied just as quietly. Then for everyone's ears he said, "I'm glad you're here, Paige." He stepped to the side, and she came face-to-face with Victoria.

"Hello, Paige," Victoria said, clasping her hands together at her waist.

"Victoria."

Victoria's face fell but her eyes softened. She shook her head as if to deny the tone in Paige's voice.

"I didn't mean to..." She swallowed and started again. "I'm sorry for hurting you."

Paige felt some of her anger dissipate with Victoria's words.

She nodded. "Can we talk about this later. It's been a heavy week so far and we should get Nicky inside."

"Of course. You're right." Victoria took a step back toward the front door.

Paige was surprised by Victoria's quick acquiescence, made no comment as they were led through the door.

*   *   *

Paige's first introduction to her grandfather, Antonio Sable, was from the across the dinner table. She looked for any similarities between them in his face, but came up short. She figured they shared the same bronze skin with green undertones, but his eyes were so dark she could barely make out his pupils and his hair, though it was graying at the edges was dark brown.

He smiled at her with the hope she expected to see in a long-lost relative wanting to unite with their family, but there was something about his expression when he didn't think anyone was watching that made her uneasy. He was keeping something from them, and her spirit was telling her it wasn't benign.

She answered his questions carefully and listened thoughtfully. He was an intelligent man with a definite love for family, but she felt nothing more than curiosity and wonder. At one time this would have had her second-guessing herself. Now, she understood what family was, and from her experience it rarely had anything to do with whose blood was running through her veins.

The next morning Paige slipped out of bed so as not to disturb her sleeping husband. It was early, and she knew she wasn't going

292

to get back to sleep any time soon, so she decided to take a walk around the farm, keeping close to the house.

The sky was gloomy with dark gray clouds gathering in the distance making Paige happy that they'd traveled the day before. Her surroundings closest to the house were familiar since she'd been there last year, but she hadn't had the chance to take the full view of the land from different sides of the house.

She stopped to listen to the birds singing in the early light of dawn before turning the corner to the back of the house. She stumbled to a stop when she saw Victoria sitting on a bench not too far from her.

Victoria looked up, surprise registering on her face.

"Sorry to bother you. I'll go back."

"No." Victoria stood up looking ready to follow after her. "Please, don't go. You aren't bothering me. Come join me." She sat back down and patted the bench.

Paige hesitated a moment before coming to sit beside Victoria. Paige's mind was whirling until she looked out over the garden to see the sunrise and became awestruck.

"I don't get to come out here every morning, but I've noticed that the mornings I do, I have an easier time holding on to my peace during the more challenging parts of any day," Victoria spoke without looking at Paige until her next sentence.

"I've been out here every morning since I found out about Antonio." Paige wasn't sure how to take that.

"You mean since you found out that we were related?" Paige asked not wanting to mince words.

"Yes and no, but not for the reasons you're assuming." Victoria didn't continue but looked back toward the sky.

Paige figured now was as good a time as any to discuss the real reason why she'd come this week.

"I don't understand," she began quietly, taking breaths to keep her voice level.

"You talk about how much you've lost and the child, no children, God took from you, but I'm in your life, and when you find out we're blood related, you don't tell me. What am I to think?"

She watched as Victoria took a deep breath then finally turned back to her. "You could think that I was over the moon with happiness to find out that the young woman I have grown fond of is my granddaughter and my grandbaby is truly blood as well." Victoria looked down at her hands for a few seconds. "Though I don't believe I look old enough to be a great-grandmother."

Paige might have smiled at the vain statement if her heart weren't exposed.

"Then why keep it from me?"

"We weren't keeping it from you. We were trying to assess the validity of the claim and find out why a man whom I haven't seen in over forty years would contact me out of the blue and give me information about a son I thought was lost to me."

Paige didn't know how to feel about her admission so she kept quiet.

"We also thought he may have an ulterior motive because he was very interested in meeting you and Melanie. We didn't want to put you through any more emotional distress at this time."

That caught Paige off guard, but she chose to address the more obvious point first. "But you were willing to put my daughter through it?"

"She doesn't know anything and Mason is here. He and I would've made sure Antonio wasn't alone with Vivian if the man meant her any harm."

Paige continued to stare at the woman. "I don't know anything, either."

Victoria opened and shut her mouth. The knuckles of the hands gripping each other in her lap whitened.

"But you didn't come to me so how could you know that?" Paige continued.

"I wouldn't," Victoria said with contrition, but her eyes met Paige's and remained fixed.

"Why?" Paige couldn't help repeating the question.

"I considered everything you were going through as a new bride and with Brandon's illness. If his claims were false I didn't see any reason to alert you."

"And when they were proven to be true?" Paige asked.

Victoria's shrug was more an action of defeat than complacency.

"I'm not saying it was the right thing to do, but my reasons were purely for your benefit." Victoria paused for a moment. "I really am happy we are related. I already secretly considered you an honorary daughter."

"You can understand my skepticism with you choosing to disclose that now. The timing is convenient."

"Yes, well my timing hasn't always been perfect," Victoria said with a self-deprecating tone.

"Take your wedding day for example." Victoria smirked. "It has been brought to my attention that I could have worked harder to find a more appropriate time to try and dissuade you from entering into a situation that would bring you so much pain."

Paige couldn't help but smile at that. "I always liked Richard."

.   Victoria stared at her. "How did you know?"

"It had to be Richard. I can't imagine you telling anyone else what you did. I'm surprised you shared it with him," Paige said.

Victoria nodded in agreement.

"I'm sorry, Paige. I made a mistake." Paige could see the pleading in her eyes and was telling the truth when she said she was surprised Victoria had shared what she'd said to her on her wedding day.

"I need you to respect me enough as an adult woman not to keep the truth from me, no matter how you think it will affect me. I want your promise that you won't do this again, Victoria," Paige said, knowing that Victoria's response would be a turning point in their relationship.

Victoria was quiet for a moment. "It's hard for me not to worry." Paige stiffened.

Victoria took a deep breath. "But if it means that much to you, I will have to respect your wishes." Victoria tightened her lips for a second. "I promise that from now on I will share any information I find out that may concern you."

Paige watched her for a few seconds more then nodded in satisfaction.

Maybe Victoria was telling her the truth. Paige turned back to watch the last seconds of the sunrise as she considered forgiving Victoria. It actually didn't take much thought. She didn't have the time nor energy to make Victoria squirm any more than she already had. She had better things to concentrate on these days.

"You were wrong. Marrying Brandon has brought me more joy than I could have imagined. Does it look like I'm setting myself up for extraordinary pain? Maybe, but then what would love be worth if it didn't hurt when you lost it?"

"You are one of strongest women I know," Victoria stated in response.

Paige scrunched up her nose at her grandmother. "Just one?"

Victoria's shrug this time was lighter. "I'm leaving room for Vivian."

"Huh. Good idea."

They sat there in companionable silence for a while before Paige said anything else.

"Next time come to me with information that might concern me," Paige said as firmly as she could.

Victoria nodded. "Do you think there will be a next time?"

"With the way people have come out of the woodwork since I've met your family. I'm pretty sure," Paige said trying to be glib.

"Our family," Victoria said, placing her hand on Paige's between them. "There is no time that you call me that I won't be there for you."

Paige ignored the lump that crept into her throat and smiled. "Thanks, Grandma."

She saw Victoria shiver and laughed.

"How about Grandmother?" Victoria asked.

"Okay, Grandmother," Paige said, looking Victoria in the eyes.

Victoria swallowed and squeezed her hand before looking back over the garden. Paige followed suit, and they sat there for a little while   longer.

CHAPTER 20

Mason wasn't surprised by the feeling the farm evoked in him. The last time he'd visited the place Rachael was healthy and full of life. Though he agreed to have her body brought back to Oklahoma to be laid in the family plot, the funeral and reception were held at the church of Rachael's youth.

There were way too many memories of her at the farm. He saw her everywhere. The barn where she'd introduced him to horse grooming and riding, the fields she'd helped tend, the woods behind the barn where they laughed, discussed their future, and where he pulled her into long kisses that left them both breathless. Even now he could see her glancing at him over her shoulder with her red hair floating around her and a smile on her lips as she guided him up to the house.

The fact that he actually placed his feet back on this property was a testament to his strength of will and love for his daughter.

The week had been fueled with high-running emotions and concern once Richard's investigators came back with proof that Antonio was hunting for information. Victoria and Richard said they had a feeling who was behind Antonio's sudden interest in his granddaughter and her mother, but weren't willing to say any names until they were sure.

The few times he'd run into Paige and Brandon away from the dinner table caught him off guard. He'd walk into the barn or seek out the peacefulness of the old oaks beyond the cultivated land and find them sitting side by side and talking with the comfort of a couple who'd spent decades together. They seemed to know each other on a level it had taken many years for Mason to get to with Rachael, and he knew in his bones they were close.

It seemed to be the universe's way of setting the punctuation at the end of its choice for best match. And Mason found that he was okay with that. He wanted that for Paige. He wanted her to be as happy as this world would allow. She definitely deserved it with everything she went through earlier in life.

He'd allowed himself one good look at her when she'd arrived with Brandon and their friends. Though she was still as beautiful as he remembered, there was slight smudges under her eyes and she'd lost weight. The glow of her eyes that looked to be powered from within was a little less vibrant, but he chalked it up to what he'd heard was a long week for her. As the days passed, the light in her eyes returned to some degree, but still paled in comparison to a few months before.

He wondered again what kind of God would allow his children to suffer when all he had to do was touch and heal them. Brandon was a decent guy. His ideas of chivalry were a bit warped, but other than that Mason liked the guy. He wouldn't go shouting it off any mountaintops, but everything the man said showed him to be honorable and kind.

Mason took it upon himself to run interference any time he noticed that Paige was alone with Antonio. She didn't look uncomfortable, just put out, but that was enough for Mason. Whatever he could do to make her stay pleasant enough to get her to extend her visit, he would do. He was happy to extend the support as everyone else seemed to be doing in their own small way. He could tell that Brandon was relieved by the show of love and protection everyone was providing. Thought he tried to hide it, Mason could tell his illness was taking its toll on his strength. Every now and then he would encourage Paige to go off with the twins or with Robin and Nicky and he would make his way to their room for a couple of hours.

Mason would see the worry cross Paige's and Dominy's features at those times before they shut it down or pulled a shutter over their eyes but it would take a few seconds for them to return to the conversation around them. He remembered those moments well and didn't envy them one bit.

Thankfully, his daughter and Gladys were oblivious enough to enjoy themselves. He tried to keep an eye on them as they roamed the farm, but he was happy to see that either the farmhands or Nathan, the foreman, looked after them. Vivian needed these carefree days. She had been way too solemn lately and though he knew he'd been responsible for some of it he didn't like it.

He'd spoken to Tabitha a couple of times but with her sister back in town she was a little preoccupied and their conversations were short. He shared as much as he thought was appropriate regarding the farm and his situation, but he couldn't help feeling the distance between them. He hoped when he got back they could get back on track.

Mason stood at the sunroom sliding door and watched as Paige walked aimlessly around the garden. She was so deep in thought he wasn't sure she actually took in the beauty around her. He couldn't tell whether she was serene or just incredibly sad. There was a heaviness that settled around her which he could understand, but he wondered how she could smile, laugh, or comfort others as he'd seen her do that week with such a burden weighing her down.

Richard had taken Brandon, Dominy, and himself out sightseeing earlier in the day. Antonio had begged off, claiming he had some calls to make. The women and girls had gone off on their own excursion arriving back only a half hour before.

Antonio was now taking a ride and everyone else was taking a midday siesta. Everyone except him and Paige. Mason took the opportunity to walk around the house and take in its lines without judging eyes on him. He grudgingly gave Victoria credit for changes she'd made to modernize the house since the last time he'd been there. He pushed away the thought, not at all interested in where it was going.

He slowly opened the door so as not to startle Paige, but she looked up from the bench she was sitting on in the center of the vibrant colors. If he were a photographer he would have begged her not to move, but he wasn't, so even though he wanted to give her the same request he knew it would come out wrong.

He walked out hoping she wouldn't consider his presence a nuisance. The vibrant colors made him smile they reminded him so much of Rachael. Walking up to the bench he looked down at Paige.

"May I join you?" he asked, gesturing at the bench.

"Sure."

He sat down on the opposite side and watched as she leaned forward with her elbows on her knees and continued to take in the beauty around them.

"How are you?" he asked, not taking his eyes from her. Paige gave his question considerable thought before answering.

"I'm okay." Her voice told him she meant it and he was relieved.

"That's good to know."

"And you?" She looked over her shoulder at him. "How are you doing?"

He didn't know why he was surprised that she returned his question, but he wasn't ready for it. "I've been very busy. Work is a little hectic. I didn't realize how much I missed the industry until I was really present at work, not just showing up physically." He shut his mouth to keep himself from rambling.

Paige sat back looking at him as if she'd never see him before. She turned her body toward him. "I have a question for you. You don't have to answer it if you don't want to." She said the last sentence quickly.

He could guess what she wanted to know and hoped he had the courage to be honest with her.

"Sure. What's up?"

She still looked unsure, so he tapped the back of her hand to reassured her.

"It's been a little more than three years since your wife died, right?"

"Yes."

"How long." She stopped looking as though she were trying to find the right words. "How long did it take after Rachael passed for you to stop wishing you could be with her?"

"I still do, but I have a child to think about and that helps more than it hurts."

"How could it hurt?"

He cocked his head to the side. "Mmm, well because Vivian has a lot of the same mannerisms and looks like her when she's happy or excited. At first it was hard to look at but once the pain was less acute I thought of it more as a gift. Rachael had left pieces of herself behind imprinted on my daughter."

"I know you said you had Vivian to think of, but when she wasn't around and you let yourself feel." She took a deep breath. "How bad was it?"

He looked her straight in the eyes, asking for permission to be completely honest with her. She nodded.

"It was excruciating."

Paige said nothing but didn't look away.

"If I hadn't had Vivian and if some of what Rachael said to me before she died didn't resonate deeply, I would have tried to join her."

"What did she say; if you feel like sharing?"

"Your life is a gift. If you squander it or try to throw it away we will never see each other again."

"How could she be sure?"

"I don't know if she was, but because she had a deeper relationship with God. I couldn't chance her being right."

"Did it really keep you from trying?"

"Yes, but not from thinking about it. I considered a great many scenarios, including causing myself irreparable damage then asking forgiveness."

"Yeah. I had that same thought," Paige said. The look in her eyes letting him know she had stepped into the past.

Knowing it wasn't a good time in her life, he tried to pull her back to the present quickly.

"I think it's different for people who have loved ones' support and surround them when they are newly grieving."

"Maybe," she said thoughtfully.

"If they accept the help," he said staring pointedly at her.

Paige nodded her understanding. "You said you weren't present until recently, but you wanted to date me a year ago. Was that real or were you rebounding?"

He did not want to answer that question, but he didn't want to venture back to the conversation either.

"It was real, and I believe if I'd been considered the 'best man' at the time I might have shaken the fog of grief off sooner."

Paige looked at him oddly.

"What?" he asked.

"Well, please don't be upset."

"You know that never works, Paige. People always get upset when you start a sentence like that."

"Okay," she said and sat back against the bench looking around the garden.

"But now I'm curious so that won't work either."

"I think I would rather you be curious than upset," Paige said with a smirk.

"Okay. I promise not to get upset." He bumped her shoulder.

"You can't promise that." She looked at him.

"Then why did you ask me not to be?" He wiggled his eyebrows.

303

Paige laughed. "When you say it like that it sounds ridiculous."

"Just tell me what you were going to say." He let a little of his impatience show.

She watched him for a moment. He suspected she was gaging his real mood.

"One night a few months ago Vivian called me, upset. I listened, and we talked for a while. During her impassioned replay of what happened to upset her she let it slip that you were seeing a counselor of sorts."

Mason's mind balked at the thought of Paige knowing he was seeing a therapist. The embarrassed heat that turned to anger a few seconds later caught him off guard and he had to stand up to put more space between them. The last thing he wanted was for Paige to think he wasn't strong. The sad thing was, he'd talked more about his feeling for Paige than he had about losing Rachael.

"I see one off and on," Paige said loud enough for him to hear through his thoughts.

He turned back to her, not sure if he'd heard her correctly. "What?"

"I said I see a therapist from time to time," she said, looking a little embarrassed.

He didn't feel calm enough to sit back down but she had his attention.

"I was just wondering if seeing a therapist helped you with your grief and allowed you to start living your life again instead of just watching it?" she asked, growing more and more quiet as her sentence went on until he could barely hear her. Curiosity overrode his initial anger and he sat back down.

"Well, that was part of it," he said hesitantly. "When Rachael first passed away, one of my neighbors whose wife had died gave me Dr. Seagrate's card. I put it away and didn't consider using it until I had a change of thought last year."

"What changed your mind?"

He glanced at her then down at his hands. There was no way he was going to share the fact that losing her was a catalyst for seeking the therapy he needed to move forward in a more healthy manner.

"Vivian. I wanted to be a better father for her."

"I think things happened the way they did for the best. For a number of reasons," she added.

"Okay. I'll bite. What do you mean by things?"

"I mean regarding us choosing to be friends," Paige said matter-of-factly.

He didn't see it quite the same way but simply nodded.

"I don't believe you were ready for another relationship when we met. You needed to talk to someone, especially if it couldn't be God."

He rolled his eyes but he smiled ruefully. "There you go with God again."

"Yep, and I will continue to go with God." She played with his words, but he knew she was serious.

"Why have you been seeing a therapist?"

"Off and on," she interjected.

"Off and on."

She was quiet for a moment, and he figured she was putting her thoughts together. "As I told you a while ago, after I had the twins I was in very bad shape mentally. My therapist diagnosed me with post-traumatic stress disorder. When I shared what I was going through, she said I needed to feel safe, and I developed a coping mechanism to help with that." She put up air quotes as she talked what her therapist said.

"What were your coping mechanisms?" he asked, hoping she would continue to be open with him.

She hesitated. "I become compulsive about certain things." The inflection in her voice told him she wasn't done, so he waited remaining as still and quiet as possible.

"And a bit obsessive as well." She took a deep breath.

"You have obsessive compulsive disorder?"

"No, just tendencies. There is a difference because mine comes from a need to control my environment when I feel like there are too many parts of my life out of order."

He was surprised. She always seemed like she had things together and how could she claim that God was her healing and strength.

"When was your last episode?" He hoped he was using the correct language. The last thing he wanted to do was insult her.

She glanced his way but didn't keep his gaze. She rubbed her forehead with her fingertips and took a deep breath. "Right before the girls came for their birthday week." She winced and stiffened a little. It looked like she was preparing to be reprimanded. If she only knew, he was the last person who would judge her.

He knew she was waiting for him to say something, but there was really only one that he thought he could share.

"I always saw you as some super woman. It's good to know you have a weakness or two."

She stared at him as if expecting more, but when he didn't say anything else she breathed out deeply and gave him a wan smile.

"No, I am not, nor do I ever want to be super woman, and I have more than two weaknesses."

"Really? How many?"

"More than two," she said in a tone that told him she was not going down that road.

He had a thought and considered how to express it so as not to sound judgmental. "As a child of God, you have told me that God has helped you through a great deal of pain, anger, and distrust in your life. Why not whatever causes you to become compulsive and obsessive about things?"

Paige stared down at the ground rubbing her hands together. "I did seek Him in regards to that and He gave me ways to combat it through prayer and trusting Him to handle everything concerning me. Through constant prayer and soul searching I learned to perceive my surroundings differently and gain a control I didn't think I had before." She took another breath.

"Since last year when I met you and learned about Vivian I was already facing my life and role in Gladys' life. I was blindsided with the news regarding my sister/mother and Brandon's illness. I forgot to check for triggers or what I like to call taking a soul check. I spent so much time reacting and not enough time communicating with Him. I started looking at all the things that were going on around me and became overwhelmed.

One might think trusting God is a blanket concept but it's more of a moment to moment relationship with God. There may be one situation that you can easily trust God in. There is no second thought to it. Then there are other situations where your first impulse is to take the helm, and it takes a person, place, or failing to remind you that He is the God of all.

He can't lie, He can't fail, but it's so hard to remember when so much failure is lying at your feet, and you've heard so many lies from people who are supposed to represent Him." She stopped, giving him a sheepish look.

"I'm so sorry. I didn't mean for it to come out preachy. I really only wanted to explain that when I step out of line it isn't Him, it's me?"

"Why can't He keep you from stepping out of line?"

"Then there would be no need for heaven or hell, least of all my story. If He could keep me from making decisions even if they are bad ones, there is no victory in that. We might as well be robots. I don't know about you, but I would rather have Vivian come to me and tell me she loved me out of her own heart rather than demand that she do so every day. It means more when she comes on her own, and God feels the same."

"I see what you mean." And he did. Right then in the middle of a garden of flowers he knew that the woman Paige was couldn't be duplicated and he'd tried. As beautiful as Tabitha was her conviction in what she believed didn't shine through in every conversation, and as crazy as it seemed, her apologetic manner when debating with him when it came to God irritated him. It all brought him to one irrevocable point. He wasn't over Paige, and all of the second-guessing and inability to just appreciate the moments he had with Tabitha made sense. He was both elated by the feeling of clarity and shaken by his inability to emotionally separate himself from the one woman he couldn't have. Not just because she was married but because of the God that stood between them.

He blinked a couple of times trying to right his world.

"Are you alright?" Paige was peering into his eyes.

He finally blinked her into focus. "Yes. Sorry. Yes," he stuttered. "I'm sorry." He looked down at his watch to make the lie he was about to tell more believable. "I was supposed to wake Vivian and Gladys up a half an hour ago so they could ride before dinner. They won't be too happy if they miss this opportunity because I didn't keep my word."

"Okay," she said, looking at him as if trying to read through him. "Thank you for talking to me and not judging me." She smiled shyly, and he felt the crack begin in his heart. Subconsciously, he placed his hand on his chest and got up so he could move away.

"Not a problem." Was all that came out before his throat closed up. He waved and turned toward the sliding glass door hoping he wouldn't come across anyone between the door and his room since he didn't think he could hold back the tears before he made it to his room.

What kind of decent human being loves a woman married to a terminally ill man. He didn't need to wait for death. He was already in his own personal hell.

He walked in long, quick strides to the sliding glass door and came face-to-face with Brandon. If he'd begun to wonder if God was maybe on his side he knew without a doubt at that moment that God's sense of humor sucked.

He looked down giving Brandon a perfunctory greeting and moved to go around him but Brandon's hand on his shoulder had him coming up short.

He took a deep breath. If he was doing to get his licks in it might as well be right now. Brandon couldn't say anything to him that he wasn't already saying to himself. He raised his head and looked into Brandon's face.

"Are you okay?" Brandon's concern was almost his undoing.

"Naw, man. I have a killer headache. I'm heading upstairs for a while."

"Sure. Here, let me pray for you," Brandon said, turning him so he could place both hands on his shoulders.

"It's okay…" he said desperately close to tears. What little hell was this?

"Heavenly Father, I thank you for my brother Mason."

Ahh, Je.. Mason stopped the thought hoping he'd interrupted it in time. Saying Jesus' name in vain during prayer was something even he wouldn't do.

"Thank you for his life and love for his daughter. Thank you for merging his life with Paige's and mine and making us family."

He felt the first tear begin to slide down his cheek, but he couldn't wipe it away without drawing attention to his movement. He'd just stepped into a nightmare.

"Lord, I speak healing upon him right now."

Oh, he was definitely in trouble. What kind of curse came with allowing someone to pray for you for an illness you didn't have.

"Touch his heart, mind, and body, Lord. Get his attention the only way you can, shake up his life and show him Your love in such a way that He can't deny that you've been with him even if he hasn't acknowledged you.

Did this man know what he was praying? Mason asked himself as he continued to stand there in horrified fascination.

"I ask for your mercy and grace, Father, as you answer your daughter Vivian's prayers."

What. What did he mean by that?

"I thank you for everything that you're doing now and will be doing in our lives. In Jesus' name, Amen," Brandon finished, but didn't release Mason.

"Whether you like it or not. You are my brother, and if you are in need of anything you can call me. I'm just putting that out there again."

"How do you do that? How can you offer me help when you're the one who needs it?" Mason wanted to kick himself as soon as the last word was out of his mouth.

Brandon removed his hands and cocked his head to the side. "What do you think I need, Mason?"

"Time?"

Brandon smiled, but it was the saddest smile Mason had ever seen in his life. "I have exactly the amount of time I'm supposed to have. I've known for a while that it's been unfair."

Mason was about to swallow back another lump aware that he'd forgotten the tears making tracks down his cheeks.

"It's been unfair because if life was fair, I would have died nine years ago the first time I was diagnosed with cancer."

Mason was struck mute. This man was unreal.

"But God healed me and gave me enough time to meet, fall in love with, and marry the most remarkable woman I've ever met. I've been blessed beyond my wildest dreams."

Mason couldn't possibly feel smaller than he did right now but more than that he knew Paige chose right.

He gave Brandon what he was sure was a watery smile.

"Thanks, man."

"None needed. I hope you feel better soon."

Mason turned to go to his room, sure he would never meet anyone else like Brandon and that it was a shame that he wouldn't be in his life longer.

CHAPTER 21

Melanie rubbed the back of her neck as the revelations of the last few days sat heavily upon her shoulders. Her hand was joined by Marc's who kneaded her neck and shoulders to help relieve some of the tension from the last couple of hours.

"We can always stop this and go back," Marc said, glancing at her quickly.

"No. It was set up this way. Once I went into that deposit box I would set off a chain reaction that would either save my family or..." She didn't finish because they had discussed it before. If things went wrong she could go to jail for aiding and abetting. Mark squeezed the back of her neck gently before releasing it and pulling his hand away.

"How long do we have for you to pick up the next clue?"

"Two days."

"I suggest we go back to the hotel and rest then get something to eat before getting back on the road."

Though the thought sounded appealing she wanted to visit one more place before they left the city where her life started going wrong.

"One more stop and I promise to rest."

His quick look at her spoke volumes before he returned his attention to the road.

"I promise. Just one more place."

She heard Marc's reluctant sigh. "Where are we going?"

"The hospital," she said without looking at him, but saw him glance at her quickly from her peripheral vision.

312

"That's very dangerous. You could be recognized."

"It's been twenty-seven years. If you ask me, it's been two years too late. I should have come back when Lilith became ill, but I kept hiding like I've been doing all of my life." She looked over at Marc. "Besides, you said all of the records set up to steer people in the wrong direction were still in place."

"Exactly, so I don't understand why you would jeopardize everything by going back there."

"It's the closest I've been to him since... since..." She now couldn't finish the sentence she'd denied herself from speaking out loud for decades.

Marc took one of his hands off the wheel to place on hers. "You can see him, you know. All you have to do is ask."

"No," Melanie said, shaking her head. "It's too dangerous. All I can do is get close enough to send Brian a message. He needs to know that Grace has found some way to manipulate Antonio." She rubbed her forehead as she shook her head. "You told me he was having financial problems after his father failed to name him his immediate successor, but I never thought he could be convinced to turn on his own son."

"It isn't clear that he's convinced Brian is alive." Marc exited the freeway, letting go of her hand to make a left turn onto the street leading to State General Hospital. "Like I said, if anyone went in search of information on Brian we would know about it. We've planted both leads and dead ends throughout the family files," Marc said.

"Yes. Information that led Paige to confront me on my lawn, threatening to disown me and sue me for custody of the grandchild I've raised as my own."

"I told you, we left that particular piece of information in place as an alert to see how deep people were digging."

"Yes. Too bad there were no alerts in place to warn me about Victoria and Richard's investigators," she said with a wan smile. "I know they are doing their job and doing it very well, but I wish they had been just a little less competent."

Marc was quiet for a moment and Melanie looked over at him.

"Do you ever wonder that with everything that has happened, if it's time to tell Paige?" Melanie opened her mouth, but Marc continued before she could speak. "There are an awful lot of coincidences. What are the odds of Paige's daughter being adopted by Brian's mother's family? Even more, that Vivian and Paige would be reunited due to Vivian's need for a kidney?"

Melanie was quiet as she admitted to herself that she too considered all the revelations that had come forth due to causes out of her control over the last year to be too coincidental. She wondered, not for the first time, if it were God that was maneuvering the situations to bring their family together.

"If God's hand is in this there is nothing I can do to change that. I welcome it because He knows what it will take to keep my family safe. It would be a dream come true to have everyone in the same room again."

"I know, baby. Never doubt the power of prayer," Marc said, pulling into the hospital parking structure.

"You've been praying for me to be reunited with all of my family?" she asked as Marc put the car in park.

"Always, but now Paige, Vivian, and Victoria are praying for it as well. I am not saying that God hasn't listened to yours or my prayers, but our voices have been joined by at least two who have very close relationships with God." Marc turned toward her.

"I'm just saying to be open to what He is doing. Don't do anything to hinder His works, but also continue to be diligent with your safety. Remember that this is only part of the reason for you giving up a life with your children. There are still people out there looking for you so they can use you and Paige to get to Grace, and from what she's shown us of herself, she won't even come to your aid if your life is in danger. She is out for vengeance against the

Sable family, and you will only be collateral damage if you or your family get caught in the crossfire.

Do you know how much I love you? I couldn't do any of this without you. Not only because of your connections but because you give me the courage I need to keep from giving up.

Don't underestimate your strength, Mel. You are one of the strongest people I know. There aren't too many people who would give up their dreams and their children at such a young age.

I know you were content to live beside Paige as her sister and watch her grow." He snorted.

"You were basically acting as her mother, while Grace continued to scheme and plot on how to destroy what you hold dear. I know it pains you every day not to know your son. What mother who has sacrificed so much for the well-being of their child wouldn't want to know that their sacrifice was not in vain. You missed so much of his life, but he had that life because of what you did.

You did what you had to do to keep your family safe. Your separation gave all of you a higher chance to survive and hide successfully. It has been twenty-seven years and they haven't found your whole family yet. I think this trip is risky, but I understand your need to warn Brian."

Melanie cupped his cheek and drew toward him for a kiss. "Thank you for that. I know we've been through most of this before, but I am so grateful to have you in my life. Don't think for one moment that I haven't forgotten what you gave up for me."

"What? You mean that twelve-hour-a-day job full of stress and cold meals in unmarked vehicles waiting to obtain just enough information to justify a warrant." He wiggled his eyebrows at her.

"I'd do it again in a heartbeat. I am married to the love of my life. I have a daughter/granddaughter who adores me even at thirteen and a sister-in-law/daughter who thinks I'm a pretty great guy. I have a decent desk job which is perfectly fine since my wife comes with more than enough drama." He winked at her.

"I love you, Mel, and I'm with you until the end of this life."

She kissed him again with all of the feelings his admission evoked with her. She wrapped her harms around his neck hugging him as close to her as possible. When they finally pulled apart they were both breathing heavily.

"Don't start something you can't finish Mrs. Miller," Marc said saucily, his breath mingling with hers.

"Don't worry. I plan on finishing this later." She ran her hand along his jaw one more time before moving away and opening her door.

"Remember to be aware of your surroundings."

"I remember," Mel said through a sigh. She knew he was worried, so she capitulated easily. "I will just be a few minutes. Then we will go back to the hotel to rest, or not" She smiled at him before opening her door. "Eat and head to New Orleans."

Melanie exited the car and walked to the hospital where she had gained and lost so much. Mel considered again what Paige would do if she found out she had a twin brother and father in another part of the country. Would she forgive her? Could she forgive her?

Mel shook her head to push away the thoughts as she walked in the hospital and took the elevator up to the maternity and nursery.

CHAPTER 22

He was tired. So tired he could barely think sometimes. The last week had weighed on Brandon. Not just his body but on his mind as well. It took a certain amount of mental acuity and energy to keep dodging Dominy. He knew his friend wanted to talk, and Brandon originally wanted to wait until the last minute before Dominy and his family were leaving, to have that talk. Brandon knew Dominy wouldn't take the news well if he accepted it at all. When Richard called to invite Paige and him to use his company's plane he felt as though God was smiling down at him. It was the perfect setup because Dominy couldn't walk out on him if they got into a disagreement and things didn't go Dominy's way. And things just weren't going to go his way this time unless God changed his mind.

Brandon had gone out with Dominy, Robin, and Nicky the Monday afternoon Paige was out of town. He knew the meeting with her new publisher had been a big concern for her. She tried to play it off like she was just excited, but the deal with the publisher she was being released from had gone downhill after she told them of her wish to also write in another genre, and he knew that had to leave a sour taste in her mouth.

Carmen was a lifesaver. Her ability to maneuver Paige's career around and find a publisher willing to buy her out of her contract and give Paige the acknowledgments she needed as a legitimate best-selling writer made him almost happier than Paige. There was a spark in her eye as she kissed him goodbye that he hadn't seen for a while.

He spent Monday out with Dominy, Robin, and Nicky, never staying out of hearing range from one or the other for long. Every time Dominy tried to get him away he made sure they spoke of lighthearted things like his family and new niece. He asked Dominy about his work, and the changes he would be making soon to accommodate his new lifestyle. But when Dominy tried to bring up Brandon's health and his plans for the future, Brandon would always deflect or change the subject.

They had a great time playing tourist in Los Angeles. He took Dominy and his family to Universal Studios. It was the perfect place to share laughs, and memories, and experience new things without being able to get into deep discussions.

On Tuesday morning he had a doctor's appointment so he canceled when Dominy called to see if he would join them for breakfast. He told him he had some office work to finish, but would join them for lunch.

Brandon could tell by Dr. Connor's expression that it wasn't going to be an encouraging visit, but he answered his questions and thoughts with their monthly routine. He saw the the surprise in the man's eyes when he told the doctor he wasn't experiencing any pain.

"Any headaches?" the doctor asked.

"No," Brandon responded quickly

"Any dizziness or blurry vision?" Dr. Connor volleyed.

"None."

Any muscle aches or pains?

"No," Brandon said, noticing Dr. Connor's frown.

"Any stomach cramping or bloating?"

"Nope."

"Wow. I must say that that is good news." The doctor's eyebrows were raised.

"I am tired, though. I can't seem to get through more than six to eight hours without needing to take a nap," Brandon said, leaning forward in his chair.

"That is to be expected, and you will be experiencing more fatigue and lethargy as this takes its course."

Brandon nodded, not completely discouraged. Is there something I can take? Some type of supplement that will help?

"I will up your vitamin B dosage and give you a energy cocktail, but I'm afraid there isn't too much more I can do other than advise you to get as much rest as possible." He ended the statement with a shrug.

Dr. Connor then went over his labs with him and the news just got worse. There were trace amounts of cancer cells found in different areas of his brain. All were superficial and close to the skull. From his expression, Dr. Connor seemed to think that was a ray of sunshine through the gray clouds he'd just pulled over Brandon. Unfortunately, it cut Dr. Connor's original time frame for him in half. And the room for Brandon got noticeably darker.

As he left the office he tried give himself a pep talk and push away some of the doctor's prediction, but it was hard. He knew the doctor could only speculate. The only one who had a right to give his body an expiration date was God. He wanted more time, but he would have to do what he needed in the time he was given, and that would be to show Paige in every word, act, and moment that they were together how much he loved her. He would do the same for his family and Dominy, if the stubborn man allowed. Then he would give his goodbyes.

So much easier said than done.

Each day he spent with Dominy and his family he tried to stop and memorize certain things about them. He made a point to say weird things so he could catch Dominy's expressions, mannerisms, his funny banter, and his wisecracks.

He also watched Robin with Nikki and wished for the hundredth time that there was a way he could give that to Paige, but the disease ravaging his body and all the chemicals used to try and stem the cancer made him conceiving close to impossible.

Tuesday evening he drove to the airport to pick up Paige. The feeling he got when he spotted her among the crowd of luggage toters made his chest tight and his eyes burn. He loved this woman.

This woman who fought to stay by his side, married him, nurtured him, and loved him was getting a raw deal. He would be leaving her. But there was nothing to do about it except try to make sure she was taken care of when the time came—both financially, and with families, and friends.

Brandon knew his family would huddle around her. But he hoped that Victoria and Richard would make sure Paige spent very little time alone at home. Brandon also hoped that Mason had taken their talk on his wedding day seriously. It wasn't easy for him to encourage another man to take care of the love of his life. He wanted to be selfish and have Paige promise to only ever love him, but he loved her, and he wanted her to be as happy as she could be without him. His ego told him it would be darn near impossible, but he was hoping she would give it a try.

Of course, he could admit that he was jealous. He knew Mason's feelings for Paige ran deep, otherwise he never would have approached him with such a crazy request. It wasn't fair to any of them, especially Mason right now, but if he loved Paige as much as Brandon thought, he wouldn't be able to stay away for long. He only hoped Mason would heed his warning about getting his spiritual life straight. He sometimes wished the tables were turned, but he wouldn't wish this life-sucking disease on anyone.

The Branchett farm/ranch was beautiful. It would have been the ideal location for a second honeymoon, sans Mason and the girls, and if the situation were different. The house was more than spacious, and he didn't have to worry about bumping into anyone if he didn't want to. The first morning he allowed Richard to give him and Paige the ten-cent tour. The place was much bigger than he first thought, and by the time they were done, he was exhausted.

After an early lunch which was only made slightly awkward by Antonio's questions toward Paige, who seemed to have virtually no clue what he was trying to get out of her, they were in their room when the fatigue hit him. He told Paige to go out with the girls and he would take a nap. She stared at him before walking to him where he was leaning up against one of the high bedposts. She came up on the balls of her feet and pressed a light kiss to his lips.

Before lowering herself she whispered, "Don't nap too long. You won't be able to go to sleep tonight." She clucked her tongue. "On second thought…" She kissed him again, deeper, leaning into him so that he could feel her warmth. When she began to pull away, he followed her, needing just a few more seconds of her scent and breath. He wrapped his arms around her waist pulling her in closer before reluctantly letting her go.

"Yeah" She looked up at him, dazed. "Keep that thought right there." She smiled at him with damp, swollen lips, and if she hadn't moved away when she did he would have snatched her up so he could do more damage.

"Laytta," she said at the door, looking at him over her shoulder and wiggled her fingers. Her antics made him chuckle, but he hoped she wasn't playing, and he definitely planned to keep those thoughts he had when she was in his arms.

He was sleeping hard when a knock came an hour later. He hoped it was part of his dream, but when it came again he slowly rolled over and called out, "Come in."

Dominy peeked his head around the door and Brandon stifled a groan.

"Mind if I come in? Robin and Nicky are out with the girls, and I thought we could go down and relax."

"I was relaxed," Brandon said but gave in at his friend's look. "Okay." He yawned wide and went to look for his shoes.

"You've been sleeping a lot lately."

"Yep," he said knowing where the conversation was going.

"Have you talked to your doctor about it?'

"Yep. He prescribed me with a few things. I think it will take a few more days before they kick in, though." He could tell Dominy wasn't expecting that answer by his hesitation and blink. The guy was as transparent as plastic wrap.

They went down to the kitchen and got themselves drinks then walked to the family room where there was a big-screen TV pointed at a sectional, leather couch. They took seats in the middle and set their drinks down on the divider. Dominy pressed a button that allowed his seat to recline, and after a moment of searching Brandon did the same. Dominy picked up the remote and turned on the television like he did it every day.

"How do you know about the remote and the chair?"

"I was down here earlier and got bored by myself so I went up to get you."

"Where're the guys?"

"They went into town at the last minute, but I told them I still had a bit of jet lag."

Brandon nodded but the lump that formed in his throat wouldn't allow him to say anything.

He took a long drink of his water and leaned back in the chair silently watching a football game playing on low. A set-up if he ever saw one.

"Have you talked to Victoria about this?"

"This... meaning...?"

"The cancer," Dominy said quietly.

Brandon didn't mean to be a heel, but he needed Dominy to at least address his illness for what it was before he could talk to him about the inevitable affects the disease was going to have on his body.

"Yes. Paige spoke to her on her wedding day." He didn't glance over at Dominy, knowing what he was about to say would rock him. "Victoria went up to Paige's room a few hours before the ceremony and tried to dissuade her from marrying me." He did look that time and was rewarded with an openmouthed Dominy.

"Yep." He nodded once then returned his gaze to the television.

"It seems she wanted to rescue Paige from the heartache of marrying someone who didn't have long to live."

There was silence for a few minutes before Dominy spoke.

"How did she know?"

"It seems that Victoria likes to keep tabs on people she cares about. She had one of her investigators get my latest records to see if she could find a doctor who could treat me."

He saw Dominy lean forward in his seat at that news. "And did she find one?"

Brandon turned to him wondering if he'd been speaking to himself. "No." He drew it out. "That's why she came to Paige and tried to discourage her."

"That..." Dominy started, but Brandon interrupted him.

"Woman who was looking out for Paige before she knew they were related and asked her husband to fly us here in his company jet," Brandon interjected.

"Yeah, I guess." He blew out a deep breath. "So, what're you going to do?"

Brandon turned most of his body toward his friend and looked him straight in the eye. "Dominy, I'm dying."

"But what about your pastors? Can't they get everyone together and pray?"

"I'm sure I am on a few prayer lists, but if this is what God wants, there isn't much more that I can do than make sure I am prepared in every way possible."

Dominy stared at him in panic, and as the moments ticked by the overly bright light in his eyes changed to something that looked like utter despair. Yeah, Brandon knew that feeling. Dominy leaned back in his seat turning back to the television. Brandon watched him out of the corner of his eye when Dominy began blinking furiously. Yep. He'd been there too.

The game was well into the second half before Dominy spoke again. "What are you going to do? Are you taken care of? Is Paige?"

Brandon held up a hand to slow Dominy's questions. "Everything is taken care of. I was able to get a decent rate on life insurance after my five-year mark of being free of cancer the first time. My parents grudgingly told me they would do anything I asked, so they're coming to Los Angeles in a couple of weeks."

"How are you so calm about this?" Dominy asked, leaning forward, glancing at him with his elbows on his knees and his hands cradling his head. "I used to think I wanted to know when I would die, but not like this." He shook his head. "How have you not lost your mind by now?"

Brandon was actually amazed at how Dominy was taking the news. He'd given him the first half hour thinking Dominy was just in shock and that he would come out of it ranting and raving, but his friend seemed oddly resigned.

"Well, I have had a lot more time to get used to it. You were so adamant about the outcome of this bout with cancer, I waited to share this last report because I didn't want to have to fight you and Paige. I need your strength, right now," he said without looking away from Dominy.

Brandon hoped his friend could respect his wishes. It really was getting tiring fighting with Paige on what he was accepting and actively doing to lengthen his time. He'd prayed so many times for God to give her the understanding he'd been unable to. He didn't want to leave her out of any part of his journey but if she continued to fight him he would have to keep certain parts to himself. It would

324

break his heart not to be able to share some of the revelations God shared with him regarding his transition especially when they'd shared everything else.

"You've been there for me every time I needed you," Dominy said, sitting back against the cushions. He never broke eye contact with Brandon. "You are the brother I wished for when I was young. I'm here for however long you need me." He got up from the couch to stand in front of Brandon. "Just ask and you've got it."

Brandon looked up unable to say anything. His throat had closed up, and he wondered what he'd done to deserve such a great friend. He stood up and embraced Dominy, returning his friend's hug in strength and length. By the time they released each other neither one's eyes were dry.

"I might be asking for trouble," Brandon said after they'd returned to their seats. "But I thought you would take it much harder." He looked over at Dominy.

Dominy rubbed his hands together. "Don't fool yourself, Brandon. I'm devastated. I can't imagine my life without you, but I don't know anyone else who has God's ear as you do. If you have done everything you can to convince Him to give you more time, then all I can do is try not to waste what we have left." Dominy swiped at his eyes.

"Now that I'm a father, I see things a little differently. Nicky has shown me so many things about myself and about this life. It is precious, not because of the things we can obtain, but because of the thoughts, memories, and emotions we can share with each other. They are all gifts."

"I couldn't have said it better. You may have a future as a pastor, yet," Brandon said.

Dominy screwed up his face. "There you go, ruining a perfectly good moment. You know I was going deep with that, and you had to threaten me with a pastoral occupation."

Brandon laughed and shook his head. "My bad, Dominy. My bad."

Dominy blew out an exasperated sigh, but the twitching of his lips kept Brandon laughing for few more minutes.

An hour later, when they heard movement in the house Dominy turned to him one more time with an earnest expression. "I'll take care of Paige. You don't have to worry about her."

"I would expect nothing less, brother," Brandon replied, his heart swelling.

Dominy nodded once and turned back to the television until Robin walked in with Nicky then he got up and wrapped them both in a hug, kissing them both on the tops of their heads.

Brandon got up feeling oddly lighter and went in search of his wife.

* * *

Toward the end of the week Brandon found himself walking through the house and gardens more. Victoria and Richard's house was full of places to sit and watch what was going on at the farm. One afternoon after a short nap he decided to join Paige who'd shared her love for the garden. When he rounded the couch in the living room to the sliding glass doors he saw Mason and Paige sitting on a bench in the center.

He didn't think anything of it until Mason reached out to squeeze Paige's hand. Brandon stepped back so he wouldn't be seen observing them. Since they'd arrived on the farm Paige had been serene and though he'd felt a measure of relief at her change in demeanor he wasn't confident it would last and wasn't sure as to what brought it on. He told himself he would only watch until he was sure she was truly alright.

He got his answer a few minutes later when his wife gave Mason a tremulous smile with bright eyes. He would have turned away if it weren't for Mason's expression of confusion as he got up and walked away from Paige. The wrecked look accompanied by the shameful way he held his head told Brandon that Mason was struggling with his feelings. He was fighting.

When Mason walked through the door blinking rapidly Brandon stood there wondering if God was joking with what he'd just told him to do. He stepped forward catching the surprise then hesitation on Mason's face and his heart went out to him. Brandon knew what he was asking of Mason wasn't fair, but he hoped what God wanted him to pray would at least bring Mason peace.

*   *   *

Brandon wasn't sure how to lead into the conversation he wanted to have with Paige so he jumped right into it as they got ready for bed.

"I saw you talking to Mason in the garden today," he said, sitting on the edge of the bed to take off his shoes. The rustling Paige was making as she took off her dress stopped. He could feel her looking at him but he didn't look up.

"Yes. He came out while I was walking around and thinking." She lifted her dress over her head.

"What were you thinking about?" he asked, slowing his movements even more.

"A lot of things." She walked over to the closet and searched for a hanger. "Like Gladys coming home to us when she leaves here, getting her ready for school."

"Oh, so you two were talking about how to enroll Gladys?" he asked, hoping the look he remembered seeing on her face was one of curiosity.

He raised his head catching her gaze as she walked to the dresser. "No. We talked about something different."

"Oh?" he said, knowing the word said more than he wished to give away.

Paige stopped in her tracks and turned around to face him. "Brandon Tatum, are you jealous?"

"No," he lied.

She continued to stare at him, making him squirm. He began to unbutton his sleeves.

"You are," Paige said, walking closer and peering at him as if looking through a fishbowl. Her head tipped to the side. "What do you have to be jealous of?" she asked, turning the tables on him.

He thought of the irony of her actions as he considered her question. *What was it about her expression in the garden that bothered him, and would it have bothered him as much if she were talking to anyone besides Mason?*

He opened his mouth and closed it, wanting to make sure his answer was as truthful as possible. He went through a number of possible causes, but the last one sent a pain through his heart. He was stuck. If he shared what was truly bothering him it would work against his desire for her to find happiness when he was gone.

"Brandon?"

"Yes?" he stalled.

"Why are you jealous of Mason talking to me?" She came to sit next to him which made him feel ashamed.

He shook his head. "I'm not jealous of Mason talking to you." He took a deep breath feeling caught by his own mouth. "I'm jealous of the time he gets with you."

He heard her intake of breath. "But I love you..." she began, and he knew she misunderstood him.

He turned to her taking her hand. "I know, baby. If there is something I'm absolutely sure about, it is that you love me. I also know that Mason respects our marriage." He rubbed his head in frustration trying to find the words. "I pray and hope you fall in love again when I'm gone. I would be selfish not to." He had to keep it general. "But seeing you and Mason talking this afternoon reminded me of my prayer and that I have everything I could ever want right here in my hand." He rubbed her hand with his. "The one thing I don't have that any man might have with you, is time."

"You never know. He may have even less time with me." Paige quirked.

"Not funny," he said, looking at her, thinking of his doctor's visit, but he pushed the thought aside quickly.

She looked somewhat abashed.

"I want a lifelong love for you, but I'm crazy jealous of the man who will get to spend that time with you," he said finally getting to the point.

He felt her get off the bed, but instead of letting go of his hand she held it tighter and knelt beside his feet facing him. "You are my present and whatever future we get. You are the man who showed me how to be free in expressing my love for you. You are the one I fell in love with when I didn't think I had any room in my life for it. No one will ever be able to take your place." She put her hand to her heart. "It is here for an eternity."

He took in her earnest expression and her words and was mollified.

"That's what this is really about, right, me replacing you or forgetting you?"

He considered her question and shook his head again in the negative. "No," he said watching her features shift. "I just really want more time with you."

"She leaned in placing her hand on his cheek. You said something very wise a couple of weeks ago."

He sniffed. "Just one thing in two weeks?" he said in mock offense.

She patted his cheek firmly. "Focus."

He tamped down on the urge to rub the spot.

"You told me that it isn't the amount of time that's important, but what we do with it. It's the memories we make and the expressions of love we share. You were right." She sat back on her heels for a moment wringing her hands together.

"I'm sorry I wasted so much of our time pouting, raging, throwing tantrums, and just being a big crybaby."

He reached down and brought her up to sit next to him. "Paige," he began but she interrupted him.

"No, let me say this. I know I haven't handled this well, and I could justify my actions by expressing my love, but that doesn't make it right." She rubbed her fingers along his long ones. "We were thirty thousand miles high when I was shaken out of my pity party, and it occurred to me that all life was fragile, and therefore an even more precious gift. I'm sorry it took me so long to get my head out of the sand."

"Okay. I've listened to you, now I need you to listen to me."

"No matter what else happens, I want you to promise me that you will not regret our lives together." He held up a finger when she opened her mouth.

"That means you don't regret time lost, or emotional outbursts we have had. We live for the moment and take in as much as we can together."

She stared at him for a moment then nodded. "No regrets."

"No regrets," he repeated. Then wrapped his arm around her shoulder and kissed her temple.

*   *   *

The day before they were due to leave, Brandon woke up with Paige half on him. She'd gradually moved closer to him during sleep each night they were married. He was now used to waking up with her arm thrown around his waist, her head on his chest, her body plastered to his side, and one of her legs wrapped around his. He lay there for a half an hour allowing her warmth to seep into his bones while he took in the scent and feel of her. When the sun touched the window seal he knew it was late enough to wake her and began running his hands up and down her back.

She stretched like a cat in his arms as she usually did when he woke her this way. She kept her head on his chest so her morning breath wouldn't hit him. He understood the courtesy but would have preferred seeing her eyes when she woke.

"Good morning," she said, her sleep-roughened voice bringing out his possessiveness. He continued to run his hands across her skin as he responded. This gorgeous woman was his wife. The one he had the pleasure of waking up to morning after morning. She was the one he got to hold in his arms when they went to sleep at night. He knew what made her laugh and cry. He knew some of the most private things about her and she knew the same about him. He hugged her to him a little tighter, but she shifted and the thoughts left him.

"You, my love, are breathtaking," he said, waiting for her to turn to him. She moved and looked up at him with those beautiful golden eyes that coaxed him from the sidelines of his life. She smiled at him. "Really? You couldn't even see me."

"No, but you were laying on my solar plexus so you really were breathtaking," he responded with a grin.

She smacked his shoulder. "Funny guy."

He shrugged. "I'm just sayin'."

"That's okay," she said, trying to move away in a voice that said it was anything but.

He held her to him not allowing her to put too much room between them.

"Don't get huffy. I was joking... a little," he continued before she could reply. "I love being your personal pillow."

He watched as she looked everywhere but at him. She squirmed a little, but when her efforts to slip out of his grasp remained futile she stopped.

"You will never get away," he said.

331

She must have heard the change in his voice because she looked into his eyes.

"You have embedded yourself into very fiber of my being." He stared into her eyes. "Just like the way you sleep wrapped around me; there is no place in my heart, mind, and spirit that you have not touched. I know I've said this before, but I feel more alive with you than I ever have in my life. Thank you for being the beautiful woman you are, and thank you for sharing yourself with me."

He watched as the tips of her ears pinkened then lowered his head to kiss her forehead.

"Thank you," she said in return after a few swallows. "I feel the same way, and I wouldn't change any part of my life before you because it all brought me to you."

Her words rocked him to the core. He didn't have the words to respond, so he lifted her up so he could kiss her.

Minutes later he whispered, "How about we skip breakfast and stay in bed a little longer."

She looked him in the eyes, concern skittering across her features. "Are you tired?"

"No. I just want to hold you for a while," he said with sincerity."

"Well, then, by all means. Hold on."

"I will," he said, meaning it in more ways than one.

CHAPTER 23

She pushed the door open as she had hundreds of times, hoping he was close so she wouldn't have to venture too far into the house, but as all the other times she heard him call from the back of the house and was propelled forward by her need to soothe him.

The place was stifling, and she had to crouch to find cooler air as she continued. She ran her hand along the wall to familiarize herself with the rooms as a cloud of smoke seemed to float from the ceiling. She slowly moved around a corner and a veil seemed to lift from her eyes. She was in a nursery room. The animals, clouds, and balloons painted on the walls attested to it just as the two cribs lined up next to each other against the wall did.

It suddenly became imperative that she see who was in the cribs but the floor began to pull at her. She looked down to see nothing but sand around her ankles. Each step was a fight, and she moved at a snail's pace until she was finally in front of the first crib. The pink blanket inside covered a screaming baby girl. She reached in to soothe her and the child immediately quieted. She blinked at her with golden eyes and smiled until a cry rang out from the other crib.

Mel cooed at the baby when she began to fret, and once again she went still except her eyes turned toward the crib next to hers. Mel's attention was also drawn to the crib. She stepped to the side peering over the railing still hearing the cries of the baby but seeing nothing but a blue blanket.

"Mel."

She was wrenched from the dream by Marc's hand on her shoulder. She blinked at him trying to ground herself in the present.

"Are you alright?" Marc frowned over at her.

"Um, yes," she answered, looking around her at the street they were parked on. "Where are we?" She hated the shakiness of her voice that mirrored what was going on in her body.

"New Orleans near the address that was on the paper you took from the safety deposit box." She stared at him.

"How long have I been sleep?" she asked, trying to orient herself.

"About three hours. I just drove through," he said as he continued to watch her.

"What time is it?" She rubbed her eyes pushing the remnants of the dream to the back of her mind.

"Seven thirty. I thought you might want to get breakfast first."

She gave him a grateful smile and looked around him at the diner across the street. "That would be wonderful."

He offered her a wan smile. "Do you want to talk about it?"

"What?" she replied, distracted with getting her purse and jacket. She would have loved to freshen up, but Marc didn't want to get a room until after they finished the business they'd been led there to take care of. She checked her jacket for the paper and key she'd carried around since leaving the bank in Colorado Springs.

"The dream you were having when I woke you." She looked up to see him staring at her.

"What? How'd you know…" Her voice trailed off as she realized his look of concern. "What did I say?" she asked, looking back through the front windshield of the car they'd bought from a private seller found on Craigslist. It was an older model vehicle with a roomy interior. It reminded her of her second car which was what led her to choose it out of the dozens of ads in the area.

"Most of it was incoherent, but at the end you were kind of cooing. I'm not sure how to explain it."

Her stomach flipped at his words. He'd gotten it right. She had been cooing.

334

"I was dreaming of them in their cribs, but even though I could hear B.J. crying, when I got to his crib he was gone."

Marc rubbed her shoulder and she relaxed a little. "It doesn't have to mean anything. They are forefront in your mind. It would be odd if you didn't dream about them."

She tried to allow his words to soothe her but the dream had left her shaky. Even in her dreams she couldn't see B.J. anymore. It was as if her son never existed.

"I checked out the address on the way here. It's a postal annex so the suite number is probably one of those mailboxes people use to have their mail diverted. It doesn't open for an hour and a half so we have plenty of time to eat." She gave him a perfunctory nod.

"Once you've retrieved whatever's in the box we can either get a room for a few hours or get back on the road and call Gladys."

Mel perked up. "I want to call my baby. I'll drive for a while if we're led out of town." She felt some of her energy return. They hadn't seen nor talked to Gladys since dropping her off at the airport in Florida. They'd taken a two-week vacation in Orlando, Florida visiting Disney World's parks. The look on Gladys' face when they announced their plan was priceless. For two weeks all they had to worry about was putting on enough sunscreen, where to eat, and slightly aching feet. It was fantastic and bittersweet knowing it might be the last time they were all together for a few months.

Mel reached for her door looking at Marc over her shoulder. "Come on, lets get some breakfast. I'm starved.

The diner was a decent size with tables and chairs spaced out around the big square room for a little privacy. The walls were painted a cheery yellow with red accents throughout. The smells coming from the kitchen made her mouth water.

Neither said a word until they'd been led to their seats and had given their drink orders. Marc started on a whisper. "Brian's medical file was flagged."

"Wait. I thought Mya got that information months ago," Melanie said, speaking of the planted information about Brian and his fictitious stay in the mental ward, while his grandfather set up new identities for Brian and his son and found a double who could come home to the Grossenbergs for a while.

"Yes. Mya picked those up a while ago. I'm talking about the real file sealed by the military."

"How?" Melanie began but the lightbulb went off in her head. "Grace."

"Yep." Marc nodded.

"What's she looking for, now?"

"DNA," Marc said quietly.

Melanie gasped.

"I think she's trying to test it against the remains Antonio has," he said.

"Is there anything we can do to delay or stop her?"

"It depends on how far she's gotten. You are going to have to prepare yourself. Those insinuations Antonio made in regards to Brian being alive and him finding a viable sample to test the remains against may become a reality."

Mel groaned. They'd been so careful. She wasn't sure whether Antonio was baiting Victoria and Richard for information or to gain an ally but she'd underestimated his resourcefulness.

Whose side was he really on?

From what she'd been told right before she had to let go of her childhood love, Brian would be secretly groomed to take his grandfather's place. The man had to be in his seventies by now. She didn't know about him, but if she were in her seventies, she would seriously be considering retirement.

Melanie considered that fateful night she'd met Luca Sable and was told what to expect as soon as she gave birth. It shocked and angered her that he would want to take not only her love away but her son, but once he was done sharing some of the plans her mother had for Brian and her son she relented and followed his instructions to the letter.

When Grace left the next day on one of her many "business trips," a very pregnant Melanie allowed Mr. Sable's doctors to examine her and her twins. Deeming them close enough to term at eight months she allowed them to induce labor then she and Brian were taken to State General Hospital by his parents. Melanie gave birth to a son and a daughter, only the son was born almost two hours before her girl due to complications. Paige was breech and Melanie had started bleeding profusely.

Thinking she was going to die, Melanie begged them to allow Brian into the delivery room. Hoping it would soothe her they let him in. She urged him to take Paige too and seeing the look of stark terror on his face she knew he would do what he could.

She'd woken up almost a day later with her mother at her side holding her baby girl. Grace told her that by the time she'd reached the hospital she'd been told that Melanie's boy hadn't made it and Melanie was in critical condition. When Grace came back to sit with her the next day she told her Brian and his family were gone, and she and her mother were moving across town. Having been warned about her mother's deceit she'd broken into bittersweet tears of relief and sorrow for what she'd lost.

Those first few days were excruciating. She'd gotten to hold her son only once, and she felt his absence as though she'd lost part of her heart. Brian's disappearance had cut almost as deep, but she held out hope that he would find a way to contact her.

Three months later she finally heard from Brian via a message passed to her by a little old lady while she was shopping with her mom. She read it as soon as she could put Paige down for her nap. It read, *I am safe and so is our son. My grandfather said you are family now and will be protected.* Then he gave her one clue if she needed to reach him in an emergency and wished her a good life. She cried for days after that, and when asked what sprung the latest outpouring of tears she told her mom she was crying for her son. When word got back to her two weeks later that Brian had killed himself she cried even harder knowing he was truly out of her life.

Melanie put her head in her hands. They had taken so many precautions, but nothing was foolproof. The fear that caused the hairs on the back of her neck to lift had her wanting to get up and run, but Marc seeing the look in her eyes placed his hand on hers.

"I'm not going to promise anything but I will be there for you and will continue to try and muddy the waters enough to lead Grace around in circles for a while.

An hour and a half later with a full stomach and hopes of speaking to her little girl soon, Mel entered the postal annex and walked straight for the wall of boxes. She scanned the numbered boxes looking for a match to the suite number on the paper she'd looked at enough times to memorize. When she spotted it her heart rate picked up. She knew it would probably only take her to another spot in the country, but it was one step closer to Brian which meant it was one step closer to her boy, even if the odds of seeing him were close to nil.

She found the corresponding box number and took a deep breath before using the key from the safety deposit box. There was only one piece of mail in the box and it was addressed to a Mr. Norris, postmarked from within Louisiana, with no return address. Mel smiled thinking of Brian's penchant for Chuck Norris movies. She locked the box back up and left as quickly as she came.

Once she was back in the car she only spared Marc a glance before opening the envelope.

"Where are you sending us now?" she whispered as she pulled the slip of paper from the envelope. After glancing at it she showed it to Marc.

"Oregon? You've got to be kidding." Marc groaned.

"You said the old man was thorough. If Brian was anything like him we will be at this for a while," Mel said giving Marc an apologetic smile.

Marc looked at his watch letting out a deep breath. "We can handle this one of two ways. Since we are now driving back across the country, we can get on the road now and call Gladys a half an hour outside of New Orleans, then continue driving for a few hours before settling in for the night. Or we can get a room now, sleep for a few hours, then get on the road and call."

Mel knew her answer before he'd finished. "Let's get on the road now. We can call Gladys then keep driving. I'll drive, so you can get some rest before we stop for lunch." Marc simply nodded and opened his door to switch places with her.

"Is there anything you want to see or experience before we leave New Orleans?" Marc asked once they were situated.

Mel shook her head in the negative. This wasn't a pleasure trip. This was business, and the lives of her children were threatened more each day it took for her to get close enough to Brian to leave a message.

CHAPTER 24

Victoria sat back in her chair staring at the irrefutable proof that Antonio and Grace were more than well acquainted. Boy, that woman sure got around.

Stupid man.

She shook her head switching to another photo of Antonio and Grace kissing. The photos were from a little more than a decade ago. She wondered how long it went on then became indignant over the fact that the boy she thought the world of would fall so low. If she didn't know before that he wasn't ever the man she saw through her rose-colored glasses as a young adult, she knew now.

She put the pictures away and got ready for the dinner that would mark the end of some of her guests' visits. The house had been full for a week and she loved it. She got to cater to Paige and Brandon, and it seemed to feed her heart to do big and small things for them and their friends. Little Nicky was one of the most adorable babies she'd had the pleasure of being around in a while, and it brought back good memories of her Brian who had also been such a mild-mannered infant.

Richard came into the bedroom as she was laying out her dress for the evening. He walked right to her kissing her cheeks and allowing his lips to linger at her forehead. She looked up when he moved away. "What was that for?"

He shrugged. Then gave her a squeeze. "I missed you and wanted to show you some love."

"Well, I'm all for that." She watched him looking at her. "What were you doing when this urge came over you.

"I don't know," he said, putting his hands in his pockets as he sauntered over to the closet. "I was talking with Brandon about some of the upgrades recently made on the irrigation system in the south pasture. Somehow, we got on the subject of churches and how different denominations are structured. He has so much knowledge." Richard shook his head. "I've barely gotten to know him, and I already know I will miss him."

She watched his head bow for a few seconds, and her heart went out to her husband, but instead of going to him she sat on the edge of the bed. She'd been wrong. Over the last few days she'd also grown closer to Brandon. His ready smile, calm demeanor, and easygoing nature was only surpassed by his obvious love for her Paige.

He'd shown her in less than a week that the love they shared for each other had no expiration date. He loved her holding back nothing. When Brandon looked at Paige the love in his eyes was so open and transparent it affected everyone who witnessed it. He proved her wrong with every gesture, word, and touch that it wasn't the time that mattered but what one did with it.

She finally got up, walked over to Richard and embraced him from behind. "Who would have thought that a newly married couple could teach us so much," she said into his back.

"Yeah," was all Richard said in return.

Dinner was lively with everyone talking and laughing around the twelve-seater, formal dining table. Everyone's attire was a cut above casual and they looked beautiful. Victoria watched everybody interacting with each other and counted dinner as a success. She took it in with a feeling of peace and accomplishment knowing that this might be the last time all of these people were here together like this. She sat at the opposite end of her husband who was bracketed by Paige and Brandon. Dominy sat next to him with Robin and Nicky across from him. Vivian sat next to Nicky to help feed him and Gladys next to her. Next to Dominy was Paul then Antonio, Mason and Mary sat to her left.

She'd worked hard for what she had and so had her husband. They had property in different cities, successful businesses, and plenty of money, but she felt wealthier at that moment than she had at any other time in her life. She gave God a word of thanks for the people around that table and what they'd brought to her life. When she felt the back of her eyes begin to burn she returned her focus to her food and worked to regain her composure.

As a surprise, Victoria had hired a small live band that played jazz and set them up in the side courtyard next to the garden, so the guests could dance and sit back and listen. Victoria took a few turns with Richard then danced with Brandon, Paul, and Dominy before she sat down for the rest of the evening claiming tiredness, but really she just wanted to sit back and take it all in.

She felt it when Richard sat down next to her. "You did good."

She smiled after glancing at him briefly then looked at the couples swaying back and forth on the makeshift dance floor. "Yes I did, didn't I." Richard took her hand and squeezed it, bringing her close to tears but she refused to give into them. She still had a reputation to protect.

Later that evening after seeing Mary and Paul off and saying good night to the others, she and Richard invited Antonio to have a late-night drink with them in her study.

"How did you enjoy your stay?" Victoria asked Antonio.

"It was pleasant. Your farm is incredible." He crossed his legs as he sat on her couch sipping at his cognac. "As I have told you before. I'm sure you're proud of what you have accomplished here."

Victoria wasn't sure, but she could swear that his words shared more than one meaning. "Yes. It took a lot of blood, sweat, and tears to get this place to where it is now." She looked over at Richard sitting in the club chair across from her. He gave her an imperceptible nod.

"I make sure I do extensive research before I introduce any new chemical to anything on my farm. I try to make sure that nothing gets in that will poison the crops. Otherwise I wouldn't be a good farmer, would I?"

"That is correct."

"So were you able to glean what you needed?"

He shrugged. "Enough. She is a beautiful woman." What I didn't expect though was the Pitbull."

Victoria looked at him in confusion.

"Mason never let me get closer than arm's length when I thought she and I were alone. You'd think he was her husband instead of Brandon.

"She's his daughter's mother."

"Yes, but that was only a recent revelation. He protects her as if..." He smiled... "Well, let's say he acts as if he were also the biological father."

Victoria saw behind the careful façade in that one smile.

"Family protects family. If nothing else you taught me that."

"I want you to stop whatever it is you're looking for and with whom you're looking with."

"Is that a threat?"

"No. I'm just giving you some advice and I hope you listen." She got up walking over to her desk to retrieve the envelope of pictures. She walked back to him handing him the envelope.

He frowned up at her. "What is this?"

She just nodded and went back to her seat to watch him open the envelope. When he did so his face paled. He sifted through the pictures, and his initial gray pallor began to redden. "Where did you get these?"

"That isn't as important as why they exist in the first place."

Antonio continued to stare at the pictures for some time before speaking. "I'm not going to try to explain how it happened, but before it was over I regretted it and then even more when she came back in my life a few months ago with an ultimatum." His hands shook.

"Which was?"

He let out a deep sigh. "To draw you in, get you to approach me and feed you information."

Victoria glanced at Richard, quickly exchanging messages.

"False information?"

"No. Not all of it. I was to compel you to gather your family here which included Paige and Melanie."

"Why especially those two?"

"Grace believes Melanie has been hiding something from her."

"These are pretty extreme measures even for Grace to go through just because she thinks Melanie is keeping something from her."

"I thought the same thing until I kept coming up against dead ends when I tried to obtain my son's medical records. Someone is protecting his information like Solomon's tomb. Why would you protect a dead person's records?"

Victoria's heart skipped and forced herself to calm. She'd been here before and it hurt every time it led to nothing. She didn't want to speak.

"Tell us why you think someone would hide or protect a dead person's records?" Richard asked, and she sent him a grateful look.

"It's no secret that my dad, Luca, hasn't fully handed over the reins to the business to me, yet."

"Well, from what I remember, he liked to play God."

Antonio quirked a smile at her. "Still does." He let out a breath. "I have jumped through hoops for that man and have done everything he's asked, but he refused to confirm or sign documents making me the official CEO."

344

He nodded at the photos he'd thrown on the coffee table between them. "That happened at a particularly low point and it may jeopardize everything I've worked for almost all my life."

In that moment Victoria felt sorry for the man who at once seemed to have it all.

"What are you saying, Antonio?"

"I think my dad has been grooming someone else for the position. I know it's a long shot, but I wouldn't put it past him to have been working behind the scenes all this time." He leaned forward looking back and forth between them.

"Some of the information I shared with you a couple of months ago I discovered as I said, but some I acquired from Brenda/Grace. When she set out to blackmail me I did a little more digging." He gestured to the photos.

"I can't attest to the authenticity of everything, but I do know that Brian is Paige's father, and Melanie is Paige's mother. What I didn't tell you was something I recently discovered that should make Brenda/Grace a great deal more vulnerable than she is," Antonio stated.

"Stop beating around the bush," Victoria said impatiently.

"Brenda/Grace was kicked out of witness protection when proof came forward that she'd hired a man to kill Brian."

"What?" Victoria asked before she could stifle her surprise.

"I don't know the details, but I came upon the information because I knew about her cooperation with the government in the first place," said Antonio.

"Why is she not in jail?" Victoria said flustered.

"Something about tainted evidence and the man for hire went missing. It never went to trial." Antonio said rubbing his forehead.

Victoria closed her eyes taking a few deep breaths before she realized the room was quiet. She opened them and looked at Antonio expectantly.

He continued, "If Brenda/Grace was no longer under government protection, how is it she and her daughter have survived this long without any threats on their lives? There's only one person I know who has the power to keep all the other organizations she betrayed at bay." He sat back.

"Luca," Victoria and Richard said in unison.

Antonio nodded without triumph.

"What do you want?" Victoria asked.

"I want to be out from under that woman's boot, but I have to be honest. I don't think you or your Richard can help me. Only one person may have what it takes to help me, but no one can find her."

He was talking about Melanie. Victoria thought.

"What does she have?" Richard asked.

"If he's alive, Melanie may know where Brian is." Antonio said to Victoria.

Victoria tried hard not to put hope in what he said, but try as she might, she couldn't keep her heart for reaching for that distant dream.

*   *   *

Victoria hugged Paige one more time before releasing her. "Remember, I'm only a call away and if I don't hear from you within a week I'll be on a plane. That's not a threat; it's a promise."

Paige laughed. "I'll make sure to call you."

Victoria watched Paige's expression change. "I admit, I came here wanting to put you in your place for keeping me out of the loop, but I understand your misguided attempt at protecting me." She smiled softening her words.

It was Victoria's turn to laugh. "Thank you for your understanding."

"*Thank you,* Grandmother."

Victoria drew in breath at Paige's use of her title and worked hard not to burst into tears. Instead, she hugged Paige to her again marveling at the fact that this beautiful, strong woman was family. She sniffed back a tear and let her go.

"Go. You're going to miss your flight." She started pushing Paige toward the waiting jet.

Paige started laughing and yelled over her shoulder when the engines started up. "It's your husband's company jet."

"That's Granddad to you," Victoria called back.

"That's not helping your case," Paige said before moving toward the jet.

"Talk to you soon," Victoria yelled.

Paige turned and placed her hand to the side of her head in the universal sign of a phone receiver.

Victoria slowly walked back to the car and watched the plane travel down the runway and take off before leaving the small airstrip. Only then did she let the tears fall.

CHAPTER 25

Richard woke up earlier than usual with a thought that couldn't fully be grasped or squelched. The gradual shifting from the dark sky to light and colorful sunrise were missed on Richard as he went back over the details of Mya's report on Melanie. For so many years she looked the part of loyal daughter and lapdog to Grace, and within days of their initial meeting with Antonio she up and disappeared, leaving Gladys with Paige indefinitely. What was he missing? Was Antonio really onto something?

He knew that no matter how hard she tried, his wife wouldn't be able to keep her hopes from rising. His job was to help them come true or to see that when they fell, there would be a cushion.

"You all are up early this morning," Richard said in greeting as he walked into the kitchen passing each of them and bestowing a kiss on their heads. He sat across from his wife at the round table. "We were too excited to sleep!" exclaimed Vivian. "We have a lot of work to do," she said, looking over at Gladys for confirmation, and Gladys nodded before taking another bite of her eggs.

"Really; and what is going to keep you so busy this morning?"

"We are going to help with the chores. Cows get up early, so we had to get up extra early, so we could eat before Malcom could show Gladys and I how to milk them. After that we are going to the northeast field. I think Robert calls it zone number six."

Richard prided himself in knowing all of the hands, both temporary and full time, who helped work their land but Richard drew a blank at Robert's name and face. He turned his puzzled gaze to Victoria.

348

"Robert is Nathan's grandnephew. He's here for a few weeks before going back to school in Bolin Green, Ohio. He told his uncle he wanted to know what life was like on a farm. He's considering biological engineering and wanted to see if agricultural engineering was something he wanted to pursue."

"What college is he enrolled in?"

"He's going to be a junior in high school," Victoria said with a raised eyebrow.

Richard was surprised by her answer and glanced around the table to see two sets of silver eyes watching him. He hoped his father radar was just being hypersensitive.

"What did you say his name was again?" he asked nonchalantly at no one in particular as Martha set a plate of eggs, sausage, and fruit in front of him. He smiled his thanks.

"Robert," Vivian and Gladys said in unison.

He took in their smiles then looked over at Victoria to see if they were playing a trick on him. She raised her eyebrows and took a bite of her grits.

He said grace over his food and began eating to give himself something to do while he devised a plan to secretly kill and hide Robert's body.

"Where are we going today?" he asked no one in particular.

It was day six of entertaining the twins alone. The adults had left the previous Sunday with Victoria and Richard offering to keep the girls an extra week. It would still give the girls enough time to get ready for the new school year, but it would also allow Gladys' arrival back at Paige's to coincide with Brandon's family's arrival.

Paige called Victoria a couple of days after returning home to let her know that Brandon put in his resignation. He said he wasn't able to give his job one hundred percent anymore. He was just too tired. Paige said he was sleeping longer than he had during their visit at the farm but he wasn't in pain.

When Victoria asked if she needed help Paige let her know that Brandon's mom was arriving in a couple days, and the rest of the family would follow later in the month. No matter what Paige or Brandon said, Ava Tatum wouldn't be deterred.

"We're going to a rodeo," Gladys said proudly.

"Really," Richard stated with nonchalance.

"Yes, and I'm going to dunk for apples," she continued.

Richard worked to keep his lips from twitching. "Bob."

Gladys looked at him in confusion. "Who's Bob?"

Vivian laughed, and he caught the smile on Victoria's lips before she hid it behind her cup of coffee.

"It's called bobbing for apples."

Gladys' brows furrowed more. "But aren't you dunking your head in the barrel to get them?"

"Well, hopefully not your whole head. Just your face and teeth."

"That doesn't sound as easy as Viv made it seem." She gave her sister an accusing look.

Vivian merely shrugged and kept eating.

"Have you bobbed for apples before, Vivian?" he asked.

"When I was really really little. I think six."

This girl was precious. She was still really really young, but he kept his mouth shut.

"It was one of the games at a birthday I went to." She tapped her forefinger on her lips as though she were deep in thought. "It was more like a wide, shallow tub, so the bobbing was pretty minimal." She ended the sentence with a shrug and bit into her toast.

He didn't even try to control the grin that lifted his lips.

"Okay, what do you want to do besides go bobbing for apples?"

"Vivian wants to watch the bull riding event, and I want to see the barrel races," Glady quipped.

A phone rang, and Richard checked his pockets for his cell, but it was blank when he retrieved it. He looked around the table to see everyone else mirroring his movements then Gladys put her phone up to her ear. "Hello?" Her face broke into a grin.

"May I be excused?"

"Sure," Victoria answered, and Gladys ran out of the room.

Richard looked at Vivian who grew quiet, then Victoria. "It must be Paige," he assumed.

"It's Melanie," Vivian said staring at her plate.

Richard was immediately on alert. "How do you know?"

"Because every time she calls, Gladys leaves the room, and the phone always rings with Gladys' default ringtone. Like her phone doesn't register who the call is from. She has a special ringtone for everyone else."

Richard and Victoria exchanged knowing glances.

"Is Melanie in trouble? Is that why she left Gladys with Paige?" Vivian asked

"I don't know," Victoria answered. "Why? Is that what Gladys thinks?"

Vivian shrugged. "I don't know. She won't talk about her."

Richard wanted to wipe the worried look from Vivian's face but wasn't sure what to say. He didn't know why he assumed Melanie wasn't speaking to Gladys either. She was her daughter in almost every sense of the word.

"I don't want her to get in trouble," Vivian said, her chin beginning to tremble.

"Who, honey?" Victoria asked

"Gladys." Vivian answered with a sniff.

"I don't see why she would," Victoria said in a soothing tone.

"Because she's lying. Daddy said not telling someone something you know that they would want to hear is the same as lying," Vivian announced, her face crumbling.

Victoria got up and was holding Vivian before Richard could rise from his chair.

"Aww, no one is getting into trouble." Victoria rubbed her back. "You're right. When someone asks you a question, if you willingly withhold information so that they think you mean something else, that is a sin and yes, a lie." Victoria took a deep breath. "I don't believe Gladys refuses to talk about Melanie to hurt you or be deceptive. Maybe Melanie asked her not to talk about their conversations, and Gladys is trying to keep her promise?"

"Why would her mom do that if she wasn't in trouble?"

Richard saw Victoria's arms briefly tighten around Vivian. "I don't know, honey, but we can pray for her."

Vivian looked up at Victoria with wide eyes. "Right now?"

Victoria looked at Richard over Vivian's head, and if it wasn't such a sensitive subject he would have chuckled at Victoria's wide-eyed look.

"Um, sure."

Vivian took Victoria's hands and bowed her head waiting for Victoria to begin.

Victoria sent him an imploring look, but he gestured for her to begin.

He watched as Victoria cleared her throat and took a deep breath, but he bowed his head when she began

"Dear Lord..." Victoria paused for a moment. "I thank you for giving Richard and myself more time to spend with Vivian and Gladys. They are a joy. I want to ask you to comfort Vivian right now. Please soothe the hurt in her heart that her sister may have caused. I ask that you also comfort Gladys right now from the hurt she may feel from not being able to be with her mom. Um... please protect Melanie and Marc while they are away. Don't allow them to be harmed and keep them from danger. Bring them back to Gladys as soon as possible." Victoria paused again so long he was tempted to open his eyes, but she spoke again on a breath. "In Jesus' name. Amen.

"Amen."

He and Vivian said in unison. He watched Vivian hug Victoria tighter.

"Thank you for the really good prayer, Gran."

Victoria seeming at a loss for words shrugged and kissed the top of her head.

They finished breakfast in silence, but he couldn't help noticing the small smile that played at Victoria's lips.

When Vivian finished, she jumped up with her plate and told them she was going to run to the barn. Richard waved her away then sat back and watched Victoria until she pointedly looked back at him.

He repeated Vivian's words with a smile. "Really good prayer, Gran."

Victoria's smile grew wider, but she only nodded her head.

After watching the girls with the young Robert, Richard searched out Victoria who was weeding in her garden. He sat on the center bench, content to watch her work for a while.

"What do you think we should do about Melanie?"

Victoria sat back and took off her gloves. She tipped her wide-brimmed hat up so she could meet his eyes.

"I honestly don't know," she said shaking her head.

"I want answers so badly, but I don't want to use Gladys to get them."

He rubbed his forehead. "I really don't think Gladys has them anyway. She just gets to talk to her mom every now and then from what I believe is a burner phone, and if Marc is as smart as I think he is, it isn't the same one."

"I think we should wait for Melanie to come back."

Her statement surprised him.

"Really? I thought you would be anxious to see if she knows where Brian is."

Victoria was quiet for a few seconds. "If she does, she's protecting him for a reason. Do I really want to risk his safety?

Besides we don't even know if that is why she disappeared in the first place. It's all speculation."

"I'm proud of you."

"Why?"

He shrugged. "You are showing a great deal of restraint."

"Richard. Not even six months ago I thought he was dead. If there is a chance Brian is still alive, I don't want to do anything to jeopardize that."

Richard nodded. "Well said."

"I'm fine, Richard," she said, pulling her gloves back on. "Two years ago I thought life and God cheated me out of being a mother, but in light of what we've learned lately I wonder if He is using my loss to bring my attention to what I've gained."

"Like what?" He had a feeling he already knew, but he wanted to hear it from her.

She looked him straight in the eye. "You, for one."

He wasn't expecting that.

"I almost lost you because I couldn't let go of my anger and pain, but you forgave me." She gave him a lopsided grin. "And now through rather peculiar circumstances I have been united with my granddaughter. There was nothing I could have done to bring that about. I know because I've tried with our investigators only to hit dead ends. If God wants to bring our family together, who am I to get in His way."

Richard watched his wife go back to work on the outlying weeds and breathed a sigh of relief and thanks. He didn't know if his wife knew what she just said, but he heard a woman who had finally put her trust and her families' well-being in the hands of the only Being who could protect them all.

He was looking forward to seeing what else God would do because He had just performed a miracle and answered Richard's prayer.

CHAPTER 26

She was in Wyoming. How had her life made so many unexpected twists and turns as to bring her to Casper, Wyoming?

Melanie sat cross-legged on the bed flipping through book titles on her tablet while she waited for Marc to come back to the room with lunch. She needed something to take her mind off her constant worries.

She wanted to be with her children. It hurt worse each day not to be near them, but she had committed three months ago to see this through, and if she gave up now it would all be in vain. She couldn't just up and leave this crazy cross-country scavenger hunt. She'd known by New Orleans that their movement from place to place was being tracked. They weren't being followed per se, but each place she was led to left a trail that Brian could check up on.

The safety deposit box she had to sign to open, the piece of mail she took from mailbox, and the key and lure keychain she took from the owner of the bait shop at a small campground just off of the Oregon Trail, who'd looked at her quizzically before having her sign his ledger. The key went to a lockbox at Nathan's Tack & Lockbox Storage—that's what the keychain said—in Milwaukee, WI where they found two pictures that nearly stopped her heart and the friendship bracelet she'd made Brian for Christmas the year they were together.

She slowly picked up the first picture that had yellowed with age. "It was one of Brian holding Brian Jr. B.J. couldn't have been more than eight months at the time. He was a beautiful baby with his honey-colored skin and silky, loose curls. He had Brian's deep-brown eyes. He was smiling up at the person taking the picture, his pudgy hand reaching for the camera. The second picture showed a boy of about twelve with a mop of brown curls reaching his ears on the sides and collar in the back. She shook her head, the picture blurring slightly through her tears. *His hair is too long.* She thought endearingly. B.J was lanky. He looked as though he'd recently had a growth spurt. His caramel-colored skin matched Paige's at that age, and his chin jutted out in pride as he held a football in his hands. "Thank you for this," she whispered into the small storage space.

She rolled the bracelet around in her fingers remembering one of the best Christmases she'd had as a child. Christmas Eve she'd snuck out of her room at eleven fifty p.m. and met Brian at their shared back fence. He climbed over to her side, and they sat in the grass with their backs against the fence in the only part of her backyard that wasn't illuminated by the patio light. They talked about their day, and family—or lack thereof—who would be coming over for dinner the next day.

Melanie's family had been invited to join the Grossenbergs for Christmas dinner, but her parents wanted their last Christmas in two years, quietly.

At midnight, Melanie and Brian exchanged presents. Melanie had worked for weeks on the threaded bracelet interlacing the colors so their initials were placed side by side on his wrist. He'd given her a knit cap with wolf ears and a pair of earrings she'd shown interest in one Saturday afternoon. They had walked the mall waiting for his mom to pick them up after a movie they'd gone to with a group of kids. She'd kept those earrings for years in a small box in the corner of her hope chest.

Brian shared that he wanted to see Old Faithful at Yellowstone National Park. He was fascinated by its ability to spout water more than ninety feet in the air. He said he would take her there if she continued to be nice to him. By the next Christmas neither family lived in that neighborhood.

Not seeing anything else in the box she turned the pictures over. The one with baby B.J. read, *He's got your chin. I also hope he's as faithful as you.* On the back of the second picture she found the following question. *Do you remember the Christmas morning we spent together? I got my wish. I told André in the gift shop, all about it Wednesday.*

Melanie stared at the two pictures for more than ten minutes before she was absolutely sure of where to go next. She just needed to double-check that a guy named André worked at the Yellowstone National Park Geyser's gift shop on Wednesdays.

So here she was in Wyoming on Tuesday afternoon trying to talk herself out of giving up her search and running to her child's side in what had to be the hardest time in her life.

Gladys was now back with Paige and Brandon, and Gladys had reported that Brandon's health wasn't good, but she was excited about school on the West Coast, and Paige had taken her out shopping for supplies and clothes. It sat wrong with Melanie. That had been her job. She and Gladys would make a day of it, spending hours going from store to store then to a restaurant and finally to the movies if they had the energy to sit through one without falling asleep—which they still hadn't been able to do—but it was fun trying.

This year Paige got to do it, and she couldn't begrudge her the opportunity. From what Gladys told her, Brandon's side of the family had come into town and were taking turns spending time with Brandon. Gladys had at no time been asked to give up her room but would share if from time to time with Brandon's mother, Ava.

Brandon stayed home most of the time moving slowly between rooms. Paige shared with Gladys that the cancer riddling Brandon's body had spread to his pituitary gland causing him to have to go through a saline IV treatment each day due to his inability to retain water. She said though he tried to eat; his appetite was almost

357

nonexistent. It didn't stop everyone from trying to tempt him with his favorite foods.

Gladys told Melanie she gained five pounds her first week back; the food was so good. It was yet another reason why Mel was conflicted. No child needed to be forced to live in that type of situation. She was glad Brandon's family was there to add support for all of them.

Melanie also received reports from one of Marc's friends who, as a favor, was keeping an eye on Paige and Brandon. When Marc shared that piece of information with her the night before, it had gone a long way in smoothing some of her feathers he'd ruffled with his double-oh-seven-style approach to reaching the campsite in Oregon over a week ago.

If she ever went back to teaching she would be able to give her students firsthand insight on some of the places she'd been forced to visit due to Marc's antics. Like part of the Oregon Trail Marc tricked her into hiking.

She didn't say anything when Marc chose to have them leave the car at the small resort he'd discovered near the trail. She didn't say anything about the backpack full of food, warm clothing, and water she'd had to carry. She did, however, have quite a bit to say to him after seven miles when her feet were so tired, every tree looked like a great place to rest for a few hours, and there were a lot of trees along this part of the Oregon Trail.

Marc had the nerve and lack of foresight to say, "Wow. I'm impressed. You lasted three hours." Then he'd handed her his water canister which she took a long swig of before accidently—on purpose—spilled some on him. He tried to jump out of the way, but her juggling guaranteed that he would not escape unscathed. When she finally righted the bottle the front of his shirt and jeans were soaked. She tried to look genuinely apologetic, but was sure the smile she couldn't fully hide thwarted that endeavor.

He gave her a disgruntled look before taking off his backpack and retrieving a dry shirt. "Feel better?"

She really did, but she just shrugged as he changed shirts.

"I thought it would be best if we hiked to the address you were given since it belongs to a small campground. That way we'd have a good excuse to keep moving after picking up the next message. Besides when do you think we will get the chance again to hike part of the Oregon Trail?"

"Hopefully never," she murmured.

"Exactly," he said before putting his backpack on and continuing on.

The sound of the lock turning brought her out of her thoughts. She looked up to see Marc step through the door, his hands filled with bags. She got up off the bed to help him. "How much food did you get?"

He waved her back and moved to the small table in the corner. "I have it. Could you go to the bathroom to get us some napkins. I think they forgot ours."

She turned taking three steps before the type of shock only cold water could render hit her between the shoulder blades. She cried out and turned only to get tagged with another stream of water to her chest. That's when she spotted Marc standing in the middle of the room with a water gun the size of a AK-47.

"Youuuuuu. I can't believe you!" she yelled and sputtered at the same time.

"Really." He seemed to ponder her outburst. "I don't know why. I never thought of myself as a pushover. You had to know I would get you back." He looked at her as though questioning her sanity.

"It was an accident," she lied.

"Yes, and so was this." He looked her up and down and began grinning like a loon.

She stomped her foot and promptly burst out laughing. "I can't stand you, sometimes," she said between breaths and pulling her top away from her skin.

Marc placed a hand on his chest. "Don't say that. You'll hurt my feelings." His hand started moving around his torso as if searching for something.

"What's wrong? What are you looking for?" she said, finally gaining control of her laughter.

"My feeling." He looked down at the floor. "I thought I brought it with me." He seemed to give up and shrugged. "I must have left it in the car."

She walked to the bed, picked up a pillow and threw it at him as hard as she could. "Feel that?"

"Hey!" he exclaimed, narrowly dodging the cushion-turned-missile.

She beat a hasty retreat to the bathroom when she saw him bend to pick up the pillow. She heard the thud a second after she closed.

*   *   *

Wednesday morning Melanie and Marc were the first customers to enter the store serving those who visited the geysers. They walked around the store for ten minutes before she made her way to the counter.

She glanced at his name tag, grateful she wouldn't have to ask around for André.

"Hi, André? She phrased it as question to make sure he wasn't borrowing someone's tag.

"Yes? How can I help you?"

"She leaned in to make it hard to be overheard. "My name is Mel. Melanie." She searched his face for recognition, but it remained pleasantly expectant.

"I had a childhood friend who shared with me, one Christmas, his dream of coming here to see Old Faithful." She thought she saw his jaw tighten but couldn't be sure.

"I was told that if I came this way, I should ask for André." He stared at her for a moment.

"You said your name was..." His sentence faded into a question.

"Melanie. He knew me as Melanie Morganson."

"How'd he tell you about me?"

She retrieved the photos from an envelope in her purse and handed him the one with Brian's message regarding him. Then watched him read it.

He looked up and passed the photo back to her. "Wait here. I have something for you."

When he moved away she turned to see Marc lingering at a nearby display of postcards of Yellowstone Park.

"You okay?" He stage whispered.

"Yes," she replied in the same manner and turned back to the counter.

A minute later André came back with a legal-sized envelope. "Can you tell me how long you've had this?"

"Nope," he said and smiled briefly.

"Okay. Thank you." She lifted the envelope in salute. "When or if you two talk again. Could you tell him I might need to go home soon to comfort my daughter?"

André gave her a blank stare, and she gave it back to him for a few seconds before turning around and leaving the store.

Melanie waited until they were back in the hotel before she opened the envelope. She and Marc sat side by side on the bed, both anticipating and dreading the next message. She reached in, pulling out a few pieces of paper and a small notebook. She picked up a small sheet on top of the others and read it to herself.

"Ever been to Montana?" she asked Marc.

361

"No," he replied.
"Well,   here's   your   chance.

CHAPTER 27

Mason couldn't understand the silent treatment he'd gotten from Tabitha since he'd returned to Chicago. He'd left her on very good terms with hopes of deepening their relationship. Mason had even called her during his visit with the Branchetts, and nothing seemed to have changed. She was as sweet and flirty as ever.

He'd called her the day after he arrived home, but she never returned his call. He'd stopped by her apartment when he spotted her car out front one afternoon, but no one answered the door.

He left a few more messages as the days went by, but he no longer held out any hope in speaking to her.

He couldn't say he was devastated. Curious? Yes. Relieved? A little, if he were honest. He was a little hurt that she would think so little of him that she could just disappear on him.

Mason went back to work, happy for once that Vivian was staying an extra week with Victoria and Richard. He scheduled a couple of therapy sessions with Dr. Seagrate, worked on a few things around the house he'd promised to get to but never made the time. Toward the end of the week he called Brandon and Paige because he couldn't stop thinking of them. There was a bond that solidified between them while at the farm that he couldn't deny.

"Hey, man. How're you doing?" Mason began when Brandon answered the phone.

"Pretty good. I am now a retired man. I don't know what I will do with myself," Brandon said with a smile in his voice. At first Mason didn't know what to say. He knew Brandon most likely had to quit due to his health, but if he was presenting it as a perk, then that's how Mason would accept it.

"Nice. How many people get to retire in their thirties?"

"To be honest, I'm not sure thirty-something people should retire. I have entirely too many ideas and thoughts to sit still."

"Maybe you and Paige can write something together."

"That's an interesting idea, but I don't know about infringing on her career like that. I'll give it some consideration though."

"Meanwhile, you said your family would be coming into town."

"Yes. My mom is coming next week, and the rest will be taking turns throughout the next month or two."

"Oh, we'll see," Mason said as if the problem had already fixed itself. "You will be spending so much time trying to entertain them you won't have too many quiet moments to ponder the wonders of the world."

"Is that what you do when you aren't working?"

Mason thought about his question and decided to be candid. "The only time I've taken off from work was right after Rachael died. I was having a hard time juggling Vivian, work, and everything else. I could have slept through the next couple of years if it weren't for Vivian. It was so hard just getting out of bed in the morning." He realized he may have shared too much when he was met with silence on the other line when he finished.

"Brandon?"

"Yeah." He sounded preoccupied.

"I have to say though that I was angry with God and the world for taking her away. My growing grudge against God at the time had a lot to do with my depression."

"What about now?"

Mason took a deep breath. He'd walked right into that.

"What do you mean?"

Brandon chuckled. "How is your grudge against God, now?"

Mason gave his question true consideration before answering. "I saw and experienced some things during this last visit with the Branchetts that have me questioning my determination to keep as much space between me and God as possible.

Mason heard a cough that sounded suspiciously like a laugh from the other side of the line.

"Are you okay?"

"Yes. I'm just trying to absorb what you said and figure a way to respond without offending you."

Mason didn't know whether to encourage the conversation or end it.

"Whatever. Just say it."

"You sure?"

"If you think I'll get upset, hang up on you, and never call you again, you won't be that lucky."

Brandon chuckled. "Okay. Listen to what I am saying because I don't want you to take this out of context." Brandon paused. "I think Vivian is a very blessed child. God has taken care of her and made sure she's not without someone in her life to nurture her relationship with Him. First your wife then Paige. He is keeping Vivian close, and she is fortunate and blessed for it. She's a special child with a beautiful and open heart."

Brandon paused again, and Mason got the feeling the next thing he said wouldn't be as flattering.

"You, Mason, are blind and not a little bit selfish if you really believe what you said about keeping space between you and God."

He heard Brandon take a deep breath. "May I ask you a question?"

Mason, blindsided by the change in Brandon's voice as well as what he'd said only a few seconds before said yes.

"What drew you to your wife, Rachael, besides her looks? What was it about her that made you want to be near her and marry her?"

Mason took a deep breath. He hadn't thought about it for a while. It had hurt too much. He let out the breath. "From the moment I met Rachael she felt like a breath of fresh air. She was never afraid to tell me what she thought of me, of her beliefs, of life. Her love for life was addicting. I had never met anyone who got so much pleasure just waking up. She was on a life-long mission of discovery to see what she'd missed the day before." He paused to see if the accompanying pang that usually came with his thoughts was on delay, but when he was only embraced by warm feelings of nostalgia he smiled to himself.

"She was the same way with her love for God. She would try to respect my feelings toward Him, but every now and then she would be bursting with it and tell me I would just have to sit there while she shared something special God told her or she realized while reading the Bible, walking on our property, or during her prayer time."

He swallowed. "Sometimes when she finished talking I purposely put on a blank face and acted like I didn't completely understand what she was saying. It wasn't to hurt her, but so she wouldn't hope that my true reaction would lead to reconciliation or a request by me for redemption." He rubbed his head realizing just how selfish his actions were and how many times he missed sharing something with her. He remembered the look of sadness in her eyes when she thought he couldn't see what she did.

"Sorry, baby," he whispered to himself. Another thought came to him, and he saw that Brandon had pegged him perfectly.

"I also didn't want to give God any credit for the beauty He gave her." He hated the shame he felt over doing something he'd considered justified at the time.

Brandon was quiet allowing him to work through some of the feelings.

"Now can you tell me what draws you to Paige?" Brandon asked, his voice full of emotion, but not the type he expected.

Brandon didn't ask 'What draws you to my wife?" but what drew him to Paige and the emotion choking him sounded like deep sorrow.

"Um." He couldn't believe he was going to answer this question. "I don't think I started trying to dig myself out of my depression until I met Paige. She looked straight through to my soul the first time we met, and I felt that maybe it wasn't as dark in there as I thought."

Mason wanted Brandon to tell him to shut up or stop talking about his wife, but he got only silence, so after a few moments he continued.

"There were some similarities between Rachael and Paige, especially when it came to God." Please forgive me, Rachael, he spoke to himself.

"But where Rachael's relationship with God seemed to be one long honeymoon. Paige's relationship with God seems more real. She seems to have ups and downs with Him. She said she didn't have a problem asking Him questions or pouting when she doesn't get her way, but she has to come back to Him, open to hear Him, because she can't imagine going back to a life without Him.

She once told me that she couldn't be with a man she couldn't talk about God with because she loved God more."

"Yes. That sounds like Paige," Brandon finally responded with affection. "Did you believe her when she told you that?"

"I did," he said.

"Then why did you continue to pursue her knowing you would be cheating her?" Brandon asked.

Mason had to admit he had a point, but say as much.

"Love isn't that logical."

Brandon laughed, but there was no humor in it. "Love is more than emotion, Mason. It isn't only reactionary; you do it on purpose. You choose how you represent your love. You choose to give the one you love anything in your power to give or you choose to make them settle. They have a say, and they can choose to take you as you are, or hold out for everything they have been waiting for. My wife chose to settle for less time with me, but I will move every mountain I can to show her it will be the only concession she has to make for marrying me."

Mason had nothing to say about Brandon's diatribe. He felt like he had been put in his place, but Brandon had said nothing he could argue with. It made it hard to talk at all but he didn't have to worry about that.

"Look, Paige just got home, but I want to say one more thing." Mason hoped it didn't cut like his last few words.

"Okay."

"I think you are drawn to women with strong relationships with God because it allows you to get close enough to Him without having to commit to acknowledging Him. I don't think that revelation will rock you because you all but admitted it already. What you will have to come to grips with is that I believe God allowed it because He would rather speak to you though others than not at all.

I think another reason you had such a hard time after Rachael died was because it wasn't just her you were missing."

Mason just sat there with his mouth open and his guts splayed wide.

"Thank you for calling, Mason. I enjoyed our talk. If you want. I'll give you a call in a couple days."

Mason didn't know what he considered less painful—a mouthful of teeth needing root canals or another call with Brandon.

He opened his mouth to say so but out came, "Sure."

"Okay. I'll talk to you later."

"Okay," Mason reciprocated then pressed the end call button, considering briefly of changing his number.

Over the next week Mason gave what Brandon said some serious thought. What did that say about him if Brandon was right.

He brought it up to his therapist, and Dr. Seagrate suggested he continue to have "these talks" with Brandon.

"He may be onto something. Did you consider that it might be why you had reservations about your relationship with Tabitha? You told me she would capitulate easily when you expressed your dislike in discussing God."

Mason laid his head in his hands. "What does this say about me?"

"That you had a bad experience with someone you loved who misrepresented someone else you love, and the betrayal was felt so deep the choice was to bury it and deal with it later, or face it with the fear of ending up like your mom." Dr. Seagrate shrugged. "You're a fighter. You just chose to delay the battle."

Mason continued to talk to Brandon over the next few weeks. Their conversations grew shorter, but no less thought provoking. The focus left Rachael and Paige, moving to Vivian, and finally himself and his relationship with Victoria. He didn't know why he didn't see it coming, but he was surprised when Brandon brought it up one late night when neither of them could sleep.

"I know that you give me certain concessions because I won't be here too much longer to tell your secrets, but if you could give me one more, I want to talk about Victoria."

Mason didn't know what to address first, Brandon's poor choice of words or the subject of Victoria. Before he could decide, Brandon continued as if he'd been given permission.

"You and Victoria have a lot of great qualities in common. You both value family, are loyal and loving, but you are stubborn, have trouble letting go of control, and will sacrifice precious things for your pride."

Mason thought Brandon was wrong. He wouldn't have sacrificed Rachael's life for pride. He would have done anything she asked. "Like what, he asked, ready to argue his point."

"Time, Mason. You sacrifice time."

All the wind went out of his sails. Brandon was right, but there were so many harsh words and feelings between him and Victoria. His five-day visit at their house had been the longest they had gone in each other's presence without full-out insulting each other. There had been a few tense moments, but they were nothing compared to last year.

"And I bet you want me to make the first move," Mason said, working hard not to sound disgruntled.

"It would guarantee when the preparation could begin on your relationship," Brandon said matter-of-factly.

"Point taken," Mason said. He tried to swallow past the taste the thought of apologizing to Victoria gave him. She had tried to take his child. The thought heated his belly.

"You are only responsible for *your* actions not hers. You don't forgive to make the other person kneel before you or give them a pass. You forgive, so you can free yourself from the anger and pain they caused. Forgiveness is for you. The stress and bodily harm you do in keeping your feelings of hate bottled up for them will do you more damage than the glares and words you hurl at them."

Brandon chuckled. "You have me sounding like a preacher, but I will pass on something my dad said to me, 'If you put the unforgiveness on the table, your hand is open to pick up peace.'"

"You have two hands. No offense to your dad's illustration," Mason quipped.

"None taken, but hopefully you have love in the other hand," Brandon said yawning.

"I'll talk to you later, Brandon. Get some sleep."

"You too, Mason," Brandon replied, then ended the connection.

Mason slowly lowered the phone from his ear.

It would figure that he would grow to really like Brandon now. It also showed him again that Paige had chosen the better man.

Truly.   What   was   God   thinking

CHAPTER 28

It was odd, Brandon thought. He'd known for over a year about the cancer, yet it wasn't until recently that he felt like his life was on fast forward. One moment he would feel God's peace all around him, and he would consider welcoming what would happen next. Then a moment would come along, like his family crowding around their dining room table laughing and joking, and he wanted to wrestle with the inevitable just enough to get some extra minutes or hours with them—with Paige

It was selfish; he knew it, but his body didn't have a problem declaring all-out war on the cancer cells, which was why his doctor said he'd become so tired. His body was trying to survive any way it knew how, so it would put certain areas on reserve causing him to have to rest while it fought.

With the rapid loss of strength he knew the day was fast approaching. He felt it almost every time he woke up. Still, he had to thank God for keeping the pain away and keeping His word not to draw it out.

He couldn't help but worry about Paige. She was putting up a good front, and he knew something very profound happened to her on the plane as she'd said, but he could see the sadness in her eyes when she thought he wasn't looking and though it had lessened greatly she still had the tendency to count her steps or the front door locks. His family was great. He didn't know if he could be as calm as he was without them. They rallied around him without making him feel like an invalid —sick person and kept Paige just busy enough when she wasn't writing to make her feel needed and a modicum of control. They were exactly what he needed.

One of the first conversations he remembered his family having with Paige was what her writing time was. It made him feel good that they respected and treated her writing time in her office just like work hours for her. Even still, she only worked for four hours at a time instead of her usual six or eight-hour stints.

He shared his concern in her falling behind one night, and she gave him a particularly mischievous smile letting him know what she and Carmen had devised to keep her from missing her first few deadlines. He kissed her, proud of her forethought and choosing such a savvy agent.

His family, not wanting to overwhelm Paige—he was used to it—came in increments of one to three at a time. Ava came in by herself the first week the family was to arrive, saying they didn't want to bombard them with the entire clan.

She said she was there for however long they needed her and would be with them for the first week but staying at a distant cousin's house about ten miles away after Gladys got back, if that was all right. The rest of the family would come and go, staying a week at a time, their stays sometimes overlapping but by with no more than four or five visiting at one time. They'd worked out a schedule just to spend time with him a couple of months before, but no one expected he would go downhill so fast.

He saw the relief in Paige's body after Ava shared their plan with her, even if she was able to mask her expression.

He thanked his mom profusely when Paige went to her office later that day.

"Baby, we're here to make life easier for you two, not harder. If there is anything we haven't thought of, let me know, and I'll send out smoke signals to the tribe." He chuckled at their common reference to their family. With six siblings and their individual families, planning family reunions was a daunting task, but his mother said everyone had made themselves available and communicated individually to make sure their visiting would overlap as little as possible.

It made him grateful to have a family that loved him and each other so deeply.

Two weeks after they returned from Oklahoma Dominy came back and stayed for a couple of days. He and Brandon spent one afternoon reminiscing. They laughed at some of Dominy's antics when they were young, when Dominy met Robin, and the rough time Brandon had when he'd met Paige. Brandon's older brother Elias Jr. teased him something fierce during that retelling, pantomiming Dominy's dramatization of his and Paige's separation and the fight behind it earlier in the year. Brandon was a good sport about most of it, grimacing at the thought of what would have happened if Paige hadn't been so determined to see their relationship through. He would have missed out on so much. *Thank you for her, God.* He thought. *I just don't have the words to tell you how much she means to me, but I guess you already know.*

Pastor Lawrence and First Lady Menagerie came over twice a week to pray or have Bible study. The first night his dad, Elias Sr. was in town for Bible study went so long due to their discussions on each verse of 2 Kings Chapter 2. Brandon thought it ironic that they would discuss the story of Elijah getting ready to leave Elisha, and Elisha begging him to stay, but when he looked up at them when the scriptures were announced everyone was concentrating on finding the pages.

He sat there listening to the two wisest men he knew debating over different points in the scripture until he fell asleep. A little time later his father shook his shoulder. He peeled his eyes open noting the apologetic look. "Sorry to wake you, but I don't think the recliner will be the most comfortable place for you to spend the night."

"Thanks, Pop." He pushed the lever to bring the footrest down.

"I was curious," he said slowly.

"Yes."

"Tonight's scripture, did you think it was ironic that Pastor Lawrence would choose that one?" His father seemed to ponder that for a moment.

"In what way?"

Brandon blinked at him. "In the way that God was taking Elijah, and Elisha was asking him not to go."

His father smiled. "Do you think Pastor Lawrence was asking you to stay?"

Brandon shook his head to the negative wondering if he was missing something.

"I wouldn't presume to think of myself as Elisha," Brandon said.

"Why not?" his dad asked him.

"Well, because you and Pastor Lawrence are mighty men of God that I can learn a great deal from," Brandon said it like it was a given.

His dad moved to sit in the closest chair before looking him squarely in the eyes. "You, my son, are a mighty man of God. You might be young, but I don't know too many men twice your age who could handle what you have in your life with such humility, obedience, and grace." His father took off his glasses and retrieved a handkerchief from his back pocket before speaking. "You inspire me, son."

Brandon was taken aback by his father's words. He wanted to ask him to repeat himself, but he was too stunned to speak.

His dad started chuckling and ran his hand across his face. "I'm sorry. I never told you that straight to your face. It was wrong for me to assume that one of the many people I've told over the years would have shared that with you."

Flummoxed, Brandon continued to stare.

His dad cleared his throat. "It was no secret why you left. You have always been your own person. When you were young you were very singular. You saw things differently and had an innate sensitivity toward people's feelings. I saw it before Peyton died, but it become more apparent afterward. I thought you had a very lonely road in front of you, but one day you brought home a sickly looking little boy with eyes too big for his head and introduced him as your new best friend."

Brandon couldn't help but laugh at his father's description of young Dominy.

"We figured if he lived through the winter you two would be friends for life."

Brandon smiled wanly. "Well, he got lucky."

"I don't think he will ever consider it luck," his father said, his expression growing somber.

"He is blessed to have you in his life and vice versa, and he will miss you greatly when you're gone because you befriended him when he felt invisible."

"Dad." Brandon put up a hand for his father to stop because the tears that welled up were fighting to be released.

"You need to hear this, son. You have been so strong for so many. You try to bring levity to this situation every chance you get to make everyone feel better. I admire that, but right now I am speaking to you face-to-face, and I want to tell you that you have been a huge source of pride in my life. It would devastate me if you left here not knowing just how much I love you, and how sorry I am that it is coming this late."

The huge lump in Brandon's throat shut off any form of communication other than a nod.

His dad got up, approached him, and kissed the top of his head. For a man who wasn't overly affectionate the gesture resonated through Brandon, and the composure he was fighting for left him.

He began balling like a baby, and his father's arms enclosed around his shoulders holding him tightly as he shook.

"Please forgive this old, foolish man."

Brandon nodded and just held on to his father's arms until the worst of the stormy emotions passed. When he was finally able to take a deep breath his father's handkerchief appeared in front of his face. That darned handkerchief, how many times had he seen his father pull one out for blubbering women and children. He almost started all over again but held it back with a chuckle.

"What is it?"

"I never thought I would be the recipient of one of your handkerchiefs."

His father returned his watery smile. "I never thought you needed it."

Brandon shrugged.

"Right." His father's shoulders slumped, and he began to move away.

Brandon caught his wrist and held fast. "I'm sorry for leaving as I did. Communication goes both ways. I should have told you that I felt like your shoes left huge imprints."

"I knew that. I wasn't going to try to keep you, but I didn't want you to feel that you had to run away. I wanted you to feel you could come back at any time."

"Thanks, Dad."

His dad kissed his head again and moved back to his seat.

"So I should dispel your misinterpretation of Pastor Lawrence's choice for the scripture tonight? He was telling you that you remind him of Elijah. He shared the conversation you had with God regarding this bout of cancer. That though you accepted His decision to allow this disease to take its course, you negotiated how you were to leave this earth, and you believe He will honor it." His father looked at him in fascination.

He nodded. "Yes, and He has. I have no pain and aside from the few pounds I've lost to my lack of appetite there has been no noticeable change. I told Mom I want an open casket at the funeral."

His father quirked a smile at him. "How did she handle that?"

Brandon shook his head, smiling back. "Not well."

"Yes, well," his father said as he tipped his head to the side. "A mother's love." He let the sentence hang there.

"What kept you from considering that you might die suddenly from an accident?"

"Because He wants the glory from this.

The next few weeks became a revolving door of friends and family coming in and out of town. He felt like he was having one huge birthday party. He asked that him and Paige have the late evenings. No visitors after eight o'clock which earned them a nod of approval from the hospice nurse that started coming by after the latest lab results. He didn't need blood work to tell him that the cancer had spread throughout his brain.

He felt sluggish even the first thing in the morning, and it took more and more concentration to keep from slurring his words, but it didn't keep him from lying in bed with Paige at night and talking about anything and everything until his lids grew too heavy to stay open.

It came on a cool and crisp morning in the middle of October. He woke up feeling odd, like he was tethered to his body by a thread. He opened his eyes with more effort than the day before. He turned his head to see Paige still sleeping soundly. He lay there just staring at the peaceful beauty next to him until she took a deep breath and opened her eyes. He watched the sleep fall away as she smiled at him. It was always worth waiting for. He smiled back trying to hide its importance, but he knew he'd failed when her smile fell away and her eyes misted over.

"Soon?"

He swallowed. "Yes."

She placed her hands together under her cheek and took in all of his features, her eyes bouncing around his face. He knew she was committing this moment to memory.

He chuckled. "Not yet, though."

She let out a breathy chuckle. "Okay. I'm going to the bathroom. Stay there."

"Yes, ma'am."

And that began a day of Paige, Ava, Margaret who'd arrived earlier that morning, Elias Sr., and Dominy who had come back in town the day before, sticking to him like glue. If one of them left the room they would tell him not to go anywhere. It became a running joke after Paige had shared her morning scare.

It was mostly quiet, and he felt a deeper peace than he could ever remember feeling. All day long, but that evening it intensified to the point where he hesitated to speak in fear that it would shatter it. Nothing did, though.

He summoned each one of his loved ones in for a long hug. Then kissed them and told them he would see them again soon. It was slow going because no one wanted to let him go and his speech was impeded.

One by one they left the bedroom until there was only him and Paige who was sitting in a chair across the room. He lifted and crooked a finger at her.

"Come lay next to me." Brandon said patting the bed with his fingers.

"I don't want to disturb you."

"The only way you will disturb me is if you don't come lay down."

She walked to the bed, slipped off her shoes and slowly climbed in bed next to him. She was too far, so he frowned at her, and she scooted closer but not enough for his liking. He growled at her and she giggled but moved so she was flush up against his side. It wasn't until then that he sighed and relaxed.

"You and I have had quite a journey." He took a breath. "I knew you were special, but I didn't expect to live so much in so little time." He took another few breaths and Paige took his hand.

"Like the dream I had when we first met." He waited impatiently until he caught his breath. "I truly started living the moment you came into my life.

He smiled slowly though she couldn't see it. "You are a force to be reckoned with." He paused.

"I love you, Paige Tatum."

"I love you too, Brandon Tatum."

"No regrets?" He turned to watch her.

"Not a one," she said with small smile that failed to reach her eyes. He wondered if he'd miss that.

"Good." He stared at her for a moment. "You can do this. You're stronger than you think." He squeezed her hand.

"You have family that will hold you up when you feel weak." He waited until she nodded before continuing. "Don't forget that."

She shook then nodded and he leaned toward her enough for her to realize he wanted to kiss her.

He lay back feeling his energy draining. He closed his eyes and summoned enough strength to finish what he wanted to say.

"You know, true love cannot be lost or severed," he whispered. "You are in my heart, and I will take you with me just as you will keep me and my love for you in your heart." He fought the fatigue that was trying to pull him into sleep.

"Thank you for the gift of your love."

"Thank you, baby." He heard her respond just before sleep overtook him.

Sometime later he woke to a presence. It was like nothing he'd felt before. It both pressed him to the mattress and beckoned him forth. He barely felt Paige's head on his shoulder, and he wanted to shake her to see if she felt it. It was consuming, and pure, and sweet, and… beautiful.

"I have fought a good fight." He whispered. "I have finished my course. I have kept the faith; Henceforth there is laid up for me a crown of righteousness, which the Lord, the righteous judge, shall give me at that day: and not to me only, but unto all them also that love his appearing."

He felt himself being lifted and the thread anchoring him to his body released. He closed his eyes to the sweetest feeling of well-being.   He   was   going   home.

CHAPTER 29

Paige woke to a vibration. She opened her eyes noticing briefly that the small light in the corner was on.

"I have finished my course," she felt and heard Brandon whisper. "I have kept the faith." She stilled hoping it wasn't what she thought.

"Henceforth there is laid up for me a crown of righteousness..."

His voice grew more whispery with each word till she had to strain to hear him, but she didn't dare move.

"Which the Lord, the righteous judge, shall give me at that day: and not to me only, but unto all them also that love his appearing."

His breathing became labored at the end of the scripture then she felt his body relax. She lay there, each minute feeling like an hour. She wanted to shake him awake but just couldn't move.

She watched his torso rise with an intake of air and lower one last time. She stared at his chest hoping it would expand again, but when seconds went by she closed her eyes to concentrate on his heartbeat which stopped soon after that. Then she felt it. He was gone. His body was still on the bed, but his presence was gone.

"Come back," she croaked. "Come back. I don't think I'm strong enough for this."

She squeezed her eyes shut, but couldn't stop the tears and then she was crying uncontrollably. She was vaguely aware of someone coming into the room. A hand touched her shoulder, but she burrowed into the body on the bed.

She was scooped up, and she fought to stay but whoever held her was stronger. She cried harder, begging for Brandon to come back. She felt a prick on her arm and a lethargy took over her body and pulled her down into darkness.

Paige woke up feeling groggy, but she didn't remember taking anything the night before. She blinked and found herself disoriented. She wasn't in her room. She was in the twins' rooms. She felt the bed dip behind her. "Brandon, why am I..." The memories started forward like an out of control reel of film.

Brandon died, and she didn't handle it well.

She slowly turned to see two pairs of silver eyes peeking at her over her shoulder.

"Hi, Mati," they said in unison. Their eyes wide with concern. She realized what they'd heard and sent them a wry smile as she turned over to show them she was okay.

"Hey, babies." She pushed a few strands of hair from her forehead. "How are you?"

They looked at each other then back at her. "You've been asleep for a very long time. We were getting worried. She sat up gingerly feeling stiff and an overpowering urge to go to the bathroom.

"Could you give me a moment." She spotted her robe at the end of Gladys' bed. She pushed herself to the edge, donning the robe. She got up on extremely wobbly legs and took the arm Vivian offered. Gladys opened the door, peeking out before giving Vivian an all-clear sign.

Vivian helped her cross the hall to the restroom, and she took care of business and gargled with some mouthwash since her tongue felt like she'd been licking rugs.

She opened the door coming face-to-face with a concerned-looking Ava. "Hello," she said, feeling uncertain.

"How are you feeling?"

She took stock of her body and emotions and felt... nothing. Well not really nothing. She felt detached.

"Um, was I given something?" She leaned in not wanting to be overheard.

"You were upset, so they had to sedate you to keep you from hurting yourself," Ava said as she guided her back to the twins' room but the girls were gone.

Paige sat in one of the desk chairs and Ava leaned against the desk. "What's the last thing you remember? She recalled feeling a deep sense of loss.

"Brandon died," she said succinctly.

Ava gave her an odd look, and she knew what she was thinking. Paige was thinking it too.

"I think I've lost my feelings."

"What do you mean?"

"I feel detached from everything. It feels more like a dream even though I know it all happened. I'm expecting Brandon to walk through the door at any moment and ask me why I slept in the girls' room last night. Paige couldn't help looking at the door for a few seconds before returning her attention to Ava who was now looking very uncomfortable.

"What is it?"

"You've been asleep for two and a half days."

"Two and a half?" Paige repeated hoping it would register, but nothing happened. Panic began to set in.

"Don't worry. You haven't missed much. The hospice nurse was already here, so they cleaned and dressed the body, and the mortuary picked it up. Brandon planned ahead, so the programs are being printed as soon as we have a date for the funeral.

Why hasn't it been set, yet?"

Ava cocked her head to the side. "Because we were waiting for you to wake up."

Paige ran her fingers along her forehead. "Okay. What would you like me to do?"

"Nothing, really. It's all be taken care of. There are a few friends that arrived today. We were going to have dinner at a family restaurant or order takeout." She stared at Paige for a moment who stared right back.

"If we have everyone meet at the restaurant you will have the place mostly to yourself. Whereas if we do takeout you may be relegated to one of the bedrooms if you don't feel like being around a lot of people."

Paige thought about her choices thankful to be given one. Ava was such a lifesaver. Paige was sure Brandon's mother was grieving just as much, if not more, but she and Brandon's family had everything handled.

"It would be nice to get myself reoriented in relative silence. Who's in town?"

"Well, you've seen Vivian, so Mason is here along with Dominy, who is staying; Margaret, Sarah, and Makayla arrived last night. The boys will arrive in the morning. Oh yes..." Ava's expression darkened briefly.

"Victoria and Richard arrived yesterday. Victoria demanded to see you before she would leave. She even called a doctor who made house calls because she was worried about how much sedative you were given. She was sure you should have woken up before yesterday," Ava said, changing her accent to mimic Victoria's during the last part of her sentence.

Paige smiled, now used to Victoria's overbearing nature. "She ruffles everyone's feathers the first time they meet, but she isn't so bad once you get to know her." What had she just said?

"I see you believe that as much as I do," Ava said, watching her intently.

Paige returned the stare taking in the lines at the corners of Ava's eyes and lips. She realized how selfish she was being. She took Ava's hand in hers. "How are you doing? I'm so sorry for your loss."

Ava blinked once then twice. "Aww, sweetie." Ava removed her hand to pat Paige's. "It's hard. I won't deny it. I may have held on to him tighter after his younger sister died which kept him under me longer, but he didn't complain. I believe he knew even when he was young." She swallowed and nodded.

Paige waited as her new mother pushed back the tears, and she wondered how she went from overwhelming devastation and panic to this numbness that allowed her to recognize and comfort someone else, then she prayed it would last for a while.

"You can hold me tighter if you want," Paige said, hoping the woman would take her up on her offer.

Ava gave her a huge watery smile and pulled her in for a hug. "God blessed my boy with a rare and beautiful wife and me with a special daughter." Ava pulled back, taking Paige's face in her hands.

Their foreheads came together, and Paige breathed in Ava's scent of cocoa butter then sighed. After a few moments Ava leaned away and patted Paige's knees as if she were a little girl.

"So the family and I will take everyone out to dinner. "Is there anyone you would like to stay here with you?"

"Can the twins stay? I'll order some pizza. We can do a sleepover…" She allowed the sentence to fade at Ava's peculiar look. "What?"

"I meant what adult would you like to stay here with you?"

"Do you think I need a babysitter?"

"No," Ava said, drawing out the word. "But I would feel better if you did."

To appease Ava and take that strange look off of her face Paige agreed. "Will you stay?"

Ava nodded her head. "Okay." She patted Paige's hand before standing up. "Okay." Then she walked out the door.

An hour and a half later Paige was sitting on the couch bookended by Vivian and Gladys, half watching one of her favorite action films. The twins had ordered combination pizza of which she picked off half of the toppings before taking three bites. It tasted like cardboard. It seemed as though all of her senses were numb.

She ignored Ava's disapproving nod and snuggled in between the girls with a throw to keep warm. She smelled their heads taking in their individual scents and wrapped her arms around them.

That's how Victoria and Richard found them when Ava let them in an hour later. Paige's arms had gone to sleep under the weight of her daughter's heads which became heavy when they fell asleep. She loathed to move so she didn't and just smiled when Victoria and Richard entered the room and sat across from her.

"How are you? We came by yesterday, but you were asleep. They almost didn't let us in, but I wouldn't leave until I saw you," Victoria said in one breath.

"I heard," Paige responded quietly so as not to wake the girls.

"Vivian called us to tell us about Brandon," Victoria said in a slightly accusatory tone.

Paige looked over at Richard who hadn't said a word. "Hello, Granddad." She sent him a small smile.

His chin trembled before he tightened his jaw. "Hello, baby girl."

She watched as Victoria took in the girls' sleeping figures. "How long have they been asleep?"

"Mmmm, maybe a half hour," Paige said, looking down at each of them.

Victoria made a move to stand. "Your arms must have lost circulation by now. Let me take them to bed."

Paige squeezed them slightly. "Would you take away my comfort?"

Victoria stopped, hovering at the edge of her seat staring at Paige. "I didn't mean... I only wanted to..."

Victoria looked slightly panicked, and Paige's heart went out to her. She probably wasn't comfortable unless she could take control of things especially when her children were involved.

"I'm going to make you a deal," Paige said without moving.

"If you don't question or change the arrangements that Brandon made with his and my family for his funeral or try to push his and my family around, I will come to you a week after the will is read, and I will let you take care of me for a month."

Victoria seemed to take that into consideration. "May I take care of security at the funeral?"

Paige figured she could make that concession. "You may."

"May I help with the reception? I know a great caterer in this area."

Paige looked at her. "Ava?" she called out, squeezing the girls when they moved.

"Yes?" Ava said from behind her.

"Victoria, this is Ava, my mom. Ava, this is Victoria, my grandmother."

"We've met," they said in unison, not looking too happy.

Paige looked up at Ava standing over her. "Has the food and place been confirmed for the repast?"

"The place has, but the food hasn't. We should have an answer in the next couple of days."

"Victoria would love to contribute to the arrangements, but I told her that we handled a lot of the planning with Brandon. She knows a caterer in the area. Could you share the menu with her, so she can see if they can meet the order?" Ava's lips twitched only once before she answered Paige.

"Yes I can." She looked at Victoria. "I'll get you a copy. By the way would you like something to drink while you sit with Paige."

"That would be nice," Victoria answered before looking over at Richard. "Would you like something?"

"Water would be great," he answered back.

"I'll come with you," Victoria said, getting up from the couch and following after Ava.

"You are amazing," Richard said, looking at Paige. "You have had that effect on her from the beginning. I remember some of the things she told with me about you when she met you in the hospital."

Paige shrugged a shoulder. "It sounds funny, but she reminds me of myself both when I was angry at the world, and when I gave my life to Christ and was so eager to help it hurt to sit still."

"I know you hear this a great deal, but you really are wise for your years."

She didn't smile but continued to stare at him. "It comes with a price."

"Yes. I guess it does. You seem to be handling it well."

"No. I'm afraid I'm not handling it at all." She double-checked to see that the girls were still asleep.

"Ever since I woke up today. I've felt a sense of detachment. I can't say I'm numb because I hurt for those who are hurting. Did it feel like you were waiting for Rachael to come back home?"

"No. I got no such reprieve. It registered every day from the moment I saw her body on the bed in the hospital. But I've heard of it happening to others. Eventually, it wears off, though. I hope you have loved ones around you if or when it does."

"Me too."

*   *   *

The next morning Paige woke up much the same way she had the day before. Before full consciousness came she smelled and felt Brandon as if he were right next to her, but when she opened her eyes she was brought back to the present. She waited a few seconds sure that this time pain would come with the realization of Brandon's death, but when it didn't, she blew out a breath.

She turned to see Gladys and Vivian peeking over her shoulder again. "Good morning, girls," she said, turning over in Gladys' bed. She still didn't have the courage to go into her bedroom.

Gladys put her finger to her lips. Paige noticed then that neither girl was talking. She frowned showing her curiosity, and Gladys brought a tablet from around her back. She put her finger up to her lips again before turning its face to Paige.

Paige gasped before she remembered to keep quiet. On the screen was Melanie. Gladys handed her the earplugs attached to the tablet. Paige looked at Gladys briefly.

"They're new," Gladys whispered.

Paige nodded placing them in her ears.

"Hey, small fry," Mel said using Paige's childhood endearment."

"Hi."

"I'm so sorry. I got in touch as soon as I could once you were awake. Please believe me. I would be there if I could."

Paige glanced at Gladys who was looking on expectantly.

"I know you must have a lot of questions, and I will answer them as soon as I get back, but until then I have to ask you not to share with anyone especially Grace that you've communicated with me."

"Why?" Paige asked.

"Because someone's life depends on it."

"Are you okay?" She wanted to know if Mel was in trouble but didn't want to upset Gladys.

"Yes. If I can keep my whereabouts a secret," Mel said and Paige nodded.

"You are strong, Paige. You will get through this."

Paige just nodded.

"I wish I could hug you and make it all better right now."

Paige smiled at the childish sentiment, but if a hug could bring Brandon she would be all for it.

"I love you," Mel said with tears in her eyes. She kissed her lips and touched her side of the screen.

Paige smiled again at the gesture. "I love you too."

Mel waved goodbye and the screen went dark.

Paige took a deep breath wishing Mel was closer than a video call away. Mel knew her. She could tell her why she'd shut down emotionally.

Paige handed the tablet back to Gladys. "Thank you." She looked at her girls who stood in front of her like a pair of centurions.

"Out with it. What's going through those pretty little heads?"

"Are you really okay? Vivian asked.

"You don't cry," Gladys said and was jabbed by Vivian.

"You don't really smile either," Vivian said as if that made it better.

Paige took a breath and tried to explain how she felt so that her children could understand. Once she was done, both of them looked more panicked than put as ease. She resisted the temptation to roll her eyes.

"I'm okay, girls. I will have family around me at all times so when this wears off. I will not be alone."

"What if it never wears off?"

"Nothing like this lasts forever," she said, feeling like she'd just spoken into her own life.

The next few days went by with her drifting around sitting on the sidelines of her life. She greeted and thanked people for their condolences alongside Ava. She'd seen Mason in the background watching her a few times, but other than the first time she saw and hugged him he stayed on the opposite side of whatever room they were in. He looked haggard with blueish shadows under his eyes. She remembered his eyes looking red-rimmed and puffy when he came by the first time and wondered what would cause him to take

Brandon's death so hard. She hadn't known them to be particularly close.

The day of the funeral came, and Paige felt a sense of foreboding. After today people would start to disperse and then the day would come when she was alone. She'd put off the inevitable by promising to stay at Victoria and Richard's, but soon she would be right back where she started.

She pushed the thoughts aside and went on automatic pilot until she found herself sandwiched between Ava and Gladys on the front row and looked up to see Pastor Lawrence at the pulpit.

"I have the honor of giving the eulogy for a mighty man of God today. He is a man who many thought highly of, the only difference being that the closer they were to him the more they loved him. I was more fortunate than some and less than others." He rubbed his head.

"I knew of Brandon a lot longer than I knew him as a friend, and I have to say that I felt cheated when he passed. I felt like the whole world was cheated. Here was a man who sought God out daily rather than wait for the Spirit to prompt him or life to bring him to their knees. A man who lived for God through not one, but two bouts of cancer, finding the love of his life and marrying her knowing they'd only have a short time together.

Brandon's life story wasn't a long one but at thirty-two, it was a full one. He gave his life to Jesus Christ at seven years old because he wanted to make sure he would see his younger sister again, who died the previous summer. At nineteen he was diagnosed with liver cancer and was healed, but not before having to drop out of college and start over. He not only sailed through his college courses, he obtained a job in the pharmaceutical industry that allowed him to travel, meet people, and share the gospel whenever he was off the clock.

Was his life easy? Not at all. How many of you could surrender your life to God to the point where you could still praise Him after receiving a life-altering diagnosis? How about receiving that diagnosis right after finding the love of your life? Would you get angry? I'm sure Brandon did. Would you try and bargain with God for more time? I'm sure he did that too. Would you fear the thought of dying slowly and in pain? Yes. He did that too. Was he a saint? Ah, no." Pastor Lawrence chuckled.

"He could be prideful. Like me. But where I was struggling to keep my reputation, Brandon was struggling to give up his life." Pastor Lawrence shook his head slowly, the smile fading a little.

Yet he stayed right there at God's feet and gave God his anger, his fear, and his desperation. Then he got up, married the woman he loved, and lived more in those six months than most of us will in six decades, and he did it with peace." Pastor Lawrence looked up at Paige, and the lump slowly grew in her throat.

"Why? Because he surrendered his life to God in life, here on earth, and the time he had left on it. So much so that in his relationship with God he felt comfortable enough to ask for a favor. He asked God if he would allow him to leave the earth with a healthy-looking body. Of course, it wasn't. His insides were riddled with disease, but he didn't want to waste away slowly as the body lost its battle.

Brandon wanted an open casket because even in the death of his body he wanted to show us that God honors His promises."

Pastor Lawrence stopped for a moment wiping his eyes then looking back out at the crowd within the church. Paige saw his eyes meeting countless others.

"You may be given ninety years on this earth or you may be given two. You may even leave here and never see tomorrow. But whether you are blessed with nine decades, nine years or nine minutes on this earth, you will spend an eternity either with God or without Him.

"For me and many of you, it's no question where we want to spend eternity. But life with God doesn't have to wait until you leave this earth. You can have a relationship with him, now. He can give you peace, now. He can take away the anger, broken-heartedness and fear, now.

"Brandon's story doesn't have to be rare, though it will remain special. It can become a given. Don't just seek God for eternal life. Start living with Him right now."

Pastor Lawrence had made Brandon's life an alter call, much as she had done just more than a year ago. She closed her eyes to hold back the tears then opened them again knowing it would be in vain. There were staunching tears from the joy of souls being won over for Christ.

Throughout the closing prayer and invitation for people to accept Jesus into their hearts she cried, but when she felt Gladys' body trembling she looked up to see the child crying and lifting her hands to God in praise. She followed the child's gaze as her eyes moved down the aisle, and her heart began to sing at the sight of Mason holding Vivian's hand walking toward the altar.

She put a hand over her mouth to stifle a shout and watched as Pastor Lawrence came to meet him and enfold him in his arms.

"Look at what your life did, baby," she whispered to Brandon as she looked up at the ceiling then at all the people at the altar. "Thank you, God for what you did and are doing." Then she joined the rest in praising God.

EPILOGUE

"Grace. Grace Morganson is that you?" Victoria asked, pulling Richard's attention from the security placed at the doors of the church.

The woman turned around and Richard caught his breath. "Vickie." He said wanting to warn her to remember where they were and it wouldn't be civilized – no matter how convenient – to drag a dead body across the front lawn of a church. He felt the briefest squeeze of her hand and didn't find it a bit reassuring.

They had devised a plan with Antonio before he left the farm, to use Grace's scheming and planning against her. The last thing he needed was for Victoria to get into a shouting match and give away something.

"It's me, Victoria Branchett," Victoria said loudly walking toward the woman, waving her arm, basically calling everyone's attention to them.

Richard tried to catch up to his wife and maybe intervene, but Victoria's next words almost had him stumbling.

"I met you a few months ago at Brandon and Paige's wedding reception," she said almost cheerily except Richard knew her cheery voice, and this was clearly an imposter.

As recognition seeped into Grace's eyes a sneer creeped upon her lips.

"Yes. I remember you now. Your Richard's..."

"Wife. Yes," Victoria interrupted. "I don't think Paige would want you here," Victoria said, taking her volume down so the conversation would stay between them.

"I don't care what you think," the woman said haughtily.

"I don't want you here," Victoria said slowly seeming to revel in saying the words.

"I definitely don't care what you want. I'm going in," Grace said, making to move around Victoria.

Victoria repositioned herself and stared the woman down, then turned to the man at the door who closed it, then whispered something in his mouthpiece.

"I have twenty bucks and Ethan at the door that says you won't get anywhere near Paige today." Victoria continued to stand there blocking the way when a gleam entered her eyes, and Richard watched as the situation shift to another level.

"It's funny how you keep showing up at these family functions... uninvited," Victoria taunted. "Does that not tell you anything?" Victoria crossed her arms, and Richard started looking around to see what was taking backup so long.

"I don't even know why you're here. You didn't show any concern for her while she was nursing Brandon." Victoria stopped and looked at the silent woman.

When a woman like Grace got silent in the middle of an argument she was biding her time for the bomb she was going to drop, and he had a sneaking suspicion of what it would be.

Victoria tilted her head. "You're here for Melanie. Well you march right back through the black hole you crawled out of because she isn't here. We haven't seen her since the wedding.

"I know my girls. They are close. There is nothing that would keep Melanie from Paige," Grace said with too much confidence.

"Well I guess you don't know them as well as you think you do." Victoria slowly gestured around the front of the church.

"You're welcome to walk around the perimeter of the church, but I will personally make sure you don't gain entrance. Paige doesn't need you or your brand of evil. She has family who loves her in there," Victoria said before moving away, but Grace's hand shot out to grab her, and Richard intercepted it by grabbing her wrist.

"You can exchange words with my wife all day, but the moment you put your hands on her it becomes me who you have to deal with." He pushed her hand back toward her while moving to fully block Victoria from her sight.

"You know it took a while for me to figure it out, but no two people could have the same soulless eyes. He leaned forward. "I know who you are, Brenda." He watched her eyes go wide them narrow. "Leave my family alone." He said.

"Or you'll do what?" She sneered.

"Or I will find the one person that hates you more than my wife right now who has nothing to lose by sharing your real identity. And I will start with the picture Ethan just took of you." He shut his mouth to keep from divulging anything important.

Brenda/Grace turned to see Ethan with his cell phone poised at her.

She hissed and turned back. "If there were such a person, and there isn't, you wouldn't just be putting my life in danger, but my daughters'." Her sentence turned into a purr.

He shrugged as she had earlier. "Maybe, but they have one thing you don't to keep them safe."

"Ha."

He leaned back staring at the crazed woman.?

"What is it that's supposed to keep them safe?"

"Family, Brenda. Family."

He walked around the seething woman taking his wife's hand.

He ignored Victoria's questioning gaze until they were out of earshot.

"I'll tell you about it after we take care of our granddaughter."

"Okay, Richard," Victoria said.

Richard looked over to see if she would acquiesce that easily and saw her bright smile.

"Victoria?" He encompassed his whole question in her name.

"I didn't kill her." She said in answer and he sighed in relief, knowing that she had control of herself. And was still willing to follow the plan.

He smiled back and placed his arm around her shoulder as they made their way to the church door, and the security that was finally coming from around the back. He sent them an apologetic look letting them know it did not bode well for them when Victoria spoke to them later.

*

Mason's life had once again formed itself around a routine of work, an occasional therapy session, taking Vivian to school, and getting home early enough to try a so-called healthy and easy dinner recipe. His new routine also included going to church with his daughter twice a month. The other two Sundays he would go to some of his favorite architectural sites and have a talk with God.

It had been a month since the funeral, and his decision to open up communication with God for the first time since he was fifteen had been both easy and hard. Thoughts would come to him unbidden sometimes when he was close to sleep or in the shower, and he would have an urge to open his Bible to figure out the questions that popped in his head. Sometimes he would talk to God about parts of his day or things that perplexed him. It was like getting reacquainted with a friend he hadn't seen for decades but odd because the visits weren't always convenient. Through it, though, he was finding pockets of peace that reminded him of his last few conversations with Brandon. How he missed his friend.

He'd given Paige a courtesy call here and there just to check up on her after the will was read. Brandon had left him a package that Mason brought home and placed in his nightstand drawer. It was irrational, but Mason felt that if he opened the package it would mean Brandon was really gone. While it remained unopened there was something of Brandon waiting for him.

"Daddy, I'm ready," Vivian's voice rang out pulling him from his thoughts. This Sunday they were going to church together instead of him dropping her off. He picked up his Bible and went to join her as they walked out to the car.

Mason wasn't one for sitting in one space every Sunday. He usually let Vivian choose but this Sunday when he spotted a familiar head sitting in the pews toward the middle of the church he ushered Vivian into the pews closer to the back. His heartbeat began to quicken not because he was so happy to see Tabitha but because it was the first time he'd seen her since he left for Oklahoma months ago, and if he was going to get the information he wanted it would have to happen today.

He watched as another woman came to sit next to her who also looked familiar, but he couldn't place her. Vivian pulled his attention away from them when she took his hand and pulled him to a standing position for the Bible reading.

He tried to focus on the service with a glance every once in a while at the women.

Just before the service ended he hugged his child for courage and gave her the keys to the car letting her know that he needed to speak to someone. She gave him a puzzled look but didn't say anything. When the service ended he ushered his daughter out and stood some ways from the entrance, so Tabitha would have to pass him to get out.

When she stepped out he blew out a deep breath and called her name. When she looked in his direction he saw hurt and anger flash in her eyes. Okay. He wasn't expecting that. He waved at her to join him. The woman next to her whispered in her ear, and after a few seconds Tabitha squared her shoulders. Oh, he knew that wasn't good. He didn't have to be an experienced dater to see she was gearing up for a fight. He glanced around to make sure Vivian had gone straight to the car and thankfully she had.

"Tabitha. You are looking well," he said when she finally came to stand before him.

"Mason," she said with an icy tone he didn't recognize.

"Uh, I'm sorry to bother you, but I wanted to know if you would ever give me an explanation for not answering my calls, texts, or notes. Are you alright?"

A moment's hesitation entered her eyes before they turned to green-tinted ice.

"This is my sister Shannon," she said, turning slightly to the woman she'd once mentioned to him. He couldn't shake the feeling that he'd seen Shannon before. He reached out to shake her hand, and she accepted it before she started chuckling.

"He's good," she said to Tabitha.

Mason felt like he'd stepped into the middle of a movie he knew nothing about.

"You don't remember?" Shannon asked.

He peered at her trying hard to put the feeling with the face.

"It was early this year. We ran into each other at the bar and grill down the street from your place. We had a few too many drinks, and you took me back to your place." Mason's stomach dipped, and the note on his mirror came into view in his mind.

Mason saw the smile tip the corners of Shannon's mouth and wondered, even drunk, how he would get close to this woman. He looked back over at Tabitha not missing the hurt this time. "I was in a really bad place after the holidays last year." He put his hands in his pockets. "I didn't handle it right, but for what it's worth, it was the last time." He looked between the two women. "Obviously it was one time too many."

He wanted to get a little closer to Tabitha to stress his sorrow for hurting her this way, but as he leaned toward her she backed. He stopped immediately and straightened. "Please believe me when I say I'm really sorry, and I never knowingly would have hurt you this way. I hope you can forgive me, and give the man who is worthy of you a chance to make you happy." Her eyes softened a little and she nodded.

He gave her a small apologetic smile and turned to walk to his car. After a couple of steps he heard Tabitha's sister ask her if she was going to let him get away without going off on him. He tensed for the dressing down he knew he deserved but she said, "Yes." He breathed a sigh of relief and continued walking to his car feeling like the lowest of men.

*   *   *

Two days later after his conscience had its way with him, he needed a fortitude he didn't seem to be getting from his talks with God. He sat on the edge of his bed for an hour before he opened his nightstand drawer and pulled out the package Brandon had left him. He sat there for another fifteen minutes before he opened the legal envelope, pulling out a small leather journal.

He had to take a deep breath to slow his heartbeat. He was almost more afraid of what he would find between these pages than approaching Tabitha.

He opened the book to the first page and was happy he was already sitting. The title "My Redemption" took his breath away, so he had nothing left when he read the next line. *To Mason Jenson, the other Better Man.*

He read that one line over and over.

He was still sitting in the same position when there was a knock at his door ten minutes later.

"I'm home, Daddy," Vivian called through the door. "Mirabelle is here, and we are going to do our homework at the table."

He swallowed so that his voice sounded normal. "Very good, dear. Tell Mirabelle I said 'Hi.' I'll be out in a few."

400

Silence met him for a few seconds, and he wondered if he overdid it.

"Okay, Daddy. I love you," Vivian responded.

"I love you too, hon." He took a deep breath when he heard Vivian move away from the door.

He went back to staring at the title and dedication for a few minutes more letting Brandon's words wash over him.

Then he turned the page.

*

Melanie smiled over at Marc. They were close—she could feel it. The ferry from New York to Maine was a new experience, and she tried hard to take in everything, but she couldn't stop the restless shaking her legs were doing. "It's okay." She took Marc's hand and squeezed it tightly as the dock came into view.

She didn't know what was different about this time. She'd thought they were close when they'd left Wyoming for Montana. She expected that message to come with directions to a person or device she could use to communicate openly with Brian. Instead she was handed a package at the southwest border and sent away.

She could barely wait until they entered the hotel room before opening the envelope. She dumped the contents on the bed and gasped at the passports and IDs. She opened one of the passport booklets to her picture. Her hair was done into the bun she'd worn two weeks before."

"Milwaukee," they said in unison, looking at one another. She picked up the other passport and found Marc's picture.

She smiled at him. "They're out of the country."

"Where're we going?" Marc asked when she picked up the small paper laying among the pieces of identification.

"We're going to Victoria, British Columbia," she said, but frowned at the directions.

The instructions say to use our own identification to leave the United States by bus and use the ones that were just provided us to enter Canada in three weeks.

Her heart sank. Three weeks. From what Gladys said, Brandon barely had three days let alone three weeks. Marc must have seen the struggle on her face because he came closer and hugged her to him.

They spent the next couple of days getting ready to make the trip to Canada and during their first week in Victoria, Melanie was able to video call Paige. Her heart nearly burst from her chest when her daughter's face came onto the screen. She wanted to reach out and hug her, scream, cry, and rant at what Grace had yet again taken from them, but she did none of that. She spoke calmly, promised to be back as soon as possible and sent her a kiss the only way she could.

They hopped around Canada for another two weeks and reentered the United States on the other side of the country in Vermont. They traveled down to Long Island, New York and were now taking the ferry up to Maine.

She got up, moving to the railing as they pulled up to the dock. She scanned every flat surface looking for anyone who even reminded her of the dark-haired, dark-eyed boy. She knew it was irrational, but she couldn't help it.

They exited and walked toward the wharf, hand in hand, her heart in her throat. This was it. They hadn't been given any other instructions. She continued to scan the faces of the people in front of her until they reached the edge.

She looked at Marc to see if she missed something. She saw him stiffen and followed his gaze over shoulder. She turned and came face-to-face with a older version of the beautiful boy she remembered with the fathomless, dark eyes.

"Hello, Mel," he said, his full mouth quirking into the same lopsided grin she remembered from years before.

"Brian," she whispered on an exhale.

~The End ~

This is the end of this book but not the end of the story.
The Promise to Zion Series will continue with
Promises Fulfilled

ACKNOWEDGEMENTS

To my friends who have read almost every page I have ever written, thank you for our motivation and patience with me. I promise not to hold my characters hostage again.

To my friends who make the hours pass by like minutes,
you are more valuable than gold to me.
Kerri, Aziza, Nicole, LaNeisha, Jackie, Cheryl, Llara, Cathy,
BriAnna and Barbara. See how rich I am.

To my husband who makes my heart smile especially on the rainy days. I am blessed to share this life with you.

DEAR READERS

It took me almost four years to write this book. There was a certain character I wasn't ready to let go of even though God made it clear to me early on what His plan was for this book.

I am a romantic. I adore happy endings and though I recognized God's desire to express the ultimate happy ending of being reunited with his children in this story, I must admit that I hoped for a delay.

Of all my characters I have to say that Brandon Tatum became my hero in this book. He showed me that appreciating life for the gift it is does not mean losing sight of the promise of eternity with God.

There is still plenty of room in this series for the happily ever after I desire plus there will be a couple of breakout books that share the lives of Dominy and Robin and Marc and Melanie before the timeline of My Beauty for Your Ashes.

I hope you continue this journey with me in the fourth installment *Promises Fulfilled.*

Thank you for reading and I hope you share your thoughts with me on this series or my others.

Please send your questions or thoughts to me at tawcarlisle@gmail.com

You can also visit my website at www.tawcarlisle.com

I can be found at www.twitter.com/traciwcarlisle

and www.facebook.com/traciwoodencarlisle as well.

Until next time,
Keep reading and expand your dreams
Traci Wooden-Carlisle

MY BOOKS

Promises of Zion series

My Beauty for Your Ashes
My Oil of Joy for Your Mourning
My Garment of Praise for Your Spirit of Heaviness
Stolen Promises

Next in the series:
Promises Fulfilled

Chandler County Series
Missing Destiny
Missing Us
Missing the Gift
(Novella) Missing Under the Mistletoe

Chances Series
Chances Are

Made in the USA
Las Vegas, NV
06 March 2024

86746321R00239